The Crown of Blood and Fire

CONNOR ASHLEY

CARRIE HARRIS

inked entertainment

Also by the authors

Co-written Novels

- Assassin's Revenge series:

The Crown of Blood and Fire

The Throne of Dawn and Destiny (forthcoming)

The Queen of Sand and Snow (forthcoming)

Also by Connor Ashley:

- Danika Frost series (with Charlotte Page):

Chosen

Inked

Also by Carrie Harris:

- Elder God Dance Squad

- Tryst

- The Supernaturals of Las Vegas series:

Thrall

Prey

Wish

Arrow

For my parents, David and Debbie.
- Connor

For Lee and Mary Ellen Harris
- Carrie

Chapter One

Larina Dracomeer stood up in the saddle, hoping to spot the smoky fires of the Praetorian Keep. No luck. Sighing, she sank back down, shoulders hunched with disappointment and uncontrollable shivering. She would have much rather stayed in Roshai, enjoying the cool shade of the tents and the tang of spices in the air, but she'd had no choice but to return home. She had no choice about a lot of things.

Over the first leg of the trip, she'd dawdled, reveling in the combination of good weather and delightful freedom. She'd ridden across the hot sands of Roshai and through the overgrown woods of Dunheim, where a pack of dire lizards attacked her drakon. It had been touch and go for a while, but Zemora seemed fine now. She loved the snowy mountain terrain, and she capered around as flakes fell

1

from the sky, pausing to stick her nose into the nearest drift at every opportunity.

Back in Dunheim, the stablemaster had strongly suggested trading Zemora in for a nice, dumb horse. But Zemora's toughness and intelligence more than made up for the occasional annoyance. Drakons had the build of a large draft horse with the scales and crests of the dragons they supposedly descended from, and even the weakest one could run a horse into the ground without breaking a sweat. Besides, Larina had so few people she could trust. She couldn't afford to lose another.

Larina pulled the fur collar of her cloak a bit tighter against the chill and surveyed her surroundings. Each slope appeared identical to the last, but she thought the keep lurked over the next ridge. Impatient, she stood in the saddle to look again as Zemora tried to inhale a convenient snowbank, snorting and hissing in delight. Beyond, she could just barely make out the grey curl of smoke above the trees. Relief spread some much-needed warmth through her bones, pierced with dread. Just a few minutes longer, and they'd be back in the keep. She might live there, but she could never call it home.

Zemora staggered, her smooth gait faltering. Larina leaned over in the saddle to scan the ground. Normally, the drakon avoided trip hazards, but she must have been too busy dancing around to notice. Larina grinned, opening her mouth to tease the creature. But before she could, the drakon collapsed, dropping to her belly in the snow. Momentum carried Larina into a snowdrift, cold flakes sticking to her cheeks. She paid them no mind.

"Zemora!" she cried, scrambling toward the drakon on her knees.

The drakon lifted her head weakly, and Larina's heart plummeted. The healer had assured her that Zemora would suffer no further ill effects from the dire lizards' poison, but she must have missed something. Or she'd been a hack, all too eager to divest Larina of her gold in exchange for a temporary cure. Because drakons didn't just collapse. Once, when they'd been fleeing for their lives, Zemora had carried Larina across a scorching desert with a dozen arrow shafts stuck in her hide. Only the most critical of injuries could fell her.

If only they'd reached the keep sooner the skilled healers there could help the beast. Larina considered running for it, but that would take too long. By the time she returned, Zemora might already be gone, and Larina would not leave her to face the Dark God alone. Her hands went to her belt, laced with herbal pouches. Perhaps she could create some concoction that might get them home, or at least make Zemora more comfortable as she crossed from the lands of the living into the Great Oasis beyond. But Larina's skills were in dealing death, not preventing it. She would try, because she owed Zemora her life, but she did not expect success.

Zemora's head dropped back down onto the ground, and Larina wracked her mind for something—anything—to help. Some small luxury to offer. She scooped up a handful of snow, holding it to the creature's mouth.

"Go ahead," she said, swallowing hard against her tears. "Eat as much snow as you want, you stubborn beast."

She turned her attention to her belt, running her fingers over the pouches. A tincture of Nightvale might slow Zemora's metabolism long enough for her to get help, but dosing a drakon would be very different than a human. If Larina got it wrong, she could put Zemora to sleep forever.

As she tried to work out the conversion to make the potion, Zemora began to wheeze. All of the numbers flew out of Larina's head and she spat out a curse, slamming her hand against the snowy ground. The poison had worked too fast. If Zemora's windpipe was already closing, it was too late. Larina would have to listen to her friend choke and die, with no comfort to offer other than her company. Her hand went to her blade, chill with the knowledge of what she had to do. She could offer a quick and efficient death. It would nearly break her, but that didn't matter much now.

Zemora wheezed and flailed in the snow, the motion uncharacteristically uncoordinated. The noise pierced Larina's mournful haze and she frowned. If she didn't know better, she'd think Zemora was laughing. Her eyes locked onto the drakon's face.

"Please tell me this is another one of your awful pranks," she begged. "I won't even be mad this time."

Zemora nudged her hard, pushing her over into a snowbank, her sharp, amused bray filling the air. Larina sprawled in the snow, her limbs numb with relief.

"You are the evilest..." But Larina couldn't finish. She dipped her head to wipe away a tear, taking a moment to compose herself. "Honestly, you have an awful sense of humor."

But Zemora paid her no mind. Instead, she thrashed about, flailing in the snow. It took Larina a moment to realize that the beast was making snow dragons. Zemora had watched the children of Gateway make them when they stopped for the night in the last town at the edge of the mountain trail. Larina flew to her feet, brushing the snow from her legs.

"Play while you can, you imp," she said, chuckling despite herself. Her eyes fell on the curl of smoke, now clearly visible above the trees. "There won't be much joking in the keep."

Worry wrapped her in its clutches, and not for the first time, she considered turning around. She could disappear. She had bolt holes ready and waiting. No one would find her. But people she cared about would bear the punishment, and Larina knew it. She couldn't leave them to that fate.

She sighed heavily, and Zemora's scaly head crept over her shoulder. The drakon had picked up on her plummeting mood, and its quiet presence made Larina feel just a bit better. Whatever happened, at least Zemora would support her. No matter what.

"Come on," said Larina, stroking Zemora's neck ridges. "I suppose it's time."

Zemora snorted, tossing her head.

"Yeah," said Larina. "I don't want to go either."

Their mirth faded as they finally approached the gates of the Praetorian headquarters. By all rights, Larina ought to feel gratitude at belonging, or maybe pride at all she'd accomplished. Instead, weariness consumed her as she rode into the small settlement. There would be no laughter here. Even Zemora behaved within these walls. Usually.

The guards closed the gates behind her. Larina dismounted onto the neat cobblestones of the small visitor's courtyard, standing next to Zemora with her hands visible at her sides. Archers watched her from their spots atop the tall wooden walls, arrows trained on her heart. Although they knew her by sight, they would not lower their guard until the gatekeeper cleared her. The Praetorian Guard had enemies, and the extensive security kept its members safe, so Larina didn't complain. None of them did.

The gatekeeper's voice came from somewhere behind her.

"Reagan. What are the properties of Tears of Sorrow?"

"The roots of Tears of Sorrow, if ground into a powder, can cure the drops. However, the leaves are extremely poisonous. Ingestion causes the insides to turn to liquid and seep out the eyes and ears," she replied.

"Good. What did you have for your birthday treat last year?" asked the unseen keeper.

"Jeweled honeycomb. It's my favorite," she answered.

This time, when the gatekeeper spoke, Larina could hear the smile in her voice.

"Welcome home, Reagan," she said.

"It's good to be here," replied Larina, lying through her teeth. She hated the constant need to be someone she wasn't. But someday, the lies would pay off. They had to.

The archers lowered their bows, losing all interest in her. Larina didn't bother to turn around. No matter how fast she moved—and as the most skilled Praetorian alive, she could move very fast indeed—she could never catch sight of the gatekeeper. She'd given up trying.

A stable girl approached, reaching for Zemora's reins. Larina didn't envy her job. Stubborn horses were no joke, but they made the average drakon look like a baby in arms. Zemora's intelligence and mischievousness far exceeded the standards for the breed, and when she got it into her head to be difficult, she couldn't be budged. Hopefully she wouldn't give the girl too much trouble.

"Be good," Larina whispered in the drakon's ear.

Zemora snorted and tossed her head as the stable girl led her away. Larina watched them go, unable to shake the worry that had taken hold of her out on the snowy slopes. With effort, she set it aside for later, entering the main grounds of the keep. Walls of wood and stone ringed the huge, self-sufficient structure. Grassy paddocks at the back of the settlement housed livestock and, when weather permitted, hardy crops suitable for the harsh climate. As little as Larina liked the place, its order appealed to her. Garret, their leader, required everything to be neat and well-maintained. Slovenly bodyguards didn't attract clients, and everyone in the Six Realms knew that the Praetorians provided the best security money could buy. They had to keep up appearances.

She stopped to warm her hands at the fire in a larger courtyard at one end of the oblong keep. A cluster of Praetorians stood off to her left, praying over a prone body wrapped in white linen on a bench. As she watched, a tall, well-muscled young man with deep ochre skin and tight dark curls cut a lock of wispy white hair from the corpse. He would add it to his prayer braid later. Larina had one too, a thick strand twisted with locks of hair from everyone they'd lost since she'd come here. Grey and brown, black and white. Someday her hair would be added to the prayer braids of her comrades. Perhaps then they'd realize that she'd been lying to them all this time. She'd be dead. The prospect didn't bother her; she'd made peace with the inevitability of death a long time ago.

The mourner touched the lock of hair to his forehead and lips before backing away from the rest of those gathered. His eyes lit upon Larina's watching form, brightening as he registered her presence. He gestured in silent inquiry. Larina debated for a moment before joining him. She'd pay her respects later.

The two of them remained silent until they'd wandered almost all the way to the opposite end of the keep, near the animal pens where they could converse without interruption. He stopped at one of the paddocks, leaning on the railing with studied nonchalance. Larina dropped down onto a bench next to him, relishing the chance to rest her aching legs.

A few feet away, a pair of piglets rooted silently at the ground. The keep's animals never made a peep. Larina didn't like it. Animals should be free and noisy and happy, but the animals in these pens weren't any of those things. Perhaps they could sense the death that hung around each and every resident, the presence of the Dark God hovering over their shoulders. She turned her back on them and tried not to scowl.

"You okay?" asked Nix.

"It's been a day," she said. It would be tacky to complain about silent pigs and naughty drakons when one of their fellow Praetorian guardsmen sat in state in the courtyard, so she waved away his inquiring glance. "Who died?"

He sighed. "Valerian. He went on a bodyguard detail with a caravan in the mountains of Oramis last week and got snatched by a ptero. It dropped him off a cliff and managed to eat most of the soft bits before the rest of the guards managed to drive it away. What a waste."

"Scales and tongues," Larina swore.

"You can say that again." Nix sat down on the bench and lifted a foot to inspect his boot, picking at the frayed seam running around the base of the scaled leather. "I'd ask if you completed your mission, but the Shadow never fails."

"Stop teasing me or I'll punch you in the mouth."

"You'll try."

A lazy smile spread across his face. After a moment, Larina answered it with one of her own. She jabbed him lightly on the arm.

"I missed you, you big lug. No one else mouths off to me like you do," she said.

"That's because you're scary." He gave her an overdone look of mock horror before his expression went serious. "Speaking of scary, every time I see him, Garret reminds me that he wants to see you as soon as you arrive."

"Scales and tongues," Larina repeated, but the curse

lacked the necessary heat to be truly effective. She leaned back against the stone wall and watched the pigs for a moment, delaying the inevitable.

"Reagan...?" Nix asked.

She pushed away from the wall, wanting to avoid his questions at all costs. Someday, he'd ask her something she couldn't answer. Someday, he'd figure out the truth about her. But not today.

"I'm just tired," she explained. "Zemora drove me to the brink of insanity on the way here. She learned how to make snow dragons."

The distraction technique worked. Nix grinned.

"Snow dragons?" he asked.

"Not well, mind you." She pushed off the wall. "I should go see Garret. Wouldn't want to get you in trouble."

Nix hitched a shoulder. "I wouldn't mind. Maybe I'd luck out and they'd boot me from the guild."

"That's not how it works, and we both know it." Their eyes met in a moment of complete understanding. "I'll see you later," Larina continued.

She walked off past the piglets, who watched her with silent hopefulness, but she had no food to offer. Before she made it too far, Nix called after her.

"I'm glad you're back, Reagan."

She paused. "It's good to see you too."

. . .

Garret's office dominated most of the third floor of the tallest structure in the settlement, just to prove a point about his power and influence. The cramped and twisting stairwell leading up to his room gave her vertigo, and Larina suspected that it had been designed that way on purpose. She spent a moment at the top to reorient herself before rapping on the sturdy door, unwilling to give him any advantage in conversation. After all, he didn't need it. The man was wily enough on his own.

"Enter," he called in his deep bass voice.

As she pushed open the door, a welcome blast of warm air hit her in the face. A cheery fire blazed in the hearth, but the heat it gave off didn't do much to dissipate the chill that overtook her in the presence of the head of the Praetorian Guild. Garret Montange was a dangerous man. He looked the part, his powerful build unaffected by age. His tanned face might have been more weathered than it had been when she'd first arrived at the keep, but his eyes still noticed everything.

"My child," he said, pinning her with that harsh grey gaze.

Then he fell silent. Garret spoke as little as possible, stretching out the silence until it spoke volumes. People got nervous under the weight of his silent stare. Rumors of his anger and his exacting ways increased their nervousness until they babbled out their secrets to relieve the tension. Guild members and clients alike scurried to make him happy, eager to fill the stillness with assurances of their loyalty and skill. But Larina saw through the attempts at manipulation. The overheated office with the piles of gold heaped on the desk no longer intimidated her. Now she understood why he stoked the fire and arranged the chairs so that it lit her face and left his mostly in shadow. His every move had been designed to throw her off balance, and she wouldn't fall into that trap ever again.

"The job is done," she said, sitting down on the edge of the desk and tossing a leather pouch down between them with a heavy clink.

Her nonchalance took him aback, but he recovered swiftly, picking up the pouch and counting up the coins. He made a show of pulling out his portion—70 percent for him and a mere 30 percent for the guard who had risked life and limb to earn it, but Larina didn't complain. As her star had risen in the guild, he'd been eager to find reasons to censure her, and she'd learned to be just defiant enough without giving him an excuse to keep her from the field.

Speaking of the field, she'd already tired of the frigid keep and the people in it, with the exception of Nix. The sooner she could leave, the better.

"Do you have any work for me?" she asked.

"Stay and rest a while," Garret suggested magnanimously. "Visit the baths. You must be tired and sore from your long trip."

"I prefer to work."

He leaned back and pretended to consider. "Well, there is a royal envoy coming tomorrow. Perhaps I might consider you for that appointment."

A royal envoy? Her heart leaped. It took every ounce of self-control she possessed not to pounce across the desk, grab Garret by his collar, and shake the information out of him. But she had to play by the rules of the guild, at least for now. So she waited for a breath, and then a second one, until she could speak without her heart choking her.

"You know I'm the best. They don't call me the Shadow for nothing," she said.

"I've heard the nickname," he admitted.

"Where is the envoy from?" she asked idly. "I've heard some rumors of upheaval in Illoria."

"Really?" He arched a grizzled brow. "I'll have to look into that. But no, not Illoria. Oramis."

"Southern Oramis, I hope?"

"Crestwynd City."

Larina pretended disappointment while her insides flip flopped. She had to bite the inside of her cheek to keep from screaming aloud. After all this time, her waiting would pay off.

"Oh well," she said, sighing. "Somewhere warmer would be nicer, but beggars can't be choosers. I'll take the job off your hands if you like."

Garret leaned back in his seat again, folding his hands behind his head, giving the appearance of extreme relaxation when she knew he remained as alert and conniving as ever. Larina never pushed when it came to jobs, not like this. Although she'd tried to conceal it, her obvious eagerness had caught his attention.

"Oh?" he asked.

She'd piqued his curiosity, and now he probed. He'd try to turn the situation to his advantage, but she didn't care what she had to sacrifice in order to get this job. She would give anything. All of her life had led up to this very moment. By the grace of the Dark God, she would have her revenge.

She saw no reason to dissemble, not now. "I want the job. What do I need to do to earn it?" she said.

The corner of his mouth twitched. "I'm afraid I don't know. The envoys want to make their own selection."

"Bodyguard or assassination?"

"A bit of both, I think."

Larina smiled, showing her teeth. "Right up my alley, then. They must have heard of me. Everyone's heard of the Shadow."

"Probably. You'll still have to impress them."

She balled her fists. "Oh, I will."

Chapter Two

After her meeting with Garret, Larina stopped in the stairway and gave herself a moment to get back under control. She couldn't manage to wrap her mind around the possibility that after all this time, she might finally have the opportunity to return home once more. To set things right. Her hands wouldn't stop shaking with the need to go now, before the chance passed her by.

To distract herself, she got to work, hoping that physical labor and familiar sights might calm her. She visited the stables to ensure that Zemora hadn't been giving the stable hands too much trouble and dropped her saddle off at the workshop to have the billet strap replaced. Then she swung by to inspect her small bedchamber. The simple space contained only a single bed and a small chest of drawers with a few articles of clothing inside. A few bits and bobs she'd picked up on her travels sat atop it: a pretty rock that sparkled when you held it up to the light, a piece of glass that gave the impression that it held a flame in its depths, and a handmade doll with a bright dress that a kind woman in Moradin had given her in payment for a favor. She refused expensive gifts or turned them over to Garret as required in her contract, so her meager possessions gave no indication that the chamber belonged to the Praetorian Guild's most decorated member. She owned little of value.

She'd been gone so long that dust blanketed the entire chamber, making her cough when she shook out the thin blanket atop the bed. Cleaning out the room took up most of the afternoon, and then a nice warm bath washed the dust from her hair and the chill from her bones. A quick glance in the small looking glass reminded her that she should dye her hair again. She'd handle that tonight, before the roots became too obvious. She went down to the evening meal feeling almost calm. Tonight, she would make a plan. The job in Crestwynd City would be hers.

As she made her way through the halls, the other Praetorians gave way before her with a tiresome yet familiar deference. Some touched the tips of their fingers to their chins in a sign of respect. They feared her, but they didn't dare to befriend her. In her wake, she could hear conversation and laughter start up again. Her guildmates had bonded into a tight-knit group, linked by a complicated web of relationships. They had secret love affairs that weren't secret at all and forged bonds that lasted lifetimes. She envied it.

She had Nix, of course, and she didn't take him for granted. She valued his true friendship more than she would a hundred sycophants. But still, sometimes she wondered what being one of the crowd would be like, just for a single day. It was a silly daydream, the kind of melancholy brought on by the drama of the past few hours. But she couldn't keep from feeling it.

As she stepped out of the dormitory hallway and into the courtyard, a teenager with a shock of short red hair stepped out to intercept her. Her slight figure had been swallowed up by an oversized leather tunic held up by bits of overworked rope. Although Larina only had a year or two on her, the top of the girl's head barely reached the Shadow's shoulder.

"Reagan," she said, her voice tight with excitement. "Have you thought about sparring with me?"

Larina huffed with amusement. "Sorry. I've had other things on my mind."

"Well, will you?"

"Fee, I told you, I don't spar."

She headed toward the dining hall with Fee at her heels, all eager persistence. Although she could barely hear the girl in all the noise, Fee began to argue her case in a breathless monologue.

"They say that if you want to be the best, you have to train with the best, and of course everyone knows that you're the best, and I realize that you don't spar, but I don't see how I'll get to be the best if I can't see you train, and it's not like I can come watch you work, although if that was an option, of course I would take it, and..."

If Larina didn't stop her, she wouldn't get a moment of silence during the entire meal. That might be a welcome change, though; often she sat alone at table. Fee might be annoying verging on pushy, but she had nerve.

Larina held up her hand to stem the tide of words and took a plate from the kitchen maid. She handed it to Fee, who stared down at the food like she had no idea where it had come from or what she was supposed to do with it.

"Here's why I don't spar," Larina explained. "When you spar, you pull your strikes. If you go slowly enough, you can still follow through, but both partners have to be master level fighters in order to train at speed. You're no master. To train with you, I'd have to pull my strikes. Slow down. And if I do that enough times, I might get into the habit. I might do it in the field. You see why I can't do that, right?"

Fee sighed. "I guess. But no one wants to train with me because I'm so small. I'll never become a brawler at this rate."

"Why would you want to? You think people call me the Shadow because I'm a brawler? Three quarters of the Praetorian Guard could pick me up and throw me through a wall if I let them get close enough to do it. I'm the Shadow because I figured out my strengths and made the most of them. Do that, and you're golden."

Fee cocked her head as she mulled this over.

"Okay. I'll do that. Thanks for the food," she said.

"Don't mention it."

Larina caught the attention of the kitchen staff and requested a second plate. She took it to the rowdy corner where the keep's children sat, throwing food at each other. The crèche contained about fifteen or so students at present. They lived and trained in the keep, learning martial arts, letters, and trades until they grew old enough to apprentice. Those with the knack for battle or intrigue would become Praetorians; others would work in the keep. Officially, they could choose to leave, but everyone knew the truth. Anyone who chose to leave paid the price one way or another.

She settled down at the end of the children's table. They were busy squabbling over a cookie to the dismay of their overwhelmed minders and didn't notice her. She began to eat in silence, her attention focused on the children. Maksim had grown thin, and he'd picked his meat apart rather than actually eating anything. Niola's ragged nails suggested she'd been biting them again. Tinker wouldn't stop talking. He directed a nonstop barrage of noise at Enku despite the fact that the smaller boy hid in the corner, making himself as tiny as possible.

As Larina watched, Tinker pushed the plate toward Enku, encouraging the frail boy to eat something, anything. Tinker had always been a force of nature. He wouldn't let up once he made up his mind. Resigned, Enku reached for his sweetbread, his sleeve falling away to expose a wrist mottled with wicked bruises.

Larina's lips drew away from her teeth in a silent snarl. She had a soft spot for all the children, but Enku in particular tugged at her heartstrings. His brown eyes seemed too big for his tiny face, and on the first day he'd met her, he'd blinked at her in owlish curiosity and proceeded to climb straight into her lap. Adults might treat her with fear or deference, but the children didn't care about her reputation. They didn't care about the trail of dead bodies she left behind. They only cared that she made them feel safe.

She needed to get one of the children alone if she wanted to find out the source of Enku's mistreatment. After years of training, she could go unnoticed if she wished. Most green recruits tried too hard, making themselves more conspicuous by their obvious desire to go unseen, but Larina had mastered the art of keeping her face hidden without making an issue of it. She kept her head turned at just the right angle so that the sweep of her hair hid her face from view as she ate. The children weren't scanning faces anyway. They were too busy bickering over the desserts, and their beleaguered crèche-minders had their hands so full that they wouldn't have noticed if the Black God himself had hopped up on the table and started dancing.

No one in the rowdy group noticed when Larina shadowed them toward the crèche. They failed to spot her when they stopped to take a head count at the door. No one even realized when she snagged Tinker out of line, wrapping a hand over the boy's mouth to cut off his startled exclamation. He struggled for a moment, stronger than his size would indicate, but she adjusted her hold easily, turning him to face her. When he realized who had picked him up, he went limp with relief. She released him, holding a finger to her lips, and led him around the corner. For once, he followed her instructions. Usually, he argued and questioned and pestered until she wanted to tear her hair out at the roots.

She led him to one of the darkened classrooms. As soon as the door latched behind them, he flew into her arms, squeezing her tight. She reveled in the rare embrace even as it made her worry.

"Have you forgotten everything I taught you about breaking a hold?" she asked in gruff tones, holding him at arm's length.

Tinker's mouth opened and closed, but no words came out.

"We'll have to do another training session," she said.

She made a mental note to arrange another training session with the crèche minders. The children studied combat technique three times a week, but she found the program to be completely inadequate. The skills they learned would be useful to full-grown guards, when they really needed techniques designed for small frames. Right now, they needed to know how to escape, not how to fight. She'd tried to make her argument by abducting every single child from the crèche one-by-one in the space of a single weekend, but Garret credited her skill rather than blaming their training. He'd missed the point entirely. Garret's security measures all focused outwards, leaving the children vulnerable to inside threats. Short of taking over the crèche herself, she couldn't do much to fix it beyond the occasional lesson.

"When? Soon?"

He yawned so hard his body shook, cramming the back of his fist into his mouth to stifle the noise. She huffed in amusement at the dramatic display. Tinker was never tired when he could be exhausted.

"Staying up late playing games?"

"No."

He stared at the ground. This nervous reticence was atypical for the boy, who even spoke in his sleep. On a normal day, the words would tumble out of his mouth with scarcely a breath between them as he prattled on about the latest contraption he'd built, what he ate for breakfast, the conversation he had with the kitchen maid, and whatever else crossed his mind. When he clammed up, it meant trouble.

Larina crouched down to look him in the eyes.

"I can't help if you don't tell me what's wrong," she said.

He tried to hold it in, but the words came out in a fearful burst.

"It's Sleth. He's been coming at night. Me and some of the older kids have been staying awake to protect the young ones, but it's really hard, Reagan. It was my turn last night, and I fell asleep, and he took Enku away all night. Now Enku won't eat or talk or anything, and... it's all my fault."

He launched himself back into Larina's arms, shaking with the effort of holding back his tears. She held him tight, imagining all of the things she'd do to Sleth. It didn't matter that he was one of the most decorated members of the guard. It didn't matter that he was her senior, and technically outranked her. She'd had enough. Garret had promised he'd put a stop to Sleth's perversions after her many complaints, and she'd considered the matter resolved. If it wasn't, she would end it herself, regardless of the consequences.

"I will make him stop. I promise," she said.

"But he might hurt you," Tinker said in a tiny voice. "I don't want you to be hurt, Reagan. You're my friend."

"But I'm also the Shadow. I kill monsters like him," she

said. "You leave it all to me. Now let me get you back to the crèche before you get into trouble."

He nodded, wiping his face with the back of a hand. Her pledge had reassured him. Within moments he had returned to his usual self, chattering away about some new game he'd invented. She smiled and nodded in all of the right places, but she barely heard a word.

After she returned Tinker to the crèche, she had a few words with the teachers. Although she didn't expect them to stand up to Sleth, the crèche did have rules, and Garret liked to see them observed. He would be very disappointed to learn that children were lost in the middle of the night. She left them quaking in their boots and went off in search of Nix. He might not have the clout she carried, but he hadn't been so brainwashed by love of the guild that he would turn a blind eye to something so wrong. As expected, he offered ready help as well as a few choice swear words.

By the time night fell, she'd hidden herself in Sleth's bedchamber.

She had never visited there, nor had she wanted to. Sleth made her skin crawl, even before she'd discovered his disgusting proclivities. The man was sickly pale and gaunt to the point of emaciation. She'd heard the stories about how most of his scars had been self-inflicted in some kind of perverse ritualistic ceremony and disbelieved them until she learned how depraved he truly was. She did not want to think of what he might have done with Enku, but she couldn't help it. As she balanced atop the decorative curtain sconces, cloaked in the shadows that gathered in the upper corners of the room, her eyes kept going to the shackles on the wall beneath her. Those large iron restraints wouldn't hold Enku's tiny arms. She wanted to believe that, but she could not take the chance.

The door creaked open, and Sleth crept in. He hummed with vile self-satisfaction, and her stomach roiled at the thought of what kinds of things might make him feel like singing. He never intimidated when he could batter, never battered when he could strike outright, and his missions almost always ended in bloodshed and glee.

Once again, she pictured the bruises on Enku's wrists. She wondered what other injuries he might be hiding. The crèche-minders had said they would tend to him. They had more skill at healing than she did, and so she'd left them to it, but she had to admit that she'd had a deeper motivation than that. She'd fled because she couldn't stand to see the boy's pain. She cared too much.

Now the memory of those injuries spurred her. Like a breath, she dropped from her hiding spot, landing just behind Sleth and putting her knife to his throat. He managed to draw his own blade but couldn't bring it to bear on her. Still, it impressed her. Most of her marks never even touched their weapons at all. She did not specialize in flashy attacks or lengthy physical struggles. Like a shadow, she hid in wait, and when she struck, it was only done when she knew her success was certain. She made up for her lack of strength with preparation and stealth. People like Sleth never saw her coming until it was too late.

She plucked the weapon from his hand before he could do something stupid with it. His eyes rolled back in his head as he tried to look at her without getting his throat slit.

"Reagan," he said, a grating pleasantness in his voice. "Are you here to proposition me?"

"I wouldn't fall so low," she hissed in his ear.

"Have you been hired to kill me?"

"No."

"Then you're in trouble, my sweet." She could hear the oily smile in his voice even though she couldn't see it. "Entering my room, why, that's a breach of guild protocol. Pulling a blade on me, that's another. You're in for it now, Shadow."

She let her blade graze his skin. He sucked a breath in, stiffening in her grasp, but she knew how to move with him. He wouldn't break free of her that easy.

"You left marks on Enku, Sleth. I told you last time; I will not stand for it anymore. Leave the children alone."

"Oh dear, what will you do?" he asked in mock fear.

"I'd take your balls, but someone already beat me to it."

She paused to consider her words to the eunuch. A statement needed to be made, but what? Sleth took pleasure in pain, and she would give him nothing that would please him. But she had to do something. With a quick, decisive slice of her knife, she cut free the long prayer braid that snaked from the back of his otherwise bald head. Then she pushed him away, dangling the braid before him. He blanched when he realized what she'd done. The prayer braid was a mark of honor for a Praetorian. The long, thick braids testified to years of service and survival in a brutal industry, and Larina had just taken that from him, cutting his hair off as if he lay dead in the courtyard next to Valerian.

"See, Sleth?" she said. Her voice came out cold and calm, her heartbeat slow and steady. "You're already gone. You died the moment you touched those children. You only walk around now because I allow you to. The next time you touch them, I'll take your head. Do you understand me?"

His eyes glittered with wild rage, and when he shouted at her, spittle flew into her face.

"You crazy whore! Give me back my braid!"

When he flew at her, she slapped him across the face like a hysterical child. In the shocked silence that followed, she let herself out of his chambers, her point made.

Chapter Three

Darkness blanketed the valley by the time Larina climbed the steep steps to the keep's north-western lookout tower. Overhead, stars twinkled in the cloudless sky, and the three moons clustered above, painting the ground with their watery rose-colored light. At the top of the stairs, she paused to admire the view. Although she hated the keep as a matter of principle, she'd always liked it up here.

Nix turned to watch her approach from his spot at the top, his face obscured by a long black scarf in a vain attempt to repel the biting wind. A roaring fire in the stove warmed his back, but she knew from experience that hour upon hour of staring out at the frozen mountain peaks would freeze your face clean off. She'd forgotten a scarf of her own, but at least she'd brought warm cups of chocolate. The steam would drive away the chill for a while.

She offered Nix his cup, and he smiled, holding out a scarf in return. They exchanged gifts with a silent smile. It had always been like this. Somehow, they always knew what the other needed.

"Nice night," she observed, wrapping the scarf around her neck. "Sorry I'm late."

He waved the apology away. "Did your errand go well?" he asked.

"The message was received, I think." She responded with deliberate care. Nix had known her plans for Sleth, but she couldn't tell him the details here. Anyone on the stairway could hear. "And yours?"

"I decided to visit the crèche before I reported for duty tonight. All of the children were in better spirits this evening. It did my heart good to see it," he said.

A weight lifted off Larina's shoulders. Nix wouldn't lie to her, not about something this important. If he assured her of Enku's safety, then she could truly relax. She took a sip of chocolate and looked out over the mountains.

"I always forget how pretty it is up here," she said.

"My people would say that you could walk right up the moonlight to the Great Oasis itself."

"I don't know if we deserve that." She smiled to soften her words. "I think the likes of you and I would be headed for the Great Below with the rest of the death dealers and scoundrels."

"You're no scoundrel," he scoffed.

"Neither are you."

"Touché."

They clinked their mugs together and drank. After a moment of quiet contemplation, he said, "I've been thinking about it, though. What I'll do when I leave, I mean. I'm thinking I could join a real guard unit somewhere, instead of just pretending to bodyguard and sneaking around on the sly. We'd be good at that after all the Praetorian training, don't you think?"

"I think I'd go slowly mad from boredom."

He flashed a look at her out of the corner of his green eyes. "Wouldn't a little boredom be better than this?"

"Keep your voice down," she hissed, flicking her eyes toward the dark stairwell. Though she saw no hint of movement in its shadowy depths, that didn't mean no one lurked there. After the stunt she'd just pulled with Sleth, he would be itching for vengeance. She didn't want to give him the opportunity.

Nix set his cup down on the ledge and gripped her by the shoulders. Normally, she didn't like to be touched, and she pulled away instinctively, but Nix held on. He moved close, pitching his voice low.

"Reagan, please hear me out," he said, and she stilled. He deserved that, at the least, after everything they'd been through together. "You are a true friend. We might not be blood, but you're my kin nonetheless."

"You're mine too. And you have no idea how much that means to me."

"Then please believe me when I say that I'm serious. I will leave the guild. I never wanted this life. The only reason I'm here is because Garret bought me from that trader. If I hadn't been sold into slavery. If I'd been wanted or loved..."

"Don't you dare say that! For all you know, your family has never stopped looking for you," she said in stern tones.

He straightened. "Which is why I have to go."

She hadn't been trying to say that at all, but now she couldn't figure out how to argue against it. She pulled away from him and took a sip of her chocolate, trying to marshal her thoughts. But before she could put together a compelling argument, he pushed his advantage.

"You should come with me," he said.

She startled, her chocolate sloshing over the brim of the cup.

"Excuse me?"

"Come with me. You hate this place. You despise Garret. You don't believe in the Dark God, and I'm fairly sure you're not in it for the money."

"Scales and tongues, no!"

"Then come with me."

Larina considered it for a moment. A normal life, working

as a guard in some nameless town, living as brother and sister with Nix. She could settle down with some laborer and have his babies. It would be a nice life, but she knew she wouldn't be content. Not without her revenge. If Nix managed to leave the guild against all odds, he would have to go alone.

"I can't," she said.

Hurt flickered over Nix's face.

"Can't or won't?"

She wracked her brain for something that could justify her delay. Something he'd believe.

"If I leave now, Sleth will retaliate against the children, and I can't allow that to happen. I have to make sure he's truly stopped before I even think of going anywhere," she said.

"Ah. Of course."

"That should give you time to plan, though. And then when the time is right, I'll... come with you."

"Sure. Of course you will, Reagan."

From the look on his face, both of them knew she lied. But neither of them wanted to admit it.

Loud noises woke Larina in the middle of the night. Darkness cloaked the room. Somewhere outside her door, people shouted and things crashed. She squeezed Kon-kon, her stuffed drakon, to her chest and began to cry. The air tasted bad, like burnt toast. It scratched the back of her throat.

"Mimi?" she called, her voice shaking and scratchy.

But Miriam, her nurse, didn't answer. That was very strange. Mimi slept in the room right next to Larina's and could always be counted on in the event of a nightmare or a midnight snack run. Maybe she had heard Larina crying. Maybe she went to fetch a glass of milk to soothe Larina's throat. Maybe one of the new servants had forgotten to open the chimney flue. Smoke stung Larina's eyes. That poor servant must be in an awful lot of trouble; she could hear the angry shouting all the way in here. Maybe she should tell the warder to give them another chance. As Mimi always said, everybody made mistakes.

She slid out of her bed. Normally, the stone froze her feet, but today it was warm to the touch. She didn't even need her slippers. With Kon-kon tucked under one arm, she went to the door of the bedchamber and tugged it open all by herself. She was very strong for just a five-year-old. Everybody said so.

A great gout of smoke smacked her in the face when she opened the door, making her cough. It swirled in the air. Tears streamed from her stinging eyes; she could barely see anything. She tripped over something on the ground and wiped her eyes, trying to see.

A dead guard stared up at her, his sightless eyes seeming to lock onto hers.

Larina would have screamed, but the smoke turned it into a strangled cough instead. She toppled to the ground, scrambling away from the dead man on all fours.

It had to be a bad dream. She tried to reassure herself that Mimi would wake her up any second now, but she struggled to believe it. Gripped by fear, she scrambled up to her feet and ran, clutching Kon-kon with panicky strength.

Ahead, the hallway opened up to a wide courtyard. Her room stood on the third floor, and sometimes during big parties, she'd sneak out to the railing to spy on the festivities below. Mimi always caught her, but sometimes they'd watch together for a little while before going back to bed. This time, there was no party to see. This time, when she peeked through the gap between the smooth stone plinths, she saw her mother's long red plait and pretty rose-colored gown. Blood splattered the beautiful fabric. Instead of a psaltery that spilled a gentle melody that delighted the ears, Mother held a sword that shook in her grip.

That didn't seem right at all. Mother didn't fight. She said only savages solved problems with swordplay. Larina didn't know what savages were, but they sounded bad. She opened her mouth to call to her mother.

On the ground at the back of the courtyard, Father and her brother Gerun sprawled motionless in a pool of blood. Their broken bodies and slack, staring eyes made Larina want to throw up. The cry for help died in her throat.

She sank to her knees, shaking all over as Mama fought

against a man much larger than her. A man in full armor against her silks. A man who looked like Chancellor Elrin, but of course that made no sense, because he was one of Mama's most trusted advisors. He wouldn't try to hit her with a sword. This must be an evil twin. Maybe a doppelganger. She knew what those were. They were in her storybooks, and they were very, very bad.

She wanted to wake up now. She bit her tongue hard enough to draw blood, but nothing happened. Maybe this was real.

"There you are!" The breathless voice belonged to Iliana, her big sister. Larina leaped into her arms, clutching her with a strength borne of hysteria. Iliana squeezed her right back, snatching her up and backtracking with desperate speed. A breathless shriek of pain followed their flight. Chancellor Elrin's evil twin must have done something to hurt Mama. Larina screamed for her mother, but Iliana didn't slow down.

"Hush! Quiet!" she hissed, but Larina couldn't be silent. Her five-year-old mind could handle no more.

They turned the corner. Where there had been smoke before, flames now licked at the walls. Iliana hesitated, and suddenly a soldier in black leathers came up behind them with a sword. At first, Larina was relieved to see him, but then his lips drew back from his teeth in an angry snarl, and he pointed the weapon at them. Its edge ran red with blood. Iliana put Larina down and shoved her roughly toward the flaming hallway.

"Go, Larina!" she said. "Run! Run now and hide!"

"But Iliana..." Larina protested. She didn't want to be by herself again. The fire terrified her.

The soldier grabbed Iliana, who struggled even though she didn't even have a sword. Larina didn't want to watch, but she couldn't tear herself away. She stood there frozen as the monstrous guard ran her sister through with his blade. Iliana shrieked like a teakettle on the boil and crumpled to the ground. Larina stared at her, hoping she'd move, but it didn't look like she'd ever move again. The guard grinned as he took a step toward her, her sister's blood dripping from his blade.

She hugged Kon-kon with all of her might and dashed into the flames. Behind her, the guard swore and leaped after her. She had to be fast. Her feet burned on the hot stones, and still, she ran. Something crashed behind her. The guard screamed, pinned beneath a pile of burning rubble. She saw tapestries burning, the door to Miriam's room bright with flames. Larina's nightgown caught fire from the rogue flames and sent red pokers of pain down her left arm and back. She shrieked in agony and at the stark realization that she was trapped.

The door to her room opened, and another soldier came out. He leaned down, but instead of pulling out a sword and killing her like the rest of her family, he yanked her into her room. It took her a panicked moment before she recognized him: Captain Flynn, her mother's bodyguard. He pulled the canopy down off her bed and smothered the flames with it. She couldn't stop crying, and her burnt skin stabbed her with bright darts of pain, but she didn't care. She hugged him as hard as she had hugged anything ever.

"It's okay, little one," he said over and over again, "But hush. You can't let them hear you."

She nodded and tried to cry as silently as she could.

"I should look for Iliana," he murmured. "One last time."

Larina shook her head. "The bad guard hurt her. She's dead. I'm the only one left in my whole family, Captain Flynn. I've got nobody now."

He kissed her forehead. "That's not true. You have me."

Larina jerked awake. With effort, she pushed the vivid memory of the dream away and allowed the drab reality of her surroundings to assert itself. Her cell at the keep was nothing like her room at the castle so long ago. This cold, hard bed would never compare to the cushy softness of her canopied chamber where Mama would sometimes sing her to sleep, accompanied by the tinny melody of her psaltery. Larina didn't want it to. It would be easier if she could forget, but the dreams still kept coming after all these years.

She'd done everything she could to stop them. Removed every bit of softness from the room, every bit of personalization or history that might remind her of home. After all, she'd come here with nothing but the half-burned clothes on her back. Kon-kon, her constant companion through so many adventures, had been lost in that last madcap dash down the burning corridor.

Restless, she stood and went to the window, looking out over the road. As a senior member of the guild, Larina could have traded up for a larger chamber with a better view. A curtained bed like Sleth's fancy getup. But that would remind her of things best left in the past. Instead of the pretty mountains, the chamber looked out on the distant road. The cold that seeped in around the glass made her scars ache. On most days, she didn't notice them, but they reasserted themselves after her dreams, like memories reanimated the dead nerves, just for a moment.

But maybe, just maybe, settling the score once and for all would put that all to rest.

A flicker of movement in the distance caught her attention. A splash of red on the horizon. She watched, transfixed, over the course of the next hour as the tiny spot resolved into a visible shape.

A flag.

The royal envoy of King Elrin Castestil approached from the south, its standard a red gash against the pristine white plains.

Her moment of vengeance was at hand, after all this time.

"Mother. Father. Iliana. Gerun. Captain Flynn," she whispered. "By the grace of the Dark God, I will set the scales to balance. I swear it."

Her palms stung. She wiped away the drops of blood on the windowsill, a testament to how hard her nails had dug into her skin as she prayed. She knew the prayers would fall on deaf ears. Her god hovered at her side, but he required her to be his hand in all things.

This time, it would be her pleasure.

Chapter Four

Garret met with clients in his office, if they came to the keep at all. Most of the time, they sent couriers with orders carried in tightly-sealed pouches. The guild's skills could only be bought by the richest members of the six realms, and only the very richest were privy to the Praetorian's true purpose. Most of the populace labored under the false pretense that the Praetorian Guild was nothing but an organization of elite bodyguards. Very few knew that the Praetorians were assassins as well as guards, and anyone who dared spill the secret didn't survive long.

A royal envoy determined to pick their guardsmen would garner everyone's interest, not just hers. The rumor mill had been going around the keep with such force that even she had heard the whispers. She could not risk anyone staking their claim before she could make hers. Garret might know of her interest, but he wouldn't save the job for her, especially if he saw an opportunity to take her down a peg.

She rose early, saw to a restless Zemora in the stables, and then settled down in the great hall to clean her blades. Garret wouldn't be able to resist the opportunity to show off, and this opulent room, with its towering chandeliers and carved chair that hinted at royalty without quite edging into impertinence, would make his point. He and his employees offered unparalleled skill worthy of respect. Larina held no love for the man, but she had to admit that she'd learned plenty about negotiation by watching him at work.

Shortly after she entered, other Praetorians began to trickle in. Some brought things to busy themselves with, as she had. Others leaned against pillars or took seats at the long wooden tables and tried to look casual. Some engaged in quiet conversation, but none tried to speak with her.

When Sleth arrived, the room fell silent.

No one stared at the blank space where his prayer braid ought to be. In fact, they looked everywhere but there. At the broad-timbered ceilings. At the flickering chandeliers. Down at their own booted feet.

Sleth bared his teeth. He seemed to be trying to make up for the absence with an excess of menace. But Larina's knife had cut him deeper than if she'd buried it in his heart.

Even the most agnostic Praetorians wore a prayer braid, which was only removed after death. Then every Praetorian would take a few strands for themselves, weaving them into their own hair. Some might call the practice barbaric, but not Larina. To her, it was a way to carry the lost—and some measure of their strength—forward through the hard times.

Larina had taken that from him. The room now held thirty people by her hurried count. Sleth alone had no twist of hair that curled over his shoulder. It was as if he had died but still walked among them. Only Larina's iron-clad self-control kept her from shivering at the thought.

Nix stumbled through the doors, bleary-eyed and only half-awake, dissolving the tension with a wave of amused snickers. He had never been a morning person. Once, she'd woken him up too early, and he'd tried to stab her. Emphasis on *tried*.

"Did you just roll out of bed?" she asked.

He grumbled something that might have been words, slouched down next to her, and put his head down onto the table. He would fall asleep if she let him. Instead, she began sharpening a blade right next to his head.

"You are a cruel woman," he said without moving.

"You're welcome."

Before Nix could complain further, the doors opened again. Garret entered, the proud tilt of his chin and puff of his chest on full display. He'd dressed up for the occasion in a black leather vest and pants over the softest silk. Rings sparkled on his fingers, and his grey beard had been neatly trimmed. Everything about him suggested power held at bay.

He paused and turned to the still-open door. The standard-bearer entered first, carrying a flag that to this day caused bile to rise in Larina's throat. The red flag of Elrin's rule featured a silver shield decorated with two crossed swords and a single flame floating above them, and it mocked her with its symbolism. Despite his lies, she knew blood and fire were the only reasons he sat on the throne instead of her parents.

A swell of anticipation built up inside her, which she quashed with firm resolve. Elrin himself would not have come. He wasn't the most popular of kings, making the trip too risky to take. This, then, was her job: to take the measure of his people, to figure out what they wanted, and convince them that she was the only person who could provide it. They would hand her Elrin's head on a platter, even if they did not know it.

First came the guards, about twenty in all. It was overkill, and Garret's lip curled as he surveyed the troops. The average townsperson might be impressed by the numbers and the crisp perfection of the red uniforms, but any one of the Praetorians could have taken on ten of the guards and lived, and they all knew it. As a result, the display failed to impress.

Then the first envoy stalked in, sweeping his eyes over the room with haughty derision. He had long greasy hair tied back in a leather thong and a spotty face, but his uniform with its many medals and regalia gleamed in spit-shined perfection. Although he'd reached middle age, his muscles strained at its seams. He carried two swords, one on each hip, and fairly sizeable blades from the look of them. She evaluated him with a speed borne of frequent practice: the way he kept his weight forward on his toes, the stiff set to his shoulders and neck, the way he turned his body to the right to look at the woman beside him instead of twisting his neck. He might be a mountain of a man, but he had his weaknesses.

The woman had drawn attention from the moment she walked in. Her pale, clingy dress made the most of her youthful, curvaceous figure and luscious black hair. Rather than shirk from her beauty, she put it on full display. Her challenging gaze reminded them all that they were welcome to look all they wanted, but no more.

"Welcome to the Praetorian Guild," said Garret, breaking the silence. "As you can see, most of our available members are already here. May I offer you refreshment or entertainment after your long journey, or would you prefer to get straight to business?"

He addressed the male envoy, but Larina would have bet that Garret had made the wrong call for once. The stocky brute might be the muscle, but she didn't think he called the shots on this journey.

The woman stepped forward. As she did so, something about her changed. Although her body and face remained as gorgeous as ever, she no longer appeared quite as inviting as she had moments before. Now, she seemed as cold and remote as the three moons on a winter's night.

"We may begin. I am Yasmeen, the king's sorceress and advisor," she said.

Larina and Nix exchanged the briefest of skeptical glances. Magic had died over a century ago, and anyone claiming to have magical power these days had to be a fool or a cheat. Sometimes both.

"My fellow envoy is Captain Bastian of the king's guard," she said, gesturing to the giant man, who inclined his head without an ounce of respect evident in the gesture.

"We have come on an appointment from the king himself to hire an assassin for a very important job." Yasmeen paused, a smile playing on her pouty lips. "You may be surprised that we are aware of the true nature of your guild. But we have long known that while you pretend to protect lives, your true skill is in taking them. Spy work. Assassination. It is for this reason that I am here."

She scanned the room, taking in the rapt faces of otherwise-jaded assassins who were captivated by her performance. Even Nix had begun to look a little dazed, and he tended to be immune to overdone feminine charms. Larina poked him under the table with the hilt of one of her daggers, and he startled.

"We will take only a single Praetorian, and we will not accept just anyone for our purpose," continued Yasmeen in her throaty voice. She didn't move. She didn't need motion to hold their attention. "Only the best will do. This is why we require a display of your abilities to determine our selection. Reputation means nothing to us. We wish to evaluate your worthiness for ourselves."

Garret stepped forward, clearly wanting to retain some semblance of control over this most important client. He clasped his hands behind his back in a show of restraint, but his intention was evident to everyone there.

"As you request, so shall it be," he said. "Do we have any volunteers who would like to compete for this project?"

More than a few eyes went to Larina as if drawn there on strings. Few of them wanted to compete with the Shadow. Almost everyone in the six realms had heard of her, mostly in the form of stories told to frighten young children. She disliked her boogeyman reputation, but it couldn't be helped. She had a job to do, and so she did it.

Sleth didn't spare her a single glance. He stood from his bench and stepped forward with a combination of deference and menace.

"This job is mine," he said, his burning eyes daring anyone in the room to challenge his claim.

Larina watched as many of her fellow assassins visibly withdrew from consideration. They didn't want to face Sleth, with his known tendencies toward sadism. He wouldn't hold back in a competition out of kindness or loyalty. He'd tear them down and enjoy it. She'd intended to hold back, not wanting to seem too eager, but anger at Sleth and everything he represented drove her to her feet.

"The job is *mine*," she said, staring him down.

Yasmeen glanced between the two of them with a pleased smile.

"Anyone else?" asked Garret. He didn't look as happy as Yasmeen. He wanted a spectacle, and his assassins weren't giving it to him. He scowled, and Fee shot to her feet, eager as always even though she couldn't have been more outclassed.

"I'll try," she said.

Larina didn't like that. Sleth would go through Fee like a hot knife through butter. He licked his lips like he was thinking that himself. Nix grunted in disgust, pushing to his feet.

"Why not?" he said, glaring at Sleth. "I'd like a chance to blow off some steam."

Sleth grinned.

Garret surveyed the rest of the room. "Anyone else?" he paused, frowning. "Well, I suppose most of you *do* have other commitments. Very well, then. You'll have your pick of these four. Shall we have a tournament of sorts? Allow them to fight it out among themselves? Last one standing gets the job?"

Bastian smiled for the first time since he entered the room, displaying a mouth full of bad teeth. "That sounds like fun," he said.

Ever the showman, Garret arranged for the tournament to be held in the training pit at noon the following day. In the interim, the simple dirt ring had been brushed clean of snow and debris, and somber black pennants flew at each combatant's entrance. The surrounding stands, usually bare wood, now bore black cushions to match. Tapestries hung from the partitions that separated spectators from combatants, finely woven black lengths with the silver shield insignia of the Praetorian Guild worked upon them.

Praetorians filled the stands and spilled into the aisles. As Larina stood at the center of the ring with the other three contenders, awaiting their instructors, she wondered if anyone manned the walls of the keep, or if they had been left defenseless in Garret's desperation to impress the royals. Even the children of the crèche had come to watch, claiming a prime spot in the front row to her left. Enku and Tinker kept shouting her name and making wild thumbs up gestures every time she glanced in their direction.

A light snow began to fall as they waited. Larina eyed the roped off row of cushions waiting front and center, reserved for Garret and the envoys. Then she looked up at the sky. The low clouds loomed, heavy with moisture. The sooner they got this over with and returned inside to the warmth of a fire, the better.

"I hope they get here soon," said Nix, echoing her thoughts aloud. "I'm freezing my stones off."

Fee tittered.

"Please don't talk about your stones, Nix," Larina shot back. "I'll be sick."

"Will you shut up?" snarled Sleth from his spot on the opposite end, as far from Larina as possible.

"I'm just saying that I'd like to get this over with before we freeze," said Larina. She refused to be drawn into an argument with Sleth. Especially not here. Not now.

"In a hurry to lose, are you?" he asked.

She smiled. "On the contrary. We both know you don't have a prayer."

She fingered the braid she held in her pocket. It would be bad form to pull it out and wave it in front of his face, but by the Trickster's stones, the idea tempted her. Sleth didn't make a sound, but his sour expression suggested the point had found its mark.

Garret chose this moment to make his appearance, saving the applicants from the embarrassment of a messy public altercation. With a significant amount of pomp and no less circumstance, he led Yasmeen and Bastian to their cushioned seats, waiting until they had settled to their satisfaction. This task accomplished, he turned to address the crowd, his voice carrying easily over their silent attentiveness. The Praetorians knew their places in this situation, and even the children were well behaved when Garret was involved.

"Today promises to be an interesting competition for the Praetorian Guild," he proclaimed, clasping his hands in front of him. He appeared stern yet nurturing now, projecting the impression of a fatherly figure who truly cared about who won the job when she knew he couldn't have cared less so long as his cut arrived safely. He must be playing some longer game here, trying to win the favor of the royal family long-term. It might come in handy on a rainy day.

"We have before us a representative selection of what the Praetorian Guild has to offer. Experienced operatives." His eyes fixed on Sleth; "Eager new blood." They moved on to Fee; "Power and muscle." Then Nix; "And nimble cunning." Finally, they focused on Larina. His gaze bore into her, and not for the first time, she wondered if he had any inkling of her true identity. But if he'd held such power over her, Garret would have said something long ago. "A Praetorian must adapt to their surroundings, and this is especially true of a royal appointment. Therefore, I have decided that this tournament will require you to employ fighting styles outside of your usual preferences. The first match will be between Sleth the Silent and

Reagan the Shadow in a bare-knuckle brawl. The win conditions are as follows: yield or be unable to continue, and you lose. Leave the combat circle—or be removed from it—and you lose."

The crowd broke out into excited murmurs. In a voice that carried over the din, Bastian said, "A bare-knuckle fight between the two of them? It'll be over in two seconds. She's just a little girl."

But Yasmeen simply shook her head, leaning forward to size up the contenders. Larina didn't much care who the onlookers favored. She knew her skills. On the surface, the challenge didn't give either of them an advantage. Neither she nor Sleth had much skill at bare knuckle brawling, whereas both Nix and Fee looked disappointed not to be taking part. But the last win condition fell solidly into her wheelhouse. She could out grapple Sleth, and both of them knew it. His knife-in-the-back style didn't suit the situation, which wouldn't allow him to circle around her unseen. His only hope would be to try to muscle her out of the ring. He wasn't a big man, but he outweighed her. It could happen.

In a battle like this, the first moment would make all the difference. She had to put him off kilter. Take the initiative from him. Win the battle before it started. So, as Garret signaled for them to take their places, she made a big show of freeing her prayer braid from the rest of her hair and dropping to one knee before the rapt crowd. She'd never been the pious sort, but for the first time in her life, she clasped the braid in her hands as she prayed aloud.

"Dark Father, watch over me in the coming battle. Fallen brothers and sisters, lend me your strength," she said.

As prayers went, this one couldn't have been simpler, but the words did the trick. Sleth lacked a braid with which to pray. He couldn't speak to the gods or to their lost guild-mates, and she'd just drawn everyone's attention to that fact. His flat eyes glittered with hate as he stared at her braid. She left it hanging down the front of her tunic instead of tucking it back down into her collar or smoothing it into the leather thong that held her hair from her face while she worked. Sleth couldn't stop staring at it, his jaw working. He would try to take the braid first. It had become even more important than winning, a symbol of her power over him.

"Begin!"

Garret's shout cut the silence. Sleth charged at her with a recklessness borne of fury. Larina sidestepped and used his momentum to launch him toward the boundary of the ring. He twisted catlike in her grip, edging away just in time, and the battle truly began. Even with the minor advantage she'd managed to create, she could not risk underestimating him. His skill and experience made him dangerous. They circled each other, looking for weaknesses.

He attacked with a flurry of blows, forcing Larina to draw on all of her considerable skills to evade. The circle didn't give them much room to move around. She dropped low, trying to anchor her center of gravity and grab onto him to grapple, but Sleth had launched into some manic berserker mode. He wouldn't be able to keep it up long, but he wouldn't need to.

Tinker, Enku, and the other children began chanting her name, loud and insistent. Larina could hear them over her shoulder, too close for comfort, could see the line marking the edge of the circle just behind her right heel. She had nowhere to go. If Sleth won this battle, he would use his newfound status to hurt the children. He would not let her stand in the way, and she couldn't allow that to happen under any circumstances.

This time, when he launched another wild barrage of punches, instead of trying to dodge them, she picked her moment and stepped inside, moving closer rather than trying to get away. She took one hard blow, twisting to absorb it with her shoulder, and then she stood within his defenses. She slammed an uppercut into his chin. Then another. He staggered but recovered quickly, grabbing her by the hair as if still trying to take her braid. She didn't realize his true intentions until he held a dagger to her ribs. Their bodies shielded the illegal weapon from view of Garret and the envoys, who watched with eager interest. At least Bastian no longer scoffed at her martial skills.

The dagger would disqualify him from the competition if

he stabbed her, but that did her no good if she'd already died. She would get no vengeance that way. The blade's edge scored her skin. There would be no defending against it without injury; he'd gotten too close. She should have known that he would cheat. She *had* known, but she'd been so focused on the prize that she hadn't planned for it well enough. If she survived this, she would learn from the mistake.

She needed space. Just enough to disarm him. Something that would make him recoil. But he delighted in awful things, so what would disgust a man like him?

Without taking the time to think about it, she leaned forward to kiss him. As much as the idea disgusted her, she knew full well that her approach would repel him. He recoiled from her approaching lips as she expected, and that minute movement gave her the advantage she needed. She hit his knife hand with the flat of her palm, driving the blade toward his belly, stepped back, and kicked the offending weapon free. It landed on the dirt with a clatter. Sleth had been knocked off balance now, both mentally and physically. She rolled, using her momentum to launch him into a throw.

Sleth spun through the air, snarling with fury. He landed just outside the circle, next to the knife he'd tried to kill her with. She waited, all senses alert for a renewed attack. He might dash at her with the blade even though the fight was over, intent on revenge.

But he didn't come. Instead, he snatched up his blade and stalked out of the arena with a snarl of disgust.

Garret rose to his feet and nodded once. She would get no more from him when it came to compliments.

"I declare Reagan the Shadow the winner of this round," he said.

Larina couldn't resist it. She met Bastian's eyes and curtsied. Yasmeen's mouth quirked as she applauded, and the rest of the crowd joined in.

Chapter Five

After winning her round with Sleth, Larina watched unsurprised as Nix beat Fee without any apparent effort. The girl would be good with a little seasoning, but at the moment her eagerness and idealism made her predictable. She'd spent too much time sparring and not enough in actual fights where nothing went by the rules and the standard attacks and counters failed to work as expected. To make matters worse for her, she tried to muscle her way through the match when Nix had more mass in his arms than she carried in her entire body. Hopefully the lesson would drive Larina's words home and she would learn to accept her weaknesses, or she'd never become a true Praetorian.

Guilt washed over Larina as Nix pinned Fee to the dirt for the third time, winning the match. If Larina had trained her, she could have saved the younger girl the humiliation. She remembered the desperation that came with being the smallest one in the training group, the underestimated little thing that the other kids dismissed as destined for the kitchen. She knew what it was like to have to prove yourself twenty times over. But as much as she wanted to save Fee, she couldn't. All the Praetorians had to find their own style before they could take on guard work or assassination. The keep produced warriors rather than soldiers—you found your strength and learned how to use it, or you died trying.

She mulled this over, toying with her prayer braid as Nix bowed and accepted his applause. When he took a seat next to her, he didn't even breathe hard. She clapped him on the back.

"Nice work," she said.

He shrugged. Fee had made her way to the benches where the children sat, climbed up on the wall before them, and began shaking all their hands with determined good nature.

"Don't flatter me. You know she wasn't much of a chal-lenge," he responded.

"The challenge was making it look good. I'd say you did a fine job of that."

This won a hint of a smile from him, and he bumped her arm with his.

"I won't throw our fight, though," he said. "This could

be my opportunity, Reagan. To make all those dreams I've been talking about come true. Just like we talked about."

Her heart sank. Did he want her to step out of the way? She couldn't do that, not for all the riches in the world. But that couldn't be explained without telling him too much.

"It's important to me too," she said. "I can't throw this match either, not even for you."

Maybe the strain of the situation had gotten to him, because Nix entered uncharted territory. No matter how strange her behavior, how secretive her demeanor, he'd always let it go. But now he looked her straight in the eyes.

"Why not?" he asked.

She faltered. "I...can't say more."

His generous mouth flattened into a displeased line, and he turned his back on her as Garret called them to the pit once again. They would fight with staffs, pitting her speed against his strength. Neither of them used the weapon if they could help it; it lacked stealth and took too long to kill. They both preferred a quick strike with a blade over the disabling blunt force of a staff. At least the choice offered no advantage.

Garret gave them time to select their weapons from the rack he'd had carted over from the armory. Larina chose a lightweight but sturdy weapon of incredibly rare su-guo from the Barren Isles. It would maximize her speed without breaking easily like most light woods did. Nix selected a heavy oak. He'd try to use the weight and length to overpower her.

Once they'd taken their places, Garret called for the battle to begin with little fanfare. This time, Larina didn't play the same games she had with Sleth. It would have been all too easy to throw Nix off kilter—she knew him so well—but she couldn't bring herself to stoop that low. She might need this job, but she wouldn't manipulate her only friend to get it. If Nix beat her fair and square, she would follow the caravan back to Crestwynd City, losing herself within its numbers. After all, the envoys had brought many guards. But after everything she and Nix had been through, she couldn't sacrifice their friendship on the altar of her vengeance.

The battle raged on. At one point, Nix caught her in the ribs with the butt of his staff. He pulled the strike, but she still wondered if he'd cracked them. Every breath she took lit her left side on fire. It brought to mind another flame, another burning sensation, another day when she simply had to keep going no matter how much she wanted to stop and lie down. It was time. Time to release every restraint she'd ever put on herself, every attempt to hide, to make herself smaller, to hold back and preserve her strength for the right opportunity. The moment had come for her to give everything she had. Her ultimate triumph awaited. Her staff became a blur of movement. She launched into a furious attack, completely unlike her usual carefully calculated combat approach. That hadn't worked. She had to try something new.

Nix didn't expect it. He knew how she fought, and he'd done a good job of countering it. But this wild and atypical onslaught caught him off guard. Under normal circumstances, he would have parried it easily, but her first lucky blow caught him on his temple. She pulled it, not wanting to truly hurt him, but it dazed him, nonetheless. He backed away under the barrage of strikes. Stumbled.

She saw her opening and took it. With a quick motion, her staff swept his feet out from under him, reversed, and came to a halt pointing at his windpipe.

"Do you yield?" she asked, panting.

Nix blinked. It took him a moment to realize what had happened. Larina met him with pleading eyes, unable to convey just how much she *needed* this opportunity. How long she'd waited for this moment, and the promise she'd made to her family. Nix hesitated as he stared back at her, but finally he nodded, his mouth turning down a little in disappointment.

"I yield," he said.

She withdrew the staff and stepped back, feeling more than a little ashamed of herself. Behind her, she could hear Garret proclaiming her the winner, but at the moment, she couldn't bring herself to celebrate. She held her hand out to Nix to help him up, and he just stared at it. For a moment, they remained there, frozen, both refusing to move. Then, with a sigh, Nix took her offer of assistance and allowed her to haul him up. Her ribs screeched in protest, but she didn't care.

He sighed again, staring down at his shoes.

"I'm sorry," she said. "I wish I could explain. But it's something I have to do."

"Yeah. I'll just find another way, I guess."

He tried to sound positive, but she could see through the mask to his disappointment. He would understand when it all came out, and he would honestly be able to say that he hadn't known about her true identity, or any of her plans. It would keep him safe.

He still grasped her hand in his, though, so they would be okay. He lifted it and turned her to face the crowd. The kids in the crèche went wild. Bastian applauded with obvious boredom. Yasmeen gave her an approving nod.

"Reagan," said Garret, gesturing to her. "Come meet with us in my office."

Larina told herself she'd make a better impression if she cleaned up before the meeting, but in reality, she needed a break to settle her nerves. After all of these years, she would come face-to-face with the usurper who had slaughtered her family and stolen her life. She would have a chance to set things right and put their spirits to rest. By the grace of the Dark God, she would give them peace at last.

She changed into a clean shirt, moving with deliberation due to her various aches and pains. Her hair stuck out in all directions, matted with dust. Plaiting it hurt her ribs, but the neat effect made the pain worthwhile. By the time she'd finished, she'd settled into an icy calm. She had done hundreds of jobs, and this one would be no different. She would find the usurper's weaknesses and exploit them as she always did. Then, for the first time since her family had been murdered, she could rest easy knowing that the scales had been balanced and their deaths avenged.

Although she didn't expect to need them, she strapped on her belt with its pouches of herbs and tinctures and spent a moment sheathing a variety of knives into their various places along its length. It would be in her best interest to win Bastian's respect if she could. Looking the part would help him see past the pretty face and trust in her skills as she needed him to. After a quick review in the small looking glass, she pulled her uniform cloak on and left the room.

When she arrived at Garret's office, the envoys sat before the fire with lavish furs draped over their laps and trays of food at their elbows. As Larina entered the room, Bastian shoved a cake into his mouth without taking a bite.

"There you are," said Garret. His voice carried only a mild rebuke, but his eyes flashed with annoyance. "I was beginning to wonder if we would have to hunt you down."

"My apologies," she replied. "I thought you might

appreciate it if I took a moment to freshen up after the tournament. It wouldn't have been pleasant to occupy a small space with me after all of that fighting and sweating."

"That was kind of you, Shadow," said Yasmeen.

Bastian belched.

"I suppose you want to know what your job is, eh?" he asked.

Larina took up a resting stance before them, hands clasped behind her back, feet relaxed and open. She inclined her head to listen, making a show of respect. Not that Bastian noticed. The food consumed his attention. He hadn't even looked at her yet.

"It would be helpful to learn the specifics, yes," she said.

Yasmeen, in stark contrast to Bastian, watched Larina like a hawk. The woman's frank evaluation had begun the moment she'd stepped in the room. Larina had to be careful to keep her face smooth and impassive under the close attention.

"I will get right to the point, then. We have kept the information quiet for the moment," said Yasmeen, "but Queen Cleora is dead. We suspect an assassin."

Larina flicked a glance at Garret, who returned the look with steady impassiveness. It hadn't been a Praetorian job, or they would have known about it. The murderer had been a resident of the castle or an independent killer.

Neither would pose much threat to Larina, but she filed the theories away for later.

"I am sorry to hear that," she said. "How might I help?"

"We would like you to protect the heir to the throne. What happened to the queen must not befall the heir," continued Yasmeen.

Bastian snorted. "I still say the King's Guard will protect the prince as we always have. But if hiring one of these Praetorians will make you all sleep better at night, then fine."

Yasmeen ignored him, and Larina refused to get drawn into the middle of that argument. Instead, she focused on the sorceress's words.

"A true bodyguard's job after all, then?" she asked.

It surprised her. Elrin had murdered so many to get the throne; she'd assumed that he'd want a Praetorian to kill for him. But the specifics didn't matter much. Not to her.

"If we have an assassin on the loose, then who better to stop them than another, more skilled, assassin?" asked Yasmeen.

"Reagan is the best of the best," said Garret. "I trained her myself."

Even though she'd taken the assignment under false pretenses, she couldn't keep from thinking through the task. Hiring an assassin to anticipate an assassin would challenge her skills in a new and interesting way.

"I could evaluate the defenses in a manner that the typical guardsmen cannot. I excel at identifying weaknesses," she observed.

"Yes, we saw that," said Bastian.

She hadn't expected a compliment from the man. But his expression didn't reflect admiration. On the contrary, he glowered at her. Interesting.

"When do we leave?" she asked.

"Tomorrow morning at first light. I do not wish to waste any more time. Be ready," Yasmeen ordered.

"Oh, I could be ready tonight," said Larina. "Now, if I had to."

Bastian held out the tray to her.

"Good. Then you can refill this," he said.

He shoved the tray into her hands. Startled, she looked to Garret for guidance. He gestured toward the door as if to urge her into action. She smothered a sigh and went in search of more food.

Chapter Six

Once she'd finally been released from waiting on Bastian—a power game if she'd ever seen one—Larina had preparations to make. She instructed the stable hands to ready Zemora for the long cross-country journey and stopped by the crèche to thank the children for their support and discuss their protection with their instructors. Then she went in search of Nix.

He wasn't in his chambers, nor having a snack in the dining hall. She didn't see him training, and why would he after the workout they'd had? He hadn't drawn guard duty that evening and hadn't been sent out on a job. So he had to be here somewhere, but everywhere she searched came up empty.

On instinct, she returned to the animal pens where they so often sat to talk. Nix lounged on a bench next to an enclosure of zoats—scaled creatures with the approximate anatomy and appearance of goats but with a supple hide perfect for armory. As she watched, he scratched one underneath its chin to its evident satisfaction. It closed its slitted eyes, letting out a trill of pleasure.

Without a word, she walked over and sat down next to him.

"I suppose you'll be leaving soon," he said.

"Tomorrow morning. I suppose you want an explanation?" she asked.

"For what?"

His voice rang with obviously false nonchalance.

"Please don't do that," she said. "I don't want to leave on a sour note. Not with you."

"I feel special."

He delivered the line deadpan, but the corner of his mouth lifted despite his best efforts to keep it down. She jabbed him with her elbow, smiling.

"You should. How's the head?" she asked.

"Hurts. Can you take a full breath yet?"

"Are you kidding? That won't happen for another week or so. Don't tell anyone and damage my reputation."

"I wouldn't dream of it, Shadow."

They sat in silence for a moment before the zoat broke it with its insistent bleating, eager for more attention. Larina began petting it, and it quieted, nuzzling her hand. She liked the smooth feeling of its scales.

"I would tell you if I could," she said.

Nix considered her a moment before he answered, his shuttered face giving no clue to his emotions.

"I've known for a long time that you have your secrets, Reagan. You know my past. About the slavers, about my family. But I know almost nothing about you, and I've always respected that. I've always thought that someday, you'd trust me enough to confide in me. That hasn't changed."

"It's not a matter of trust. If it was, I would have told you everything long ago."

"That's good to hear. But what is it, then?"

"I promised not to tell. The man I made the vow to is dead, but I gave him my word, and it didn't die with him."

It wasn't the whole truth, of course, but it was true enough. Nix nodded, his expression relaxing.

"I can respect that. I won't pester you about it any longer."

"Thanks. And I really am sorry."

He waved off the apology. "I'll find another way. But you'd better get going. Pack all your pretty dresses since you'll be at court." He paused and pretended to consider her. "Oh wait. I forgot who I was talking to. You don't do pretty."

"I've done pretty before," she protested. "I just don't like it. Remember that job in Roshai with the dancing troupe?"

He laughed. "How could I forget? Get out of here before we get lost down memory lane. Bring me something nice from Oramis to make up for stealing *my* job out from underneath me."

"Yeah, yeah. Whatever you say."

She gave the zoat one last pet and stood up. Then, surprising them both, she gave Nix a quick, awkward hug. This might be the last time they saw each other, even though Nix didn't know it, and the possibility stabbed her in the heart. Ignoring the curiosity written clearly on his face, she spun on her heels and left before her emotions betrayed her.

Despite Nix's teasing, it took Larina longer to pack than expected. Although she lived simply, she'd amassed quite a large collection of weaponry and herbal stores, all of which needed to be packed properly for transport. She favored simple clothing—trousers and tunics cut for movement and without adornment that could be used against her in a fight. But over the years, she'd collected a wide variety of disguises. She could slip beneath notice as a servant girl or a beggar. She could fit into the bustling market stalls of Roshai and the cool tile-covered palaces of Illoria. Of course, she wouldn't need all of her outfits, but she selected a few that might come in handy.

It finally dawned on her that tomorrow morning, she

would be leaving the keep, possibly for the last time. The road would end at Crestwynd City. She hadn't set foot inside its walls since the day of the fire. She hadn't heard her real name spoken aloud since then, because she could no longer be Larina Dracomeer. From that day on, Captain Flynn had called her Reagan, claiming her as his illegitimate daughter. He'd said that he could never replace her father, but he'd protect her with his life.

Shortly after they'd arrived here, he'd died.

She'd been to Oramis plenty of times since but always avoided the capital. If she stepped foot inside its walls, she knew she wouldn't be able to resist the urge to search for the king. And he would be too well-guarded, even for someone with her singular talents. She needed a way inside, so she avoided the temptation and waited for her opportunity with painstaking patience. The king would leave the safety of the castle walls for some parade, some festival, some occasion of state, and then she would make her move. But the years had ticked on with no chance in sight.

Now she had it, and she could only hope herself equal to the challenge. All of her training would amount to nothing if she fell apart at the first sight of the courtyard where her mother had been slaughtered, or the throne room where she used to play catch with her siblings. She had prepared for every possibility, but she didn't think anyone could be ready for grief and the memories it would almost certainly bring with it.

Her packing completed, Larina glanced about the room with an unexpected pang of regret. As much as she disliked the keep, it had been her home for years, and she would miss parts of it, at least. Late nights spent on the crèche floor, telling stories to soothe the children to sleep. Early mornings in the training yard with Nix, exchanging playful barbs while they pushed each other to be better, to do more. The familiar passages that she'd paced night after night, practicing her skills until she could pass even the most paranoid of Praetorians undetected. Regardless of what happened, she would never return here again. The realization hurt more than she would have expected.

Latching the door, she took out her dagger and pried loose a stone near the head of her bed. In the small nook behind it rested a small vial of dye and small velvet pouch. Thorough as always, she closed up the hiding place before opening the pouch to examine its contents: a purple conculium from the mines of the Orami Mountains. An intricately worked silver dragon wrapped its body around the precious stone, securing it to the chain. Her mother had given it to her on her fifth birthday, and she'd felt very grown up wearing it. It had belonged to her grandmother, Queen Rosamina, a long time ago.

She could not allow anyone to see it, but she refused to leave the only memento she had of her family behind. Only the ultra-rich could afford conculium, and this piece in particular bore the emblem of the Dracomeer family. Most people would assume that she'd stolen it or—even worse—realize that she hadn't. So she placed it back into its pouch and packed it away with exquisite care before coating her hair in the fragrant solution that would cover up her natural color. Once it dried, she settled back down onto the bed.

It took a long time before she fell asleep, her slumber bringing dreams of fire and blood.

The next morning found her bleary with exhaustion as she secured her bags to Zemora's saddle. The drakon danced around the courtyard, eager to get on the road. While Larina couldn't begrudge the animal its happiness, she wished Zemora would hold still just long enough for her to tie a knot. But the drakon wouldn't cooperate. After the third time she dropped one of her herb bags, she bit back a curse. The envoys made their preparations just a short distance away, and she didn't want to draw any attention to her trouble. She needed them to develop the utmost confidence in her skills.

She reached for the reins, but Zemora danced away, showing her long incisors in a delighted grin. Normally, Larina loved the animal's playfulness, but not today. She wanted to finish her preparations and set forth before her nerves got the best of her.

"Come on," she muttered, "*please*, Zemora."

She took a step toward the drakon, who shied away from her again, setting her tack to jingling. The noise attracted Yasmeen's attention.

"Everything okay?" asked the sorceress, a furrow of concern between her brows.

"Just fine," Larina replied, forcing a smile. "I'll be ready to go in a few minutes."

She turned back to Zemora and debated darting forward to grab the reins. If Zemora decided to bolt, she'd end up looking like a fool. But she couldn't carry her bags all the way to Oramis, either. As she was contemplating her options, Nix emerged from the kitchens. She went to say goodbye to him.

"Zemora is being her usual difficult self," she murmured. "Can you grab me something from the kitchen to bribe her with?"

He grinned, clasping her hand. As they shook, he slipped something chilly into her palm. Carrots.

"I was watching you out the window from my spot by the nice warm fire," he explained.

"Rub it in, why don't you?" she said, shivering as she imagined the cold bite of the wind.

"See if I help you ever again."

"Oh, and thank you."

She flashed him a grateful smile and lured her recalcitrant animal over. Placated by vegetables, Zemora trotted over as docile as you please. Nix helped her tie the remainder of her bags onto the harness.

"Thanks," murmured Larina.

"You okay?" he asked, just as quietly. "You look a little ragged."

She nodded. Funny how she'd spent all of this time missing her family when she'd had some right here. Nix was *family*. They might not share the same blood, but the bond couldn't be denied. Even after she'd snatched something he'd wanted out from underneath him without a single explanation, he had her back and always would.

"Nix, can you help me tie this on?" she asked, gesturing to one of her pouches.

The item in question hung securely from the saddle, but Nix didn't hesitate. He came to her side, arching his brows in wordless inquiry.

"If you'll just hold onto it for me, I'll bind it more securely," she said, loud enough to justify their activity in the event that anyone watched them.

He did as she asked. Then, with their bodies blocking the view, Larina's hands dipped into the pouch and brought out the velvet bag containing her grandmother's necklace, pressing it into Nix's hands. He tucked it into a pocket and nodded as if to say that he'd handle whatever she'd passed on to him. She only wished she could see his face when he saw the priceless jewel. Maybe this wasn't in her original plan, but it eased her mind to know that she'd set the scales straight between them. She'd taken his opportunity to leave the guild when she won the competition, but her gift could afford him a better one. One that also provided answers to questions she'd been unable to reveal. But all of her secrets would come out now, and so she saw no reason to continue to protect him from them.

"Need help with anything else?" he asked, indicating her bags but meaning something else entirely.

"I think I've got it from here, thanks."

Her heart eased. Nix would know what to do with the necklace. He had connections throughout the six realms who could melt down the gold and sell the stone. Her heart hurt at the thought of giving up this last connection to her family, but Nix had earned it, and even if she did manage to beat the odds and survive this trip, she would never be able to wear the jewel. Better to put it to good use than leave it moldering in its pouch.

"Actually, there is one last thing," she said. "Will you take over the children's training? The crèche-minders said they would take extra care to keep them safe, but we both know how well that promise will hold. Fee said she would help too. I ran into her this morning."

"Of course. Have you suggested that they skip their baths? Sleth hates dirt. I rolled in the mud when we were young to avoid his attention, remember?" said Nix. "If that doesn't work, they may need to try more direct measures. I'll make sure they're equipped to defend themselves."

"Thank you," she said.

Now she could leave without regret. Nix could be trusted. With the money he made from the necklace, he might even take Enku and Tinker, to keep them safe from Garret's need for vengeance. He would not allow them to be made into one more lesson on the benefits of loyalty, bodies flapping on the pikes mounted just outside the walls. She imagined the three of them leading a quiet, normal life in some small, unassuming town well beyond the reach of Sleth and Garret. That idea warmed her, and the last twinge of guilt over unfinished tasks slipped away.

"I guess that's it, then," she said.

"Farewell, Reagan," said Nix. "And good luck."

"Goodbye, brother," said Larina, and she meant it.

His mouth hung open, but he couldn't find a word to speak. That didn't matter. She'd said her piece.

She hadn't expected to feel anything but relief when she mounted up and exited the gates of the keep for the last time. But to her surprise, tears pricked at her eyes. She would miss Nix with the same bone-deep longing that she held for her parents and siblings. For the rest of her life— however long that might be—she would carry him in her heart.

But now she had a job to do. She set her jaw and looked to the horizon as the caravan set out across the snowy landscape.

Chapter Seven

An unexpected storm blew in the afternoon the caravan left the keep, pelting the riders with stinging sleet. Their progress slowed to a crawl as their mounts attempted to navigate the treacherous paths, and even Zemora ceased her antics, plodding along with elaborate caution. The accompanying winds made conversation difficult, which bothered Larina none. She had no desire to make friends, and although information about the castle would be helpful to her cause, it could wait. The silent plod through the snowy passes gave her some much needed time to work through her excitement and fear over the job to come. By the time they descended into Gateway, calmness gripped her once again.

The road became a bit easier after they left the town, which was a blessing given that they needed to make up time or they'd miss their ship. Larina didn't much like sailing. She didn't exactly get seasick but spent the entire time on board wishing she could vomit and get it over with. At least this route would shorten the amount of time they spent freezing their faces off in the mountains. She yearned for the more temperate climes of Oramis, where at least she'd be able to feel the tips of her fingers.

The caravan pushed their drakons hard to make it the port city of East Morad in time. Larina considered it lucky that the entire group had been outfitted with drakons, because they wouldn't have made it in time on horses. Zemora had quickly established herself as a leader among the herd, teaching them to make snow dragons and throwing apples at them during breaks. Larina couldn't decide if Zemora meant to play a prank or make a power play. Over the course of the trip, the other drakons became her devotees, so the plan—whatever it was—had worked.

After the breathless and icy travel, the envoys took refuge at a portside inn that had been reserved for their party. The contingency of guards bedded down in the warm bunkhouse, and Larina heard whispered plans of a cask of ale being brought in for the night, which she didn't begrudge them. Body guarding was difficult work, and on more than a few assignments, she would have been down there with them, drinking just enough to remain inconspicuous and envying their easy camaraderie.

But her situation couldn't have been more different this

time. She took a gloriously warm bath in front of the fire of her single room, driving the last of the chill from her bones. Then, dressed in a clean but simple tunic and trousers, her knife belt strapped at her waist in the unlikely event of trouble, she went downstairs to take dinner with the envoys.

The innkeeper spared no expense on her illustrious guests, offering them dish upon dish: rabbit stew, fried vegetables, and a lightly broiled fish that Larina particularly enjoyed. She picked at the meal regardless, knowing that soon enough her stomach would be rocking on the ship. She drank even less.

Bastian, on the other hand, indulged himself. He drank and ate until he had to have been bursting and then asked for more, shouting at the soft-spoken innkeeper like she was a dog to be brought to heel. With every moment spent in his company, Larina liked him less and less.

While the innkeeper scurried to slake his appetites, he peered at Larina's plate, which still held a slab of untouched meat. "You gonna eat that?" he asked.

"No, please help yourself," she offered, pushing it toward him.

"Don't mind if I do."

The innkeeper returned to the table, her plump golden face gone pale with worry. "Is there a problem with your food, mistress? I will be happy to correct it," she said, dry-washing her hands on her apron.

"No, good innkeeper, not at all," replied Larina with a smile. "You've fed me so well that I couldn't possibly eat another bite, and I hate to see good food go to waste. Did you cook the meal yourself? I thought the fish in particular was excellent."

She engaged the relieved innkeeper in conversation throughout the remainder of the meal, distracting her from Bastian, who had moved from gorging on food to downing tankard after tankard of ale. Perhaps he had a hollow leg? Larina didn't know how else to explain where he put it all.

Throughout the meal, Yasmeen remained silent and watchful. She ate little and paid no mind to Bastian's display of ill manners. Larina's intervention with the innkeeper won her an approving nod, but otherwise, the supposed sorceress kept her opinions to herself.

Finally, Bastian declared himself in desperate need of a chamber pot. Under the innkeeper's careful ministration, he made his uneven way toward the back of the building, leaving Larina and Yasmeen in blessed silence.

If Nix had been at the table, Larina would have made a variety of cutting remarks to him about Bastian's boorish behavior, but of course she couldn't take such liberties with Yasmeen. Praetorians didn't befriend their clients, especially not royal envoys. She was here as an employee, not as a friend.

So it surprised her when Yasmeen said, "He is good at his job, but that man has the manners of a molting zoat."

The corner of Larina's mouth quirked before she managed to get it under control. The sorceress was more correct than she probably realized. Bastian was undoubtedly an ass, but he knew his stuff. Every evening at camp had been an exercise in organization, every cog functioning in perfect precision. That level of skill didn't happen by accident. It had to be drilled into a group. Bastian might have no manners, but he ran the guard well. So she had to concede the point, even if she did not feel free to express her opinions aloud.

"It isn't for me to say, my lady," she responded.

"You don't trust me yet." Yasmeen paused to take a sip of vidka, a clear liquor that Moradin was famous for. She took a moment to savor it, rather than gulping it down by the bucket as Bastian had done. "A wise choice, but I hope we will soon get beyond that. It is beneficial to have friends in the court."

"I've been in similar places, and I know exactly what you mean. Castles are full of undercurrents, and it's impossible to pick them up in a short period of time without someone to orient you to what is truly going on."

Yasmeen nodded. "So you have done palace work before. May I ask where, or is that a tightly guarded secret?"

"I have not worked for any of the royal families themselves, but I've done work in their great houses. I don't suppose it would be too much to say that I've worked in the Yellow Palace of Roshai and tasted the sea air at

Castle Illorian. But it has been some time since I visited either."

"I would be very pleased to hear about them sometime, as much as you can tell. Of course I am happy to serve my king in any capacity he asks, but also, I'm grateful to be chosen for this task. I long for travel." Yasmeen's husky voice, usually so strong, faltered for the first time. "But I have not had a chance." She shook herself from some reverie and renewed her focus on Larina. "But enough about me. I wish to learn more about you. Where do you come from? How did you come to join the guild?"

Of course Larina couldn't tell her the truth. At the keep, she had refused to answer such questions, but she could not afford to pass up this opportunity to make Yasmeen an ally and potential resource in the castle. Underneath it all, the sorceress seemed lonely. Larina recognized it all too well, the mark of a woman whose reputation kept her apart, regardless of her own desires.

But she had to say something, and she had to remember it later, so she told Nix's history in place of her own.

"Slavers took me when I was very young. I don't remember much of my family. Flashes, smells, a few bits of music. The slavers kept me for a couple of years until I hamstrung one of them with a knife I lifted from his boot. Then they sold me to the guild. They offered a good price in their eagerness to rid themselves of me."

Yasmeen frowned. "You're a Praetorian slave? I didn't know they held to such a barbaric practice."

Larina had seen Nix answer this question before, and she tried to summon up all of the pain and pride she'd seen on his face then and wear it for herself. It wasn't difficult. Her heart ached for him.

"I am no one's slave," she said, staring Yasmeen down.

The sorceress offered a conciliatory smile. "I didn't mean to offend. Far from it. I myself was sold to a procurer by my own mother when I was six, for a bag of rice."

Larina couldn't keep from blanching. "I'm sorry. I didn't know."

"Actually, it is a pleasure to speak with someone who I know won't look down on me after hearing the truth."

"I won't," Larina promised, and meant it. "How did you climb from... *that* to where you are now?"

"From child prostitute to advisor to the king, you mean?" Yasmeen shrugged. "Probably in much the same way you rose to your prominence in the guild. I clawed my way to the top."

"Did you use your sorcery?"

Larina didn't believe in her so-called magic, but she wanted to see how Yasmeen would react. Magic had been gone from the world long before either of them had drawn a breath, ever since the Shattering, when a magical explosion in the Barren Isles drained the world of its power. She had to be lying, but Larina understood why she might do such a thing. Her so-called magical powers had saved her from a life of unimaginable horrors and brought her to...

To Elrin. Larina had made a dangerous mistake, empathizing so much with Yasmeen that she forgot to whom the woman had pledged her fealty. She couldn't afford such a blatant error, not for a moment.

Yasmeen watched her, her brown eyes deep with sadness. "You don't believe in my magic," she said, misreading the emotions that flickered over Larina's face.

"It doesn't matter what I believe. I respect you and your position."

"I appreciate that. It is more than some offer. But still, you must know what it is like to be set apart." Yasmeen sighed. "I notice that even you hesitate to touch me."

"I don't touch you because I have manners, not because I am afraid you will use your magic against me." But Yasmeen frowned, her brow creased with doubt, and Larina knew she had to go further to preserve the growing camaraderie between them. Her desire to do so had nothing to do with her personal feelings. "Here. I'll prove it to you."

She reached across the table that separated them and, for a moment, placed her hand over Yasmeen's. The sorceress's skin radiated a chill despite her close proximity to the fire. Her fingers closed over Larina's for just a moment before releasing them.

"That was a kind gesture," she said. "I appreciate your trust."

Larina didn't think much of it. After all, blood magic, like all the other schools of power, had died out when the magic drained from the world. The risk of Yasmeen pulling a knife and trying to plunge it into her heart exceeded the chance she'd take control of Larina's body with a touch. Any power Yasmeen exhibited would most likely be alchemical in nature. Some extraordinary things could be accomplished by a determined herbalist. Larina only knew enough to mix herbal recipes she'd memorized, but she'd studied with skilled herbalists at the keep who studied new herbs and developed their own concoctions. Regardless of their source, she hadn't been lying when she said she respected Yasmeen's abilities.

"Thank you for speaking with me," Larina said. "I've enjoyed it. Most people don't think of the Shadow as the kind of person they'd like to converse with over dinner."

Yasmeen let out a tinkling laugh. "Ah, well. Most people don't think of a sorceress that way either. Any time, Reagan."

"Thank you again, Yasmeen." Larina pushed back from the table before her emotions could run any further away with her than they already had. She would have to work hard from now on to steel herself against Yasmeen, because she had to admit the truth: she liked this woman. "I'd best get to bed. We have an early start tomorrow."

"Pleasant dreams, then."

Larina tidied up her dishes but couldn't figure out where to put them, so she set them in neat stacks on the empty bar. Then she went up the long stairway that led to their rooms. One of the guards, a young man with beer on his breath but clear eyes and a steady gaze, gave her a nod from his spot at the bottom. The guards kept to their duties, even in this place of apparent safety. It would make her job more difficult, but she would manage.

At the top of the stairs, the captain of the guard stepped out to intercept her. He stank of booze and onions and sweat, an unpleasant combination that made her draw away. But he closed the distance between them, breathing his rank breath right into her face.

"What were you talking about?" he demanded.

"I beg your pardon?" she asked, unruffled.

"You and the sorceress." He jabbed a thumb down the hallway. "I heard you blabbering. What were you saying? Was it about me?"

"No, Bastian, we weren't discussing you," she said with the kind of infinite patience she usually reserved for recalcitrant children in the crèche. "Let me pass."

"No." He put a hand on her shoulder and gave her a little push. "Tell me what you were talking about first."

She'd known from their first meeting that there would be a confrontation between them. Bastian had made it clear that he considered her presence unnecessary and that he saw her as a threat. Had his guards been on duty when the queen was murdered? If so, it would explain his behavior. He would see her presence as an indictment of his abilities, and he would seek at every turn to discredit her.

She could not let him undermine her. If she gave way now, things would only get worse. He would redouble his efforts to push her around. By the time they reached their destination, she would be effectively powerless to make any decisions on her own, and she needed to retain her independence if she was going to assassinate the usurper.

"Well?" he spat into her face. "Answer me. I'm waiting."

"I will not." She stared him down. "You are not my superior nor my client, and I have no responsibility to divulge anything to you. I will, however, consider it an aggressive action if you lay a finger upon me again, and I'll cut it off for you."

"I'd like to see you try, little chick," he said, grinning.

In a flash, her knife came to her hand, the blade at his belly. He had no time to react. She'd been ready to draw ever since she'd smelled him on the stairs. For him, the aggressive act had probably seemed all too sudden, but she'd been waiting for this moment all along.

"Or maybe I'll carve my name into your stomach," she suggested. She didn't like this sort of intimidation, but she couldn't afford to trade barbs with Bastian the entire time she worked in Crestwynd City. She had to goad him into challenging her now or backing down for good. That meant pressing harder than she would have otherwise. "Shall I?"

"You wouldn't dare," he said, but he didn't sound too sure.

"That's the problem, Bastian," she replied in honeyed tones. "You have no idea what I'm capable of. So it's best if we keep things cool and professional between us, don't you think?" She paused, and when he made no response beyond glowering at her, she nodded. "You have a nice night now."

He didn't respond but allowed her to pass. Her shoulder blades itched the entire way to her room, and all of her senses remained on high alert for any signs of approach, but he never made a move. Still, she double-checked the locks on her door before turning in for the night.

Chapter Eight

The cramped walls of the passageway squeezed the air from Larina's lungs. The place smelled of must and damp, and something in the distance dripped, each metallic plink frightening her all over again. She'd lost Kon-kon. He'd be scared without her to take care of him, but she couldn't go back. The bad men would kill her like the rest of her family.

Her lower lip trembled in the darkness, and fat wet tears snaked down her face, but she didn't make a sound. Captain Flynn had told her to be quiet. The bad men might be chasing them, and the slightest noise could give them away. They didn't know about the passageway, and he wanted to keep it that way, he said. He'd even taken off his boots so his feet wouldn't make any sound when he walked. It would have been funny to see always-proper

Captain Flynn marching around in his stockings under different circumstances, but she didn't feel like laughing at all.

"Hold here for a moment," whispered Captain Flynn. She came to an immediate halt as he stopped in front of her. Mama had taught her to listen to the guards, and now she understood why.

Captain Flynn did something to the wall, and part of it swung outwards, letting in a gust of air. When the smoky blast hit her, Larina burst into a spasm of coughing. Panicked, Captain Flynn covered her mouth with his rough hand until the fit passed.

"Sorry," she whispered, clearing her throat.

His eyes softened in his blackened face, and he patted her on the head. "It's okay. You are being very brave. I will climb up to take a look around, and then I'll lift you out. It might take a moment, so don't you be afraid. Just be quiet and wait right here."

She nodded. In the dim light from the open door, he took in the fresh tear tracks and the blistered shoulder where her nightdress had burned away. He didn't comment. Instead, he put a smile on his face that looked funny to Larina, like he didn't really feel like smiling at all, but he tried to anyway. His eyes glistened with tears. She didn't want him to cry, so she tried to smile back.

He turned away, brushing at his eyes.

"I'll be right back," he said without looking at her.

It took him two tries to pull himself out of the passage. It wasn't really that high up, but maybe he'd gotten tired after all that running. Perhaps that explained why he hadn't carried her. She watched as he disappeared over the edge, and prayed.

"Great Mother, please make Captain Flynn be safe," she whispered. "And make me safe too."

Iliana would have said it better. Her big sister talked to the Great Mother constantly, and she'd always lectured Larina about using the "proper respect" for the goddess. But Larina thought the Great Mother would understand that she was only a little girl and wouldn't mind the plain prayers.

It worked, too. Captain Flynn's head popped through the door right after she'd finished praying. His eyes searched for Larina in the dark, and he was relieved when he spotted her.

"I found a horse and cart," he said. "You can ride in the back, all cozy in a blanket where no one will see you. Can you stay hidden for me?"

Larina knew how to hide. Sometimes it seemed like no one wanted her around, but she didn't think she should have to sit in her bedroom by herself while the rest of the family danced at balls and had fancy dinners. She'd become very good at sneaking around the castle, just so she could have a little taste of the fun. She nodded. She could hide in a blanket and cart, no problem.

"Good, little one. Now, this might hurt, but I have to lift you up. I'll do it quick. Can you stay quiet, even if it hurts?"

Larina nodded again, and he took her right hand in both of his, and he pulled. The motion tugged at the burned left half of her body, and she let out a little yelp before clamping her mouth shut. Tears streamed down her face as he lifted her into the light.

As he set her down, his eyes became frantic again, as he saw her nightdress. A big red smear ran up the front. When she touched it, wetness stained her fingers. Captain Flynn looked down at the opening to the secret passageway, set into the ground of an alleyway a few blocks from the castle. A carmine puddle at its lip shone in the light of the two moons.

"Ah," he said. That was all.

Larina sniffed at her hand. Blood. It soaked the ground right where Captain Flynn had stretched out to pull her out. He must really care about her to lie down in a pool of blood like that. He had it all over him now, too.

"Come," he said, taking her hand. "The cart is just over here."

Silent with growing shock, Larina went with him. Behind her, the castle that she used to call home burned uncontrollably, painting the sky with orange.

. . .

Larina did not like the mountains one bit. Even though Captain Flynn had stopped to pick up some supplies he'd hidden at a warehouse, including a lot of blankets to wrap her up in, she shivered with a cold that worked its way down to the bone. Her arm and back no longer stabbed at her with burning pain. Instead, they always felt chilled despite the herbal salve the captain put on her every morning and night. It smelled like mint tea. For a little while, it made her forget about the pain.

Captain Flynn worried her. He had a bad cut on his tummy, and even though he'd told her it was just a scratch, she knew better. It needed stitching, and she would have offered to do it, but Mama had only just begun to teach her needlework. Her stitches danced all around in unsteady lines, unlike Mama's neat rows. She couldn't do that to Captain Flynn, and besides, she didn't think his supplies included needles and thread.

She could only hope that they got to their destination before she turned into a block of ice, or he grew too weak to go on. His face had gone all gray, and although he'd insisted on doing everything for her the first couple of nights, his protests had gotten weaker. She'd gathered the wood for last night's fire all by herself and started it too, despite her new fear of the flames.

She looked up at the moon. Now, only one hung in the sky: Gloria, the eldest of the three sisters, ripe and rosy like a peach. Larina had always liked Gloria the best. In her

Moon Goddess storybook, Gloria was caring and kind, but she always took a stand if someone tried to hurt her sisters. She stopped them, just like Larina had to stop Chancellor Elrin when she grew up.

"Captain Flynn?" she asked from her spot in the back of the cart. He no longer made her hide now that they'd left Oramis far behind. Now would be a good time to ask the question that had been growing in her mind ever since they'd snuck out of Crestwynd City in the dead of night. "Is Chancellor Elrin going to come after me?"

Captain Flynn considered this for a moment. "He would if he knew you lived. But if our luck holds, he thinks you died in the fire. That is what everyone said at the last village. So long as the Chancellor believes it, and we don't tell anyone your real name, you will be safe where we're going. I promise you."

"Is Chancellor Elrin a bad man?" she pushed further.

"Yes." The cart went over a bump, and Captain Flynn grunted in pain. He did that a lot now. "I wish we had known it sooner. I suspected over these last few weeks, and I told your mother to be careful, but I couldn't prove anything. I failed."

He dabbed at his eyes. He hadn't cried since they'd left. Larina had plenty of times, although she tried to hide it by burrowing in the blankets. He always picked up on her sadness despite her attempts at secrecy, reaching through the layers of itchy wool to stroke her tangled hair.

"I believe in you," she said. Her mama always used to say that to her when she complained about impossible tasks. Mama always said she could do anything. Of course, she also said Larina wasn't *allowed* to do things even if she *could* do them, which was very confusing. But still, the words had made Larina feel better then, and she hoped they would make Captain Flynn feel better now.

"Thank you," he said.

They crested the hill they'd been climbing for the past hour, and now Larina could see smoke winding over the trees. It was a cook fire kind of smoke, not a castle burning kind. Now she could tell the difference.

"Do you see that?" she asked. "Smoke!"

Captain Flynn nodded. "Now, remember what I told you?"

"My name is Reagan, and I'm your daughter. You didn't tell anybody about me before, but now you're bringing me to your old school. Am I going to go to the school too?" she asked. "I've never been to a school before."

"No, child. This school is not for you. I forbid it. And Garret is going to have to accept that, whether he likes it or not."

Larina didn't know anyone named Garret, but she didn't care. She would have accepted anything he said at that moment if only it meant she could leave the cart for good and be warm again.

The wooden walls of the keep rose before them. It was

so big, almost as big as her castle, but she couldn't say things like that anymore. She had to pretend that she grew up in Crestwynd City with her mother, who died in the fire and fighting. Then Captain Flynn brought her to this school. She knew the story well by now. They'd practiced and practiced, and Captain Flynn called her a very good actress.

He wasn't her Papa, but she loved him anyway. Some of the castle guards could be a little mean, but he had always been patient with her. She was glad he'd been the one to save her. She climbed up on the bench next to him as they pulled through the open gates into a small, sparse courtyard, and hugged him.

He grunted and then went limp in her arms. She struggled in vain to hold onto him, but his weight proved to be too much. He slid off the bench and onto the dirt floor of the courtyard. Red stained the front of his leathers and dribbled from his mouth.

Larina climbed down after him and tried to wake him up, but he wouldn't awaken. Not even when the guards came to help. Not even when she called his name, or when her tears fell onto his slack face.

Captain Flynn was dead. She recognized death now, because she saw it every night in her dreams. She laid her head on his lifeless chest and cried for all she had lost.

.   .   .

Tears still streamed down Larina's face when she awoke in her cabin on the Venture. It took her a moment to orient herself. Even after all these years, her dreams came as detailed as they had right after it all happened. Her subconscious wouldn't let her forget any of it, not until she balanced the scales. The Dark God willing, that day would come soon.

She dashed the tears away with an impatient hand and stood from her gently rocking bunk. Her stomach didn't exactly love her surroundings, but she had to admit the Venture was the steadiest ship she'd ever been on. Captain Dormano had one eye, an appalling vocabulary, and the lightest touch at the helm she'd ever seen. If all ship travel was as smooth as this trip had been, she wouldn't ride her drakon everywhere.

By the light of the lantern seated in its holder on the wall, she dressed swiftly. Although she had no duties aboard ship, she needed to stay in shape, and she'd devoted quite a bit of time to her growing friendship with Yasmeen. She might still doubt the sorceress's powers, but her support would be a definite benefit.

She'd found midmorning to be the best time for training. If she waited long enough, she could avoid the crew during their morning chores and take her lunch afterwards in an empty mess. Not that she minded the sailors. They barely paid their passengers any attention, and when they did, they treated them with the same gruff deference. But that would fade if she made herself a nuisance.

She ate a leisurely breakfast of steaming porridge and dried fruit before ascending the ladder to the upper deck. There, she could get in some calisthenics and a little light weapon work without getting underfoot of anyone. To her dismay, she found Bastian and two of his lackeys lounging on the benches when she arrived. Most of the guardsmen were professional and well trained, but this pair shared Bastian's temper as well as his disdain for her.

The captain smirked. "Don't you ever rest, little missy?" he asked. He'd taken to calling her insulting names in an attempt to goad her into some kind of confrontation. So far, she'd resisted the urge to lop something off of him. A finger maybe, or a toe. Nothing truly necessary. A skirmish with him would give her an opportunity to evaluate his skill. She'd never seen him in action, although she knew what kind of fighter he'd be: very straightforward, with a reliance on brawn and a tendency to play dirty if opportunity allowed. To be frank, she expected him to be a better captain than combatant.

"I train daily, as your guards do," she said, giving the men in question a respectful nod despite their desultory appearance.

"We should spar," he suggested, standing up from his bench and stretching. "It would do me good, after all this sitting."

She shook her head. "Thank you for the offer, but I don't spar."

"Of course you don't."

"No, I honestly don't. Some Praetorians do, but I dislike the practice. It trains you to pull your strikes. It's not a habit I wish to develop. I train with practice weaponry or on a dummy, so that when the time comes, I won't hesitate to strike a killing blow, if such a thing is called for."

"So, what?" he demanded, more irate than the topic warranted. "Are you suggesting that my guards and I are soft because we spar? That we won't hesitate to kill when necessary?"

"No. That isn't what I said."

She hoped her matter-of-fact tone would head him off, but he had already made up his mind to be offended. His face flushed with anger, and his hands clenched into fists as he approached her.

"Well then, what do you mean? Because I will not stand for an insult to my guards. I've trained them myself, and I'm damned good at what I do," he sputtered.

"I agree with you."

This took him off guard, and for a moment she hoped she had forestalled this confrontation after all. But he had been looking for a reason to pick a fight with her, and based on the mulish expression on his face, he wouldn't be satisfied until he'd had his touch. Very well, then. She would give it to him.

"You're just saying that to throw me off balance, but you won't manipulate me that easy, wench," he said, grabbing at her collar as if to pull her close.

She didn't know what he intended to do with her. Perhaps he just wanted to yell in her face. Intimidate her a little. Show his men that he held the power on this ship. But he was Elrin's man, and Elrin was a butcher. If he saw an opportunity to strike, he might just take it.

She removed his hand from her tunic. The fluid movements of her body were as natural to her as breathing as she stepped around him, pulling him off balance, making him work to keep his feet rather than continuing his act of aggression against her. Then she twisted, turning his arm in the socket until his body had no choice but to go with it. He flipped over onto the ground, the wind knocked out of him, and with the speed of a striking viper she leaped atop him, the blade of her knife at his throat. She let it cut him, just enough to prove her seriousness.

He froze, his eyes wide. At the edges of her vision, she could see the guards, half standing now, unsure whether or not to intervene.

"I don't spar," she explained in polite, conversational tones, "because I don't train like you do. Guards often have to subdue or contain, but Praetorians don't. I may wear the hat of a guardsman from time to time, but at my core, I'm a trained killer. That's why I don't spar. Because sparring is about *not* killing, and I don't leave my enemies alive to stab me in the back."

She rolled off him, coming up to stand a safe distance away, ready for anything.

"That's why I won't spar with your guards, nor with you. Because if I'm threatened, I don't settle it in the sparring ring. I kill. It's what I'm best at. I wouldn't want to do that to you," she continued.

Bastian regained his feet, his eyes narrowing at this thinly veiled threat, but he didn't speak. Just looked daggers in her direction. She didn't care. He could hate her all he wanted, so long as he stayed out of her way.

"Does that make more sense now?" she asked, making a show of politeness. "Your sparring sessions are very well done, just not within my area of expertise."

Bastian glanced at the shocked faces of his lackeys and nodded, grabbing at the opportunity to save some face.

"Yes, well, if you ever want us to teach you sparring, you let us know," he grumbled.

"That is very kind of you. If you'll excuse me."

Given the circumstances, Larina decided it would be wise to hold off on training until later. If she remained on deck, it would be an invitation to further confrontation. So she bowed her head respectfully and made her exit.

As she turned the corner, she came face-to-face with Yasmeen, who was wrapped in a silvery cloak that all but disappeared in the misty sea air. The sorceress's pinched expression suggested she had overheard their confrontation with little pleasure. She gestured for Larina to follow her to a secluded spot near the aft of the ship where eavesdroppers would be unlikely. En route, Larina planned her response to the lecture she would almost certainly receive: she'd had no choice but to engage somehow, and her actions had been calculated to stop future conflicts. No more and no less. She did not intend to challenge Bastian's authority or start a competition between them.

Yasmeen leaned on the railing, looking out over the still water to the dim shapes of the land beyond. It reminded Larina of a faerie-scape from her childhood storybooks, something unreal and imagined in the distance, like an oasis lost travelers saw on the distant sands.

"I've always wondered what's on the Barren Isles," said Yasmeen, to Larina's surprise. It certainly wasn't the topic she'd expected. "After all this time, do you think anything lives there?"

"I thought the land was declared dead after the Shattering."

Yasmeen clucked her tongue. "I know that. I'm no idiot. But those shapes look like trees, don't they? If the trees have come back, perhaps other things have as well."

Larina squinted in the mist. Perpetual fog shrouded the island, making it impossible to get a good look at it. But only a fool would risk setting foot on that cursed ground.

Everyone who had tried had never returned, and even sailors who skirted too close wasted away in slow stages that even the most accomplished apothecaries and healers couldn't combat.

"Maybe," Larina conceded. "I wouldn't risk going there myself, though."

"It's too bad." The sorceress looked pensive. "I would like to read some of their books. The library at Kata held quite a few tomes on magical theory that no longer exist elsewhere."

"I wouldn't mind harvesting some su-guo myself, but it's not worth the risk."

Yasmeen turned, fixing Larina with a stare. "Speaking of risk, you'd better watch it where Bastian is concerned."

This sounded less like an official upbraiding and more like a worried friend. Larina blinked.

"I'm sorry?" she asked.

"He may be an oaf, but he is dangerous. He has the ear of the king, and you'll have to work with him as a member of the guard."

"Praetorians are outside of the chain of command."

"True, but the king will listen to Bastian when it comes to matters of his safety," countered Yasmeen. "Making an enemy of him would be unwise."

"He had his mind made up about me before we even met. To him, I'm a threat, and he'll seek to remove me if he can, regardless of my actions. What would you have me do that I haven't done?" asked Larina.

Yasmeen considered for a moment and sighed. "I suppose you're right. Conflict between the two of you might have been inevitable. But if you have the opportunity to soothe his ego in the future, I advise you take it. He responds well to that kind of thing, and it might get him off your back."

"I will. Thank you."

"If he tries something with you again, you could think about cutting out his tongue," suggested Yasmeen.

If Larina hadn't been shocked before, she certainly was now.

"I beg your pardon?"

"At least then we'd have some peace and quiet around here. That man doesn't know how to shut his mouth."

Larina searched Yasmeen's face, looking for a hint of a smile or something to suggest whether she truly intended this cold-blooded suggestion. But the pale face under the silvery cloak was smooth and expressionless.

"You jest, yes?" she asked.

"So you like his tongue?" asked Yasmeen in arch tones.

Larina let out a disgusted bleat, and the sorceress threw back her head and let out a peal of merry laughter.

"I got you!" she said.

"Yes, you did," said Larina, unable to suppress a snicker. "I vow my revenge upon you!"

She'd meant it as a joke, but the mere thought of vengeance brought to mind things that Larina didn't want to think about at the moment. She would rather enjoy the fact that she had made an unexpected friend. The vengeance could wait until they broke land. For now, she would allow herself this one pleasure.

It couldn't hurt.

Chapter Nine

The remaining days of travel passed without incident. The morning after Larina's confrontation with Bastian, she climbed to the upper deck to find Yasmeen already established on the bench where the men had awaited her the day before. Although neither the captain nor his toadies made an appearance that morning, Larina appreciated the backup. Neither woman commented on it, but from that day forward, the sorceress lounged on the deck when she arrived, reading a book or looking out over the glittering ocean waters. They left for the galley together to grab a bite to eat after Larina finished her workouts, whiling away the hours over idle conversation.

During this time, Larina barely saw the guard captain at all. According to Yasmeen, he drank late at night with a few of the sailors and then slept in until past midday. That arrangement suited her just fine; a cooling off period might help to avoid further altercations once they made land. If not, she could handle him—his ego mitigated whatever one-on-one skill he'd possessed—but she preferred to keep the peace if possible. Maiming the head of his guard would attract Elrin's attention, to say the least, and she didn't want the king to take too much interest in her. He might recognize her. She'd done as much as possible to alter her appearance, dyeing her distinctive red hair to a dull black on a regular basis. Of course the intervening years had changed her, but for all she knew, she might carry a strong familial resemblance to her mother or sister. She couldn't quite remember their faces any longer.

As the ship drew closer to Crestwynd City, their ghosts loomed over her. Yasmeen's company provided a welcome distraction from the tangle of emotions that grew in Larina's belly. They talked about safe things—people they'd once known, interesting facts they'd learned, places they'd been long ago. Larina probably ought to have steered the conversation to the court and its players to better prepare herself for the job, but she kept putting it off.

Finally, they sailed into the harbor. As they drew closer to the city, Larina had been eager to watch it grow before her, to see if anything still seemed familiar after twelve long years, but she found herself hiding away in her small room instead. She told herself that packing up her things now would save time later, but she knew that wasn't the real reason she dawdled about below decks. After all the time she'd spent longing to go home, she had made it, but what if it no longer felt like home at all? Or what if walking the castle halls brought the past flooding back to her? Her repeated nightmares still plagued her, and she didn't think she could stand it if the memories of her dying family intruded on her waking hours too. Here, she wouldn't be able to escape them. She would walk the same hallways, touch the same walls. At least it would be impossible for her to sleep in the same beds; she assumed they had all burned.

But once all of her things had been packed, she could avoid the sight of the city no longer. She went out to take her first look at the land where she'd spent the first five years of her life. Yasmeen and Bastian stood at the railing already. Her friend smiled as Larina approached, moving over to make space for her. Bastian studiously ignored her existence, which suited her just fine.

She watched as the ship slid gracefully into the harbor. The city loomed over her. It had been built in terrace-like rows that ran in concentric circles around a long-dormant volcano. The castle loomed in the center, its high, pointed towers reaching up toward fluffy white clouds. Below it, the terracotta rooftops of shops and homes shone in the midday sun.

Larina breathed in. Somehow, she'd expected the place

to stink of smoke, but of course that scent memory came from the last night she'd spent within its walls. Instead, Crestwynd City smelled of the sea, and of warm clay baked in the sun, and of its infamous baked goods. This was a city built for gourmands, with its fresh seafood, sweet pastries, and local wines. Nix had taken a few jobs here and raved about the food. Larina herself couldn't remember much about the cuisine other than the flaky, sugar-encrusted pastries that Mimi had brought to her room on a tray for breakfast each morning.

"Have you been here before?" asked Yasmeen.

She watched Larina with a knowing smile on her face, one that would have been worrisome if not for all of the time they'd spent together over the trip. Yasmeen often wore that expression. It meant nothing.

"I have traveled the length and breadth of the six realms, but I haven't had the pleasure of working in Crestwynd City," said Larina. It didn't exactly answer the question, but Yasmeen didn't seem to notice.

"It's a beautiful place," Yasmeen allowed. "I particularly enjoy the statue set in the center of the market square over there. If you watch long enough, you'll see it between the buildings. It's the Three Sisters, done all in bronze. When the light hits it just right, it glows."

Larina followed her pointing finger. She hadn't been allowed to leave the castle grounds very often, but sometimes she'd been permitted to go to market under the watchful eyes of Mimi and the guards. She'd enjoy a treat while she listened to the music played by minstrels on the street for coin, and before she returned home, she always visited the statue. The Three Sisters had ruled Oramis centuries ago, riding their dragons to the corners of the kingdom to establish order. But then the women died in battle, and the dragons vanished or simply died out after the magic they fed on drained from the world. The Orami claimed the statue to be lucky, and as a girl, Larina had never missed the opportunity to touch the hem of each sister in the hopes that something extraordinary would happen to her. It had, but not in the way that she'd hoped.

As the Venture slid into its berth at port, she spotted the statue through the maze of buildings and smiled.

"I see it," she said. "It's lucky, isn't it?"

Bastian snorted derisively from his spot further down the deck but said nothing.

"I've heard that claim," admitted Yasmeen. "But never put it to test myself. Perhaps we'll try it, if your duties allow."

"I'd like that," said Larina.

The crew rushed this way and that to bring the enormous ship in safely and secure it to the dock. Larina and the two envoys remained in place, safely out of the way. As she watched, two of the crew slid a gangplank down to the waiting hands of the dockworkers, who lashed it into place with assured movements and complicated knots. The ocean spray kicked up by the tumult of the large vessel's movement misted them as they worked, but they ignored the assuredly cold water. Although spring had finally come to warm the air, the sea would remain frigid until summer had taken hold.

Once the gangplank had been secured, one of the workers fastened a flagpole to its end. At its tip flew the standard of King Elrin: flickering flame over a pair of swords. At first, Larina assumed that this gesture paid homage to the king's representatives onboard, but as she gazed over the city once more, she had to concede that this might not be the case. Elrin's flag flew everywhere, dotting the cityscape like a spray of blood.

A hint of Larina's distaste must have shown on her face because Yasmeen touched her shoulder with gentle fingers.

"Are you okay?" she asked, concerned.

Larina nodded, but the vague response did nothing to dispel Yasmeen's anxiety, so she had to find an excuse to go with it.

"It's a bit too rocky for my taste," she said, after a pause. "This has been an exceptionally smooth voyage, but I'm usually like this on boats. Not sick exactly, but not quite well either. My stomach would much prefer to be on dry land."

"Then let's go. Bastian can have some of his soldiers fetch our bags, can't you, captain?"

"We aren't porters," Bastian began.

"But you'll do it to be gentlemanly, won't you?" Yasmeen interrupted.

She forestalled any further argument by leading Larina away toward the gangplank. Behind them, Bastian sputtered with annoyance, but as the women exited the ship, he called for some of his men to carry the "blasted luggage."

Disembarking the full contingent of guards as well as all of their mounts and supplies took time. Under different circumstances, Larina might have been impatient at the delay. After all, they didn't need all of their belongings to arrive at the castle at precisely the same time, did they? There would be no harm in splitting their party and leaving some of the guard behind to deal with the luggage. But the wait gave her the time she needed to calm herself once again. Normally, she remained unflappable no matter what the situation, and it would be tempting to think she'd begun to grow soft. But this job carried with it some uncomfortable personal emotions, and to deny their presence would only ensure that they cropped up at the most inconvenient time. She needed to deal with them as they came up, so she would.

In her early days as a Praetorian, Garret had personally trained each of the recruits, and he'd lectured them for a long time about emotions. To deny them would be fatal, he'd said. But controlling them, using them when necessary, *that* was the mark of a successful Praetorian. Although she may have grown to dislike Garret and everything he stood for, she had to admit that she'd found this lesson to be nothing but true.

So she allowed the emotions to flow through her, to exorcise themselves, and by the time she climbed up on Zemora's back to make their way through the winding streets to the castle, she could do so without feeling like the turmoil might tear her apart at any moment. Icy calm gripped her as their small procession set forth, and she could look with interest upon the vaguely familiar streets as if she truly saw them for the first time. They were quieter than she remembered, with fewer people, all of whom gave their procession with its red flags a deferential and cautious berth. After a while, Larina began to make a game of trying to catch the eye of someone they passed—anyone—but failed miserably.

The gates and portcullises stood open as they approached, and Larina wondered if perhaps the presence of Bastian at the front of their party had opened the doors for them in advance. But then she saw the crowd gathered in the inner courtyard. That explained the quiet streets, but not the wary caution with which the residents had treated their procession. She had wanted to believe that the Orami people chafed under Elrin's rule, and she'd heard rumors that suggested as much, but she didn't put much stock in rumors.

A long time ago, her mother had addressed her people from the very same balcony that hung above them now. Larina remembered standing atop it and looking down to the ground far below with dizzying effect. Now, she recognized the man who loomed over the sober crowd all too well.

Elrin. The usurper.

He looked much the same as she remembered him. His dark, reddish-brown complexion contrasted with his hair, which had gone grey in the intervening years but was still cut in the same close-cropped military style. He'd always seemed a giant in her eyes, and she'd chalked that down to the age difference. But now that she saw him anew, she realized her memory had been more accurate than she'd realized. His broad shoulders strained at his finely-cut red doublet, and he still appeared hale and hearty despite his age, which had to be somewhere in his fifties.

He loomed over the chastened crowd with an almost predatory mien. Like he might have them all clapped in chains at any moment. For a moment, she chastised herself for letting her emotions carry her away to such fanciful conclusions, but then she saw the gallows.

They sat tucked off to one side of the balcony, but had been built to maximize visibility, the high platform looming over the sizeable audience. Queen Thalia had never allowed a gallows here, not that Larina remembered. She wouldn't have used such a horrible punishment against her countrymen. She'd always said that a good ruler must care for their people, not slaughter them.

A man stood near the hanging rope. She could see how his body trembled even at this distance. Thick rope bound his hands behind his back, and his face was blotchy and bruised. He raised bleak eyes to the king, who glared back down at him.

"Traitors to the crown will not be tolerated," declared Elrin. His voice carried over the silent crowd. Larina could almost taste their fear. No one dared to even move as his eyes raked over them, her included. "Mercy is for the weak. Do you want mercy from me? Do you want me to bend and beg until our enemies sense my weakness and come to take everything we have? Of course not. I am harsh, but that harshness serves a purpose. I alone keep our shores and borders safe. I alone maintain Oramis as the jewel of the six realms. And I demand respect!"

His voice rang out with fury, and the man on the gallows quaked before it. Elrin glared down on him again, his face thunderous with rage.

"How dare you?" he demanded. "Possession of illegal items of propaganda is disrespectful of the throne, and all that I do to assure your safety."

He held up a wad of purple fabric and shook it. Larina didn't need a good look to identify the offending item. She could have picked out that banner in her sleep, and frequently she dreamed of it. A silver dragon on the field of purple. Her family's banner. She hadn't seen one in years, and now Elrin dropped it to his feet and stomped on it.

"You will pay the ultimate price," declared the king. "As will your family."

The man struggled and screamed to no avail. As the shocked crowd watched, guards led a woman and two children up onto the gallows. The kids stood in wide eyed shock and the mother cried as the guards fitted the ropes over all four of their heads. Larina could barely believe her eyes. She was the Shadow, supposedly the most bloodthirsty assassin the Praetorian Guild had ever produced, and she couldn't imagine doing such a thing.

"All those who hold allegiance to a false queen will be exterminated," Elrin declared.

His eyes swept the crowd, and although he couldn't possibly be aware of her presence there, she couldn't help but think he must be looking for her. This couldn't be a coincidence, could it? Did this kind of thing happen often? Did her family still have supporters in the city, even after all this time? Or was a new unrest growing, and the Dracomeer name being dragged out of the dark corners again?

She had to find out.

Her stomach fell to her toes as the executioner pulled the lever, and all four captives dropped through the trapdoor. At least the end came quickly with a snap and a jerk of the rope. The bodies swung to and fro, a grisly reminder of the atrocious lengths the usurper would go to in order to satisfy his thirst for domination.

Elrin turned on his toes without giving the crowd a second look. The people dispersed quietly, with looks of intense discontent on their faces, but no one dared say a word.

Not even Larina.

After the public execution, Yasmeen led Larina in the direction of the kitchen, pointing out the windows and explaining the basic layout of the castle. At first glance, the sorceress appeared callous, but Larina had spent enough time in her company over the past few days to realize that Yasmeen hid her true feelings as a matter of habit, a survival technique picked up in her years of indentured servitude. It would be impossible to tell her true thoughts—on the brutality of the king or anything else—by her public reactions.

Bastian and his men saw them as far as the kitchen gate.

"We'll drop you here," said Bastian. "I'd like to look in on the barracks before Elrin asks for me."

"Thank you for seeing to our safety," murmured Yasmeen.

Bastian nodded. The moment he'd entered the grounds, his demeanor had changed, the snarl and bravado tempered by calculation and perceptiveness. He even forgot to sneer when he looked in Larina's direction. "Praetorian," he said. "I'm sure I'll be seeing you."

"I'm sure you will," she replied in neutral tones.

With that, he led his men off. As he left, Larina watched him give succinct instructions to his guards, sending them off on various errands. For all of his bluster, it would be a mistake to underestimate his skill. He wouldn't allow her to take him unawares a second time, and she increasingly regretted allowing their rivalry to progress as far as it had.

The guards unlocked the gate and opened the heavy door within that led to the kitchens. Yasmeen led Larina through the bustling stone rooms that smelled of yeast and spices. The kitchen staff had already begun to prepare the evening meal, and the women hurried through to avoid getting in the way. Then Yasmeen took off on a winding route through the building and up the spiral staircase to the second floor, Larina trailing behind and trying not to gawk.

So much was different. So much remained the same. Every once in a while, she spotted a familiar tapestry hung on the wall, or a piece of sculpture that rang some bell of memory within her. But of course she couldn't ask to examine every piece of art displayed throughout the halls, not without explaining why, so she kept going without knowing for sure if her recollections led her false. Perhaps later she would get a better look at them and jog her memory properly.

They climbed up to the third floor. The courtyard where her parents had died was gone now, its grasses and winding paths paved over and ominously decorated with a standing display of heavy armor. The corridor that led to her old bedroom was now carpeted in a luxurious red, with little ornamentation. Her mother had hung musical instruments from all across the six realms in the recessed alcoves that dotted the walls, but now they stood empty except for utilitarian lanterns.

"The royal family's rooms are down there," Yasmeen explained, pointing. Larina could see no fewer than six guards without turning her head. Elrin certainly was paranoid these days. Perhaps the loss of his queen or the increasing agitation of his people had gotten to him.

"Guest quarters are this way," the sorceress continued, leading Larina a short distance away. "I am just down the hall. Close enough to be summoned at night in the event of an emergency. Bastian also rooms here, but he often bunks in the barracks with his men. You can use this room to change, and the baths are at the end of the hall. If you're in need of anything, you can ring for the girl. The bell's just inside the door. We're to clean up and dress for dinner. I've arranged for something to be brought for you since our bags are delayed."

Larina nodded. "How much time do we have?"

"An hour. It seems like a long time, but I could soak for ages," Yasmeen said, drawing the last word out to exaggerate it. "It will be nice to get the ship out of my hair."

"Oh yes," Larina teased. "You're such a mess that I can barely stand to be seen in public with you."

Yasmeen blinked. "You're mocking me."

"I'm just teasing."

The sorceress turned toward her room, but not quickly enough to hide her smile. "I'll forgive you this time. Be ready in an hour," she said.

"I will."

Larina let herself into her room and took a quick look around. The small, well-appointed chamber housed a wide, soft bed made up with luxurious blankets, a heavy chest with a key in the lock, and a small dresser decorated with intricate scrollwork. Sheepskin rugs sat next to the bed, waiting for bare feet in the mornings. Along one wall ran an intricate tapestry depicting a dragon in flight, its copper scales glinting in the sun. Its tail curled around itself as it made a figure-eight in the sky. Larina ran her fingers over it, marveling at the skill it must have taken to create such a thing. She didn't recognize it, and that above all else set her mind at ease. At least here in this chamber, she could avoid the ghosts of her past. She didn't remember the room at all, nor anything within it.

At the end of the bed hung a dress. She could only assume that Yasmeen intended it for her, and one glance convinced her that she wouldn't be wearing it. The beaded bodice wouldn't allow her to breathe, let alone move if the situation required it, and the long skirts would allow no access to her knives unless she wanted to strap one to her leg and hike up the dress every time danger presented itself. She turned toward the door, where a small silver bell hung on a string that disappeared into a hole in the stone. When she pulled it, a matching bell would ring down in the serving quarters, alerting them to her needs. This, she remembered all too well. She tugged on the bell with an intense feeling of déjà vu, half expecting Miriam, her old nurse, to come bustling in with a tray of sugar rolls—her favorite sweet—and a glass of milk.

But of course that didn't happen. Mimi had been of advanced age back then and would be long gone by now, Larina assumed, if she'd made it out of the fire in the first place. Instead, a young girl with her serving dress tugged down low to show off her curves came flouncing in.

"I can't wear this," said Larina. "Do you know where my chests are?"

"They won't be here for at least another hour, miss," said the girl. "Does the dress not fit? I can have some others brought up."

"Can you find me leggings and a tunic? I'll wear them with my cloak."

She'd brought it along with her, sealed in a pouch. It might smell a little musty, but she could air it out while she took her bath.

The girl tilted her head, looking at her like she'd grown another head. "You want to wear leggings and a tunic instead of that dress?" she asked incredulously.

"I have a job to do," Larina explained. "I can't move in that thing."

"Oh."

The girl was mollified now that she knew—or assumed—that Larina would prefer the finery if only she had a choice. She swiped up the dress with a practiced hand. "You'll be wanting plain colors then, I assume?" she asked.

"The darker the better," said Larina.

The girl nodded, paused, and said, "What is your job, miss?"

"I'm a Praetorian Guard. Can I count on you to find me something suitable?"

The girl's eyes widened, likely eager to ask questions about the guard and all of its imagined excitements. But one pointed glance at the dress reminded the girl of her duties. She nodded, setting her curls to bouncing.

"Yes, miss. Of course, miss. I'm Viola, if you need anything else."

"Just towels, please."

"They're in the baths. This way, let me show you."

With eager deference, Viola got her situated in the baths and hurried off to find her something suitable to wear. Larina, ever cautious, took a moment to inspect the space and place her knives at the ready before sinking into the steaming water. She needed to have all of her wits about her. In just a short while, she would come face-to-face with the usurper, and she could not afford to fail so close to her target.

Out of the bath, she wrapped herself in a cushy robe left for her. When she returned to her room, she saw that Viola had delivered a pair of black breeches, a dark purple tunic, and a pair of fine black knee high boots. She dressed quickly, plaited her hair, and put on her cloak and belt. It took a little time to figure out the best places to hide her knives, but finally, she was ready.

Yasmeen stepped out of her room at the same time as Larina. The sorceress wore a diaphanous gown of powder blue that looked like it might float away with her at any moment. Larina gave her an approving smile while the sorceress looked amused in turn.

"Someday, I'll see you in a dress, and then I'll probably faint from shock," she declared.

"It doesn't happen often," Larina allowed. "If it's necessary for the job, I'll dress up. But I'm always working. Even when I'm not working, I could be working."

Yasmeen arched a perfect brow. "What do you mean by that, exactly?"

"The Praetorian Guard has a reputation. Even if I'm not on a job, I carry it with me wherever I go," said Larina.

"I hope this isn't overstepping my place, but I had the

impression that you aren't completely satisfied with the guild. Was I wrong?"

Larina paused to consider the question. Had she spoken out somehow in a way that she shouldn't have? She decided not. Nix read her mind on occasion too. That kind of thing must happen in friendships.

"I don't think complete satisfaction is in my character," she admitted. "But you're not wrong. Garret and I don't always see eye-to-eye. I have definite opinions on how things should be done."

Yasmeen laughed. "I bet you do. You'll have to tell me about them sometime. But for now, let's get to dinner before the food gets cold."

Together, they walked through the chilly halls to the dining room. Larina steeled herself before the large wooden doors. This room she remembered quite well, with its long tables and thick purple curtains. This section of the castle had gone untouched by the fire and shouldn't have changed much. Unconsciously, she rubbed at her left arm. The burn marks were difficult to spot at a distance thanks to Garret's skilled herbalists, but the shiny skin still felt tight and uneven. It hurt sometimes, a phantom pain that Larina suspected came from her mind more than her body but still found herself unable to combat.

The guards gave them respectful nods before allowing them through. The room beyond the heavy doors matched Larina's memories closely, but of course the purple curtains had been replaced with bright red ones, and Elrin's flag hung above the high table as a constant reminder of who ruled over them. A few people sat scattered about the room, eating in silence. This scene didn't resemble the crowded, vibrant dinners she remembered from her girlhood, with the entire royal family in attendance and the tables packed to bursting with visitors and high staff. She remembered music and heat and the constant press of voices, and sometimes there had been dancing. But now the room had the aura of a crypt.

Yasmeen led her inside without noticing her hesitation. Only one person occupied a seat at the high table, and the sorceress led her straight toward him, bypassing the long tables full of delicacies no one had shown up to enjoy.

"Dezrick!" chirped Yasmeen. "I'm glad you're here. I have someone to introduce."

Larina eyed him with interest as they approached. Prince Dezrick was ostensibly her charge, and she would have to protect him—or at least give the appearance thereof —while she determined how to get to the king. She'd played with him a few times in her youth, enjoying raucous games of stones and towers and hide and seek while Elrin and her father talked trade agreements and border patrols. But she didn't remember much of him, and of course they both had changed quite a bit since then. He'd been close to her age, although she didn't remember exactly how old. But it put him in his late teens now.

She didn't remember his mother at all, but the resemblance to his father was clear in his rust-brown skin and dark eyes with their long lashes. He wore his hair longer than Elrin, the neat braids brushing his shoulders. He had the same sharp features, but the full lips did not at all resemble his father's thin, angry mouth. Perhaps those had come from Queen Cleora.

He glared at Yasmeen. "What do you want?" he asked, his voice flat.

Yasmeen didn't respond at all to the rudeness. She carried along as if he had proclaimed his delight to see them.

"I wanted to introduce Reagan of the Praetorian Guild. Your father has hired her to stand as your bodyguard in light of the...recent developments." Yasmeen's voice faltered over this last phrase, struggling to find the right words for the situation.

Dezrick barely glanced at Larina as she stepped forward and bowed her head.

"I need no bodyguard," he declared.

Yasmeen opened her mouth to respond, but Larina spoke first. She'd dealt with charges like this; he would run roughshod all over her if she allowed him the space for it, and she would be unable to pursue her true objectives if she remained at a mercy to his whims. She had to establish control early.

"The king believes you do," she said. "I promise you'll find me no interference to your usual pursuits."

Dezrick glanced at her again before turning his attention back to Yasmeen as if she hadn't spoken. "Send her back," he ordered.

Yasmeen made a show of settling into her chair. "Reagan, please, have a seat," she said, gesturing to a spot further down the table, away from Dezrick and his awful manners. "And if you'd like her to be sent back, that's simple, Your Highness. Just order your father to do it."

Dezrick choked on his drink, spraying the table. His face flushed in angry embarrassment as he dabbed at the wet spots on his clothes with his napkin. Yasmeen said nothing, and Larina followed suit, watching to see what move he would make next. He eyed his plate, still nearly full of glossy vegetables covered in a creamy sauce, thick-crusted bread, and a variety of delicate pastries with fancy candied decorations on top. The sweets filled almost half of the space. Larina might have found that endearing if the young man in possession of the food hadn't been acting like a spoiled brat.

"I don't need a bodyguard," he repeated, his expression mulish.

Yasmeen remained unruffled. "After what happened to Queen Cleora—"

"Don't say her name!" he interrupted, pushing away from the table. "This conversation is over."

Larina kept her expression neutral as the prince stomped off. Automatically, she evaluated him as he moved, looking for the tell-tale signs of a skilled combatant, but she found none. He walked with a pronounced limp, his right leg lacking the range of motion necessary for a smooth stride. The sword at his hip looked more ornamental than anything else; its rich leather grip bore no indents from repeated use. He wouldn't be protecting himself. Either he was in denial about the situation or just needed to grow up.

Elrin deserved him. They deserved each other.

Larina turned back to the table. Yasmeen's expression betrayed a faint hint of exasperation beneath the impeccable manners, but the sorceress forbore to comment. "I'm so sorry for the rude display," she said. "Shall we have some dinner?"

The assassin surveyed the long, empty table. The center spot with its oversized carved chair piled with red pillows sat empty, the place setting before it untouched.

"Should we wait for the king?" she asked.

Yasmeen shook her head. "He wanted to be here but has been unavoidably detained. I hope you'll understand."

Larina didn't want to understand. These halls threatened to overwhelm her with ghosts better left buried. The specter of her own death loomed large, not as something to be feared, but as a long-overdue peace. She'd earned it. Welcomed it. But the longer she delayed, the less certain she became that she'd chosen the right path, that she would set things right. If only Elrin would show up so she could finally end this.

But of course she couldn't say any of that. She kept her expression bland, allowing none of her roiling emotions to show on her face.

"Of course. I'm sure he's busy," she said.

"Shall we?" asked Yasmeen, gesturing to the spread.

Larina smiled, making sure that the expression reached her eyes. Even a courtier's trained glance would not spot her lie. But as she filled her plate, her mind was full of visions of death. This delay would not affect the usurper's fate. The Shadow could be patient when necessary, even now.

Chapter Ten

O nce Dezrick and his sulky attitude had vacated the premises, Larina and Yasmeen enjoyed a fine meal. The quiet room suited them both. As they'd discovered on the ship, neither of them needed bustle and excitement to be content. They enjoyed quality conversation when one of them had something to say but didn't feel the need to fill the silence with meaningless chatter. Now that the rocking of the ship no longer dampened her appetite, Larina tucked into the excellent meal with gusto. Even Yasmeen did more than pick at her food.

Finally, they both pushed back from the table, sighing in contentment.

"That was..." Larina stumbled over her words. "Excellent," she finished.

Her face flushed. She'd almost pointed out that the food was as good as she remembered. Novice Praetorians made this kind of mistake, not the guild's most renowned operative. The day's experiences must have shaken her more than she'd realized. She would have to take extra care for the rest of the night.

Luckily, Yasmeen assumed that her stumble came from different origins, saving Larina from the need to come up with an excuse herself. The sorceress laughed.

"It's a little overwhelming, isn't it?" she said. "The food here is so good that sometimes I forget not everyone eats so well."

Larina nodded.

"What now?" asked Yasmeen. "Shall I show you back to your room? You'll learn the layout of the castle soon enough, but I remember getting lost so many times over my first few weeks here. It's a maze for certain."

Larina nodded, lost in thought. "Regardless of the prince's opinion, the king isn't likely to change his mind about my assignment, is he?"

"Definitely not."

"Until I get further instructions, then, I'll begin the job as I see fit. I'm here to protect the prince, and that's what I'll do."

Yasmeen tilted her head and studied Larina for a moment, long enough to make the latter concerned. The silence grew between them, until Larina worried her friend struggled to find some kind way to say something monumental.

Instead, she only said, "I admire you, Reagan. You don't let anything stand in the way of what you intend to do."

Larina bowed her head. "I'd say we have that in common, milady sorceress."

"It almost sounds like you're kidding, but I'm going to elect to take that as a compliment."

"Then you're wise as well as beautiful."

Yasmeen rolled her eyes at this. "Now you sound like a courtier. Come on. I'll show you to the prince's rooms. He'll be in a fine snit when you arrive at his door, won't he?"

"I'm sure he'll be thrilled to see me."

Larina almost asked about the prince, but of course an experienced courtier like Yasmeen wouldn't tell her anything of substance. Especially not out in the open. Perhaps if she found the right opportunity she would inquire later. They had built a bond that encouraged honesty, but of all people, Larina knew the limits of such a friendship. She might value Yasmeen's company, but she wouldn't dream of disclosing her true identity. There would be no way of knowing how far Yasmeen trusted her in return.

Instead of pursuing the topic further, Larina stood. One of the silent servants who waited at attention by the wall immediately approached to clear her place, eyes lowered with respectful deference. Yasmeen led her toward the door without acknowledging their presence, and so Larina did the same. She would make friends with the staff later. The gesture had helped her in many a job before. But at the moment, she had a prince to chastise. To her surprise, she found that she looked forward to the experience.

The corridor outside of Prince Dezrick's door was surprisingly empty, a fact that Larina filed away for later. Had Bastian reassigned the prince's guards when she'd arrived, or had the younger royal gone unguarded until now? Each option came with its own questions. None of them were good.

She rapped on the door. Dezrick opened it a hair, took one look at her, and ordered her to go away. Then he slammed it in her face.

She rapped again.

This time, when he opened it, he put his face an inch from hers and stared her down in a manner probably meant to be threatening. But Larina had been on the receiving end of stare downs from the likes of Garret, and this little princeling didn't intimidate her in the least.

"Do I need to call the guards?" he demanded.

"That depends," she replied in the calmest of tones.

"On what?"

"On your goals. If you hope to have me removed from the premises against my will, calling the guards will do no good. While the captain has trained them well, their skills won't do much good against the average Praetorian, and I'm the best there is."

His eyes raked her figure before he let out a scornful snort. "I could pick you up with one arm," he said.

"I could kill you before you even moved. I'm sure your guards would respond well to the threat of danger, but they have to see it coming first."

"And no one sees you coming, is that it?" he asked, his dark eyes flashing with anger.

"Not unless I want them to."

She put no bravado into her tone, but she knew her skill, and her confidence must have shown through. Dezrick gave her another long look before opening the door with a grumble, gesturing for her to enter.

"You might as well come in, then," he said. "Otherwise you'll scale the walls like a jeweled lizard and hide in my curtains to spy on me."

"Jeweled lizards are poisonous. They wouldn't just hide in your curtains," she said as she entered the room.

"I didn't compare you to one on accident."

She chuffed in amusement, making a quick circuit of the room. Compared to the blissful unfamiliarity of her chambers, this suite was all too familiar. If the sofa were moved to this wall here, gauzy curtains fitted over the windows, and bookcases arranged against this wall, it would look just like her sister's room had so long ago. That door to the left led to her old bedchamber. The sight broke through Larina's carefully cultivated focus with ease. Her eyes grew watery as memory after memory assailed her. Slamming that door in her sister's face after some stupid argument. Sneaking through it late at night and curling up next to Iliana's warmth after a nightmare. The room beyond, with its tapestries and toys.

Her eyes threatened to spill over. Dezrick hadn't noticed because he was too busy sulking. But he would. She faked a sneeze, covering her mouth politely and taking the opportunity to wipe the tears away before he could mock her for them.

With effort, she tore her eyes away from the door, resuming her focus on the task at hand. The chamber said little about its inhabitant. Beyond the luxurious furnishings and tapestries, the prince had done nothing to personalize the space. She saw no evidence of martial pursuits; no swords beyond the little-used one at his hip, no practice armor tossed onto a chair or wooden staff propped up in a corner. In fact, if not for the man himself, who moved stiffly to one of the plush chairs and sat down to eye her with distrust, she would have thought the room unused. Perhaps this testified to the excellence of the household staff, but she didn't think so. Dezrick either had no personality of his own or refused to show it.

"Do you intend to loom over me all of the time like a vulture, or will you sit down?" he asked.

In lieu of an answer, she perched on the chair opposite him, tilting it to give her a better view of the doors. She didn't expect anyone to try to kill the prince, and if it happened, she wasn't sure she'd make much effort to protect him. He'd been insufferably rude so far, and given his close personal relationship to the man who had killed her family, she might not lift a finger if a hundred assassins came barging into the room. But a heady combination of professional pride and personal caution kept her alert. No one here knew her true identity, but this castle would never be safe for the likes of her.

Dezrick leaned forward, his hands on his knees, and favored her with a surprising smile. When he wasn't acting like a toddler, the prince cast a striking figure, nearly a head taller than Larina, with a slim-hipped build. He wasn't exactly handsome, but that smile would win over crowds. Too bad he was so rude.

Out of habit, she looked him over, noting his weaknesses in the event that they ever crossed blades. He would present no danger. His hands bore no callouses from hours of practice, and his slight body lacked the mass for unarmed combat. The lamed leg jutted stiffly out in front of him, its lack of muscle tone obvious through the fine velvet of his leggings.

"How long have you been spying for my father?" he asked, his light voice in contrast to his words.

The question surprised her with its ridiculousness. She would cut off her own head before she sold her soul to Elrin. She stood against everything he stood for. But she could say none of that, nor let a hint of it show on her face. She laughed aloud.

"Do you suffer from paranoia, Prince Dezrick?" she asked. "It's the only explanation I can come up with for such a ridiculous question."

He blinked. "Paranoia? No." Then he marshaled his annoyance once again, but with effort. "If you're not my father's lackey, then explain yourself."

"That's easy enough. I am a member of the Praetorian Guard. Did your father's people not inform you that I was coming?"

"This is the first I've heard of it." He waved that away. "A Praetorian, hm?"

She nodded. "Yes. Given recent events, your father has found it appropriate to hire you one of the best bodyguards in existence."

"What makes you so good?"

Larina frowned. She would have expected that an heir of such advanced age would be in the know on the true nature of the Praetorian Guild. A good king would prepare his heir to rule in the event that illness or battle struck him down prematurely. Either Dezrick had failed to learn or his father failed to teach him. She wouldn't have been surprised by either explanation.

"Well?" he pushed.

She decided to tell him. If she made an enemy of him, she'd have a more difficult time getting to the king. It would be better if he accepted both her presence and opinions without question.

"We are assassins," she said. "I meant what I said about your guards. From what I've seen, they are well-trained. But I'm not only a guard; I'm also a hired killer."

"You?" He shook his head. "You look like the average fighter would snap you like a twig."

"That's part of my advantage. I am always underestimated. No one would ever expect someone like me to present any real danger."

He shrugged, but she could sense the wheels beginning to turn in his mind. She didn't want that. A vapid, unthinking prince would be much easier to control than a spoiled one full of demands.

"What do I need an assassin for?" he asked.

"Someone got past all of those well-trained guards to hurt your mother. I'm trained to look for the weaknesses in a security detail. I'll be fixing them to ensure no one comes back for you as well. In the meantime, I'll also act as your personal bodyguard."

Dezrick snorted. "I'm unimportant. You should be watching the king."

"He hired me to watch you."

"But why?"

The question gave her pause. Now that the prince had brought it up, she realized it had been bothering her too. Why did Elrin want Dezrick protected when he clearly had a history of putting his own welfare and prosperity before everyone else's? If an assassin had killed the queen, wouldn't he expect to be the next victim rather than his son? Wouldn't he want the bodyguard for himself? She couldn't see him as a doting father, but perhaps her own experiences of him clouded her judgment. At the least, she could see him protecting his line of succession, even if he couldn't be bothered to care about the person attached to them.

"Perhaps he trusts in his own martial skills," she suggested, unsure of whether she believed it herself.

His face twisted. "I'm not much of a fighter, I will admit." He toyed with the thick golden ring on his index finger. "Never had the stomach for it."

"You get used to it after a while," she offered.

"I suppose." He stood abruptly, taking her by surprise. "Very well. I can see that you're determined to be stubborn about this, and I expect that if some villain climbs through my window, they'll pick you up and toss you out it without even breaking a sweat, but you can stay in the suite next door."

He pointed to the door that led to her old rooms.

"Oh. But I…"

She trailed off. Larina wanted nothing less than to sleep in those rooms again, but a true bodyguard wouldn't pass up an opportunity to bed down closer to her charge. In some cases, she'd insisted on sleeping on the floor with a particularly slippery client. She wouldn't do so here, because spending every waking moment with Dezrick would eliminate any possibility she had of getting to the king, but this, she couldn't pass up without arousing suspicion.

"What?" he demanded, some of the arrogant exasperation creeping back into his voice.

"We'll have to have my things brought in. They gave me another room already," she explained.

"This makes more sense. Do I have to tell you every time I leave? You won't be following me into the bath, will you? I have a private bath here in my suite."

"I can promise that I have no desire to watch over you while you bathe," she said. "Checking the suite before you enter will do."

"Good. Then go and get your things. I'm growing weary."

He dismissed her with a wave of his hand, and she went to the wooden door that used to separate her rooms from her sister's suite. It couldn't be the same door; the fire would have burnt that to a crisp. But even the scrollwork on the handle looked just like she remembered. With a heavy heart, she opened the latch and pushed the door open.

The space beyond did not hold a stick of her old furniture. Like Dezrick's rooms, the layout had been changed by some unknown designer, and Larina had to suppress the automatic urge to move things back to where they belonged. The bed should be under the window, and there ought to be a wardrobe over along that wall. But there was the stone on the ceiling that resembled a grinning face, and down there was the nook where her mother had taught her to read. She had come home after all of these years only to find home had changed so unbearably that it hurt. It was as if she and her family had never existed.

On one wall hung Elrin's red flag. She tore it from its moorings, flung it on the ground, and sank down beside it to weep.

Silvery moonlight filtered in through the window, the cold light of Amalthea, the smallest of the moon goddesses. The traitor. Larina watched the shadows creep over the ceiling, unable to relax. She'd gotten into the bed for about a minute and rolled around to give the appearance of sleep to anyone who might enter, but otherwise, she couldn't make herself rest in this room. Every time she shut her eyes, she became convinced that she smelled something burning.

All of her usual tricks to calm down in the middle of a

job didn't work. She tried meditative breathing, a skill she'd learned off a Heliotrine monk in the remote sandy steppes of Roshai. Attempts to work through her feelings logically did nothing to relieve the squeezing panic in her chest every time she closed her eyes. A soothing herbal tea made with the water left on the sideboard by some kind chambermaid quenched her thirst but otherwise offered no relief. She would get no rest tonight.

Accepting this fact calmed her nerves when nothing else had worked. The average Praetorian could function on little to no sleep for extended periods of time. She knew how to remain operational using herbal tinctures and meditative practices. It might not be the ideal situation, but she could still achieve her goal under these circumstances.

Come to think of it, she could get the whole thing over with tonight. The king's rooms were within reach; why was she waiting? The wee hours of the morning presented a prime opportunity for surprise attacks. The guards would have settled in by now, weariness gripping them as the hours ticked by with nothing to see or do. With the benefit of surprise on her hands, she could bypass them with a minimum of bloodshed and kill the king. Then she wouldn't have to agonize over the possibility of failure or sit here and stare at the familiar yet foreign outlines of her childhood bedroom in the night. By sunrise, she would either be dead, or free for the first time in her life.

Her mind made up, Larina moved with swift efficiency.

She rumpled her hair as if she'd been asleep, tugging her braid to and fro until wisps of hair stuck out. Then she pulled a dressing gown on over her tunic and leggings, took off her boots, and went out into the hallway in her stocking feet. As she walked toward the kitchens, she made note of her surroundings. A plan had started to form in her mind, and she filled it in as she went. At the top of the stairs stood a guard who jerked to attention as she approached. He eyed her with caution, but she disarmed him with a sheepish smile and asked for the location of the kitchen.

"Down these stairs and to the left, miss," he said, pointing in the correct direction. "I'd show you myself, but I'm afraid I can't leave my post. The guard at the bottom can point you on from there."

"Thanks so much," she said. "After all that travel, my schedule is all messed up. My stomach keeps grumbling so much that I can't sleep!"

"You could ring for a maid to bring you something," he offered with a hesitance that suggested he worried the suggestion might be unwelcome.

"And pull them from their beds too? I'd feel too guilty."

This time, when she smiled at the guard, he returned the gesture. It turned his craggy face into a kind one.

A few minutes later, when she returned with a piece of sugar roll and the kitchen cat tucked under one arm, he pointedly didn't ask what she was doing. But the expression on his face spoke volumes. Better to explain it away before he got too curious about her actions and mentioned them to the wrong person.

"I thought I saw a jeweled lizard in my room. It was probably just a shadow, but you can't be too careful with these things," she said, holding up the drowsing cat. "I hope the kitchen staff won't mind if I borrow him. I was hoping he could hunt it down."

"Not at all, miss. That's what he's here for. I had a younger brother who got bit by one of those bastards." He coughed into his fist. "Sorry for the language, miss."

"No worries. I hope your brother was okay?"

"He died." He fixed her with a piercing look. "Let me call someone up to search your room to be safe. I don't like sending you in there with just a cat, even if it probably was nothing but a shadow."

She waved away the concern. "I've dealt with much worse in the sands of Roshai. I used to pull sand snakes out of my bed on the regular. But I promise not to take any unnecessary risks. If kitty sniffs anything out, I'll come out here and wait with you while he takes care of it. Does that seem reasonable?"

He nodded. "Absolutely. I'll be here for another hour or so, miss. You call if you need me. My name's Herris."

"Thank you so much," she said, continuing toward her room.

She passed by an open door, firelight flickering in the

chamber beyond. The back of her neck prickled as she passed it, all senses alert for a potential attack. But the lone figure in the sitting room beyond napped peacefully in an overstuffed chair, her head tipped back, mouth gaping open.

Miriam, her old nurse.

Age had stooped her shoulders and whitened her hair to a ghostly halo, but Larina would have recognized her anywhere. Mimi had been the one constant in her childhood, the one person whose presence could always be relied on. As an adult, she understood her parents' obligations, although as a child, sometimes she'd resented them. But Mimi had always been there, and Larina had mourned her just as deeply as the rest of her family. Her heart leaped. The need to throw herself at the old woman and sob in relief and loss gripped her with such intensity that she swayed. Her throat tightened with the threat of tears, and only by digging her nails into her palms was she able to maintain control. She withdrew in silence, forcing herself to turn her back on that memory of safety and love. She could no longer afford that weakness now that she was a handmaiden of the Dark God himself.

Back inside her room, Larina took off the dressing gown, tucked her braid into her collar, and pulled on her gloves. She triple-checked her belt and knives. It might have been more satisfying to plan a bigger death for Elrin after waiting all of this time, one that would hurt, but the knives would have to do. A quick death in the night, with no one there to hold his hand and comfort him in his last moments. He would be just as shocked as her family had been.

Before she left, she took a moment to consider padding her bed as if she still slept in it but decided against the ruse. If Dezrick came knocking, he would want something specific. Spoiled royalty like him expected everyone around them to leap to attention when ordered, and sleep would not deter him. She paused to listen at the adjoining door between their rooms but heard nothing. No movement, but no snores or mumbles either. She would just have to hope he was a silent sleeper.

Although the rooms appeared to be in good repair and scrupulously cleaned, Larina took the time to oil the hinges with a small vial from her belt. When she'd opened the door, it hadn't been as silent as she liked. This time, however, it moved without a sound, allowing her to peek through the gap.

She couldn't see much from here. The hallway turned just beyond Dezrick's door, leading to Elrin's suite of rooms. But when she'd gone to Dezrick's room earlier, she'd taken the time to scope out the rest of the surroundings. The nearest guard stood just around the corner, with another pair of them clustered right outside Elrin's door. The lack of guards assigned to Dezrick intrigued Larina. Either Elrin had pulled them off the moment she'd arrived

—which didn't make sense—or he hadn't bothered with them in the first place. If Larina didn't know better, she'd suspect that Elrin wanted his son dead and gone, but then why would he have hired her? If this had been any other assignment, she would have looked into that further. As it stood, though, it would work to her advantage.

Silent as a shadow, Larina slipped out the door and latched it behind her. Although she had the passage to herself for the moment, she had little idea how often the guards patrolled. She'd marked the sound of footsteps throughout the long hours of the night around every half hour or so but didn't yet know how strict the timetable was, or how many guards patrolled, or how many she'd failed to hear. She would have to act quickly. She placed the drowsing cat in the far corner of the hallway. It wouldn't be drowsing for long.

When she was younger, Larina had imagined all kinds of complicated and daring methods to get to her victims. Wall scaling would be involved, dangling dramatically from tall towers as she crept from nook to cranny and then in through the window. Once inside, she'd engage in stirring and dramatic battle, using secret assassin weaponry never seen outside the Praetorian ranks. To her youthful dismay, she'd found early on such showy displays only made the job harder. No one survived to admire her skill anyway.

As a result, Larina had abandoned flashy plans for careful economy, finding the holes she could slip through without pomp or circumstance. She'd learned to pay painstaking attention to the details of every room she entered, and once again it paid off. En route to the kitchen, she'd made note of the wooden beams that ran down the corridor, supporting the roof. The stone ceiling arched up over them with plenty of space to move, and the beams themselves were a thick wood, certainly sturdy enough to hold her weight.

The corridor didn't allow her a great deal of space to build up speed, but she didn't need much. She ran up the wall, gaining just enough height to grab the beam that ran from one wall to the other. Splinters caught on her gloves but failed to pierce the tough leather. With feline nimbleness, she swung her feet up and climbed atop the beam.

Although she hadn't made much noise, she crept to a shadowy corner of the wall and waited there. If anyone came to investigate, they would be highly unlikely to see her there. People rarely looked up.

After a moment, one of the guards paused at the end of the hall and scanned the corridor, attracted by the noise of her movement or simply on routine patrol. He didn't see her up in the shadows, nor did he take notice of the cat curled up in the far corner. After all, what threat could a little cat be? His curiosity sated, the guard turned with crisp precision and returned back from whence he came.

It took all of her considerable balance to creep along the narrow beam while crouched to fit in the space above the rafters. With slow deliberation, she made her way over the heads of the guards to the end of the corridor.

She had nearly reached the king's door when it opened, taking her by surprise. Her shock intensified when Yasmeen stepped from the chambers, her normally perfect hair tousled and her mouth reddened from rough use. Larina had known that her friend remained loyal to the king, but the sorceress had to have more self-respect than that. Still, she could not deny what Yasmeen's disheveled appearance implied. Perhaps the king had forced her to sleep with him? Larina couldn't decide whether that would make her feel better or worse about the situation.

Yasmeen pulled her wrap tight and left without any inkling of the presence above her. Larina's eyes followed her, drawn with anger and sorrow in turn. The sorceress deserved better than him, but what choice did she have after a life of slavery and servitude? Killing him would free her, and Larina could only hope that Yasmeen would be grateful for it when everything came out.

After a few minutes, an unearthly yowl filled the air. The scalespine had done its work; Larina had dosed the cat with a perfectly harmless tincture in her room. Now that the herb had worked its way into the animal's system, it would be manic and uncontainable for the next half hour or so, after which it would promptly fall into a contented sleep. But no one else knew that. After a startled moment, all three of the guards rushed down the hall to investigate the awful noise, leaving nothing between her and the doorway.

She would have a few seconds at least, while they searched for whatever had alarmed the cat. Hopefully the king was asleep by now, sated after his rendezvous with Yasmeen. She knew from her childhood that the thick door blocked most of the noise from outside, and the suite of rooms beyond it was huge. Elrin would have to be standing at the door to hear anything happening here.

Moving in swift silence, just inches from her goal, Larina dropped to the floor. She landed in a crouch and went to the door, opening it with swift silence. The door latched behind her with a muted click. Light streamed in from the balcony where Elrin had stood just a few hours earlier and condemned a family to death. What she would do now would help even the score, for her family and for theirs.

The fire had not gotten this far, but still the new arrangement and furnishings made the space alien and unfamiliar, and it took her a moment to orient herself. That door over there led to the queen's former study. The door on the right led to the private bath. The one in the back would take her to the master bedroom.

Larina was halfway to the bedroom when the door to the study opened and Bastian stepped through.

Chapter Eleven

For one shocked moment, Larina and Bastian stared at each other from across the king's private antechamber. Wrinkles from the bedclothes creased the guard captain's face, but his eyes remained alert. For a moment, Larina considered fighting her way through him, but she quickly discarded the idea. She could best him, but it would be loud. Elrin and the guards would be alerted by the noise, and she couldn't take them all on at once.

He drew his sword and brandished it at her. "What are you doing here?" he demanded in full voice.

Larina slid into the icy calm that usually accompanied her work. The feeling refreshed her after the emotional swing she'd been on all day. She'd planned for this possibility, and she knew exactly how to handle him.

"I'm testing your security, as I was paid to do," she responded. "To be honest, I expected better."

He sputtered, closing the distance between them and holding the blade to her throat. With effort, she kept her hands down, allowing him to manhandle her. When the king threw open his doors, he saw a young woman with arms at her sides and his captain, red-faced with anger, holding a sword to her skin. The king planted his feet, striking an imperious pose.

Then he bellowed, "I demand an explanation."

"I found her in your rooms," began Bastian. He sounded confident, but then, as the words left his mouth, he looked from Larina to Elrin and back again as if trying to ascertain if the pretty young woman had been summoned to the king's presence for a private meeting in the bedchamber. "I thought you were in danger," he added in a weaker tone.

Elrin's gaze settled on Larina, and she forced herself not to flinch. He couldn't possibly recognize her. When she'd last seen him, she was a five-year-old with missing teeth and fiery red hair. With her hair dyed and the maturity that age had leant her, she looked nothing like the girl she'd been. Although she felt very small right then, looking into the eyes of the man who had stolen her family from her. It took all the willpower she had not to lose control completely, pull her blade, and thrust it into his throat. But she would settle for nothing less than a sure thing. The opportunity would come.

"Explain yourself," said the king.

"I am Reagan the Shadow, of the Praetorian Guard," she said. She remained unmoving in Bastian's grasp, making a show of how nonthreatening she could be. "My job, as I understood it, was to assist in your security. I began by testing it."

"And if you did make it to my bedchamber, what would you have done then?" he demanded.

"Waited until you awoke and advised you of the threat to your safety, as you hired me to do."

The king glowered at her. "I hired you to look after my son."

"I sent all of the guards outside of his room to chase a cat. I assumed that you would want a full security analysis, as most of our clients do. In the absence of direct instruction, I took the initiative to begin it."

Elrin considered this for a moment, nodded once, and turned his attention back to Bastian.

"Release the girl," he ordered.

"I don't like it, sire," began the captain.

"You don't like *me*," murmured Larina.

The king's keen ears picked up on the comment, as she'd hoped he would. The corner of his mouth twitched.

"And why is that?" Elrin asked in a smooth voice.

"I bested him one-on-one," explained Larina.

"You cheated!" Bastian exclaimed.

The king threw back his head and laughed in harsh amusement. "This little thing beat you in a swordfight?" he demanded. "Were you drunk?"

Bastian flushed. "No, but she *cheated*."

He would have explained more, but Elrin shushed him with a wave of the hand.

"Enough. I require sleep. Captain, return to your rooms. I expect a full reckoning of how this little girl managed to gain entry to my rooms tomorrow. You will patch these gaps in my security. Unless you need assistance?"

"Absolutely not," Bastian answered.

Moving with slow calculation, Larina grasped his hands and pulled them away from her body. Then she stepped free and curtsied for the king, her teeth clicking down on her tongue with such agitated force that she tasted blood in her mouth. With effort, she restrained herself from the deep, court-trained curtsey that her mother had drilled into her when she was four. Instead, she made her obeisance simple and hated herself for it.

"Please let me know if I can be of assistance in this endeavor, Your Majesty," she said, knowing that Bastian would do everything in his power to avoid taking her up on the offer.

The king grunted before returning to his bedchamber. In his wake, Larina half expected Bastian to try something.

She'd humiliated him in front of his men on the ship, and now she'd done it before his king. But he said nothing as he stalked over to the door and flung it open, gesturing for her to leave. His eyes shot daggers at her as she exited.

Frustration and fury gripped her as she returned to her bedchamber. She'd been so close. The opportunity would come again, but she couldn't suppress her disappointment.

After she returned to her quarters, Larina fell asleep on top of the covers. Perhaps she'd worked herself to exhaustion, but she'd trained and fought much harder, usually ending up agitated and full of post-battle nerves. This had been exactly the opposite. Coming face-to-face with the usurper after all of this time had exhausted her. He hadn't recognized her, and she hadn't lost control and launched an ill-considered attempt at his life. All in all, the experience had been a bit anti-climactic, but she didn't mind. Now she could return to her tried-and-true methods of planning a job unfettered by emotion.

She needed little sleep and managed to wake before most of the household despite her late night excursion. As the sun rose over the rooftops, she bathed and dressed in the growing light. A little green lizard skittered over the stones of her windowsill, attracted by the heat. It reminded her of her need to return the cat to its rightful place in the kitchen if the guards hadn't done so already, and so she went to hunt down the kitty and give him a treat for his assistance the night before.

These tasks done, she grabbed a flaky pastry from the staff tray set out in the kitchen, exchanging a few friendly words with the cooks and their many assistants. They accepted her compliments with politeness but were disinclined to talk as they bustled to and fro with trays of baked goods for the breakfast spread. She returned upstairs with a contented belly just in time to see Dezrick open his door and peek out as if he expected someone might leap at him. When he saw only her, he sighed.

"Come on, then," he said, heading down the hall.

He ignored her for the rest of the morning. She stood behind him as he dined in solitude, picking the pieces of spiced ham off the top of his savory roll and setting them to the side. He'd avoided all of the meat dishes on the buffet as well, Larina noticed. Once again, Elrin's place at the great table stood empty, and most of the castle residents stopped in to grab a morsel on the go. No one greeted the prince. This may have had something to do with the black cloud of ill manners that followed him everywhere. Larina wondered if father and son were equally disliked within these walls, and if so, whether she might make use of that fact. She would explore the idea later.

His breakfast finished, Dezrick stood, grunting at the porter who appeared at his shoulder to take his plate and pull out his chair. Then he stomped out without so much as a glance to see if Larina followed. It appeared that this job would not require extensive amounts of small talk, which suited her just fine. She disliked the pastime and would have hated it even more with Dezrick involved.

As an added bonus, the silence gave her time to think. Bastian would be adjusting his security arrangements at this very moment, and he'd do everything in his power to keep her out of it. Even if she was consulted on the matter, she had to assume that he'd leave out as much information as he could, since he neither liked nor trusted her. She'd have to start from scratch and make her own observations. This would likely have to wait for a few days at the least, as both the king and Bastian would be wary of her after last night. If they failed to thaw, she could manufacture an event to allow her to save someone—like Yasmeen—and set their minds at ease about her usefulness.

She continued to strategize in this manner while Dezrick led her through the castle. His leg seemed stiffer this morning, and the air hung thick and heavy with rain. He moved slower in the damp, and she made a mental note of it.

At last, he stopped at a door on the first floor, tucked away in a section of the castle she had rarely visited during her youth. If she remembered it right, this part of the castle had been full of offices and studies back then.

Dezrick pulled the door open to reveal a massive library that smelled of old books and polished wood. Shelves ringed the large space, stretching all the way to the high, vaulted ceiling. Books packed them near to bursting. Attempts had been made to contain the collection with a few standing shelves arranged in precise rows along the left-hand side, but it appeared to be a losing battle. Ornate armchairs and long tables furnished the remaining open area; one of the tables was already strewn with open books left by some eager reader.

With the shutters closed, the flickering lanterns lit the space with a warm and peaceful glow. Larina took a moment to check the windows and peer into the dark corners as a bodyguard ought to, but her mind focused less on the presence of potential predators and more on the reading nooks set beneath each window, piled with silken pillows. It would be luxurious to spend an afternoon here if not for the odious presence of a certain prince.

The annoyance in question sat down at the messy table and lost himself in the pages of his book, so she busied herself by thinking through her mental map of the castle, making adjustments to reflect the day's observations. This would come in handy later. She had always found that repetition helped her make the split decisions that separated life from death. Besides, she had nothing else to do.

The morning ticked away, minute by agonizing minute. The long silence made Larina miss Yasmeen and her agile conversation. No one entered the library, and Dezrick appeared ready to stay at this table for all eternity.

Larina walked the perimeter of the room once every hour or so to keep herself awake. These long tedious hours tended to be the worst part of bodyguard detail, but it wouldn't do to allow herself to be lulled into inattention. With her luck, Bastian and the king would show up and find her drowsing on the job.

But when the door opened, it didn't reveal those unwelcome guests at all. Instead, her old nurse Miriam came in, balancing a tray of food. The heavy tray threatened to topple her frail figure over, but she smiled as brightly as Larina remembered. The urge to rush over and hug her took such a hold over her that Larina had to avert her eyes for a moment to regain control.

"I've brought your lunch, Your Highness," said Miriam.

Her voice crackled with age, and she coughed at the end, averting her head to avoid spitting all over the food. At that very moment, she reached the edge of the woven rug that insulated the center of the room from the cold stone beneath. Her foot caught, and both the tray and the nurse went flying. Miriam slammed into one of the oversized chairs, while the tray clattered to the floor amidst a spray of broken dishes and spilled tea.

In situations like this, Larina knew her duty. As the prince's bodyguard, she was expected to ignore the fallen woman, remaining alert for any potential threats rather than allowing herself to be distracted by the tumult. But she didn't care about Dezrick. *He* certainly wouldn't help. Quite the opposite; he'd probably yell. Perhaps if she stepped in, she'd forestall the temper tantrum she knew was coming from his royal spoiledness.

So she broke protocol and went to Miriam's side. To her complete astonishment, Dezrick did the same. They leaned forward in tandem to take the old woman's elbows, meeting each other's gazes over the top of Miriam's bent head. Larina could see her shock reflected in his eyes. After a moment, Dezrick turned his attention back onto the nurse.

"Are you hurt, Miriam?" he asked with more gentleness than Larina would have given him credit for. "Can you stand?"

"I'm so sorry, Your Highness. Please, don't mind me. I'll clean up this mess in just a moment, after I've caught my breath," replied Miriam, her voice shaking.

"You'll sit down and rest a moment, and I won't hear any arguments about it either," he replied with stern kindness.

"Please don't trouble yourself. I'm just a silly old woman who needs to watch where she's going."

"I said no arguments. Let us help you up," replied Dezrick.

Together, Larina and Dezrick helped the nurse into the cushy chair she'd collided with moments before. Larina couldn't believe how light Miriam was; how frail her frame had gotten. She'd never been a big woman, but the past few years had stripped the vitality from her bones. They'd done nothing to dampen her spirit, however. She forced a shaky smile as they helped her into the chair.

Once Miriam had been deposited in the chair, Larina began to pick up the broken china from the floor, placing it on the tray. Dezrick watched her for a moment, lips pressed thin with some private thought he didn't care to share. But finally, he spoke.

"You don't need to do that," he said. "I'll ring for the staff to take care of it."

"No, no!" exclaimed Miriam. "I'll clean up and fetch a new tray. I'm feeling much better now."

Dezrick put out a hand to stop her attempts to rise, and after a moment, the nurse subsided, shaking her head at him with fond exasperation. Larina couldn't believe her eyes. Dezrick, acting like a decent human being? She would never have expected such a thing, although maybe she should have. Miriam's true kindness and determined spirit could charm anyone, if given enough time. That had to explain it.

While the prince rang the bell for assistance, Larina continued to pick up the broken shards.

"The maid will be here in a moment, Reagan. You should leave it," he said, looking down at her.

"I'm in charge of your safety, and broken crockery all

over the floor is a hazard," she replied. "It would get in the way if we needed to exit the room in a hurry."

"Hmph," he replied.

The door opened to admit a familiar chambermaid— Viola, who had helped Larina find suitable clothing the first night she'd arrived. This time, however, the serving girl didn't even notice her. Her eyes locked on Dezrick with an awe that bordered on mindless devotion. The girl was so infatuated a blind man could have seen it.

"How can I help, Highness?" she asked, dropping into a deep curtsey that showed off her cleavage.

Dezrick didn't so much as glance at her, seemingly oblivious to the effort she was making to secure his attention.

"Have this cleaned up, and bring us a new luncheon for three..." he trailed off, his eyes on Miriam. "Shall we call for a healer?"

"Don't you fuss at me, now," said Miriam, irate. "I'm quite well. Just a bit of a tumble is all."

"Very well," said Dezrick with a hint of a smile. "That will be all, then."

Viola paused, looking up at him through the fringe of her lashes, begging to be noticed. But after a moment in which no recognition came, she straightened.

"Your wish is my command," she said, heading for the door on a wave of disappointment.

Either the maid excelled at her job, or perhaps her

desire to impress the prince added extra fire to her step, because quicker than Larina had expected, the mess had been cleaned up and a new tray brought into the room. Dezrick spent the time tidying up his books to make room on the table, and Larina kept watch as she should have been doing all along. If she snuck a few glances at the elderly nurse, it was only to check on her injury. It had nothing to do with their past.

Finally, the door closed behind Viola, who promised fervently that she would be "right outside, just in case Your Highness needs anything. Anything at all." Dezrick approached the chair and offered his arm to Miriam.

"Come sit with me," he said. "We'll lunch together."

"It isn't proper," she protested, glancing at Larina.

"I insist."

With some good-natured grumbling, Miriam allowed herself to be persuaded to sit at the table with Dezrick. Once she was settled, he made up a plate for her, which she insisted would be too much even though he hadn't even filled it halfway. But he would not be dissuaded. Then he poured out the tea.

"No lemon for me, please," Miriam requested.

"I remember." After he turned his attention to filling his own plate, Dezrick added, "Are you going to sit down or what?"

It took Larina a moment to realize that he was

addressing her after the morning's long silence. She cleared her throat and repeated Miriam's protest.

"It wouldn't be proper," she replied.

"Well, you can do what you like, but you must be hungry. You won't be able to watch my every move if you faint from hunger," he said.

"Be nice, Dezrick," said Miriam.

"I *am*," he insisted.

The two of them stared at Larina until she sat down just to make them stop. Dezrick handed her a plate, and she busied herself filling it. Now that she got a whiff of the food, she realized how much her belly ached. Her meager breakfast had been too long ago, and the smell of freshly baked bread, sharp cheese, and the warm spices of the tea awakened her hunger. She dug in with gusto, hoping that keeping her mouth full would help her to avoid further conversation.

Miriam and Dezrick chatted with easy familiarity as they dined. Mimi hadn't changed a bit. She'd always spoken to Larina with respect even when others disregarded her because of her youth, and she treated Dezrick with the same fondness. Larina could barely believe the change in the prince, who treated Miriam with eager solicitousness. He appeared to be a completely different person than the stubborn brat she'd met the night before, and she began to wonder if perhaps her perception of him had been clouded by her hate for his father. But she hadn't imagined his rudeness toward Yasmeen, nor his dismissal of her. Larina didn't know what to think, so she remained silent.

"Could you pour me some more tea?" Miriam asked, turning to Larina with a kind smile. "I'm so sorry, I didn't catch your name."

Dezrick jumped in before Larina could reply herself. "That is my fault," he said. "Please excuse my poor manners. This is Reagan, a Praetorian Guard. My father hired her to watch my back in light of... recent developments."

His face fell, and for the first time, Larina saw how much the loss of his mother had hurt him. That could excuse his strange behavior. Grief did things to people. Sometimes she still felt its clinging effects herself, more so now being back in her childhood home, so she couldn't fault him for that.

Miriam put her hand to his face. Larina remembered being on the receiving end of the exact same gesture in her youth, after she woke from a bad dream or cried out in sickness. She couldn't keep from staring at the wrinkled, ashy hand of the old nurse against the burnished youthful glow of Dezrick's cheek. She wanted nothing more than to fling herself into Mimi's arms, but she turned her eyes to her plate instead, allowing him to grieve in privacy.

After a moment, he cleared his throat, and the moment passed. Larina poured Miriam some tea.

"Thank you, dear. My name is Miriam. I'm so glad you're here," Mimi said.

The old nurse offered her hand, and after a moment, Larina shook it with gentle care, loathe to inflict any additional pain. Although Miriam hadn't drawn attention to her discomfort, Larina had noticed the tension in her carriage and the way she turned her body to avoid using her left arm as much as possible. She'd hit that shoulder on the chair pretty hard.

Instead of the expected handshake and release, Miriam clung to Larina's hand with painful determination. She met Larina's blue eyes with her deep brown ones, searching her face. For one awful moment, Larina thought she'd been discovered. Maybe she did resemble her mother as she'd feared and hoped in equal measure. But the moment passed. Miriam didn't shout her name, and Dezrick didn't call for the guards to take her away in chains.

Instead, Miriam said, "Thank you for helping me, Reagan."

"It was my pleasure," replied Larina.

Miriam released her then, and Larina returned to her meal with her heart pounding in her chest. Dezrick sensed the tension in the room and turned the conversation to his boyhood exploits, a topic that Miriam quickly warmed to. The two of them teased each other with obvious fondness, allowing Larina to sink back into quiet. She watched and listened and tried not to enjoy herself. Finding a single ounce of happiness in this place—with Elrin's son, no less —would betray every memory she had of her family.

A shift in her opinion of Dezrick would complicate things. If he was following in Elrin's evil footsteps, she wouldn't feel bad about removing the king's foul influence. But if he wasn't, she would regret causing him pain.

Troubled and conflicted, Larina couldn't force down another bite. She pushed her plate away and sat in silence while the other two finished their meal. Miriam attempted a few times to draw her into the conversation, but she answered all of the questions posed to her with polite briefness, and eventually the nurse let her be, returning her attention to the prince.

Larina knew it was better this way, but it still made her heart ache.

Chapter Twelve

Dezrick took dinner in his rooms. He had an extra plate brought up for Larina as well, and she took advantage of his offer to sit and rest her aching feet. Without Miriam's unshakeable positivity, this meal lacked the easy conversation of the luncheon, but at least the silence between them lacked its earlier antagonism. Instead, Dezrick treated her with a sort of brusque politeness, and she kept her responses as brief as possible without being rude.

As she finished her meal, her eyes fell on an instrument leaning in the corner. She would have recognized its triangular shape anywhere. One knob near the tip was noticeably darker than the rest. Years ago, she'd broken it trying to get it off the wall while her mother rested.

It was her mother's psaltery. In Dezrick's room.

He noticed her sudden interest, following her intent gaze to the wall. With obvious pride, he picked up the instrument and the bows tucked behind it, offering them to her.

"Beautiful, isn't it? Do you play?" he asked.

"Not since I was a child," she said, holding her hands up in refusal. She did not want to touch her mother's favorite possession after all of this time. To find that the instrument had survived the fire pleased and saddened her at the same time. She didn't think she'd be able to control those emotions if she held it again. "But I love to listen."

"I've been trying to teach myself, but I'm not very good," he admitted. "Maybe someday I'll be able to play something without embarrassing myself."

She nodded, rising from the table, eager to escape the haunting presence of the psaltery. Every time she turned around, she saw something that made her face the horrible tragedy that befell her family once again. She'd known there would be ghosts in these walls, but nothing could have prepared her for these constant gut punches of memory.

She needed to get out of there but couldn't do so without being released by the prince.

"May I take your plate, Highness?" she asked.

"Please do. I think I'll retire early." He stood from the table and waved her away. "I promise I won't so much as take a piss without notifying you first."

"Given your en suite facilities, I'm not sure that's necessary. But I appreciate the consideration."

He didn't even seem to note her faint attempt at a joke. Lost in his own thoughts, he hobbled back to the door that led to his sleeping quarters and let himself in without another word.

Back in her bedroom, Larina busied herself with a few minor housekeeping chores. She sharpened and cleaned her knives, oiled the leather grips to keep them supple and strong, and topped off the herb vials she'd used on the cat from the larger stash in her bag. She bathed, washing and re-plaiting her hair without much fuss or fanfare. Once she'd finished, she could hear no movement from Dezrick's rooms. She hoped that he had gone to bed without delay, but she waited a bit longer to be certain.

Shortly after the click of the patrol's boots passed her door, Larina got up from her bed. This time, she padded the sheets, creating a reasonable facsimile of her body huddled under the covers. The prince had begun to show some manners, and the ruse might hold in the event that he came to request her assistance. If it didn't, she'd already made a big show of testing the security and could use that to justify her absence.

After a quick pause to arm herself, she went to the secret door Captain Flynn had used to take her to safety so many years ago. It took some doing to figure out the cleverly disguised mechanism that opened it, but she'd studied secret doors at the keep and knew what to look for. That combined with her vague memories helped her figure out what to push and where to pull.

The door slid open. A blast of stale air hit her in the face. Based on the cobwebs and dust, no one had discovered the passage in the intervening years. That didn't surprise her. No living castle resident would have known it existed, since only her immediate family and the captain had been in on the secret. When Captain Flynn first showed her the passage, she'd considered it a fun little adventure, but at the end it hadn't been fun at all.

In the thick dust, two pairs of footprints remained visible on the floor. Age and time had blurred them, but she still could make out the staggering marks of the larger footprints and the scurry of the smaller ones, evidence of her flight with Captain Flynn so many years ago. She knelt down to get a better look. The painful unevenness of the captain's prints stabbed at her heart. He must have been in agony, but he had protected her, nonetheless. She wished she could repay him somehow, but he'd left behind no family as far as she knew. Only her, his fake daughter, remained to mourn him and to set the scales straight on his behalf.

She searched for an opening mechanism on this side and tested it before pulling the door shut behind her. The absolute black of the passage pushed in on her, but she'd remembered to bring along a lantern. After lighting it, she started to make her way down the tunnel.

This time, she climbed out on her own, staring down at the empty dirt where Captain Flynn had spilled his lifeblood. Nothing remained now to mark his sacrifice, and that saddened her more than she would have expected. In an attempt to distract herself from the tears that pricked at her eyes, she looked around. The alleyway was different than she remembered, much cleaner and with a small fountain at its mouth that she didn't recall. After a quick glance around to orient herself and verify that no one had seen her climb out of the secret door, she checked the opening mechanism, then closed it up and made sure it left no hint of its existence.

For a while, she simply wandered, indulging in memories. The same small lizards scattered at her approach, abandoning their search for nighttime insects to snack upon. The same russet-colored walls lined the streets, their surfaces still warm from the long day of sunshine. The same circle of bakeries and artisans ran around the marketplace. She stopped at the statue of the Three Sisters and touched the hems of each one in turn. Larina needed all the luck she could drum up.

But there were so many differences too. Identical red flags hung on every corner in an overwhelming display of Elrin's constant presence. Her favorite shop where she'd bought candies had been replaced by a cobbler, the windows full of shoes. The flat dirt of the marketplace had been supplanted by neat cobblestones. Everywhere she turned, she found something new to wonder at. So much was the same and so much had changed.

Given the late hour, she saw next to no one on her ramblings. Once, she spotted a pair of night watchmen patrolling an adjoining street. She took a detour into a small park and allowed them to pass, eager to avoid their attention and questions. All of the shops had closed for the day, their windows shuttered tight. All except for one luthier's studio, where it appeared that the owner had left for the night without extinguishing the lantern, and a smithy.

The smithy attracted her attention and she paused to look into the window out of curiosity rather than need. But then she spotted a finely-wrought bow on the rack, displayed with a few staffs. The place must employ a woodworker as well as the smith himself, creating a one-stop-weaponry shop. She stared at the bow for a long moment, the vague outlines of a plan forming in her head. She owned a bow, of course, but stashing an extra one in the right location within the castle could give her the opportunity she needed. She wouldn't have to worry about being spotted with the weaponry en route to the job.

After a moment's consideration, she rapped at the door. She waited a long time before the latch clicked and the door opened just enough for the person inside to look out. The poor light and the cracked door made it difficult to make out their features, but Larina noted the height and build nonetheless. By their size alone, she assumed she addressed the smith.

"What do you want?" they asked in a surprisingly feminine voice.

"My apologies for disturbing you so late. I was passing by and saw your light. I wondered if you might be willing to do some business," Larina replied, keeping her hands out where they could be seen.

"And how do I know you don't intend to rob the place?"

"If I wanted to rob a shop, I wouldn't choose the one that's full of weapons."

The shape on the other side of the door paused, considering this.

"Fair enough," they said.

The door opened the rest of the way, revealing a mountain of a woman. Larina barely came up to her shoulder. She had long, blond hair streaked with gray and a face creased with smile lines. Although she was on the tail end of middle age, muscle ridged her forearms above her folded sleeves, and she held a heavy cudgel at her side like it weighed nothing.

"Madame smith," said Larina, bowing her head as the woman stepped aside to allow her to enter. "Thank you."

The shop area smelled of metal and oil, a fresh, bright

scent that enlivened Larina's senses. To her right stood a counter, emptied of wares for the night. Along the walls, racks of weaponry stood, awaiting their new owners. Although she would need to take a closer look to be certain, their lines appeared clean and strong, their designed unburdened by frippery or needless decoration.

"It's too late for a young thing like you to be alone on the streets," said the woman, frowning in concern.

"I work long hours. There's no escaping during the day."

"What do you do?"

"Private guard. I spend most of my time standing in corners and trying not to fall asleep. My name's Reagan."

"Ah." The woman took her measure, nodding in satisfaction. "Yes, I suppose you aren't as helpless as you look. I spot at least four blades on you from here."

"You have good eyes."

"I have a nose for metal." With a glimmer of humor, the woman tapped her nose. "Come on out," she called. "The girl is harmless."

A tall figure stood up from behind the shadowy counter. The young man held a hammer that rivaled the smith's in size and heft, and his coloring, build, and features left no question of his parentage. He could be no one but the smith's son. His pleasant face was closed and cautious, and he made a point of setting the hammer out where she could see it. His mother rolled her eyes in exasperation.

"I am Kyra, and this stubborn mule is my son Alaris," she said. "What can we do for you, Reagan the guard? Are you looking for a new blade to add to your collection?"

"I have plenty of those for now, although I can see that this is the place to get them if I find myself in need. I saw a bow in the window, though, and I'm in the market for the right one if I find it."

"That would be my handiwork," said Alaris, pride tinging the suspicion still on his face. "What size are you looking for?"

Larina held out her hands. He peppered her with questions about her draw, her intended use, the range and power she preferred. The more he asked, the more certain Larina became that she would find what she needed there. The young man understood the need for a weapon to fit its owner. Without that true fit, even the best-made blades wielded by highly trained fighters would never reach their full potential.

His questions completed, Alaris disappeared into the back room and came out with three bows. He set them atop the counter with a flourish and gestured.

"I think one of these will suit you. If you'd like to try them, I have some targets in the back," he offered.

The selection took just a moment. The largest of the three bows he'd offered featured a sinewy dragon carved into the handle, its tail wrapped around the weapon. It felt apt that Elrin would die at the hands of a weapon carved with her family's symbol.

"This one," she said.

"You should try them all," put in Kyra. "Test the differences."

"This is the right one," insisted Larina. "But I'll test it to be sure."

"Hmph."

With obvious disapproval, Kyra gestured for the two of them to follow, leading them into the rear of the shop. Alaris paused to let Larina go first, his caution disguised as a show of manners. In their situation, she would have done the same, so she didn't blame him in the slightest. She too was cautious, even now. But Kyra led them to the targets as promised. As she set them up, Larina caught Alaris's eye and held up the bow.

"This is beautiful work," she said.

His face lit up with the compliment.

"I spent a long time on the carving," he admitted. "I even studied dragon anatomy to get the proportions right. It's such a pity that they're extinct. I'd do just about anything to see one in the flesh."

His face glowed with excitement, and she couldn't help but smile.

"I'm not sure I share the sentiment, since an untamed

dragon without a rider would probably roast us," she replied. "But it's still gorgeous."

He shrugged, unswayed. He'd change his tune if a wild dragon ever appeared in the skies, venting its fire and rage on the people below. Larina had heard similar vows before, but the will to survive always overcame them in the moment.

Larina turned her attention to the practice space, taking note of the high walls lined with bales of hay to catch any stray projectiles shot by unskilled buyers. The smith finished her set up and gestured for her to take her mark. Before Larina stood a row of round wooden targets with freshly-painted bullseyes at their centers, flanked by a pair of well-stuffed mannequins. Larina pulled a neatly-fletched arrow from the quiver next to the shooting line. She tested the pull of the weapon, letting it tell her how it wanted to be held, seeing how it responded to minute adjustments in her shoulders and arms. It nestled into her hands like it had been built for them. When the arrow loosed, she didn't even need to look to know that the missile flew true. It buried itself in the mannequin's heart. She shot three more in quick succession, clustering them tight. The final shot split her first arrow in two.

She turned to see an impressed-looking Alaris and an impassive Kyra.

"I'll take it," she said.

Alaris burst into an excited stream of compliments and

questions. He wanted to learn to shoot with such accuracy. Where had she learned? Had she ever considered giving lessons? He would trade arrows for them if she was interested. She greeted his enthusiasm with noncommittal politeness. Under different circumstances, she might have taken him up on it—arrows could get expensive, and she'd been nothing but impressed with the quality of his work. But she didn't intend to be in Crestwynd City for long. She wouldn't have the opportunity to collect on the deal but left the door open just in case her plans changed.

Kyra watched them both with implacable calm, allowing her son's excitement to peter out. Then she said, "I'll take eighteen silver for it."

Larina nodded. "Sold."

By the surprised look on her face, the smith had expected to haggle, but Larina intended generosity. She pulled out a single gold coin, exceeding the asked price. When she handed it over, Kyra gestured.

"Come in, and I'll give you the change," she said.

"No need," Larina replied. Kyra arched an inquiring brow. "It's worth it. Your work is worth more than you're charging, and I'm hoping my purchase—and my skills—can remain discreet. Besides, I owe you for the arrow I broke."

"The arrow was worth it just to see you shoot, but I'll not argue with generosity." Kyra elbowed her son. "You hear that, Alaris? No babbling on to everyone who walks through the door about the skills of the late night archer."

He rubbed his arm, looking annoyed. "I'm not deaf."

"Then keep your mouth shut, you hear?"

"But why wouldn't you want people to know how good you are? You'd get more work as a guard that way. Better hours too, I bet."

Before Larina could manufacture a response to that, Kyra said, "Not everyone wants to brag, son. For example, I'll wager we've had a few of those Praetorian guards in here before, but they're always honor bound to keep quiet about their work."

"Sure, but I don't see how that's applicable here," said Alaris. "The Praetorians are giant mountains of men, not small things like her. No offense meant to you or your skills, miss, but they'd have to be big to protect their charges. I heard that the Shadow once fought off an entire flock of pteros himself on the steppes of Moradin. He'd need the strength of five men to do that."

The story was mostly true. She'd had a small contingent of guardsmen with her that day, most of whom had turned out to be useless. But two had helped. One had distracted the pteros by getting her head ripped off, and the other—her lover—had run screaming after her and got disembow-eled for his trouble. The flock had gone blood-mad. The resulting feast had given her the necessary time to plan a counterattack.

"I met a Praetorian once," said Kyra. "Before you were born. He barely came up to my shoulder, and I swear that his waist was no bigger around than my thigh. But I wouldn't have messed with him if you paid me, and I tended toward hot-headedness back in those days."

"You've never told me that before," Alaris protested before turning back to Larina. "Are you one? A Praetorian?"

"If I was, I wouldn't admit it," she said, not unkindly. "It's late. I'd best be going so we can all grab some sleep. But it's been a pleasure doing business with you."

Kyra nodded. "If you need us to stay open late again sometime, leave a note under the door. We're not often here at this hour, but I'll stay if I know you're coming."

"That's much appreciated," Larina replied. "Good evening."

She let herself out into the street and headed back toward the passage, taking care to make certain no one followed her. She had everything she needed now. Once she picked her location and time, she would plant the bow in place well before making the attempt. It would be easy.

Elrin would die, and not even Bastian could stop her this time. She smiled in satisfaction as she contemplated it.

Chapter Thirteen

Although she yearned to put her new purchase to good use, Larina took her time planning her next attempt on Elrin's life. This time, she would not fail. Over the next few days, she took advantage of every minute. Dezrick continued to spend most of his time in the library, poring over books with a scholar's zeal. Ever since that awkward dinner when they'd discussed her mother's psaltery, he'd treated her with cool dismissal. He didn't return to his initial spoiled behavior but instead chose not to speak to her unless absolutely necessary. Then, he said only the bare minimum, refraining from any personal comment. This left Larina free to plan during the day and make arrangements at night before grabbing a few hours' sleep and doing it all over again.

It didn't take very long to get everything into place,

although impatience threatened to consume her. She watched Elrin's bedtime habits for a week. He was very schedule-oriented, rarely deviating from his patterns with the reliability of a former military officer. She picked the perfect moment to attack and the best location from which to do it. Just in case, she set up a safe house with a few essential supplies at the ready. But she'd always known the odds, and she'd come to peace with them.

For the first time, she dared to picture it. She'd never imagined a future free of her need for revenge and from the guild that had sat at the center of her life ever since her childhood. She would be able to go anywhere and do anything so long as it didn't take her into the path of the Praetorians. Perhaps she'd go south to Roshai and hire herself out as a bodyguard for the traveling caravans, or set up a trade route herself. The desert settlements paid good money for supplies and necessities to those brave enough to dare the dangers of travel in the remote regions, and she had the skills to get in and out alive. The more she considered it, the more the idea appealed to her: a quiet life moving from one town to the next, buying and selling, beholden to no one. She could pick a new name of her own and start again. Live her own life this time.

The dream felt like a luxury she could finally afford. It sustained her through the long boring hours standing at attention in the library and the sleep-deprived nights of preparation.

The night before her second attempt on Elrin's life, Larina took the evening to rest. She put her feet up, enjoying a cup of her special blend of soothing camender tea, reserved for these moments when she prepared to take a life. But now that everything stood at the ready, she followed the old ritual of preparing herself to do her job to the best of her ability, without emotions or fear.

After she finished the drink, she stretched in her room, limbering up her muscles without taxing them too much so they would be at peak performance. Then she took herself to the baths and had a nice long soak in the steaming water. When she returned to her room, she sat at the window, looking over the rooftops onto the city below. Whatever would happen tomorrow would happen. She had done her job well. Captain Flynn would be proud.

When she went to bed, she quickly fell into a restful sleep. No nightmares plagued her that evening. For some reason, they never came the night before a planned assassination. It was as if the ghosts of her family stood at bay to allow her to do what was necessary.

The next day passed at a crawl. Larina ate well to fuel her body for the job, but she tasted little. She dwelled over every aspect of the plan, turning it, evaluating it, making certain that she knew each nook and cranny. She had prepared for every likely scenario and quite a few unlikely possibilities as well. As she stood at the end of the long table in the library and waited outside of Dezrick's doors, they played in an endless loop within her mind.

Finally, she sat down to dinner with the prince. Although they had barely spoken over the past few days, he still insisted on her dining with him in a flagrant disregard for protocol. He took her presence for granted now. She wondered what kind of man he would become without Elrin's malign influence. Would the need for vengeance against her consume him as it had her? She could only assume so, and the knowledge filled her with a strange, conflicted mix of resolution and regret. Dezrick had shown hints of decency. But she owed nothing to Elrin's son, who sat in her rightful place. She cared less about the status or power, but she couldn't get over the fact that he enjoyed the company of his family—or at least some of it. If the usurper had just deposed her family, sending them off to some remote backwater, she could have been happy, because they would have been together.

Dezrick dined in silence, an open book at his side. She recognized its cover—a treatise on responsible economic policy by Verdegris the Elder, an ancient scholar who had counseled the first king of Oramis and the first queen of the Barren Isles both in turn. The book gave her pause. It had been one of her mother's favorites.

Dezrick caught her eye on it and held the cover up for her inspection.

"It probably seems boring, but it's actually quite interesting," he said.

"I've heard that it's good but never read it myself."

"Ah." He paused and then added diffidently. "I could loan it to you once I'm done, if you like."

"Thank you. That's very kind." But she didn't want kindness from him, not right now. That would lead to guilt on her part. Besides, she wouldn't have the opportunity to read it. "Shall I take the dinner plates away?"

"Yes, please. I think I'll retire early and try and finish the book. My brain is full to bursting, and I'm eager for something light to read after this. I was thinking about picking up some of Praetor's tales."

She blinked. Praetor, the founder of the Praetorian Guard, mostly appeared in lurid stories of action and adventure, full of swooning maidens and impossibly stupid villains. They were usually printed on cheap paper for children to read and reenact later during their long hours of play. Not the kind of thing that would be found in his fine library, nor the likely choice of a scholar eager for learning.

He snickered at the confusion on her face and said, "I'm just kidding. Good night, Reagan."

"Good night, Dezrick."

Before retiring to his room, he nodded to her as if acknowledging her presence again for the first time in a long while. After a moment's consideration, she nodded back. Although the exchange left her feeling like she hadn't gotten to know the prince at all during her time here, she gathered up the plates feeling a bit better about the future. With his father out of the picture, Dezrick would be okay.

A cold rain pattered on the cobblestones as Larina emerged from the secret passage and into the dark streets of Crestwynd City later that night. Although spring had coaxed the stubborn sprouts of plants and flowers out of window boxes and garden plots, winter still refused to let go without one last reminder of its power. The pelting downpour stung Larina's skin until she pulled her cloak close about her. The Praetorian garment was reversible, and she'd chosen to turn it inside out for her purposes, so that no insignia or crest would betray her true identity to anyone who managed to spot her.

Luckily, the terrible weather decreased the possibility of that happening. Although she'd left earlier than usual, the streets had already emptied, and locked shutters covered the shop windows. Smoke curled up from the chimneys, and she could smell meat cooking somewhere in the distance, but otherwise she saw no signs of occupation on the street save a dog rooting for scraps. Even the little lizards that crawled over the walls of the buildings had sought refuge from the storm.

The castle stood removed from the bulk of the city, but a single building sat next to it: a temple devoted to the

Great Mother and all of her children. The body of the temple was a squat round building ringed with exquisite colored glass windows depicting each god in turn. In the center sat a majestic altar to the Great Mother, with a huge bell tower overhead that played songs of worship at midday. Arranged like spokes on a wheel sat smaller altars to the minor deities: the Dark God of death, the Agile Lady who danced over the lands to bring the springtime, the Gentle Shepherd who watched over all animal kind, and more.

She let herself into the temple using a window near the Dark God's altar, just another sign of his blessing. The latch needed tightening, leaving her just enough room to reach in with a carefully selected tool and lift it. She made her way through the building with the confidence of practice. Although her nighttime ramblings had assured her that no one would be here at this time, she kept her eyes and ears alert for signs of life. But she sensed nothing.

She climbed the tall steps behind the Mother's altar. A window off the bell tower took her out to a wide ledge. From there, she inched around the corner to a section of wall in dire need of repair. It appeared that the birds had been pecking at the stone, leaving an uneven surface full of handholds to take her up to the roof. En route, she stopped to retrieve the bow and its quiver of arrows from its hiding place under the eaves.

Dizzying heights no longer bothered her. Back when she'd started to climb, her heart had galloped with fear, and

Garret had sensed her reticence. He'd sent her higher and higher until the terror no longer gripped her with such strength, and now she could undertake any height secure in the knowledge of her skills. Although if she'd had her choice, she would have preferred not to undertake the climb in such a downpour. It made the tiles slippery.

As she reached the edge, her feet lost their purchase on the smooth terracotta tiles that topped the tower's roof, leaving her dangling by her fingertips. Her mind went blank, letting go of everything except for the immediate actions she must take in order to stay alive. Her feet probed for a secure spot to brace herself as her fingertips slowly lost their grip. She planted her boot into a crevasse just in time to avoid plummeting down to a messy death, then pulled herself up to safety before the experience could repeat itself.

Her hands shook with nerves, which she firmly squashed. From here on, she had no reason to worry about falling. She edged around the rooftop until she came in sight of the balcony where the usurper had sentenced a man to death immediately after she'd arrived. She'd expected him to summon her after she'd been discovered in his suite, but he'd extended no invitation, nor consulted her on any security matters. She would have asked Yasmeen about the king's apparent disinterest in Dezrick's safety or her place in it, but she'd avoided the company of the sorceress ever since she'd seen her leaving the king's rooms that night. Ostensibly, Larina had been busy protecting the prince, but she could have found the time to chat with Yasmeen if she'd wanted. She still had many questions about Elrin, but they would have to go unanswered. She could live with that.

Moving with the certainty of practice, she lowered herself down to her hiding place. The ledge supported a row of statues crammed close together, but there was just enough space between the Agile Lady and the Dark God for a small person to squeeze in. The height and the tiny amount of space available to maneuver must have combined to make Bastian dismiss the tower as a potential security risk despite its closeness, and Larina couldn't fault him for it. Many talented Praetorians simply wouldn't have fit. Once she'd squeezed herself in, she settled in to wait, huddled in her cloak against the frigid rain. If his schedule held, it would be hours before Elrin appeared on the balcony. He took a glass of wine out every night to look over the city he stole before heading to bed. The weather wouldn't deter him; he'd been out two nights earlier during another storm that blew in off the sea, watching the roiling clouds from beneath the safety of a sturdy canopy. As he stood there, she would bury an arrow in his heart.

The minutes ticked away. Her hands tingled with the cold, so she tucked them into her armpits to preserve heat and agility. It wouldn't do to miss her shot because her fingers had gone numb.

Finally, the warm light of the lanterns brought Larina to full alertness, as Elrin's servants readied his suite for his arrival. She glimpsed them through the windows, moving in efficient concert. They plumped pillows and set out what she assumed was the evening meal, a long process that required many trays and much fussing. One servant built a roaring fire; she could see its reflection in the glass. Then they departed, leaving the room empty and still once more.

Larina stretched out her fingers and warmed up her limbs. Once Elrin arrived, she wouldn't want to move lest she attract his attention. The dark, moonless night shrouded her from easy view, but at this close distance the light from the castle would illuminate her if she didn't take care. So she readied herself and then settled down into a comfortable stance with her hood shielding her eyes from the rain and her bow at the ready, trying to marshal her jittery nerves. She'd done such missions a million times before, but this one couldn't have been more different. As hard as she tried, she couldn't reach the calm stillness she usually cultivated before an assassination. But perhaps her fury and grief would lend her skill instead of stealing it. They had better, because failure was not an option.

After a painstaking eternity, Elrin himself appeared in one of the windows. He danced into and out of view as he filled a plate, daring her to take the shot. But she knew this impatience all too well. It gripped her every time she attempted to finish a job, this desire to take the first opportunity out of fear that the ideal one would never come. This time, it was more intense than ever. But experience had taught her to stick with the plan, and she would do just that.

Instead, she studied the man who had taken everything from her. In her girlhood, she'd considered him as a friend —of her mother if not herself—and someone who would always protect her. He had the imposing build of someone with strength and power, and at her young age she'd never imagined that anyone would use those attributes for ill gain. She knew better now. He'd only had the appearance of trustworthiness and never the virtue itself. Now age had deepened the harsh lines of his face into cruelness. Finally, the exterior matched the rot inside him.

Elrin disappeared from her view for a while, most likely to eat and dress for bed. She waited still, secure in the knowledge that he would return as he always did to soothe his nerves with a drink before heading to sleep. She reached for her quiver to select the perfect arrow, letting her fingers run over the fletching, waiting for the pull that would tell her this one would strike true. Some part of her wondered if the call of her weaponry had some divine magic to it, if perhaps the hand of the Dark God helped draw her to the perfect instrument of death every time.

Her fingers paused on the end of one arrow. She pulled it free and looked it over. She'd already examined each missile in this quiver, and the dim light made it difficult to see, but she checked anyway, just to be sure. The shaft was smooth and sturdy, the feathers straight and true. This arrow would find its home in Elrin's heart. She touched the tips of her fingers to her prayer braid and thought of her family. Her musical, loving mother. Her father's rare smiles and quiet soothing voice. Her sister's serene devotion. Her brother's incessant excitement. And Captain Flynn, with his grunts of pain and the soothing hands that had comforted her when she cried in the blankets of the cart that carried her away from her home. His hair had been the first addition to her braid, and she treasured it if only for that fact. She would set them all to rest now, and know that she had done her best by the few memories she retained of them. Elrin had stolen them from her, leaving her only with the vivid recollection of the day they'd died.

She nocked the arrow at the ready and waited.

Elrin appeared again, wrapped in a fine red velvet robe. He paused by the windows to pour himself a goblet of wine. Then he disappeared again. For a heart stopping moment, Larina worried he would not come out at all, but finally the door opened and the king stepped outside.

He left the door open wide behind him and walked out to the edge of the balcony with his glass in hand. On the parapets that flanked him to either side, guards stood at the ready, watching for danger, but they couldn't spot her here. The guards at his door would do him no good. It was time for him to die.

Elrin stood at the railing and looked out over her mother's city. She drew the arrow with a smooth, confident motion and took aim at his blackened heart.

A breath in. On the exhale, she would release.

A flurry of unexpected movement took her by surprise. Yasmeen ran out the open door with the giddiness of young love and flung herself into Elrin's arms just as Larina loosed the arrow, a motion as automatic to her as the breath she'd just released. She reacted in instinctive panic, jerking the bow out of line, deflecting the arrow.

The missile thunked into the stone next to the embracing couple. Larina didn't wait to watch the outcome. She already dangled off the edge of the roof. If she could get out of sight before they looked in this direction, she could escape and return to the castle to join the hunt for the assassin. No one would realize that she hunted for herself.

"Guards!" Elrin's voice thundered into the night, his voice carried in the wind. "The assassin has returned!"

Larina dropped down to the ledge below, landing on the balls of her feet. Just a few steps more, and she would be around the corner and out of sight. She hurried toward safety, but the rain made too much speed dangerous.

"There! I see him!" called Yasmeen.

Larina turned the corner and threw caution to the winds, leaping into the tower window and running for her life.

. . .

As she neared the ground floor, the temple doors flew open with an echoing bang. The guards had moved quickly, spurred by the possibility of glory and fame and the acknowledgement of a grateful king whose almost-killer had been apprehended. Swearing under her breath, Larina evaluated her situation.

Given the layout of the building, their arrival forced her to adjust her escape plan. The altar room offered no hiding place. She had to get out. She'd barred the door at the base of the steps to give herself a bit of extra time in the event that something went wrong, and now she was glad for the foresight. But the doors shuddered with such violence that it was clear they wouldn't hold long.

Frowning, Larina backtracked to a small workroom midway down the stairwell. Here, the temple staff kept the brushes and oils to polish the bells until the copper gleamed, the hooks to pull the heavy instruments down to replace their ropes, and other tools of their trade. She bypassed all of these things and went to the small window, unlatched it, and closed it behind her before dropping the twenty feet to the temple roof below. She would have preferred to latch the window behind her, leaving no indication of her escape route, but the panes fit too well. Hopefully she would get away before the guards realized where she'd gone.

The temple garden contained a variety of tall fruit trees, tended in the name of the Gardener, watcher over all growing things. She sprinted across the roof toward the largest of the trees and leaped into its branches. As early in the growing season as it was, the tree had only just begun to sprout, but it had no problems supporting her insignificant weight. Larina crossed over it and leaped to the next tree, a smaller, younger one that swayed with her movement. With effort, she maintained her balance and made the final leap to the wall that separated the temple grounds from the street beyond.

She'd gambled on the fact that this wall wouldn't be guarded if she needed to flee, not while Bastian would still be organizing his search parties. Still, she leaped down off the wall with a knife in her hand, ready for anything. But no one arrived to intercept her nor shouted a warning at her escape. For the moment, she had evaded discovery. It wouldn't last long.

As she rushed down the street, she pulled a black mask from her belt and tied it over her face, leaving only her eyes exposed. Yasmeen couldn't have gotten a good read of her features from so far away. If she had, she would have identified Larina by name if not by gender. Thanks to this mistake, the guards would be looking for a man. If she played this right, she could escape without suspicion and survive to try again.

A few blocks away, she'd hidden a bag of emergency supplies in a pen full of irritable zoats tucked behind an armor shop. She had plied the creatures with treats for a full week before they would allow her into the pen without biting her. All she had to do was reach the stash, and she'd be home free.

The rapid tromp of booted feet announced the approach of the search parties long before she could see them. She melted into the shadows underneath a row of baskets that would overflow with fruit during the market hours. Her small size gave her an advantage when it came to hiding, and the soldiers didn't think to look down into the small space, although they did a fairly good job of searching the area before moving on.

Larina waited until they were long gone before crawling out and setting off again. Twice more, she heard voices down the street and took cover, but she saw no one. The close-set buildings and curved streets made the guards' search more difficult, and she took full advantage of that.

It was easy. It all should have been easy. By all rights, Elrin should have been bleeding out onto the balcony stones at this very moment. But he wasn't, and it rankled. Larina tried to set that aside and focus, but nothing could stop the endless refrain that echoed through her mind. She'd failed. She'd *failed*.

Regret carried her down the streets away from the castle as the buildings grew smaller and less ostentatious, flitting from shadow to shadow with deft skill, avoiding the notice of a group of excited apprentices discussing their day's work on the way home. It led her around the corner toward the zoat enclosure where she'd hidden one of her supply caches. It pulled her off her game. Normally, she would have paused to scan the area, but not this time. The older couple who lived in the neat little cottage next door went to bed shortly after nightfall, their snoring audible from all the way out in the street.

A pair of guards stood right next to the zoats, only a few steps away from her hidden supplies.

For one frozen moment, they stared at each other. Then, before the closest guard could sound the alarm, Larina dashed forward, silencing him with a swift strike of her bow string against his neck. His attempted cry for help turned into a yelp of pain before her nerve strike dropped him like a brick. As he fell, she had already begun to move toward the second guard, who pulled his sword free of its scabbard. He wouldn't be calling for help. She could see him calculating his reward already, expecting that the blade would assure her surrender.

It didn't. It couldn't. Although her face was covered, she couldn't risk identification.

She charged, taking him off guard. He took a belated swipe at her, the heavy blade hurtling at an awkward angle that would present no trouble. She deflected the strike with a practiced sweep of her arm, hitting the flat of the blade and batting it aside. Bastian's men didn't know what to do against an unarmed combatant. She'd noticed that during their shipboard training sessions and chose not to draw her blade.

He tried to bring his weapon around to strike again, but she kept moving, forcing him to adjust his swing, buying precious seconds. Before he could bring the weapon around to bear again, she struck. Her pointed fingers dug into pressure points with the speed of a striking viper: neck, shoulder, inner arm. His hand went numb, the sword clattering to the ground. His unconscious body followed in slow stages, crumpling in a jerky, awkward semblance of a dance.

She hated killing guards, especially good ones. But it couldn't be helped. She dispatched them both cleanly, drawing her knife blade across their throats with a practiced flick, and sent them to the Dark God's embrace without pain. There was no time for a full remembrance, but she took a moment to slice a lock of hair from each of them and tucked it into a pouch. She would add the strands to her prayer braid if she survived long enough.

A low murmur of voices approached from the east. She couldn't get into the zoat pen and retrieve her stash now without being seen. Better to lead the guards away before returning, or skip the stash and head straight to her safe house if she could make it without detection. She disliked that plan. There was too much ground to cover between here and there for comfort.

She retreated down the alley, circling back the way she'd

come. The murmuring voices became shouts of excitement as the new contingent of guards spotted her. With a quick glance back, she evaluated her pursuers. Five men. No bows or other ranged weaponry. All she had to do was outrun them.

At the end of the alley stood a drainpipe, running up the otherwise unclimbable side of a tall mansion. The place had been designed to impose, its unbroken edifice looming tall over the street below. Ornamental crenellations hung down from above, gilded with precious metals, but they would be easily circumvented. Her hands gripped the rain-slick metal without hesitation, pulling her up off the street. As she reached the edge of the roof, the guards came into view, shouting to distant reinforcements.

Larina clambered up and pulled back from the edge, forcing them to guess her location, and crossed the mansion's long roof. The tiles clattered under her feet. The water made them slippery, slowing her down. At the opposite end of the building, a drop-off took her to the top of a series of servant out-buildings. She paused at its edge, looking back to see the guards emerging onto the mansion roof behind her. She had to lose them, and soon, or they would steer her into a trap that even she couldn't escape.

She jumped from the servant's building onto the third-floor balcony of a neighboring manse only to be greeted by a scream of fright from inside. Rather than pausing to apologize, she climbed up a pillar onto the roof and continued to run. The guards behind her reached the edge of the servant's building and paused at the gap to shout for backup, hesitant to jump.

They didn't like heights.

Larina ran along the rooftops, scaling walls and gutters, darting through the open window of someone's home and out the other side of the building without being discovered. She'd left most of her pursuers behind with the exception of a pair of stubbornly persistent guards. Their superior height and longer legs gave them pace on her, but they slowed at every jump, giving her time to make up the ground she'd lost in the straightaways.

Knowing this, she adjusted her route, taking shorter stretches of running and more leaps from one building to the next, taking longer jumps even when a shorter and easier option presented itself. The gap between her and her pursuers began to widen. She kept going, her lungs burning with exertion, but her legs did not falter. Years of training under Garret had taught her to endure pain.

A short distance ahead, the roof of another tall mansion terminated at the opening of a narrow alleyway beyond. The roof had been covered in a slick tile probably selected more for ornament than use. Her heart skipped a beat as she considered making the jump in the rain. She would have to clear almost twenty feet and then brace herself with hands and feet between the two walls or plummet to her death on the street below. It might not be possible, but she saw no other option. At least she didn't carry heavy weaponry with her today to make the job more difficult. The heavier guards wouldn't be able to follow.

If Larina had given herself the time to truly consider what she was about to do, she might not have had the courage. But with the sounds of pursuit growing louder as the cordon tightened, she went for it without hesitation. She sprinted across the slick tile, reached the end of the building, and launched herself into the air. Her foot slipped at the last moment, and immediately she knew she was in trouble. Her angle had been thrown off, leaving her hurtling toward one of the walls instead of straight up the middle as she'd intended. Moving with the automation of instinct, she pushed off, tik-toking back and forth between the alley walls as she made her way toward the ground.

It hadn't been her intended plan, but it worked. Probably better than her initial idea. Rain still pattered down on the bricks, and more than likely, an attempt to brace herself against them would have led to her sliding down to her death. At the end of the alley, she climbed up onto the roof of a candlemaker's shop, turning to look back at her pursuers. They reached the brink, staring at her across the distance. She raised a hand in a cheery wave. Enraged, one of the guards ran at the gap.

The moment he left the ground, she knew he wasn't going to make it. He'd misjudged the trajectory, jumping high when he needed to go long. As he descended, his hands and feet scrabbled against the slick surface without slowing him. She gripped her prayer braid, murmuring a blessing as he crashed to the ground with a bone-breaking impact. She couldn't see the body but no one could have survived such a fall.

What a waste of bravery.

She'd led them to their deaths like zoats to the slaughter, and she regretted that, but such things couldn't be helped. The sacrifice would be worth it if it gave her another chance at Elrin. Despite all odds, it looked like she might have escaped identification or capture. So she hurried off into the night before the sole remaining guard could summon someone to come and help him apprehend her.

When he'd joined the search, Bastian had cordoned off the neighborhood in a vain attempt to contain Larina. She'd heard a pair of guards discussing it as they passed right by the group of laborers she'd joined as they came out of a tavern, singing drunkenly at the tops of their lungs. Good. This would buy her the time she needed to disguise herself and escape to her safe house. She circled back around to approach the stash with the appropriate caution this time but saw no one other than a pair of serving girls lugging a heavy basket of linens between them. Larina offered a hand carrying it up a set of stairs, tugging a cloak out of the stack and pulling it up over her hair as they disappeared into the darkness.

The area remained quiet except for the annoyed bleating of the zoats, angry at being awoken once again. Once they smelled the carrots she'd tucked in a pouch for them, they settled, allowing her to retrieve the bag she'd hidden underneath the rafters of their meager shelter.

She changed quickly, tearing off the stolen cloak and pulling dress and apron over her sweaty and rain-spattered tunic and pants. A neat cap covered her flyaway hair. All the used clothing went into the empty bag, hidden in the straw. After a moment's consideration, she tucked the bow and arrows back up into the rafters. If the guards somehow discovered the weapon, the handiwork might be traced back to Kyra and Alaris. But she couldn't bring herself to destroy such a beautiful weapon. She might need it again. Besides, they didn't know her name.

Her Praetorian cloak would identify her without question, so she brought it with her. Once she'd dressed, she smudged her face a bit, adopting a hunched and shuffling gait. The guards wouldn't take notice of a lamed servant girl except maybe to tell her to get out of their way. They certainly wouldn't expect her to have made that jump. She could hardly believe it herself in retrospect.

In a fit of last-minute inspiration, she got down on her knees in the zoat pen and rolled around. Bits of hay and clods of damp earth stuck to her clothes and cap. The scent of zoat was unmistakable. Her disguise complete, she secured the gate behind her before making her way toward her safe house. It sat on the other side of the city, well outside of their search range. Once she made it past the market, she would be free.

When she entered the market square, a quartet of guards standing near the statue of the Three Sisters took immediate interest in her. She shrank beneath their stares, averting her eyes from the neat uniforms with their royal insignia, their impressiveness not dulled by the spatter of rain. Two of the guards approached her as she slunk across the cobblestones, calling for her to halt.

She complied. It didn't take much acting skill to appear frightened. Most of her jobs left her shaking afterwards even though she usually kept it together during their execution. It wasn't difficult to summon up the appearance of nerves.

"What are you doing here?" demanded the guard, his voice sharp and commanding.

She stared at her feet and mumbled.

"Speak up," he pressed.

The second guard chimed in, his kind blue eyes smiling at her even if his lips didn't.

"You have nothing to be afraid of," he said. "But it's strange to see you out here so late. You should be at home. The streets aren't safe."

Larina allowed her eyes to flick up to his face before

returning to the safe refuge of her feet. Then she spoke all in a rush, as if too nervous to control herself.

"I fell asleep in the zoat pen," she said. "My ma'll be likely enough to kill me when I get home. I don't think I would have woke up at all except for all the shouting. Do you know who was shouting so late?"

The first guard took a none-too-subtle sniff to corroborate her story. The scent of zoat hung around her like a cloud. He couldn't have failed to notice it. But the kind guard simply nodded.

"You're a right mess too, aren't you?" He paused. "I'll tell you what. You tell your ma that the guard kept you from going home and told you to hide in that zoat pen. We were chasing a dangerous criminal. You think she'd be angry at you then?"

She looked up at him again, allowing hope to trickle into her eyes.

"But isn't that lying?" she asked.

The first guard huffed, waving his hand in disgust before walking back to rejoin the group at the far end of the market. But the second remained with her, talking it over with patience, caring about a dirty servant girl who had nothing to offer him in exchange for his assistance. She could only hope that the guards who died were more like the former than the latter, but she would never know. Now she had more deaths to lay at Elrin's feet, more ghosts to avenge.

She thanked the guard for his kindness, overcome with guilt. She'd picked her route knowing the rain had increased the chances of someone taking a spill. She'd hoped the guards would fall back once the pursuit got dangerous, but she'd forgotten to account for the pressure they faced. They would have to return to the castle empty-handed after nearly having her in their grasp. Elrin and Bastian wouldn't be pleased, and the pressure had driven the guards to their deaths. Her skill had been obvious, but they'd engaged anyway. Fear of the king's reprisal had been more of a threat than death at her hands.

She'd always taken pride in her refusal to take innocent lives. On occasion, she'd refused a contract on moral grounds. Once, she'd even turned the tide, killing her employer when she learned without a doubt what he'd done to the young woman she'd been hired to assassinate. She'd taken his money back to the keep, and no one had realized that the wrong person had died. Not even Nix.

It was little comfort after what had just happened. Her shoulders bowed with sorrow and guilt as she entered her safe house. She ate a bit, cleaned herself up, and changed back into pants and tunic. Then she took a moment to plait the guards' hair into her braid, oiling the strands to merge them with the whole. As she did, she murmured prayers for their souls, that the Great Mother would judge them, and sort them according to their deeds. Men like him had ensured her safety as a girl, but they'd also lit her home on fire and murdered her sister before her eyes. It was diffi-cult to take their measure in such a short battle. But the pious practice brought her some semblance of peace, that regardless of their mettle, she'd offered what respect she could. Their strengths—whatever they might be—would be carried with her from this day forward.

She returned to the secret passageway with care. Guard patrols still roamed the streets, but many of the residents had joined them, roused from their beds by all of the noise. She didn't look so conspicuous now. Still, once she'd entered the passage and closed the hidden door behind her, she heaved a sigh of relief.

Back in her room, deep self-incrimination over-whelmed her. How had she been so stupid? She should have taken the shot. Yes, the sorceress had been friendly, but Elrin poisoned the land and killed its people. It didn't matter how much Larina liked her; Yasmeen's life couldn't balance out all the others the king had taken. He'd probably had the queen killed. He didn't seem much concerned about his son's safety either.

She had no proof and probably would never know for certain. But the more she thought about it, the more she regretted deflecting her shot.

The usurper would not get away from her next time. She would kill Elrin or die trying.

Chapter Fourteen

When Dezrick exited his sleeping quarters early the next morning, Larina stood at attention just inside the door to his suite, keeping watch. He was surprised to find her there, like he expected she would guard him from afar. Given his reaction, he must not have heard the commotion the night before. His windows faced the opposite side of the castle, and so the noise mustn't have carried far enough to be heard through his closed windows and heavy draperies. If this was the case, she could use it to her advantage.

"What are you doing?" he asked.

"My job." When he huffed in exasperation, she clarified. "Someone made an attempt on your father's life last night."

He jerked to attention, his eyes searching her face for some hint of the outcome. "What happened? An attempt, you said. So it was unsuccessful?"

She nodded, her face betraying nothing of the disappointment she still felt upon hearing those words. She should have taken the shot. The regret would remain with her for the rest of her life.

"What exactly happened?" he asked, sitting down at the table where they took their dinners more often than not these days. He gestured to her usual seat. "Tell me everything."

But she remained in place, shaking her head. "I would if I could, but we'll have to ask someone else for the full story. Once I heard the ruckus and realized what was happening, I came here to watch over you. I've been here all night. The only thing I know is what I overheard from the guards out in the hall."

As soon as the words left her lips, she wondered if this lie had been a mistake. Although Dezrick hadn't left his room to investigate last night, someone must have checked on the prince at some point during the night. If they challenged her story, she would have to backpedal and claim to have left the room for just a moment to guard Dezrick from a hidden position.

Dezrick frowned, his generous lips flattening in consideration. "I'll change," he said, gesturing to his dressing gown. The fine navy blue velvet shimmered in the light. "You go find out the details. You can tell me over breakfast."

She hesitated.

"I'll bolt my door while you're gone if that's what you're worried about. Besides, no one is going to try and kill me. Half of the time, my existence doesn't even register. I'm fairly certain that my father intends to rule from the grave, so my position as heir doesn't hold much weight."

He didn't sound bitter about it, only resigned. Besides, Larina reminded herself, she didn't care about his welfare, and she wanted to know what the castle gossip said about the night's activities too. It might save her from a slip that would give away her true activities.

"Okay, but stay in here. Don't open the door to anyone but me," she ordered. When he didn't respond, she pressed further. "Promise."

"I'll do as you say," he responded.

"Good. If you haven't, I won't tell you what I've found out."

He put his hand to his heart and exclaimed, "You are the most demanding guard that ever was!" on the way back to his bedroom. The joke made her lips quirk. She waited until she heard the heavy lock slide into place, checked the lock on his front door, and let herself out via the adjoining door between their rooms.

The castle sat still and silent, as if nothing untoward had happened at all. Larina supposed she could ask the guards for information, but she hadn't had much chance to befriend them. Dezrick's activities didn't leave her standing among them for hours with an opportunity to ingratiate herself. She didn't want to risk another encounter with Bastian, who might put two and two together. With reluctance, she turned toward Yasmeen's room. As far as the sorceress knew, they were still friendly, and she would likely be eager to share her information.

Larina steeled herself before knocking, setting aside her personal feelings and focusing on the job to be done. If smiling in the face of Elrin's lover would get her the information she needed, then she would do just that.

Yasmeen opened the door with placid curiosity that turned into a wide smile as soon as she saw who stood outside. She still wore her dressing gown. The same one she'd sported when Larina saw her leaving Elrin's room. But her hair rested over one shoulder in a gleaming coil, and her face was as flawless as ever. She took Larina by the hands and pulled her inside.

"I'm happy to see you, Reagan!" she exclaimed. "It's been so long since we last spoke that I was beginning to wonder what had happened to you."

"I'm sorry," replied Larina, forcing a smile. "Dezrick likes to keep to himself, which leaves me little time for socializing. This has been my first chance to get away. I hope I didn't wake you."

"Not at all. I barely slept a wink."

"Me either. Do you know what happened? Once I realized that the king's life had been threatened, I locked myself in the prince's suite and stood guard to ensure his safety. It's left me out of the loop. Can you tell me anything?"

Yasmeen put a hand to her chest. The nervous gesture didn't appear to be feigned; the hand in question shook visibly.

"It was more than just a threat to his life," she said. "He nearly died, and I with him."

"No!" exclaimed Larina. "Tell me what happened. I must know every detail if I'm to keep Dezrick safe."

So Yasmeen did.

When Dezrick emerged from his room in a bright sapphire tunic and pants, Larina already sat at the table, looking into space but seeing nothing. Yasmeen had told her everything she needed to know, and now she needed to plan anew. Would it be better to try again right away, before Bastian and his guard had a chance to get their feet under them once again? Or should she wait for a while and let them settle back into complacency? As much as she would prefer to get the entire thing over with, she suspected that the latter would prove to be the better choice.

Dezrick's reappearance interrupted this line of thinking.

"What happened?" he demanded, hurrying over to her as swiftly as his lame leg would allow.

She relayed what Yasmeen had told her, being careful to stick to only the details that the sorceress had mentioned. Someone had shot at Elrin on his balcony the night before. Yasmeen herself had been present, consulting the king on matters of a confidential magical nature, and the arrow had narrowly missed them both as they stood talking on the balcony. The would-be assassin had demonstrated preternatural agility, evading a thorough search effort orchestrated by Bastian. But Elrin was convinced that another attempt would be made soon and had doubled his guard.

"So, Prince Dezrick, I hope you'll be extra vigilant too, and not go sneaking off without me. I can't keep you safe if you don't work with me," Larina finished.

He fixed her with a gaze of utmost innocence. "I don't know what you mean. I rarely leave my rooms except to visit the library. It must be a boring assignment to someone as skilled as yourself."

"Boring isn't bad."

"Maybe. But still..." he trailed off, looking at the psaltery in the corner. "You know, it's been a while since I've been out of the castle and I need new strings for my psaltery. I think we'll go shopping today."

She gaped at him. He'd just learned that an attempt had

been made on his father's life, his mother had been assassinated too, and his first reaction was to plan a trip to the market? She couldn't have heard him correctly.

"I beg your pardon?" she inquired.

"You heard me. I'd like to go to market today."

"That is the worst idea I've ever heard."

"Far from it. Rumors will be spreading among the populace. It's my job as a part of the royal family to walk out among them where I might be seen and put their fears to rest."

Her mother had said things like this to her long ago, but she hadn't expected to hear an expression of duty from Elrin's son. She eyed him, pursing her lips.

"Besides," he continued, "I do have the best bodyguard in the entire city. If you're as good as you claim to be, I'll be just as safe there as here."

"Only if you do as I say, the moment that I say it."

"Deal."

"Okay." He smiled in triumph, but the expression faded as she added, "Although I'm not sure if we'll be able to get out the doors. If I was in charge, I'd lock the castle down, and Bastian is no slouch. He'll do the same."

"Scales and tongues," he swore, taking her by surprise. She hadn't expected such coarse language from him. "You're probably right." Dezrick fell into a contemplative silence, staring at her. It took every ounce of self-control she possessed to keep from fidgeting. "Can you keep a secret?" he asked.

Larina went on high alert, although she took care to remain relaxed on the outside. Perhaps she would learn something useful, something she could use to put the prince on the throne. Then she would not have to feel guilty about deceiving him. After all, it was for his own benefit in the end, even if he wouldn't be able to see that himself.

"That all depends on the secret."

"You need to swear," he persisted.

"You know I can't do that. If you're up to something that would put you in danger, I'm honor bound to tell the king," she replied, though Larina didn't mean a word. She owed Elrin nothing, and this secret could be of use to her. Besides, she had to admit to some curiosity. "But if it didn't put you in danger..." she prompted.

Dezrick took the hint with obvious eagerness.

"Oh, it wouldn't. Not with you there."

A grin lit up his face. Funny how the expression transformed him from a spitting image of his father in his youth to a young man in his own right. One with a sense of humor, even.

"Fine. Under those circumstances, I promise," she said.

He nodded. "There's a secret passageway in my suite. I can get us out past the guards without anyone even knowing that we're gone."

Larina kept a straight face with effort. Of course she'd known that her sister's rooms had an escape route built into them just as hers had. But how had he discovered it, if none of her family had survived to tell him of it? Perhaps her own tunnels weren't as secret as she'd thought. She had to learn more.

"Really?" she teased. "And I imagine you just discovered this by accident one day? Or figured it out by reading your books?"

"Don't make fun," he said, offended. "And yes, I did figure it out myself. I'm not stupid."

"I didn't say you were."

"Well, I did. I was…" He cleared his throat, his eyes skittering away from hers to rest on a blank spot on the wall. "My father made me clean my rooms by hand when I misbehaved. I was scrubbing the walls, and one of the stones had a smudge on it. I realized if I pushed hard enough, it moved, and then I figured the rest out from there."

They sat in silence for a moment. Larina didn't know what to say to that, so she ended up changing the subject. "I suppose it would be my duty as your bodyguard to go through that tunnel and see where it comes out. To protect your safety."

"See?" he said, smiling again. "I knew you'd see it my way."

. . .

About an hour later, Larina opened the door at the end of the passageway and took a careful look around before allowing the prince to exit. Ostensibly, she scouted the area to protect him from anyone who might seek to do him harm, but in truth, she was committing the location to memory. Dezrick's tunnel ended in a blind alley behind a spice shop whose scents hung heavy in the air, a few blocks away from the exit from her room. Memorizing this location might do her some good if the passage from her room became unusable for some reason.

Once she'd finished, she reached a hand down to help Dezrick up. Instead of refusing the assistance and making a point of climbing out himself, he accepted the offer without comment. She closed the door behind them, and together they walked out onto the main street.

As they idled from shop to shop, Larina watched the prince. He'd changed once their plans had been made, abandoning the fancy court garb for a plain tunic and trousers. His stilted manners and natural reserve had evaporated, leaving behind a bright-eyed young man who watched everything with eager frankness. She hadn't seen him smile this much since she'd arrived in the city, not if she counted every day between then and now.

He noticed her watching him and arched a brow. "What?" he asked.

"You've done this before."

"Yes."

He paused to skirt around a carter with a stubborn drakon that had stopped in the middle of the street to munch on someone's flower box. It reminded Larina of Zemora's antics. With a pang of regret, she realized that she'd only been down to the stables once in the handful of weeks since she'd arrived here. The drakon would be furious. She bit when she was angry.

Dezrick's continued comments drew her back to the present.

"I'm supposed to be the next king of Oramis," he observed in a quiet voice that she had to lean closer to hear. "But how am I supposed to do that if I know nothing about its people? If I never walk the streets and see what their lives are like?"

"Your father doesn't do that," she blurted, to her instant regret.

"No, he does not. I got the advice from books. I've been reading everything I can get my hands on about what it means to rule a country. There's quite a bit in that library. Philosophy, economics, politics, the art of war." He rubbed his lame leg, fingers massaging his thigh. The limp wasn't quite so pronounced now, but if they walked long enough, it would assert itself. "If my father won't teach me, I'll learn on my own."

"That is very wise," Larina said.

"Yeah, well... I owe you an apology," said Dezrick.

She stopped in the middle of the street, frozen by genuine shock. Carters and shopkeepers alike veered around her, shooting annoyed looks in her direction, but she ignored them. Larina stared at Dezrick, dumbfounded. His throat worked, but he struggled for words. Some people might have helped him, offering soft encouragement or empathetic statements, but Larina didn't have the skill. She could only wait.

Finally, he sighed. "There's no way to sugarcoat it. I was awful to you the day we met."

"You were," she admitted. "I thought you were a spoiled brat."

He laughed, a self-mocking sound tinged with bitterness. "You're not wrong. It comes with the crown."

"But..." she prompted.

"Yasmeen is my father's mistress. My mother is barely cold in the ground, and he's already..." He trailed off, then began again, the words bursting out of him like he'd been carrying them around for a while, desperate for someone upon which to unload them. "I think they were together while my mother was alive. Yasmeen made a few comments..." He trailed off again, his jaw working with restrained emotion. "I miss her. My mother."

"I'm sorry," Larina offered. "I know what it's like to miss family."

"Yes, you have to leave them when you join the guard, don't you?" She didn't answer, but he didn't seem to notice. He continued: "When Yasmeen introduced us, I took my anger at her out on you. I'm sorry for that. I know you're only trying to do your job."

"Don't worry about it," she said. "I repaid you by thinking very unflattering things about you. I think we're even."

Dezrick chuckled. "Fair."

They walked along in companionable silence. Dezrick stopped into a sweet shop for a treat, allowing Larina to pick. She hesitated only a moment before selecting her old favorite. He offered a sugar roll to Larina and took one for himself before passing extra treats out to a group of delighted children playing in the gutters. Then they walked on.

As Larina had expected, his limp grew worse the further they went. Rather than bring it up, she suggested they take a seat on one of the benches in a little park that sat in the middle of a circular intersection. It wasn't much, just a circular bench that ringed a fountain. At its center stood a statue of some long-forgotten noble, his name lost to time and memory. He stared mournfully toward the castle, hand outstretched as if beseeching a king who would not listen.

Larina knew the feeling.

After they sat down, Dezrick said, "You don't have to stop on my account."

"You're in pain," she replied.

"I can handle it."

"I'm sure you handle more pain than most people give you credit for."

"You're very perceptive," he replied. Then he paused. "I fell down the long stairway by the ballroom when I was eight. I had a high tolerance for pain even then, so my parents didn't realize it was broken until it was too late. It healed wrong."

"That's awful," she said, recognizing easily that there was more to this rote tale than he wanted her to believe. He would have had access to the best healers in the land. The pieces didn't fit together, but he clearly wanted to believe that they did.

He shook his head, refusing the empathy she tried so hard to give.

"No, you want to know what's awful?" He pointed at the shop that sat on the opposite corner of the intersection. It sat, quiet and still, its windows boarded up and signs torn down. She couldn't even tell what it had been. What wares some proud owner had once sold there. "That. The taxes are so high, they drive the people away. Stores are closing. People are fleeing the city. A family needs to eat. When your shops can't afford to stay open, your country is in trouble."

Larina frowned, taking a closer look at her surroundings. At night, all the shops looked the same, their windows covered and lights darkened. But now that she saw the city in the light of day, she realized that he spoke the truth. She could see three more boarded-up buildings from her spot on the bench, each down a different street. Weeds choked the tiny park they sat in, and the arm of the bench wiggled. All signs of a neglected city in decline.

"That is awful," she admitted. "But what can you do about it? Talk to your father? Make him see sense?"

Dezrick scoffed, echoing her own unspoken thoughts on the matter. "He barely realizes I'm alive. Once he knew I wouldn't be a great warrior like him, he no longer had any use for me. No, there isn't much I can do now. I come to town whenever I can. I pick businesses that look like they could use the help, and then I buy a bunch of things and give them away. Would you like to try it?"

For some reason, the idea made Larina want to tear up. But she couldn't say anything except yes.

"What shall we get?" he asked, excited. "You choose this time. I always get to choose."

She stared down at her feet, kicking them back and forth as she contemplated potential gifts. Her soft leather boots scuffed against the cobblestones.

"Shoes!" she exclaimed, catching his excitement. "Good shoes are expensive. I remember feeling so accomplished when I'd worked enough to afford my first pair."

"That's an excellent idea," he said, standing and offering her a hand. "We'll buy different sizes and give them out to anyone whose boots look in need of mending."

Larina took Dezrick's hand, and he pulled her up, his warm fingers closing over hers. Face-to-face, they grinned at each other, their excitement palpable over the pleasant task they were about to undertake.

"That is a good idea, Reagan," he said. "I'm glad you're here."

To Larina's immense surprise, she said, "Me too," and meant it.

By the time they had finished, Dezrick's purse had grown much lighter, as did their hearts. They strolled down the streets toward the alley that would take them home, neither of them in any particular hurry. Larina set a slow pace, not wanting to tax his damaged leg any further. He hadn't spoken a word of complaint the entire morning, but when he thought she wasn't looking, he'd rub his thigh, his face drawn with pain.

She wouldn't have brought it up at all if he hadn't stumbled. The leg buckled, threatening to give out entirely, and only her swift reaction stopped him from toppling to the stones. She grabbed him by the shoulder just in time, holding him upright. Dezrick rewarded her with a grateful smile.

"I may have overdone it," he admitted.

Sweat dotted his forehead, but otherwise his expression remained placid. He had become an expert at hiding his discomfort. Larina wondered if there was a trick to it, and if he would teach her. Ever since she'd arrived in Crestwynd City, the anguish in her heart threatened to burst out of her at any moment. She'd always been so self-contained, but none of her usual tricks would suffice to put her emotions back into a box where they belonged. It unnerved her.

"We could sit down for a moment," she offered.

He shook his head. "No, thank you. Once I get down, I might not get up again. Just give me a moment and we'll go on."

"Whatever you need."

Dezrick's gaze met hers. At this close distance, she could see the long lashes that ringed his kind eyes. Lines radiated from them despite his young age, reflecting years of pain. A dead mother. A father who didn't love his son and had no desire to teach him the things he needed to know as next in line for the throne. Under those circumstances, Larina couldn't blame him for his attitude or his caution.

"Tell me something to distract me," he requested. "Something about you. I know next to nothing about you."

"That's because I'm not very interesting," she demurred.

"I beg to differ. You're the first person I've met in years who talks to me like I'm a real man instead of acting like I'm nothing but a title in trousers."

"Really?" She chuckled. "Mostly, I feel like I've mouthed off to you."

"Exactly."

He ought to have been annoyed, but instead he beamed at her. Larina couldn't help it, she laughed outright.

The mirth didn't last long. It faded as she realized that as much as she wanted to offer him honesty, she couldn't. She would have to tell him the same story she'd made up for Yasmeen. Normally, lying didn't bother her, but this time, guilt sat low and heavy in her stomach. For the first time, she wondered how he would react if he learned the truth. He disagreed with his father's rule—she knew that now for sure—but the same blood still ran in their veins. It had to count for something.

"Tell me who you are," he persisted, blind to her discomfort.

"Well," she said, her gaze falling in something like shame, coming to rest on the neat stones beneath them. "I came to the guild from a slave trader when I was very young. I was a fierce little thing, and they despaired of selling me off to a grand house. I would have bit and fought everyone there. So they took me to the Praetorian Keep, high in the mountains. I took well to the training they offered me, and now here I am."

Dezrick lifted her chin with a gentle finger.

"Don't be ashamed, Reagan," he said. "The ones who should be shamed are the slavers. I abhor the practice. But you cannot be faulted for something you had no control over."

Even though he didn't know her real story, the words still touched her. They somehow offered true absolution even though they lacked the correct context, washing away some of her guilt over being the only member of her family to still draw breath. Sometimes she wished she had died with them, and someone more deserving—like pious Iliana or impish Gerun, perhaps—had lived instead. But maybe Dezrick was right. Maybe she should stop holding herself hostage.

His eyes searched her, looking for some acknowledgement. Larina nodded. She didn't trust herself enough to speak.

"Where are you from? Have you ever gone back and tried to find your people?" he asked.

"Iloria, I think. I've been there many times, but I don't remember enough to nail down what region of the country I came from, and the slavers didn't say. To undertake a search under those conditions would be impossible."

Dezrick nodded, his lips pursing with regret.

"I'm very sorry," he said.

"Thank you."

They stood there for a long, awkward moment. Finally,

Dezrick broke it, clearing his throat and observing that he could walk a bit further now. They continued toward the castle, his arm about her shoulders. She'd meant the gesture to support his faltering steps. Never in a million years would Larina have admitted that she took comfort from it as well. Not even to herself.

Chapter Fifteen

The next day, Dezrick spent a long time resting, leaving Larina to wonder if their walk had over-taxed him. She hadn't realized how much the leg bothered him, and now that she fully understood the extent of his injury, she wished she had put a stop to yesterday's rambling sooner. Still, she had enjoyed it.

Midday, he knocked on the adjoining door between their rooms and asked her to come to dinner that night as usual. She arrived at the appointed time to find the table empty of any food to consume. When Dezrick arrived, she offered to hunt down the wayward meal, but he responded with a mysterious smile.

"It's not missing. Come with me," he said.

She realized with a sinking feeling that he must mean to

dine in the main hall. Of course he had every right to do so, but she disliked the place. Elrin could arrive at any moment, and she rather liked avoiding him as much as possible. To her surprise, she also regretted the lost opportunity to converse with Dezrick. For some reason, the prince disarmed her. It wouldn't deflect her from her goal, but it did make her feel better about the potential outcome. After Elrin died, Dezrick would become king, and that would be a good thing for Oramis and her people. He cared about them, and would do his best to care for them as her mother had.

Instead of leading her to the massive dining area with the large high table, Dezrick took her to the kitchens. When they entered the expansive stone-walled room, the fluffy orange cat in the corner took one look at her and bolted for the safety of the pantry. She'd repaid him in catnip from her stores but clearly needed to bring more next time to balance the scales. At least the prince didn't notice.

A large wooden table sat in the middle of the chamber. It usually overflowed with dishes in progress—bowls of rising dough covered in cloth, platters of meat waiting to go on the spit, and piles of produce dishes in various stages of completion. But this time, the table was readied for dinner with three place settings and covered serving dishes. Larina sniffed, appreciating the spicy tang in the air. Whatever it was, it smelled delicious.

"It's Ilorian food," Dezrick explained. "My father won't allow it to be served, but my mother used to have some snuck in from time to time. She and I would eat down here in the kitchen, just like this. I've been wanting to do it since you told me your story..."

He trailed off, his expression hopeful. Even though the story of her Ilorian origins had been a falsehood, gratitude made her awkward. She shifted from foot to foot, unsure how to respond, but she didn't have to fake her answering smile.

"Thank you, Dezrick. This is incredibly kind of you. I don't know what to say."

As soon as he heard the words, he relaxed. She realized how nervous he'd been, how eager to please her. Most people rushed to make her happy out of fear or a desire to get something from her. But Dezrick didn't. He wanted to make *her* happy.

"Shall I call Miriam in? She made the arrangements for this wonderful repast, so I invited her to join us," he said.

"Oh, please do. Or I can get her if you'd like to rest your leg."

"I've had plenty. I'm fine now. Sit."

He waved her back into her seat and disappeared into the depths of the kitchen. After a short while, he returned, frowning. Larina jumped up from her seat in anticipation of a problem.

"What's wrong?" she asked.

"Nothing, nothing. Miriam has a headache. I wish she would have said something earlier. I would have waited for another day to send her off on errands. But I sent her to bed now." He indicated the table. "I guess this means it's just you and me. I hope you don't mind meatless dishes. My mother disliked meat, and I just never got a taste for it myself."

"Not at all. Iloria has some spectacular vegetarian dishes."

They sat. After they filled their plates, Dezrick asked her to tell him a bit about the land of her supposed birth.

"You've never been?" asked Larina.

"No. I would love to visit my mother's side of the family, but my father never allowed it. I wish she'd been able to go home before she died. I know she missed it."

"Why couldn't she?"

Dezrick shrugged. "Safety. It takes a lot of preparation for the royal family to travel. It just never worked out. I almost never leave the castle myself. At least, not officially."

This excuse sounded like a load of garbage, but Larina didn't say so out loud. For years she'd had this vision of Elrin as the ultimate bad guy, full of every vice ever named, intelligent and cunning in turn. But the more she learned about him, the more short-sighted she realized he was. He disregarded things he ought to be paying attention to—like his son—and spent all his effort maintaining an iron grip on his power. He seemed to think that if he relaxed his hold, all of Oramis would slip out of his fingers. For all Larina knew, he might be right. The populace was discontented, the economy faltering. The worse it got, the more Elrin would tighten his grip. Oramis would fall, and he would never realize that he was to blame.

Larina lifted her fork. "Are these your mother's favorite dishes?"

"Some of them. Those two contain meat, so we always skipped them, but they were my grandfather's favorites." He paused, sighing. "I never met him."

"He had good taste." Larina speared a piece of zoat laden with a creamy sauce and sprinkled with nuts. "I could drink a bowlful of this."

"My mother liked that sauce over vegetables. You remind me a lot of her, you know."

"Because we like the same food?"

"You're both stronger than people realize. Everyone underestimated my mother. She was quiet and kind, and my father didn't like it when she spoke in public. She was an ornamental queen, only good for breeding in his eyes. But by the time she realized it, she was already expecting. If she'd run, he would have followed her to the ends of the earth rather than lose his heir."

"That... must have been hard."

"I can't imagine it." He put down his fork, lost in

thought. "She tried to protect me, you know. She kept me from my father when I was young. I didn't realize what she was doing at the time, of course, but in retrospect... I confronted her about it later. She still couldn't bear to say a word against him."

"She was protecting him?"

"No, she was protecting me. He's a difficult man."

That was an understatement, but Larina found that it didn't surprise her. Over the short time she'd known him, Dezrick had shown his perceptiveness. He might not know the exact circumstances of his father's ascension to power—how could he?—but he understood that Elrin had faults, and that was a start. He appeared to have inherited some of his better qualities from his mother. By all rights, Larina should have hated Queen Cleora. But as Dezrick talked, she decided that she would have liked the woman had she been able to meet her on the right footing.

He picked up his fork again. "I feel like a clod for complaining about my parents when you have no recollection of yours. Please forgive me."

"Not at all. We aren't in a contest to prove who carries the deeper tragedies. I can tell that you miss her."

He nodded, wiping at his face. He hadn't cried, but they had watered up multiple times during the conversation. Larina wasn't particularly emotional herself, but tears pricked at her eyes as she watched his obvious emotion.

"Well," he said, "it's kind of you to share the meal with me. It reminds me of the good times."

"I'm glad."

Dezrick smiled at her. "I think she would have liked you."

"I think I would have liked her, too."

He beamed at that, looking so pleased that Larina found her face flushing. She'd never discussed emotions so freely; even Nix had never been quite so open with her before. For a moment, she wondered if this strange forthcomingness on his part could be a ruse designed to insinuate him into her good graces, but she discarded the idea as quickly as it had come. The meal reminded him of his mother. It was only natural that Dezrick should talk about her. Besides, he must be terribly lonely. Before Larina arrived, he must have spent all his days in the library, with no one to talk to except for Miriam on rare occasions.

His face fell, and Larina had no idea what had caused such an abrupt change in him. She especially didn't know why she cared so much, but the moment his expression changed, she found herself desperate to fix whatever had gone wrong.

"What is it?" she asked.

"Speaking of parents, I have dinner once a month with my father. We are due for our next one in three days' time."

He toyed with his half-eaten roll, his appetite vanishing in an instant. As a matter of fact, he'd gone a bit green.

"You don't get along," Larina observed in as neutral a tone as possible.

"That is an understatement," he replied.

"At least it's only once a month?"

Dezrick nodded, then forced himself to perk up with visible effort.

"And you'll be with me, won't you?" he said. "I'll have to bring you along to show what a good boy I've been, complying with his wishes for my safety."

His grin resurfaced as he contemplated this, and she found herself smiling back. She liked the idea that her very presence would make an intolerable situation more bearable. Besides, she could take advantage of this dinner. If she must attend a meal with the king, it would present the perfect opportunity to poison him.

Larina couldn't decide which realization made her happier.

Larina returned to her room full of good food and optimism. The meal had settled her nerves, allowing her to see the way forward. Direct approaches hadn't worked with Elrin, and the security net around the king had only gotten tighter since her last attempt. Although she avoided poison whenever she could, she had plenty of stock with which to accomplish the task. As much as she wished for a different opportunity, she had to take this one. It wouldn't be the satisfying death she'd wished for, in which Elrin knew without a doubt that his life had been ended by the Dracomeer blood he'd failed to extinguish. But the job would be complete, nonetheless.

Some planning would be necessary to guarantee that the deadly dose would be consumed by the intended target and no one else. Dezrick had explained that he and his father ate alone in the dining hall. The bitter twist to his mouth suggested the privacy wasn't requested so father and son could have pleasant bonding moments. As much as she disliked the mental picture that Dezrick had inspired, the arrangement worked in Larina's favor. No one else would be eating but the king and his heir, which made her job much easier. She would simply need to ensure that the prince's portions remained poison-free.

She opened the locked chest that contained her herbal stores and took stock of the neat rows of stoppered bottles. She knew their order by memory with no need to consult labels or smell the contents, although she did both for thoroughness every time she used them. Selecting a poison might inspire her on how to accomplish the job. What to use...

Her fingers paused over the container of Nightvale. A preparation of the thorny vine was often used to aid sleep, and it tasted so similar to pepper that most people couldn't tell the difference. At a high enough dose, Elrin would return to his rooms, tire early, and go to bed. He would never wake again, and no one would suspect a thing.

Except that they would. Given the recent attempts on Elrin's life and the assassination of the queen, his death would be suspicious regardless of the circumstances. Her fingers withdrew from the Nightvale as she reconsidered. It would be better to give the curious a clear explanation to point to. An accident. That would be more difficult to achieve than a clean and anonymous murder, but with a few days to arrange things, it would be possible. Larina would select something that could be easily mistaken for another herb. Something she could slip into the kitchen as if it had been prepared by mistake. She could plant a bit in the garden too, in order to make it clear that the offending plant had somehow seeded there. The gardeners might lose their jobs, but Dezrick would make certain they were well taken care of. He would approach the problem with his usual logic and knack for empathy.

Larina could work with this. Now that she had a plan, she knew exactly which poison to use. Tears of Sorrow caused a painful and obvious reaction that no one would fail to recognize, and the plant looked almost identical to marjoram, but with purplish blooms instead of white. Miriam and her cooks liked to use marjoram; she'd tasted it in almost every meal she'd had here. Frankly, the repetition had gotten a bit tedious, but now she appreciated it.

With the basics of her plan in place, the details began to

sort themselves out. Once Dezrick had retired for the evening, Larina could begin to make the necessary arrangements. In the meantime, she tidied up after herself and closed her eyes for a brief rest. Although the repeated nights of little sleep had begun to exert their toll, she was refreshed and invigorated by the certain knowledge that this would be the end of it. In three days' time, her quest would be over, her revenge accomplished. Everything would be right again.

Before she left her rooms, she put her ear to Dezrick's door and listened to ensure that he had bedded down for the evening, just as she'd done every night. To her surprise, her keen ears picked up the sound of movement from the chamber beyond. He had never stayed up this late before, and she frowned, overcome by the concern that someone had snuck into his suite. After all, someone had killed his mother.

Moving quickly, she extinguished her light and closed her windows lest a stray breeze give her away. Then she put her hand to the latch. The door inched open soundlessly, just enough for her to peer at the chamber beyond. To her surprise, she saw Dezrick himself, standing at the open passageway that led to the city. He didn't notice her intrusion. Instead, he checked his pockets and glanced around, his eyes skimming over the door between their rooms for one heart-stopping moment. But he failed to acknowledge her presence. Instead, he set off down the passage with a lantern in hand.

Although this development interfered with her plans, Larina couldn't just let him go. She had to know what he was doing. Not because she cared, but because it would be very inconvenient if he got himself killed right before she got to his father. Anything could happen to a rich man like him on the nighttime streets. She hadn't had any trouble on her nightly forays, but then again, she had the skill to avoid it. Dezrick didn't.

Larina followed at a distance, moving with an instinctive catlike grace that minimized noise and kept him within sight. At the end of the tunnel, she waited for a minute to allow him time to exit the alleyway before reopening the door. This was the riskiest moment of the operation so far; she chanced the possibility of losing him around a corner before she could catch up, but she couldn't risk him seeing the door open.

The gamble paid off. She lingered in the shadows at the mouth of the alleyway, easily picking out his figure with its distinctive gait down the road. From there, she had no problems following him. He didn't even look behind him.

To her surprise, Dezrick stopped at a familiar black-smith's shop. One that sported a light in the windows despite the late hour. He knocked just as she had only a few nights earlier and was quickly admitted.

Rather than crossing in front of the building in full

view of the windows, Larina ducked around back. She moved with careful deliberation lest she make some noise or blunder past a window and draw the attention of the occupants within. In near silence, she climbed the wall that bordered the shooting range at the back of the building. The courtyard stood still and empty, but off to the left side of the smithy, a dim light emanated from a window. She crept toward it and peeked inside.

The living space beyond overflowed with people. Most of them, Larina didn't recognize. They sat on chairs and cushions on the floor. Some leaned against the walls. Kyra stood by the door, arms folded, watching them. Alaris led Dezrick into the room, the two of them talking quietly. Larina couldn't catch the words through the glass, and she didn't have a good perspective for lip reading, but the two of them appeared to be friendly. One of the women seated on a chair with her back to the window turned her head, and to Larina's surprise, she realized it was Miriam, smiling at the rough-looking young woman seated beside her.

Larina began to wonder if she'd interrupted a gathering such as this the night she'd purchased the dragon bow. It would explain Alaris and Kyra's late presence in the building. This room sat in a part of the house that she hadn't visited. If the rest of the group had been meeting that night, would she have heard them talking from the shop area or the shooting range? Probably not.

Alaris pulled the only empty chair from the corner and

set it out for Dezrick with the air of someone doing a favor for a friend rather than a subject waiting on royalty. Dezrick smiled his thanks and sat down. As soon as he was settled, Kyra held her hands up. The room immediately quieted, all eyes turned toward her.

Her husky voice carried through the window when she spoke.

"Thank you for coming on such short notice," she said. "The king has increased the city patrols, so we'll keep this brief. I understand that the prince has some important news to relate to the group. Dezrick, can you enlighten us?"

Dezrick nodded, leaning toward the group, his elbows resting on his legs. His demeanor reminded Larina of their day in the city. He relaxed in this company, his natural reserve dissipated in the company of normal folk. In Larina's experience, most royals didn't know how to act when faced with regular people; they expected the world to bend to their exacting standards regardless of the situation. But instead of requiring the townspeople to treat him like royalty, Dezrick had become one of them.

"Thank you, Kyra," he said. "Much has happened since we last met. There has been an attempt on the king's life."

Larina could barely believe what she was hearing. Excitement thrummed through her veins, but she remained still for the moment, listening with every ounce of concentration she could muster. She knew Dezrick disliked his father, but this was something else entirely.

It was treason. Not that she could throw stones on the matter.

"Did it work?" Alaris demanded, his excitement obvious. "May the Dark God bless them, did someone get to him before we could?"

"Alas, no. The usurper did not meet his death. But he will," said Dezrick. "I pledge it to you."

Chapter Sixteen

Larina spent the entire day after the meeting in a haze of shock. Dezrick didn't realize that she'd followed him. She'd seen him safely to the entrance to his tunnel and then reentered the castle through her own to avoid detection at the other end. He'd greeted her in the morning with his now-customary politeness and went straight to the library once again. Perhaps he yawned a bit more than usual over his books, or maybe she had become more aware of the gesture now that she knew what it signified. Perhaps he'd snuck out before and she'd been completely unaware of it, distracted as she had been by her own murderous plans.

What she'd overheard left her no doubt as to his intentions. The group of rebels conspired to rid themselves and their city of the king. At one point, they had launched into bitter complaints about the things he had done. The rough-looking woman next to Miriam had lost her family to the gallows, perhaps on the day that Larina had come to town. The memory haunted her just as the loss of her own family did. Elrin had to be stopped.

In her expert opinion, the group at the blacksmith's shop didn't have what it took. While they held good intentions, they couldn't come to a consensus on a plan. Some of them wanted to recruit more people to their cause, but others argued it would attract too much attention. The rough-looking woman espoused a long and convoluted plan to recruit small groups of rebels who would communicate through secret codes left around the city at the sweet shops. The plan had so many holes that the woman got confused in the telling, and she and Alaris argued about it until Kyra threatened to dunk their heads in the trough outside. Dezrick espoused good theory—probably from his extensive reading—but had no idea how to kill a man who remained constantly under guard. Possessed with the fire of youth, Alaris wanted to storm the gates of the castle with sword in hand and hack his way through battalions of trained guards until he got to the king and lopped his head off. At least no one in the group gave that suggestion serious thought.

Larina had almost interrupted the meeting to reassure

them that they needn't worry about the actual killing because she had it handled, but what good would that do? Revealing herself would only increase the possibility that something would go wrong. Too many conspirators with good intentions and little practical experience to back them up could only hinder her efforts. So she'd kept quiet, soothed by the knowledge that once she completed her job, Dezrick would have supporters to back him up and ease the transition to his rule.

Mulling over the possibilities helped keep Larina awake the entire morning despite the long hours she'd been keeping. In fact, they distracted her completely. Dezrick snapped his fingers in front of her face. She shook herself out of her daze, her cheeks flushed with embarrassment.

"I am so sorry," she said. "Did you need something?"

"Are you sure you're okay?" he asked.

"I was just thinking, that's all. I promise it won't happen again."

Her words tumbled over themselves in her desperation to prove that she deserved to be trusted with his safety. She usually had no trouble multitasking when it came to her work. Larina needed to sleep a little tonight or she might not pull off her plan. In the meantime, she planted a reassuring smile on her lips.

Dezrick's concern didn't fade. If anything, it grew worse.

"Why don't you sit down?" he suggested, pulling out a chair for her.

"No, thank you."

"I insist."

"Dezrick," she said, "I'm your bodyguard. If I sit down, my reaction time will be just a bit slower in the event that something happens."

"Well, if you loom over me like that when I'm talking to you, I'll have a crick in my neck. So you'd be protecting me from injury if you sat down."

She shook her head in exasperation but did as he asked. He watched her with an air of self-satisfaction before pulling out a small parcel wrapped in cloth. He held it out to her.

"What is this?" she asked.

"It's my half-birthday." At her look of confusion, he clarified. "I mean, it's a gift for you. It's an Illorian tradition, isn't it? To give gifts to your closest friends on your half-birthday?"

He tensed with worry, and she hurried to reassure him.

"Oh, of course. You just took me by surprise is all."

He snickered, and she forced a chuckle. Larina hadn't received many gifts since her childhood. The Praetorian Guard didn't celebrate things like birthdays, let alone half-birthdays, and even if they had, Larina wouldn't have claimed hers. Someone might put two and two together and figure out her true identity. On rare occasions, she and Nix would pick up something small for each other while out on a job, but the gifts were always practical. If she passed through Rottenheim, which was known for its armor, she might pick up a pair of bracers for him as well as herself. If he took a job in Roshai, he'd bring back some of her favorite herbs that only grew in the region. Things like that. But she hadn't received a wrapped gift since her girlhood.

"Thank you," she said.

"Go on. Open it."

Larina untied the cloth to reveal a book bound in purple leather with a dragon stamped on the front. For one panicked moment, she wondered if this was Dezrick's way of telling her that he knew who she really was. But this dragon wasn't part of the Dracomeer crest. It crouched instead of reared.

"It's an old Illorian fable," Dezrick explained. "About a wicked king who tried to enslave the people and kill off all the dragons. They work together, man and dragon, to depose him, thus beginning the long tradition of dragon riders. Do you know it?"

"Not in detail. I'll be glad to read it."

"You like it then?"

Her eyes filled with tears, although of course she didn't let them fall. Larina Dracomeer didn't cry. But she had to admit she would miss him after the deed was done. Either she would die, or she would leave, and to her surprise she found that a part of her didn't want to. Without her quite understanding how, Dezrick had become her true friend.

He put his hand over hers, clearly concerned.

"Reagan, if I've upset you, I'm truly sorry," he began, but she cut him off before he could go any further.

"I love it. I'm more grateful than you'll ever know," she said.

"It's just a book."

"It's the first gift I've received since I entered the guild," she explained. "I don't really know what to say."

He cleared his throat, his cheeks coloring. "You're the first person I've given a half-gift to. Other than my mother, but I don't think she counts. Giving them to parents is traditional, you know."

"Oh, I think it counts anyway."

He hitched a shoulder. Then his eyes lit up.

"Sit with me a while longer and read. Like we're friends in a library, and I'm not a prince, and you're not a body-guard, and we're just two normal people reading books together. We'll pile up a stack of them in front of the door so no one can enter, and we'll sit away from the curtains so no ruffians can shoot at us, and then you can relax for just a while. Please? Say you will," he said.

Larina knew she ought to refuse, but this might be

their last time together. It couldn't hurt to oblige him. After all, the biggest danger to anyone in the castle was her.

"Just for a little while," she agreed. "After all, it is your half birthday."

When Larina reported to Dezrick's suite the next day to attend the dinner, she found him in a state of agitation. She'd never seen him so frantic before. He adjusted his collar before the looking glass no less than four times, and he changed his fancy doublet twice before she managed to convince him that he looked very fine indeed.

"I'm sure you think I'm being ridiculous," he admitted, shame-faced. "But you don't know my father. He will take every opportunity to talk me down. My clothes aren't right. My hair isn't right. My entire existence is a disappointment because I'm crippled and useless. I'm trying to minimize it as much as possible."

"If he says that, your father is a fool," Larina blurted.

Dezrick stopped, frozen with shock. Larina could hardly believe she'd said it herself. If anyone but the prince had overheard it, she could have gotten into an incredible amount of trouble. But she might as well be honest now. It might do him some good in the hard days to come, to know of her faith in him.

"Your father isn't even half the man you are," she

continued, collecting herself. "He should be proud of you. I've seen how much work you put into your studies, how much you care about your duties to Oramis. I'm proud to call you my friend, Dezrick, and if he can't see how amazing you are, that's his problem. Not your shortcoming at all."

He didn't react for a long moment. Then he cleared his throat, not meeting her eyes. She began to wonder if maybe she'd gone too far, but then he spoke in a gruff voice.

"Thank you," he said. "I needed that."

"Well," she replied, "that's what friends are for. But do you know what else you need?"

"What's that?"

"Help with your collar. It's twisted up on one side. Stand still and I'll fix it."

He tilted his head so that his long braids fell off his shoulder, exposing his neck and collar to her ministrations. The elaborate collar had truly gotten tangled, and it took some doing to arrange it just so. Larina muttered a few choice swear words under her breath, to Dezrick's amusement, before she finally managed to get it right.

"There you go," she said, looking over her handiwork. "I'm sorry it took so long. I'm not really accustomed to these collars. However do you get them on by yourself?"

He didn't answer. Instead, he edged closer, his brown eyes fixed on hers. Larina's heart pounded for some reason she didn't understand. She didn't want it to. Her lips had gone unaccountably dry; her hand trembled. Dezrick took it in his own, stilling the nervous movement. Then, his eyes never moving from hers, he brought it to his lips. They pressed against her palm, warm and soft and gentle.

In a panic, Larina snatched her hand away. Her cheeks flared, and her knees had gone liquid.

"I just realized," she said. "I should go down to the kitchen and grab something to eat before we leave. I'm so used to eating dinner with you that I nearly forgot. Isn't that silly?"

"Reagan," he said.

But she had already rushed to the door, desperate to make her escape. She could not allow herself to have feelings toward this man, not moments before she would murder his father.

"It's okay, Dezrick. I just need to grab a bite to eat and put my book away safely. Then I'll be back to take you to dinner. Don't worry. I know you'll do fine."

Her words created a wall that he couldn't penetrate. She left him no space to speak. Then she closed the door on him, allowing herself to lean against it for just one moment.

The kiss had been delightful. Perfect. It wasn't the kiss of a man bent on seduction, but one borne of genuine feeling. But it would have to be the end of things between them. It hurt, but she had no other option. Besides, he would hate her soon enough, when she killed his father right in front of him. That fact shouldn't have bothered her, but it did.

. . .

It didn't take long to run down to the kitchen and grab a bite to eat. Members of the staff dashed to and fro, prepping a special meal for the king and his son as well as the usual fare for the rest of the castle. Miriam stirred a steaming pot of soup and gave out instructions with her usual unflappable poise. Larina had been surprised to find the former nurse in charge of the kitchens, but after seeing Miriam at the meeting the other night, she had to admit that she didn't know her nurse as well as she used to. With no royal children to look after, Mimi would have had to find some occupation, and the work suited her well. The kitchen had become a warm and welcoming place under her direction, if very busy and a little heavy on the marjoram.

Miriam filled two bowls and placed them on a gleaming tray, steam filling the air with a delightful fragrance. In all of the chaos, Larina reached across the tray to straighten the napkins, dumping her vial of poison into the bowl that overflowed with chunks of meat. As she palmed the empty container, she made a show of sniffing with evident appreciation.

"Would you like a bowl before you head back up?" Miriam asked.

"I wish I had the time. But if there are leftovers, I

would love to have some. It smells divine," Larina replied. "Can I offer any help in carrying the trays up?"

"Oh, no thank you dear. Someone should be coming in to take them up any moment now. But it's kind of you to offer."

Larina took a sandwich off the servant's tray and saluted her with it. "I'm happy to help. You keep us all so well-fed. If there's ever anything I can do to repay the favor, I hope you won't hesitate to ask."

Miriam beamed at her as she took her leave.

Everything was in place now. Zemora waited for her at the safe house; Larina had taken her from the stables, explaining that she wanted to loan the mount out to make a little extra money and get Zemora some exercise. The stablemaster hadn't cared; as soon as he realized the drakon would be gone, he couldn't have been more helpful. Larina almost asked what the mischievous beast had been up to but decided she'd be better off not knowing. Zemora had made her frustration at being cooped up in the stables clear the moment Larina entered the room by flinging water into her face. Larina could only imagine what other hijinks she'd been up to.

In the event that her escape plan turned out to be unsuccessful, she'd made plans for a message containing Zemora's whereabouts to be delivered to Miriam. Her old nurse could sell the drakon and retire on the proceeds.

She returned upstairs and rapped on Dezrick's door. After a moment, he opened it, looking tense and miserable.

"We should talk," he said, but she held up a hand before he could get any further.

"After the dinner," she suggested, not unkindly. "I know you're stressed about it."

"But I wanted to apologize for—"

"You have nothing to be sorry for. Honestly."

Some of the worry drained from his face, but furrows still creased his forehead. But Dezrick nodded and tried to force a smile for her benefit.

"That is very kind of you," he said.

"You'll be fine."

They stared at each other for a long moment, his deep brown eyes boring into hers. Larina wished that things had been different. If Elrin hadn't killed her parents, she and Dezrick would have grown up side by side. They could have gotten to know each other without all the lies and hidden pain. Perhaps they would have managed more than just a single kiss on the palm. It was a nice daydream. Too bad things hadn't turned out that way.

"I guess we ought to go," he said. "I don't want to be late."

"No, of course not."

Larina followed a few steps behind, as a proper body-guard should, as they descended the stairs toward the dining hall. A pair of guards opened the doors as the prince approached. Larina offered them a polite nod and received the same gesture in return as she passed.

The king hadn't arrived yet. Inside the great room, all the tables had been cleared of settings except the high table at the center of the room. The king's place with its great carved chair dominated the space. Next to it, Dezrick's seat and place setting appeared childlike. Perhaps the slight hadn't been accidental; Elrin liked to demonstrate his power over everyone whenever he had a chance to do so.

They waited in silence. Dezrick stood behind his chair, shifting his weight in evident discomfort. Larina wished he could have sat down, but Elrin would see that as a weakness, and he needed no opening. To distract herself from worries about Dezrick—not to mention the murder at hand—she thought back to all the times she'd dined in the room as a girl, playing chase the rabbit around the tables with her father and siblings while the staff brought out the food. How full of life the castle had been! Today, she would make certain that Elrin could not take such sweet moments away from anyone else ever again. Then she would take her leave of this place forever. It was a bittersweet moment.

The doors opened, disrupting her reverie, and disgorging a full contingent of twenty or so guards. They took station against the wall opposite Larina. Although protocol dictated no exchange of nods in the presence of the king, more than a few of them met her eyes. Respect was exchanged. She hoped that the day would not end in violence, because she wouldn't relish having to kill them. The numbers might not be in her favor, but the guards hadn't prepared for someone who fought like her, and she still had quite a few tricks in her repertoire that they hadn't seen yet.

Bastian followed his guards. He'd cleaned up for the event, dressing in a neat uniform that matched his men except for the gold braid at the shoulders and the medals decorating his chest. A neat ponytail at the base of his neck kept his lank hair out of his face. He scowled, his eyes roving the room to evaluate any potential threats. They alighted on her briefly. His lips quirked, but he maintained his composure. Larina stared back, unflappable, secure in the knowledge of her superior skill.

Finally, the king entered the room, resplendent in an embroidered red tunic and leggings, a fur-trimmed cloak sweeping the ground behind him. At his hip sat his sword. Larina didn't need her memory to attest to his skill with it; the weapon was worn with extensive use. The plain, heavy blade was no ornament. In a hand-to-hand battle, he would present more danger than all his men put together, but she didn't intend to let things go that far. As soon as the soup course began, he would be dying on the floor, and no amount of swordsmanship would save him.

Elrin's eyes scanned the room just as Bastian's had. The king wore an imperious air that failed to fool Larina. The tight set of his jaw, combined with the lines of fatigue etched in his face suggested that the recent attempts on his life had rattled him. His eyes skimmed over Larina before returning to her face. For one breathless moment, she wondered if she'd been found out. Could she make it to the window before they closed in on her? Then the king turned to Bastian, his lips curled in a mocking smile. He hadn't forgotten about her nighttime excursion to his bedroom. That could have been bad if he hadn't assumed she competed with Bastian to win his favor. The king's ego blinded him to the obvious truth.

Bastian flushed under the bemused gaze of his liege. Elrin's pursed lips suggested a tide of angry words held back with effort as he busied himself with a review of his guardsmen. He ambled down the row, pausing to speak a quiet word with the shortest of the guards, a nearly colorless woman with the palest skin and eyes Larina had ever seen.

Elrin must have forgotten all about her existence up until this moment, a fact that Bastian must not have minded one bit. His presence combined with his obvious hatred made her escape less likely. Even if she had no obvious hand in the king's death, Bastian wouldn't pass up the opportunity to detain her. If Dezrick didn't stand up to him, she would be dead by morning.

It was a sacrifice she was willing to make.

Dezrick cleared his throat, a diffident sound designed to draw the king's attention. The amusement faded from the usurper's face as he regarded his son. The prince hobbled forward, the lame leg even less flexible than usual after his city rambling and nighttime excursions. With some effort, he knelt on the ground before Elrin, bowing his head. After a moment, the king's large hand cupped the back of his son's head in a gesture of fondness that surprised Larina. But his expression bore no affection at all. Elrin evaluated his son the way she'd examine a drakon at market, critically probing for strengths...and weaknesses.

Dezrick saw none of this, but his resigned expression suggested that he knew it all anyway. He struggled to his feet, keeping his eyes on the floor.

"Father," he said in formal, stiff tones that sounded nothing like his natural voice, "it is a pleasure to see you."

"Sit," Elrin gestured to the table. "I see you are unwell."

He delivered the comment with palpable disapproval, but Dezrick failed to react. Instead, he took his place at the table, waiting for his father to sit before following suit. Elrin gestured with a finger, and the guards opened the doors to allow the serving staff to enter. A tall young footman with white-blond hair approached the table with a bottle of port, pouring liberally into both glasses. Another footman with matching hair and similar features lit the candles at the center of the table with a long firestick. A young girl with a turned up nose placed baskets of fresh baked rolls on the table, enough for the royals and all of the guards combined, their warm, yeasty smell filling the air. Then Miriam herself placed the soup before the two royals, a heaping bowl laden with chunks of beef for Elrin, and a vegetarian version for his son, her kind smile going unnoticed by both.

Elrin picked up his spoon. It took all of Larina's considerable training not to tense up in anticipation. Moments like these made her dislike poison; she could only watch and hope that he didn't decide to pass on the soup course.

"I hope you have been well," Dezrick observed with elaborate politeness.

"I have been busy," Elrin replied, holding the utensil poised over the bowl. "But not too busy to check up on you. I understand that you have continued to spend all of your time in the library despite my orders to find a more suitable occupation for someone of your stature."

Dezrick froze, his hand hovering over the breadbasket. Although he tried to hide it, Larina could tell how much his father's words cut him. If Elrin could only see the error of his ways, Larina knew that Dezrick would be eager to forgive him. But the usurper would never change. The man had a rotten heart, if he even had one at all.

Elrin saw none of his son's hurt. He pressed on.

"I must remind you that if you are to rule after me, you must show the willingness to do what is necessary, regardless of the cost. Until I see this from you, I can do nothing with you. I will not recognize you as my heir, Dezrick. Not unless you do as I say," he said.

Larina watched as Dezrick's carefully constructed self-control began to crumble. His hand tensed on his roll, breaking the crust. She dreaded what would happen. She didn't want his last words to his father to be hateful, although maybe that would help exorcise some of the demons between them. At least he would know that he'd spoken his peace and stood up for himself before the end.

"What would you have me do?" he asked. "What would be good enough for you? Shall I learn the sword? Become a fierce warrior like you? If you wanted me to be a warrior, you should have taken more care about my unfortunate *fall* down the stairs."

Larina hadn't questioned Dezrick's description of his injury when he'd told her. She'd nearly gone toppling down those stairs herself as a child, racing around with her brother after the staff mopped the stone. Elrin hurt—pushed?—his son, and now he scorned him for the very injury he'd caused. Larina's opinion of the man had already been low, but it turned out that it could go lower. She pursed her lips, stemming the torrent of accusation that threatened to escape them. He would get his just desserts as soon as he took that first fatal bite.

Elrin refused to acknowledge his guilt. He smothered it with anger, throwing the spoon down on the table.

"I should have had more children," he proclaimed. "Perhaps then I would have one worthy of succeeding me. Or at least I could have a child who can stand on their own two feet without falling over. What kind of ruler can't stand before his own people? A pathetic one. You'll be dead within a month just like those feeble Dracomeers; overpowered by those with the stomach to do the difficult thing. You're weak, Dezrick. Regardless of the leg, you don't have what it takes to rule. You lack the strength to do what is necessary, to instill fear if necessary. The vermin of the city would eat you alive. You're too soft to keep them under your thumb." Elrin picked up his spoon again, his voice low but still carrying throughout the room easily. "You're just as weak as your mother."

Dezrick blanched but made no other response. Instead, he stared into his soup, slump-shouldered and bleak-eyed. Larina wanted to put her arms around him and explain all the ways that Elrin was wrong, but what good would that do? It wouldn't take the sting out of knowing that his sole remaining parent held him in such contempt.

Elrin watched the prince for a moment puffing up in satisfaction with the utter defeat he had caused. He nodded to himself, picked up his spoon, and scooped up a large chunk of beef.

He lifted it to his lips.

"Wait, Your Majesty!"

A surprisingly familiar voice called out from the open doorway that had just admitted the servants a few moments before. She would have recognized it anywhere, but its owner had no business being there.

Larina snapped her head toward the door as Sleth slithered into the room. She could not mistake his gaunt, almost skeletal figure with its bald head. When he turned to bow to the king, she saw the stub of a new-grown prayer braid at the nape of his neck. The hair hadn't grown quite long enough to braid yet, but he'd knotted a few pieces of hair onto it and plaited them into a weak little strip that flopped over one shoulder.

As he made his obeisance, Sleth glanced at her, his eyes lit with a wicked glee. Then he returned his attention to Elrin, his face sliding into a practiced subservience. He'd always treated Garret with the same smoothness, playing to the man's ego to make him dismiss whatever charge Larina or the others had laid at his feet. He'd gotten away with so much as a result, and now he'd turned those same skills on to Elrin. But how? Why? He shouldn't even be there.

"What is it?" Elrin demanded.

"You should have someone taste your food, sire," Sleth suggested. "It's standard procedure in many kingdoms."

Elrin laughed. "Are you suggesting that a member of my household would be foolish enough to try and poison me?"

"I suggest nothing. But given recent events, one can never be too careful. A man of your stature acquires enemies as naturally as breathing. Some caution seems wise under those circumstances."

Larina wanted to scream, but she remained in her place, her expression neutral. How had Sleth known that the soup was poisoned? Or did he? He would have accused her outright if he'd realized what she'd done. Her mind whirled, contemplating the possibilities.

Elrin considered the diminutive assassin without expression, then nodded. "You speak sense, Praetorian. I will follow your council," he said, beckoning to one of the footmen. Larina's stomach plummeted to her knees, but what could she do? If she spoke up, the king would have her killed. Even if she managed to escape, she wouldn't get the chance to try again. Dezrick and his rebels couldn't finish the job. She had to survive, if only to see this important task through to completion. If she could. For the first time, a pang of doubt twisted her insides. Had she finally found a job she couldn't complete? Should she strike now while everyone's attention was elsewhere? The option tempted her, but it wouldn't do. Bastian and Sleth were both positioned to intercept her. Her success wouldn't be certain, and Elrin had already slithered out of her grasp too many times for her to indulge in overconfidence.

Through force of will, Larina remained impassive as the footman took a sip of the soup. He moved with confidence, trusting that none of his fellow kitchen staff would tamper with the food they'd labored so hard to make. But he didn't realize that Larina had been out in the gardens at night, planting poison among the herbs.

The footman put the spoon down and stepped back into his place against the wall.

"There," said Elrin. "Are you satisfied?"

Before Sleth could respond, the servant coughed, tucking his mouth behind a hand. Elrin turned in his seat to look at him. Dezrick half rose from his chair, his brow creased with worry, but an impatient gesture from the king kept him from going to the boy's aid. The coughing jag worsened, foaming spittle gathering at the corner of the victim's mouth.

No one called for a healer. Either they knew death was inevitable, or they didn't care if the boy survived. Larina didn't know which was worse. Shielded by the table, Dezrick's hands clenched tight as he struggled to retain control. Even Larina, a handmaiden of the Dark God, found this death painful to witness. Her fingers crept up to her braid, sending up a wordless prayer for his soul.

The footman began to seize, his body dropping to the floor, jerking in an incessant dance. Blood spilled from his eyes. His brother could bear the agony no longer; he broke from his spot at the wall, dropping to his knees.

"Venn!" he cried, throwing himself atop his sibling's quivering form. "Please, Your Majesty. Please help him. I'll do anything."

"He's already dead," Elrin replied without a hint of empathy.

Larina dared a glance at Sleth only to find him already watching her. Her blood ran cold as she pictured his death in furious detail. He smiled. The expression carried no joy;

it was more a baring of teeth than a manifestation of happiness. He wanted to get a rise out of her. She didn't know what his game was, but she didn't much care. If she had to go through him to get to the king, so be it.

It would be her pleasure.

Chapter Seventeen

In the wake of the servant's brutal death, Dezrick shoved his soup away from him with a convulsive, panicked thrust of his hands. Reddish broth spilled across the table like blood, soaking into the fine tablecloth, leaving a stain that would never wash away. It seemed fitting that there should be some lasting mark of the tragedy that had occurred here. Larina would carry the guilt of it for the rest of her life, an unseen mark that would taint her regardless of its invisibility.

"What idiocy is this?" the king demanded of his startled captain. His voice had gone icy calm. It sent chills down Larina's spine. "Bring the kitchen staff to my throne room. You will find the one responsible for this, or you'll hang for it yourself."

Larina had never expected to empathize with Bastian,

he of the snide comments and persistent envy, but she did so now. His face tightened with tension as he looked into the disapproving face of his liege. Then he nodded, his entire body stiffening with resolve.

"I will not fail you," he declared.

Without delay, he spun on one foot and marched toward the door, gesturing for some of his guards to follow. As they exited the room, he already whispered orders. Larina could feel nothing but pity for him. He wouldn't find the culprit out there, and she had no intention of admitting her guilt. If she hadn't spoken up for the innocent servant, she certainly wouldn't do so to save the man who had sought to dominate her from the first day they'd met. Perhaps that made her a bad person too, but she'd come to grips with her morality or lack thereof long ago. As long as the end served some good, she would undertake the means necessary to get there.

Elrin stood and, without sparing a look for his son, left the table.

"Follow me," he ordered.

Dezrick didn't even glance at Larina as he fell into step behind his father. His face had gone ashy with fear as he contemplated how close he'd come to death. She would have liked to reassure him that he'd never been in danger, but of course she could do no such thing. Instead, she could only fall into her proper place behind him as the guards closed ranks around their king.

To her dismay, Sleth appeared at her elbow, beaming.

"Aren't you happy to see me?" he murmured. "You should be pleased to have another Praetorian as backup."

"I don't need backup from you or anyone else," she whispered back.

He hitched a shoulder, making a show of his nonchalance.

"I couldn't really offer it anyway. My hands are full protecting the king." He paused, glancing at her out of the corner of his eye to evaluate her reaction. It took all of her training to hide her shock at the comment, but disappointing him made the effort worth it. "After the incident with the arrow, Elrin asked Bastian to fetch him a bodyguard of his own. I'd impressed the captain enough that he sent for me. Isn't that grand?"

"Lovely," Larina replied in a flat voice that delighted him even further.

His presence complicated things. Sleth was a skilled assassin and bodyguard, and he knew many of her tricks. If he suspected that she might be behind the attempts on the king's life, he would make her job very difficult indeed. She would have to think hard on how to handle this.

The king led them to the throne room. The last time Larina had been inside these walls, her mother had sat on the great throne, the golden sun rising above her, the razor-sharp rays of light seeming to emanate from her head. But now Elrin took his place there, and a wave of anger washed over Larina. She wanted to pull him from her mother's rightful seat and slit his throat, but a horde of guards stood in the way. She would die before she reached him, so she stayed her hand.

Dezrick took his place on the dais a few steps down from his father. Larina's mother had placed chairs on the dais for her spouse and children, but Elrin offered no such comfort. Dezrick had no choice but to stand, his tilted posture the only hint of the pain he endured. Larina took a spot along the wall as close to him as protocol allowed, ready to offer an arm upon request. Although that request would never come. Dezrick wouldn't give his father the satisfaction of asking for help, and she didn't blame him.

Bastian and his guards marched through the open door, escorting the entire kitchen staff. A few of the maids cried out in fear, tears streaming down their faces unchecked. Miriam held the hand of one of the most stricken, patting it as if to communicate the assurances she couldn't make herself speak. The group stopped before the throne, the guards stepping back at a motion from Bastian, leaving the kitchen staff trembling and alone. Then the king stood, towering before them on the dais, his face twisted with fury.

"On your knees," he barked.

Most of the servants dropped to the floor. Miriam and one of the other cooks, both of advanced age, followed in painstaking stages. A girl toward the back waited with flashing eyes and only knelt when Bastian put his hand on the hilt of his sword.

"Which one of you poisoned my soup?" Elrin demanded. "Which member of my household is so duplicitous that they would try and kill me in my own home?" No one answered. "Identify the traitor among you, and I will be merciful to the innocent. You gain nothing with your silence."

"As the head of the kitchen staff, I can say with confidence that none of my people would do such a thing."

Miriam's voice rang out with strength and conviction despite the creak that old age had leant to it. She raised her eyes to the king's with quiet confidence, unbowed by his display of temper. He stalked down the steps to loom over her, glaring right down into her face.

"Some would find this an admirable sentiment, Miriam," he said. "But to me, it is nothing but naivety. The attempt was made; therefore someone must have made it. If the culprit is not identified, I shall have to punish you all."

Elrin paused, but there was no response other than the muffled crying of the maids.

"Very well. You shall all receive lashings until someone confesses," he said.

The maid next to Miriam let out a horrified, "No!" She might have said more but for the old woman's hand reaching out to grip her arm in a squeeze of warning. Then the head of the kitchen staff stood to look her king in the face. Her voice held an unexpected hint of steel when she spoke.

"This is wrong, Your Majesty. You know that," she said.

"How dare you speak to me in this manner? How dare you lecture me as if I'm a boy in the nursery! I'm your king, and I demand your respect."

He spat the words into her face, his cheeks going red with suppressed emotion.

"I respect your position, Your Majesty," replied Miriam, unruffled. "But honor must be earned, and this is not the way."

Elrin stepped back, and for a moment, Larina wondered if the rebuke had hit home. Mimi's plain speaking and quiet confidence could reach anyone. Even Larina's mother, when she had been in one of her moods, would always listen to the nurse. But Dezrick blanched. He didn't share in Larina's optimism.

"Bastian," Elrin snapped. The captain stepped forward, chin held high. "Be my hand in this. Administer my punishment. Begin with Miriam, and add a few extra lashes for her insolence."

Bastian bowed his head. "Your will shall be done, sire." Larina detected a hint of a smile on his face, and it turned her stomach. Did he carry the same twisted concept of entertainment as Sleth did, taking joy in inflicting pain and horror? Or did the opportunity to serve his king give him pleasure, satiating his desperation to earn the man's approval? Larina didn't like either option. She liked what was about to happen even less. Miriam would pay for Larina's mistake in pain and blood, and the realization made Larina loathe herself. But she could do nothing. If she confessed here and now, it would only prove to Elrin that he could hurt her through Miriam, and he would want to hurt her quite badly once he knew who she was.

"This is barbarism." Dezrick stepped into Elrin's path as he returned to his throne. "You cannot do this."

"Weak, just as I told you. Watch and learn, boy," responded the king. "Decisive actions such as these are necessary to retain power. Perhaps a firsthand lesson will reach you when my words could not."

"But it's *Miriam*," the prince persisted, grabbing at his father's arm in his eagerness to make his case.

"Enough!"

Elrin shoved Dezrick away, and the lame leg gave out underneath him, sending the prince toppling down the stairs. Larina went to his side, kneeling down to shield his pain from watching eyes.

"Leave him be," ordered the king.

Larina knew that she would be best served by not replying at all, but she couldn't help herself. Her whipsawing emotions could no longer be contained, although she still managed to hold the worst of it back.

"You hired me to protect your son from all harm," she said. "I will do my job until I am dead, or I am released from duties. My pride as a Praetorian Guard demands no less."

"I am in charge here. Have you not forgotten who hired you?"

"On the contrary. I am following your orders at this very moment," she said. "Do you wish to amend them?"

She wanted him to. For a moment, she allowed herself to imagine what would happen if she pulled out her knife right then and there and went for his throat. She pictured it sinking into his flesh, severing the artery, spraying her with blood. It was too big of a risk for her to take, but that didn't change her desire for it. The usurper's eyes narrowed as he considered her challenge, but even he couldn't find a way to justify further brutality toward his son.

"Carry on then, but stay out of my way," he said, sitting down on the throne and gesturing for Bastian to begin.

Larina tried to focus on Dezrick, but she couldn't block out the cries of pain from Miriam as the whip hit flesh. Based on his stricken expression, neither could the prince. As the beating continued, Larina pictured the moment when her knife finally slid into Elrin's flesh. The gout of blood. The shocked realization in his eyes as his life leaked from him. The thud of his body on the ground, and the satisfaction she would take in spitting on his corpse. She would take out every ounce of this pain on him, adding to the tally he would have to answer. But in the meantime, she could do nothing to spare Miriam. Instead, she and Dezrick clung to each other, waiting for the agony to end.

After the horrific floggings, Elrin sent Dezrick back to his chamber like a recalcitrant child, the remainder of the meal thankfully forgotten. To his credit, the prince failed to follow instructions. Instead, he reached into his own purse to pay for a healer from the city to tend to the injured, since the king had refused to allow the staff to care for them. Dezrick sat in the kitchen until every injured staff member had been seen, apologizing to each one with tears in his eyes. No one could doubt his sincerity or hold him accountable for his father's cruelty. No one except himself.

Larina helped where she could. Although it would be dangerous to betray too much knowledge of herbalism given the recent poisoning, standing aside would be an inexcusable cowardice. She mixed up a few hurried poultices and brought them down, claiming that her employer had provided them. A bodyguard would carry such things, so no one batted an eye, and after a quick sniff and a few questions, the young healer Dezrick had brought in from town encouraged her to apply them herself. After she did so, she made herself useful. As Larina bustled about, helping where she could, she gathered the poisonous plants from the garden and burnt the whole lot to leave no trace of what she'd done.

Once they had provided as much relief as they could, Dezrick led Larina back to his room. As soon as the door shut behind him, his solicitous calm dissolved into a fury the likes of which she had never seen in him before. He let out a strangled howl, clenching his fists in his hair. Then, before she could attempt to soothe him, he began to throw things off the nearest shelf. Books thumped against walls and slid across the floor, carried by the force of his anger. Once he'd depleted the shelf, the prince whirled around, looking for something else upon which to vent his anger. His elbow caught a ceramic inkwell, shattering it against the wall and sending shards flying in all directions. Dezrick ignored it, intent on destroying everything he could get his hands on. Finally, he reached the psaltery in the corner and picked it up.

"No!" Larina cried.

The sound shook him from his destructive reverie. Slowly, sheepishly, he returned the instrument to its stand.

"I'm done now," he said. He panted as he made his way through the mess to the table and sat down, shoulders slumped in defeat.

"You're bleeding."

Larina pulled a clean cloth from her pocket and held it to the wound at the corner of his eye. The cut wasn't as deep as the blood trail suggested. He probably didn't feel a thing. He had grown used to pain.

"Whenever I am hurt, Miriam has always taken care of

me," he said in a lifeless tone. "After my accident, the healers said I'd never walk again, but Miriam and my mother never gave up on me. Without them, I'd probably be lame."

"I—" Larina caught herself just before she shared a memory about the time that Mimi had nursed her through a frightening bout of the shaking fever. "I can tell that you truly care about her," she said instead.

The bleeding had stopped. She dabbed at the stains on his face, wanting to soothe him but not really knowing how. When it came to comfort, she had little to offer. She could kill a man from around a blind corner, mix a sleeping draught from a collection of herbs, or rig a shack to blow up at the precise time to take out a passing caravan, but she knew little about emotions and what to do with them.

"My father did it, you know." The words tumbled out of Dezrick now, like a confession to a temple priest. "He asked me to show him what I'd been learning of the sword, and even before the injury, I didn't have the knack for battle. I'd practiced because he told me to, but my heart wasn't in it. Still, I wanted him to be proud, so we took our practice swords out to the landing. I showed him what I'd learned, but I could do nothing good enough to suit him. My attacks were too soft; my parries too sloppy. He began to beat me with the wooden blade—to show me the error of my ways, he said. He hit me so hard that I fell down the stairs and shattered my leg. I screamed, but do you think he helped? Of course not. He told me he hoped the injury would teach me a lesson. He never apologized, not even when the healer said I likely wouldn't walk again. I was only eight."

Larina couldn't stand the look on his face, the grief and loss that mirrored her own. Elrin hadn't just stolen her childhood. He'd taken the prince's too.

Without stopping to second guess herself, she wrapped her arms around Dezrick's head, pulling him close. He resisted at first but then melted into her, accepting the proffered comfort. His tears warmed her belly. Her hands stroked his hair.

Then, inexplicably, he stiffened and withdrew from the embrace. Tears stained his blotchy face.

"I'm sorry," she blurted.

"I have a headache," he declared, not meeting her eyes. "I think I'll go lie down."

"O—okay," Larina stammered. "I'll be right next door if you need me."

He nodded but offered no explanation for his strange behavior. Instead, he disappeared into his bedchamber, shutting the door behind him. Larina stood there in the wake of his departure, wondering where she'd gone wrong.

Chapter Eighteen

Larina took some time to clean up the mess before returning to her room. Although she remained dressed and ready for the remainder of the evening, Dezrick didn't summon her. In fact, she had begun to think he'd gone to sleep when she heard the unmistakable sound of the door to his secret passageway opening.

Dezrick was going to another meeting.

This time, rather than following him, Larina exited through her own. From there, she followed him to the blacksmith's shop and scaled the wall to listen to the proceedings.

Unsurprisingly, poor Miriam didn't attend. The head of the kitchen staff was hopefully asleep, soothed by the herbal draught the healer had administered. Larina had set aside an extra supply to soothe the upcoming nights and guarantee that all the kitchen staff got the rest necessary for their bodies to heal.

Once Kyra called the meeting to order, Dezrick didn't even wait to be called upon. He burst out into another angry tirade, describing what had happened over a growing chorus of dismay. Alaris pounded on a table when the prince described how Miriam had been beaten, and Kyra's knuckles went white as she clenched her fists at the description of Elrin's past violence against his son. By the time Dezrick had told the full story, everyone in the room seethed with anger, hovering on the verge of riot.

"We must do something," he urged, his eyes scanning the room. "We cannot afford to waste our time with empty words any longer. When will it be enough for us to stand up and say 'no more'?"

"I'm ready," Alaris declared. "I'll give my life if it means removing the usurper from the throne."

He took a step forward, raising a fist like he was eager to head out this very moment and strike a blow against tyranny. Larina appreciated the sentiment, but Elrin would decimate them. Even with all her skill and well-laid plans, she had failed to reach him time and time again. The rebels would get themselves killed, and those deaths would be on her hands too. Just like the guard who had fallen during the nighttime chase. Just like the young servant with the poisoned soup. She could not take the weight of more innocent lives, not when she had the power to save them. Enough was enough.

Larina opened the window and dropped into the room on silent feet. Although she made no noise, the movement attracted attention as intended. Alaris drew a cudgel and would have charged at her if not for the restraining hand of his mother. Kyra, for all her restraint, held a knife in her other hand. Other people in the room had drawn various weapons if they had them, or gotten out of the way if they hadn't. Only Dezrick remained motionless, his eyes wide with surprise but free of threat.

"If you're going to take down Elrin," said Larina, "you're going to need a plan."

Alaris tried to shake off his mother's restraining grip, frowning.

"You'd better explain yourself," he demanded. "Right now."

Murmurs of agreement from the rest of the group met this proclamation. Still, Dezrick didn't move, and that fact had caught Kyra's attention. She watched the prince, her brows arched in inquiry. When he failed to speak, she prompted him aloud.

"Dezrick?" she asked.

"This is my bodyguard. The Praetorian I told you about," he explained.

"The girl who is spying on you for your father?" Alaris squinted at Larina, his brow furrowed. "You're the crack shot with the bow. The one who claimed to be a private bodyguard."

Although Larina would have been suspicious if their positions had been swapped, the fact that Dezrick didn't trust her still hurt. Ironic, considering her true purpose. But she couldn't help her feelings.

"I don't think she's his spy anymore," Dezrick proclaimed.

Larina raised her chin. "I never was."

Kyra's eyes widened.

"You're saying we should trust her after she snuck into our secret meeting and offered to advise us on how to kill the king?" she asked. "I trust *you*, Dezrick, but as for the rest, I'm unconvinced."

Dezrick approached Larina, a gesture of faith that she appreciated given the circumstances. They both knew she could kill him on the spot, and he would be powerless to do anything about it. After she struck, the group might overwhelm her with numbers if they were lucky, but the damage would already be done.

"Who are you?" Dezrick asked.

"Reagan," she said. "The Shadow." Her true name didn't matter. This one was true enough.

"Why are you here?"

"I heard you leaving. It's my job to protect you, so I followed."

Dezrick colored with shame as he realized that he'd led

her straight to the secret meeting, but he continued.

"You offer us your help. Why not turn me in to the king?" he asked.

"Elrin is no king that I recognize. Fear is no way to rule a kingdom. We both know that," she responded.

He arched a brow.

"You aren't afraid of him?"

"I am a Praetorian."

He looked at her sharply then, brow quirked in inquiry. She couldn't help but think of how they'd clung to each other when Miriam had been beaten, and about the warm comfort of his hug afterwards. She'd spoken the truth, but the reality went much deeper than that, and they both knew it. But it didn't matter. She had skills that the rebels desperately needed. After a moment, Dezrick nodded.

"I vouch for her," he said.

Alaris scoffed aloud but quieted when Kyra elbowed him. The blacksmith clearly led the rebel group, and her reaction would determine what happened next. The smith rubbed her chin, leaving a faint black smudge, a leftover of the strenuous day's work.

Kyra took a few steps toward her to talk face-to-face. Larina appreciated that. The smith looked her over with neutral, considering eyes, nodding at what she saw.

"When you came to the smithy that first night, were you truly shopping for weapons, or were you scouting out our meetings?" she asked.

"I told the truth," Larina said. "I knew nothing of your meetings until the last one. I followed Dezrick here but did not make my presence known. I wanted to think about it first."

The group burst out into shocked murmurs and impressed glances. But Dezrick stared at her woodenly, all color draining from his face. He alone seemed to grasp the implications of her statement. Had she been a true spy, they would all be hanging from Elrin's gallows at this very moment.

"Why?" Alaris burst out. "To turn us in?"

Kyra silenced him with a displeased glance. Then, to drive the point home further, she said, "If you can't hold your tongue, son, I'll have to send you outside."

With every passing moment, Larina liked her more. The rebuke didn't carry the sting of anger. Instead, the smith simply stated the reality—if the behavior persisted, she would take steps to correct it. To his credit, Alaris took it well. Cheeks flaming, he murmured an apology. For all his youthful eagerness, he didn't dig in when he knew he'd done wrong. These were good people, Larina realized. She didn't know them all, but Kyra and Dezrick wouldn't stand for anything less. To her surprise, she found herself wanting to prove her worth, not just because it could potentially help her end Elrin once and for all, but because the good opinion of these people meant something.

Kyra turned her attention back to Larina.

"Can you explain that?" she asked.

"My goals align with yours, but most people aren't thrilled to have someone barge in on their secret meetings," said Larina, unable to suppress her smile. "As we're experiencing right now. But if Dezrick is urging swift action, you need someone like me. I have skills that could be useful. Perhaps we could help each other."

Kyra nodded, considering this. As she did, Alaris interrupted again, but this time with excitement in his voice.

"I'll admit she's a heck of a shot with a bow! Scales and tongues, I've rarely seen anything like it. Last time she was here, she buried an arrow in the mannequin at distance first try," he said to Dezrick.

The prince stiffened, looking at Larina with dawning comprehension.

"It was you. The would-be assassin with the arrow," he murmured.

Despite his low tone, his voice cut through the room, stilling all movement. All eyes turned to Larina with a new curiosity. She could feel their hope and eagerness, their desire that she might be the missing piece that would finally help carry their plans to fruition. She could only hope the same, but still, it took every ounce of bravery she had to confess.

"Yes," she said, swallowing hard. "And the poison too. It was only Elrin's bowl, Dezrick. You were never in danger; I made certain of it. But it was me. I'm to blame for what happened to Miriam and her staff, and for the boy who died. It's my fault, and I'm so sorry."

Her voice cracked a bit at the end, and Dezrick shifted as if her obvious distress pulled him toward her on a string. But then, he stopped himself, looking around at the group that listened on with rapt attention. His gaze returned to her.

"You have nothing to be sorry for. The fault is my father's and his alone," he said.

"That is kind of you to say."

"It is truthful of me to say." He paused, considering. "Do you have the will to try again? As you can see, we have resources here that may be of assistance. Perhaps together we can finally remove Elrin from his throne and make Crestwynd City a safe and pleasant home for its people again."

"Dezrick has been studying the writings of Queen Thalia," said Kyra, nodding at the prince in approval. "He's determined to follow in her footsteps and do the right thing by her people, since she cannot."

The mention of her mother's name nearly broke Larina. All this time, she'd spent in the library with Dezrick, standing over his shoulder as he pored over books. Had he been reading her mother's work, even as she stood by his side? The possibility shook her, and for a moment, she considered telling them her real name. The urge quickly dissipated. Dezrick trusted her, but that goodwill might evaporate if he worried they'd fight over the throne. She desired nothing of the sort, and so she stood to gain little by claiming her true identity. It would only complicate matters.

"I think he'll be a fine king," Larina said. "I believe it with all my heart."

Dezrick blushed, and Alaris clapped him on the shoulder with enough force to nearly knock him off the chair. The room broke out into scattered laughter, breaking the tense moment. When they all settled again, something had changed. She'd been accepted as one of their own, and now they had work to do.

"I agree with the prince," Larina said. "Every day Elrin remains on the throne allows him to inflict more harm on the Orami people. The time to act is now, but to do so without a plan is to fail. Trust me; I know this from experience."

"And you have the skills to make this plan?" asked Kyra. She leaned forward, showing eagerness for the first time.

"I do. But first, I need to know what resources we have to work with. Even mundane skills can be of use. Perhaps you can sew a replica of a guard's outfit or herd a flock of angry zoats to overpower a lookout post. No skill is too small. Do you have a list of these resources?"

Kyra shook her head, embarrassment tinging her cheeks. "We never thought to make one."

"Then let's do so now. We'll use that to create our plan. I intend this attempt on Elrin's life to be the last one."

"I can get behind that," Dezrick agreed.

"Good." Larina looked around at the circle of eager faces, all hoping that they might contribute something, no matter how small, to the liberation of the country they loved. "Let's begin."

Over breakfast in his room the next morning, Dezrick kept staring at Larina when he though she wasn't looking. At first, she waited for him to speak, but it became clear that he couldn't—or wouldn't—say whatever was on his mind.

"What is it?" she asked, not unkindly. "You clearly have something to say."

"No!" he protested in embarrassment. "Nothing. It's nothing at all."

"Then why do you keep looking at me? Is my hair sticking up? If so, please just tell me. I don't pick up on subtle social cues very well."

His expression turned from sheepish to kind in slow stages.

"Your hair is fine. I'm sorry, I don't mean to make you uncomfortable. I was just marveling over what happened last night. Is it safe to discuss here, do you think?"

He paused there, looking over his shoulder as if he expected the king's men to pop out from behind the curtains or from under the table at any moment. Larina would have laughed if not for the seriousness of the situation. As much delight as the new partnership brought her, it still didn't make up for what had happened to Miriam and her staff. It didn't bring back the dead servant. When she'd finally gone to bed, the memory of the agonized cries of the surviving footman had haunted her for hours. She'd barely slept a wink.

Larina considered Dezrick's request. It would be better to set some ground rules. Although the prince didn't have Alaris's impulsive streak, he had little to no experience in subterfuge as far as she knew. If she gave him guidelines, he would follow them. He could help too, opening doors that had heretofore been closed to her. She would need the assistance now that the king was on high alert.

"Quietly, and only in here," she said. "With all the doors closed, including those to my room. I must check your rooms when we enter them, and you mustn't say a word about it until I give the all clear. We can never discuss it anywhere else. Even if you think we're alone in the library, it isn't safe to bring these topics up. Do you understand, Dezrick?"

Some people might have taken offense at being spoken to this way, especially those of royal blood, but not the prince. He even took a moment to give her request proper consideration before he nodded.

"I understand, and I will follow your wise counsel,

Praetorian." He paused, smiling. "I can hardly believe that you've joined us. With a member of the Praetorian Guard on our side, how can we fail? You've brought us hope, Reagan, and I can't tell you how much we needed it."

She sighed. "I appreciate that, but don't forget that the king has a Praetorian now, too." Although she hadn't mentioned Sleth since they'd left the throne room the night before, he'd been heavy on her mind. Calling for a second Praetorian didn't seem strange given the circumstances. The king had every reason to want a bodyguard for himself as well as his son. But the fact that no one had seen fit to notify her of Sleth's arrival nagged at her. Working in tandem, two Praetorians could protect the entire royal family from harm, but the king and Bastian had chosen to keep her in the dark. She still couldn't decide if this proved the king's utter disregard for his son or suggested something more sinister.

Dezrick's face clouded.

"Yes, what do you think—"

A gentle rap at the door interrupted him, and he fell into a stricken silence. Larina held up a finger and went to answer it. Viola stood on the other side, a hopeful smile on her face. The expression faded when she saw Larina, and she stood on tiptoe, trying to see into the chamber beyond.

"What is it, Viola?" Larina asked the maid.

"You are wanted in Yasmeen's quarters immediately, Miss Reagan."

"Is that so?" Larina searched the girl's face for some hint of duplicitousness, but other than an over eagerness to see the prince, she sensed nothing. "I cannot leave the prince unattended. Is it an emergency?"

"I don't think so..." Viola said. "But I'm happy to attend upon him in your absence."

Larina knew the girl would be more than happy to do so. She practically wriggled with excitement. The assassin quashed an amused smile and responded, "Thank you, but I meant that he's in need of a guard. Could you please ask one of the men on duty in the hall to send someone down to cover for me?"

Dezrick opened his mouth to protest, but Larina stopped him with a stern glance. Appearances needed to be kept up. A responsible bodyguard wouldn't leave their charge unprotected with a killer on the loose. Besides, his mother's death still remained unaccounted for.

"I'll get a guard then," Viola offered, disappointed.

"Thank you."

Larina had never been in Yasmeen's chamber, and its appearance took her by surprise. A gauzy curtain divided the sizable room into two distinct areas. On the left sat a fancy boudoir complete with curtained bed and overstuffed sofa. Candles and flower bouquets accented the space, lending an intimate air. In contrast, the right-hand side of the room was more utilitarian. A long table supplied with a variety of herbal equipment sat at the ready, with a musty book on a lectern alongside it. Vials of liquid preparations clustered on neat racks alongside rows of drying herbs and a pristine drakon skull. Yasmeen stirred some concoction at the table; she wore one of her usual splendid gowns with an apron tied over top to protect the precious fabric. She greeted Larina with a smile that the assassin had to force herself to return.

"Reagan!" exclaimed Yasmeen. "It's been too long. I was beginning to think you'd forgotten all about me."

"I'm sorry. I've been watching over the prince every waking moment and haven't had a chance to get away. I do miss our chats. Did you need something, or is this a social call?"

"I wanted to ask your opinion. Elrin wants me to advise him on the recent attempts on his life. He's quite displeased, as you might imagine." Yasmeen's smile became brittle and forced. "I hoped to make use of your expertise."

"How can I help?" Larina asked cautiously.

"Please. Sit." Yasmeen gestured toward the bench that ran alongside the table, and they both settled there. "I know the Praetorians have some skill with poison, and I wondered if you might have an opinion on what happened the other night. How it might have been administered."

"Well, the kitchen is extremely busy at all hours with people coming through. The staff trays are there, you know, so everyone is in and out. I picked up a sandwich yesterday myself. Anyone could have slipped the poison into the soup in all that chaos. Queen Cleora's killer is still at large, are they not? Perhaps this was the same person, still at work within the castle walls."

"Perhaps," Yasmeen allowed, drumming her nails on the table.

"It might be wise to move the staff trays to another room to limit kitchen traffic," suggested Larina. She needed to offer some sort of help, and this suggestion wouldn't make her task any more difficult. She couldn't try poison again anyway.

"Thank you, Reagan. I'll make a note of it."

"It's no problem at all. I'm glad to be asked. I'll also start checking the prince's food before he eats, to be safe."

Yasmeen startled at this suggestion, as if she hadn't yet realized that the prince could also be in danger. This made no sense. After all, Larina's job was to guard the prince, and why take the trouble to hire out a professional guard in the absence of danger? But Yasmeen's disregard for the prince fit with Larina's other observations. Dezrick was always the last item on the priority list except with Miriam. The rest of the staff spent so much time doting on Elrin that they had forgotten his son, and his wife's murder had gone all but unremarked on. It spoke volumes about Elrin's power and the fear he inspired.

"That...is a good idea," allowed Yasmeen. "That is all for now, but I plan to talk with you more moving forward.

We will have to be extra vigilant with the banquet and ball coming up."

Larina, who had been about to stand, sat down again with a thump. "What banquet? This is the first I've heard of this. Dezrick hasn't mentioned anything to me."

"Oh? Well, perhaps he's forgotten. He must know. The prince of Dunheim will be paying a visit in six days. Elrin has scheduled a variety of events in his honor, including a masked ball and banquet."

"Ah."

Although her voice remained neutral, Larina felt nothing of the sort. If not for Dunheim's support, Elrin never would have pulled off his coup. Her family would still live. At times, she'd considered taking her vengeance on the Dunn royal family, but she knew they weren't at fault. They'd merely taken advantage of the situation. Elrin had put the plan in motion. Elrin had betrayed her family's trust.

Yasmeen frowned, sensing without needing to be told that something bothered her friend. She touched Larina's hand.

"What's wrong?" she asked.

"I'm just frustrated. It's difficult for me to do my job without being informed," Larina explained. "I've barely heard from Bastian at all since I started. Isn't it his job to keep all the security staff up to date?"

Yasmeen's lips pursed, and Larina caught a sense that

the sorceress shared her annoyance, although she tried to keep it hidden. Could it be that Yasmeen and Bastian vied for the king's favor and the power that it provided? Yasmeen's personal relationship with the king did not in any way guarantee his respect or ear in important matters, and she would want to secure her position after years of slavery and uncertainty. Larina could use this to her advantage.

She pressed on. "I didn't even know about Sleth's presence in the castle. It's an important piece of information that could have helped me do my job better. But I hesitate to complain because I don't know how the court works, and as you pointed out on the trip here, reading the relationships in a royal household can make or break your success. One misstep can cost you everything."

Yasmeen nodded, picking up a packet of powder from the table and toying with it as she mulled this over. When she raised her eyes to Larina's, a new frankness filled them. Yasmeen no longer hid her worry, but put it on full display.

"I didn't know either," she admitted. "And it bothers me too. Bastian has never been my fan, and he sees you as an ally of mine, so perhaps he's trying to shut the both of us out. I intend not to allow that to happen. If I press to be included in the planning sessions, will you come? I propose that we share what we know to ensure that neither of us is blindsided."

Larina didn't need to consider the wisdom of this

arrangement. She agreed readily. Although she could not condone Yasmeen's physical relationship with the king, and she couldn't trust the woman as a result of said relationship, she needed to be involved with those planning sessions. They would provide the kind of information necessary to plan the king's demise.

He would die at the ball.

Chapter Nineteen

After Larina returned from her meeting with Yasmeen, she accompanied Dezrick to the library, where they remained for most of the day. Dezrick read his books while she stood watch. She made a mental note to compliment him on his poise later— he conducted himself as usual, without a hint of the secrets they shared. But then, as he rose to return to his room, he gathered up a few books to carry back with him, giving her a significant glance that would have caught the attention of anyone who had been there to see it. He'd found something, and the excitement of it had made him forget his subtlety.

The prince barely contained his excitement, nearly bursting into an explanation as soon as the door to his suite closed behind them. Larina forestalled this with a cautioning finger and proceeded to search the room for signs of an interloper. Finding nothing, she fixed him with an exasperated look.

"You were doing so well," she said. "Until the end. Anyone who saw your expression would have known you were excited. What would you have told them if they'd asked?"

He faltered, nonplussed by the question. "I don't know. I'm sorry, but I found something important. I think this could make all of the difference to our plans."

"I'm eager to see it, but before we do, I need to make sure you understand what I'm telling you, Dezrick." She caught his eyes with hers and held them there a moment to underscore the importance of her words. "If you do something like that again, it could cost us both our lives."

To his credit, his cheeks flushed with shame.

"I'm sorry. I promise not to do it again," he said.

Finally, Larina relaxed, taking a seat at the table next to him.

"Okay. Show me what you found, then," she requested.

He slid a heavy book across the table toward her. Age had cracked the brown leather, drying it to a brittle texture. She handled it with as much delicacy as possible, but still, bits of the binding broke off beneath her fingers. Dezrick didn't seem to mind. He urged her on with a wave of his hand.

"I marked the page," he said.

She opened the volume to the strip of parchment he'd stuck inside. The section appeared to be some kind of design plan, but Larina couldn't decipher the labels. The spidery handwriting had blurred with age, and it wasn't in any tongue she knew. Maybe Ordun, an extinct language from long, long ago, back when Oramis and Dunheim had been a single, harmonious land and dragons had flown the skies. The language had a distinctive appearance, with dotted vowels that told readers how to pronounce the short syllables, but she'd never learned it.

"These are the original plans, drawn up from when this castle was first constructed," Dezrick explained, tapping at the page with an eager finger.

"You can read it, then?" Larina asked.

"I'm good with languages. That shouldn't be surprising given how much time I spend in the library."

"No, I suppose not." She scanned the plans, searching for some familiar shape to orient herself but finding none. "Help me out here. Where is the throne room?"

"That would be..." Dezrick scooted over so he could see better, his shoulder brushing hers. "This one here. Although back then, it was the great hall. The throne was still there, but the courtiers also ate there and held raucous parties. The diaries from that time are something else to read, I'll tell you."

Larina snickered. "I bet. It looks like most of the east

wing was added later? That's why I didn't recognize the shape, I think."

He nodded. "Yes, after Oramis and Dunheim split into two countries. The first queen of Oramis built the library. She wanted to rival the great magical library at Kata, but she had a difficult time getting hers hands on the book she wanted, so she collected history and philosophy instead. We have one of the greatest collections of ancient maps in the world."

"Really?" Larina asked. "How many do you have?"

"I've never counted, to be honest. But I'd number them in the hundreds. It's less the number than the rarity, you know. Some of our maps are hundreds of years old, and a few are the only known surviving copies. I didn't realize you were interested in such dusty things."

He smiled a little to soften the words, but Larina didn't mind. She'd gulped up the trivia with a hunger that surprised her. Normally, she couldn't have cared less about mapmaking, but this was different. A piece of her heritage she'd never even known had existed. She vaguely remembered her father poring over tables strewn with old maps, and she wondered if maybe he'd added to the collection, but she could find no way to ask without inviting questions. She pointed at the plans.

"This is your suite, and the tunnel that leads out into the city, correct?" she asked. He nodded. Her finger skimmed over the page to the tunnel that led out of her room. She couldn't admit to knowing about it, but that interested her less than the other tunnels marked on the age-spotted paper. There were more than she'd realized. "And this..."

"It's another tunnel. And that one, and that one. The builders added a ton of them when they built the place. Some probably won't work, but a few of them must still be operational."

Their eyes met over the book, alight with matching excitement.

"This is how we get our people into the castle on the night of the ball," said Larina.

"Exactly," responded Dezrick.

Over the next week, Larina and Dezrick fleshed out the remainder of the plan. In the past, she'd been forced to collaborate with other Praetorians or hired muscle, and as a matter of principle, she disliked the experience. Her partners would get fixated on an idea and keep suggesting it regardless of its suitability. If shot down, they'd begin to sulk, or retaliate by rejecting perfectly good alternates. She didn't understand that mentality. If an idea worked, she wanted to use it, regardless of who had suggested it in the first place. Conversely, if a plan had problems, why waste the time on it?

Thankfully, Dezrick shared this pragmatic outlook, and

the two of them made a habit of debating suggestions over long and pleasant dinners in his room. By the end of the week, they had a variety of options that would work depending on Elrin's security plans. Once Larina met with the security team, they could select the idea that would work the best.

They went to the next rebel meeting together, and both looked forward to explaining their plans to the group. They had made true progress over the past few days, and their success seemed certain.

They arrived at the smithy just in time for the meeting to start. Larina fidgeted with a lingering awkwardness as she entered the room via the door rather than the window. It would take the other revolutionaries time to accept her, but hopefully once they saw what she'd planned, they would realize she truly meant to take the king's life. Trust often made the difference in groups such as this, and she had little time to win it. But Dezrick believed in her, and he would set an example for the others to follow.

As usual, Kyra opened the meeting but soon abdicated the speaking floor to Dezrick. He and Larina shared their plans, their listeners growing restless with excitement. When they had finished, Alaris and Kyra began to catalog the weaponry they had on hand and what would need to be made. If some of their number were to impersonate guards, they would need to carry regimental short swords adorned with the royal crest. Kyra sometimes made them for the castle, but the warder hadn't placed an order in a long time, so she had none on hand. Forging them on such short notice would be difficult but not impossible.

The meeting carried on in this manner, with each member of the group given a specific task that would help to prepare for the ball. They had multiple ways into the castle depending on where Bastian put his guards. They had backup plans and alternates. As Larina had learned, Elrin had a way of upsetting even the best laid arrangements, and this time, she intended to be ready to pivot as necessary.

As the discussion concluded, a celebratory air took hold of the room. Formerly tense expressions relaxed into smiles, and stiff shoulders dropped as they all contemplated the end to their struggles. Kyra went to the back room to fetch glasses and drink, claiming that a toast was in order. Before she could return, a knock at the front door split the silence. Everyone froze. Larina's blood went cold, and she edged closer to Dezrick. She'd been on high alert, and few people could have avoided her notice under such conditions. But Sleth still lurked in the castle, on some errand she had not been able to uncover. Perhaps he'd managed to track them despite her best efforts. Or maybe one of the many members of the resistance had turned against them, informing the king of their plans in the hope of mercy. But who? Everyone in the room wore the same expression of shock and fear. Including her.

Her mind raced through the options. She'd mapped out an escape route when she'd followed the prince here the first time, but he would be unable to keep up, and she lacked the strength to carry him. Perhaps she could hide him and lure the guards away, leading them on a wild chase while he made his way back to the entrance to the secret passage. She couldn't leave him to hang. The possibility of a world without him shook her to the core.

Then Kyra returned with a tray full of drink. Inexplicably, she smiled.

"I'm expecting a visitor," she explained before going to answer the door.

The tension in the room dissipated. Dezrick let out a shaky breath, exchanging a glance with Larina. She smiled back, trying to hide how off-kilter the experience had thrown her. Her hands shook with adrenaline. She never lost control like this. It didn't make sense. She ought to hate him for taking her spot in line for the throne, but instead, all she wanted to do was protect him.

Larina shoved this line of thought aside as Kyra returned with Miriam on her arm. The old woman moved with stiff care, and dark circles under her eyes testified to long and difficult nights, but her smile shone bright as ever. The group broke out into excited murmurs and cries of greeting, and Alaris exploded with an excited, "Why didn't you tell me?" to his mother, which she answered with, "Because everyone who knows you can read you like a book." Everyone laughed, and after a moment, Alaris joined them, nodding.

It took a long time for Miriam to make her way around the room. Everyone took the opportunity to speak a word of support, and she hugged every one of them. Dezrick's healers had done a fine job. Although Larina watched the old woman with concern, she didn't see a hint of pain as the rebels wrapped their arms around the frail body over and over again.

Then Miriam reached Dezrick. He couldn't even meet her eyes. Instead, he went down on his knees, his face twisting in pain, and bowed his head in abject shame. Tears streamed down Miriam's face as she watched him, begging for him to rise. When he finally did, the wet streaks down his face matched hers. The old nurse took him into her arms, soothing him with a firm kindness that Larina remembered all too well.

"You cannot control anyone's actions but your own, my boy," she said. "So you cannot take their responsibility from them, either. Your father did this. Not you. Taking all the responsibility for it will take you down the same dark path your father has chosen, stripping freedom from everyone in the name of protection. And you are better than that."

Miriam stroked his face, brushing the tears away. He nodded, straightening his back and lifting his shoulders, wanting to be the kind of man she would be proud of.

Larina found herself doing the same as Miriam turned to her, standing tall and smiling with all her might. She knew the next few minutes would be difficult. Miriam would hug her, and she had to keep her emotions in check. But it would be worth it to feel the embrace of her nurse again.

"I'm so glad you're feeling better," she said. "You were missed."

"I am glad Dezrick has you to keep him safe," Miriam responded. "I can rest better knowing you're at his side."

The old nurse folded her into a warm embrace, and for just a moment, Larina allowed herself to relax. She felt safe and cherished and loved, like those early days when she'd lived in this very city and her biggest worry had been how to get her brother to quit pulling her hair when no one was looking. She missed him dreadfully, but oh, how they'd fought.

After a moment, Miriam released her, kissing her on the forehead with gentle lips.

"Thank you, Mimi," murmured Larina.

The nurse's rheumy eyes sharpened. She gazed at Larina for a long, uncomfortable moment. Larina could do nothing but stand there, trying but failing to decipher what was happening. Miriam's eyes widened and a gasp escaped her lips. Her usual kind smile returned and deepened into a delighted grin. Tears fell from her eyes again and she cupped Larina's face in her weathered hands.

"You are most welcome, Larina Dracomeer," she said.

The name took the room by storm. Dezrick sprang from his chair in shock. Unflappable Kyra let out a strangled shriek. Alaris pounded on the table next to him, unable to contain his excitement. In the middle of all the chaos, Miriam and Larina stood, looking into each other's eyes. Although she wasn't much of a crier, Larina could feel the tears track down her cheeks.

"How did you know?" she asked.

"I've suspected for a while. You don't take after your mother much, but you bred true to your father's side of the family. What happened to your beautiful red hair?"

"I dye it."

Miriam nodded. "You do a good job. Good enough that I questioned what my eyes and heart were telling me until just now. No one has called me 'Mimi' for twelve years, child. But even if you hadn't, I would have known you when I held you. You always fit just right in my arms."

The kindness in her voice undid Larina's careful control. She'd spent so many years steeling herself to bear what had happened to her family. The Praetorian Guard had shaped her into an uncaring killer, and she'd welcomed it. Caring for people hurt too much, and she had hurt enough for a lifetime already. But hearing her real name spoken with kindness after so long broke open the dam that held back her emotions, and she cried as she hadn't done since she was a girl.

Once she'd spent her tears, she withdrew from Miriam's embrace, wiping her wet cheeks with embarrassment.

"I'm sorry," she said, looking around. She didn't even know what she apologized for. The unpleasant display of emotions? Not telling them the truth sooner? Both? Her eyes lit on Dezrick, who stood just inches away, his face a tangled mess of emotions. "I'm so sorry."

"Child," said Miriam, with a firmness in her voice, "we are just happy to see that someone of Queen Thalia's blood survived that awful night." She paused to look around the room, her intent gaze demanding agreement. Her stern expression made her sentiments clear: she would brook no argument over this. "But how did you survive?"

"Captain Flynn," Larina said.

She wanted to explain all he'd done for her, the pain he'd gone through just to see her safe, but her voice didn't want to cooperate. Miriam nodded with apparent understanding anyway, without the need for clarification.

"He was a good man. I will remember him in my prayers to the Great Mother from this day forward," she said, squeezing Larina's shoulder.

"So it's true?" asked Kyra, stepping toward them. Hope lit the smith's eyes from within, and she leaned forward as if that might make the desired confirmation reach her just a moment sooner.

Once the name fell from Larina's lips, she could not take it back. She could run instead, abandoning the legacy of her family and the burden of revenge behind her. But to do so would be to betray her name and shun these good people who sought to return Oramis to the way it ought to be. She couldn't leave them to face Elrin on her behalf. She had to claim her name once more.

"It's true," she said, her voice quivering. "I am Larina Dracomeer."

A moment's silence greeted her words. She didn't dare look at Dezrick. What would he think of her? Would he hate her for keeping this one secret from him, when he'd risked everything by telling her the truth? Kyra, at least, greeted the declaration with delight. After a moment, she drew her sword. Then, she went down on one knee before Larina, offering the exquisite blade to her.

"Welcome home, princess," she said. "My blade, and every one I make, is at your service."

One by one, the rest of the gathered revolutionaries followed suit, drawing their weapons and offering them to her on bended knee. Some carried weapons worn from skilled use, while others had nothing but kitchen knives. But they offered her even the simplest of weapons with the same bright hope. Larina wanted to tell them to stop this nonsense, but they needed it. They needed someone to believe in. She would be that person, but she had to make her position clear.

"I thank you for your loyalty to the memory of my mother," she said. "But I am no princess. Not anymore. I haven't come to reclaim the throne. I am here to avenge my family and to set things right, but nothing more."

Kyra's shoulders slumped in defeat, and Larina hastened to explain.

"I'm a Praetorian through and through now. I have been trained to protect life, and to take it when necessary. I am not fit to rule Oramis. I wouldn't even know how to begin."

"You're giving up on us?" asked Kyra.

"No." Larina put everything she had behind that word. "I will not stand by while Elrin corrupts the throne and the land with his murderous ways. But once he is gone, I will take my leave. You will be in good hands with Dezrick. He belongs on the throne, and I do not begrudge him it."

Unable to resist the urge, she looked at him. The prince stood there, so close and yet so far, watching her with unreadable eyes. He spoke not a word as everyone stood and moved forward in concert, eager to say something to the lost princess returned to them after all this time.

Chapter Twenty

After the meeting, Miriam needed an escort back to the castle. Larina happily obliged. Dezrick still hadn't said anything about her true identity, and the longer the silence between them stretched, the more worried she became. She didn't want him to think she intended to snatch the throne out from underneath him after he'd studied so hard to be worthy of it. But making him believe that would be difficult. She supposed she would feel the same if she were in his position.

She welcomed Miriam's chatty presence on the walk back to the secret passageway and volunteered to take the nurse down to her quarters, leaving Dezrick safe in his suite. After bidding Mimi goodnight, Larina found herself too restless to return to her room. Instead, she climbed up to the aviary where she would be unlikely to be disturbed at this hour. She'd found the place soothing as a girl but hadn't yet had a chance to revisit it. Most of the birds already slept. Black cloths covered the cages of the smaller ones, and hoods shielded the heads of the larger predators. A few feathers ruffled at her entry, but otherwise the aviary remained silent.

Animals soothed her. At the keep, she'd gone to the pens whenever she could, taking breaks between grueling training sessions to relax in their accepting presence. She'd met Nix there, and they'd struck up their unlikely friendship, the two most guarded and untrusting trainees finding understanding and acceptance in each other. She wished she could see him now and take advantage of his advice and support, which he would likely offer alongside some smart comments.

One cage sat uncovered on the table. Perhaps it had been forgotten, or its occupant was scheduled for a nighttime flight. The crowen within ruffled its feathers and gave a soft caw. Scaly growths on the black bird's feet continued up to cover its belly, only giving away to feathers on the wings, back, and head. The crowens' intelligence made them exceptional messengers. She'd used them herself on occasion.

Larina poked her fingers through the cage bars to stroke the glossy wings. The crowen's initial caution gave way to delight as she petted it, and she opened the cage, intending to pull it out. Then the aviary door opened behind her, letting out the softest of creaks as it moved. Hurriedly, she shut the cage to keep the restless crowen from escaping, expecting to see a servant or messenger with an urgent message to be sent despite the late hour.

Instead, Dezrick limped toward her. His face was drawn with pain as he lurched up the three stairs that led into the room. She wanted to help him but stopped herself at the last moment. Perhaps given recent revelations, her assistance wouldn't be welcome.

"When you didn't come back," he said, "I was worried."

Shame flooded her. She'd assumed he would be threatened, but she ought to know him better than that. She shouldn't be surprised to find that he thought only of her.

"I'm sorry," she said.

It wasn't enough. The rigid lines of his body told her that. When he raised his eyes to hers, they swam with hurt and confusion. Her stomach roiled with regret.

"Why didn't you tell me?" he asked. "Not about where you were going, but about your name. I understand why you'd hide it at first, but once you knew my position, once you knew *me*, why didn't you say something?"

"I guess I got used to hiding." She wanted to stop there, but he deserved more. She forced the words out from between numb lips. "I'd hidden for so long—and for good reason—that I couldn't even contemplate coming clean. Besides, my true name would only complicate things. Elrin needs to go, and that's all that matters to me. Dezrick, I really mean it when I say that you shouldn't be threatened. After he's gone, the throne is rightfully yours, and I'm happy for that."

He waved his hand. "I'm not worried about that. I'm not in this for the power." He paused. "But I trusted you. Don't you trust me?"

"More than anybody else. And you're right. I should have told you."

She didn't realize how much she meant it until she said it aloud. Dezrick nodded, but she didn't know if he believed her or not. He changed the subject before she could ask.

"I think I remember you. You had hair like fire."

"I dye it now. With berries. It makes a mess," she said. He offered her a faint smile but otherwise didn't respond. "Dezrick, what's wrong? If you're not worried about a power struggle between us, what's weighing on you?"

"I—" He broke off, at a loss for words, and then slowly, painfully got down on one knee before her just as he'd done with Miriam. She would not accept a gesture of fealty from him of all people and began to tell him so when he interrupted her, his voice torn with emotion. "I'm so sorry, Larina. I'm sorry for what my father did. I can't imagine what it must have been like for you to lose everything you'd known in a single night. I'm ashamed to carry the blood of the man who did that to you."

Larina swallowed against the lump in her throat, but she would not cry. She'd already done that in public today for the first time since she'd been a child, and she didn't care to repeat the experience. It made her feel weak and uncomfortably exposed.

"Like Miriam said, you can't take responsibility for his actions. None of it was your fault. Besides, you've suffered at his hands too," she said.

He winced. "I'm certain that he killed my mother," he said. "They were alone together when she died. He told that story about an assassin, but he didn't seem worried at all. Not until you showed up. It was like he knew the assassin wouldn't come back to threaten him, and how could he know that if he didn't kill her? If only I had proof, I'd confront him with it, but there's nothing. I didn't even get to see her body. Everyone knows what happened and no one will say a word about it because they're afraid of him."

Larina put her hand on his shoulder, offering what comfort she could. But she knew full well that it would never bring back the family he'd lost. The family they'd both lost.

"I'm sorry," she said. "All I can promise is that we'll avenge her. We'll avenge all of them."

His eyes met hers.

"I think she would have liked you. My mother, I mean," he said.

"And mine would have been so proud to see you

studying her writing. She would have talked your ear off about it, I imagine."

"I'm glad you're here, Larina. I won't lie and say that your confession didn't shock me, but now that it's all done, I'm happy. I don't have anyone left. But I don't feel so alone with you here," he said.

"You're not. And you won't be, I promise. If you need me, I'll be there."

"Good." He took a deep breath, leaning forward so his forehead rested against hers. "I was worried when you disappeared. I thought you'd left for good."

It was ridiculous to care about his feelings after she'd spent years plotting to kill his father. That went against her training. She shouldn't care at all, and she definitely shouldn't take comfort from the warm pressure of his head against hers, or the panicky way he snatched at her hands.

"I promise not to do that. I wouldn't leave you without a word," she said.

"Good," he repeated. "Because that would break me."

Then he kissed her. The touch was tentative at first, and Larina froze in indecision. She couldn't afford to develop feelings in the middle of a job. Such things had gotten guards killed time and time again. But she found herself kissing Dezrick back with increasing abandon. He knew her like no one had, and he accepted her. His embrace made her feel secure in a way she could only vaguely remember.

A relationship with Dezrick would be no less doomed because he called her by her real name instead of the fake one she'd worn for so long. But she couldn't help it. Because she had to admit the truth to herself.

Leaving him would break her, too.

Larina barely slept that night. She tossed and turned, troubled by new nightmares. Instead of seeing her family bleeding and broken on the ground, she saw Dezrick, Miriam, and Kyra in agony. Elrin stood over them, laughing as they died, while a five-year-old Larina struggled against Bastian's violent grip. After waking up in a cold sweat for the fourth time, she gave up on sleep, watching as the sun rose over the city, a creeping line of light that tried to reach the castle walls but was cut off by a line of stubborn clouds.

She had made a critical mistake. She'd kissed people before and enjoyed it, but never once had she been consumed by the desperate urge to hold them tight lest they disappear. The idea of losing the prince made her throat clench and her hands sweat. The possibility of harm coming to him—or to Mimi, or Kyra and the rest of the rebels—brought the same bone-deep grief that overwhelmed her when she remembered her family. She'd been so careful not to get too close to anyone, but being here had stripped her of her usual defenses, and now she would pay the price.

The kiss had been interrupted by the arrival of a harried birdkeeper who had returned to put away the forgotten crowen. Back in Dezrick's suite, they'd taken refuge in pleasantries before retiring for the night, neither of them willing to bring up what had happened. She hoped they could forget it, but she couldn't seem to let it go.

A light tap at her door interrupted this train of thought. Larina slipped her last knife into her belt and padded forward on silent feet to answer it. She clutched one of her knives in hand, just out of sight, as she opened the door. Yasmeen stood on the other side, her hand raised to knock again. Larina pocketed the knife as she looked the sorceress over. Her normally placid expression was twisted in annoyance.

"Are you dressed already then?" she asked. "Good. Come with me."

Larina flicked a glance back at the adjoining door to Dezrick's room. She'd heard no noise from him yet, no indication that he'd climbed out of bed.

"What's going on? I'll need to fetch a guard for the prince if I'm leaving," she said.

"I already asked. They're coming," Yasmeen replied, ignoring the question altogether.

The tromp of booted feet corroborated this statement. Larina waited until the guards took their places, earning an impatient sigh from Yasmeen, before following her down the hall.

"What's happening?" Larina hissed, lengthening her strides to keep up with the sorceress's hurried pace.

"Elrin just saw me in the hallway and asked me why I wasn't at this morning's security meeting. Apparently, Bastian and Sleth promised to extend the invitation to both of us, but I haven't heard a thing about it. Not until the king mentioned it, anyway. You?"

"Not a word."

"They must have conveniently forgotten." Yasmeen's smile turned icy, and for the first time, Larina realized what a dangerous enemy the sorceress would be. She'd dismissed the courtesan as nothing but a bedmate for the king whose claim of magical powers helped her maintain a tenuous hold on her freedom. But now, she recognized that Yasmeen had a keen political mind at work behind her luminous eyes. One she'd be foolish to dismiss. "Shall we remind them that we're to be included?"

"I'd be happy to," replied Larina with a humorless smile of her own.

"I thought you might."

Yasmeen led the way. They nodded to guards who stood at the ready in their immaculate uniforms, prepared to defend the structure with their lives. They passed alcoves where Larina had hidden during endless games of hide-and-seek with her brother. They descended the stairs that

Dezrick had fallen down years before, permanently damaging his body. They crossed into the new wing of the palace and approached the closed door of the library where Larina spent most of her days, standing at the prince's shoulder while he tried to learn how to lead a kingdom.

Yasmeen stopped there. A strange wave of anger coursed over Larina, that Bastian and Sleth had picked this of all places to hold their secret meeting. In her mind, the library belonged to her and Dezrick, a safe place of books and ideas where Elrin's hand hovered a little less closely. Now that illusion had been shattered.

But of course Yasmeen didn't share this sentiment. She paused to catch Larina's eye, nodded, and then stalked into the room.

At Dezrick's favorite table, Bastian and Sleth sat close together, their heads nearly touching as they looked over a plan of the castle marked with notes. Books picked at random from the shelves held down the corners. Larina glanced over them, hoping that the prince hadn't left out any particular tomes that gave a hint as to his reading topics but saw nothing but random histories still spattered with dust.

"There you are!" Yasmeen cooed as she glided toward them. "I'm so sorry that we're late. I know you must have been holding up the meeting for us."

Bastian glanced at Sleth, confusion written all over his face.

"Uh...yeah," he said. "We were wondering where you were. Weren't we?"

He sounded uncertain, but Sleth slid into the breach.

"We were just discussing whether we ought to have someone fetch you," the Praetorian said with an oily smoothness. "But I see that isn't necessary now."

"Not at all," replied Yasmeen. "I was just held up with the king—we are so close, you know—and we were talking about how accommodating you've been to his wishes that Reagan and I are involved with the security plans for the upcoming events with Dunheim. We all know how important their success is."

"Oh, yes," hissed Sleth, gesturing them forward. "All the more reason that we should begin. We have much to discuss."

Yasmeen settled into the proffered seat, but she wasn't done yet. "Yes, let's. Heads will roll if things don't go to Elrin's liking, and I would hate to take a poor report of our progress back to him. He is such a pet when he's upset. You've seen how bad his temper can be when he feels his orders aren't being heeded, haven't you, Reagan?"

Larina, who had quietly taken a seat on her other side, picked up the cue easily. "I have," she replied. "I'm sure Bastian has too. But let's not talk about that. We're all friends here, after all."

Sleth returned her chilly smile with one of his own. "Indeed," he replied. "Shall we begin?"

They all bent their heads over the plans, as if they had no desire to kill each other whatsoever.

A few hours later, Larina and Yasmeen returned upstairs. The sorceress remained silent on their walk, her beautiful features drawn inward in contemplation. Larina offered to see her to her rooms, hoping to catch a word, even though she wasn't certain what she wanted to ask or whether she'd believe anything that came out of Yasmeen's mouth. As they reached the door, Yasmeen gestured for her to step inside so that they might be able to discuss the meeting in private.

"What did you think of that?" asked the sorceress. "I have the firm feeling that they held out on us, but I'm open to an alternate interpretation."

"They were definitely unhappy to see us," admitted Larina. "But their plans were good, and even if they'd wanted to switch them out for an alternative to keep us in the dark, they didn't have the opportunity to do so. We took them by surprise."

"Was that why you asked so many questions? To confirm that they weren't lying to us?"

In truth, Larina had been testing the plans for weak spots, trying to find a way to get her people in without anyone else at the table realizing her true motive. Sleth had begun to eye her with suspicion as she'd asked query after query, and she'd turned it into a game as a result, making it obvious that she tried to annoy them with her pestering. Bastian's jealousy made it easy to goad him, and the more curt and insulting he'd gotten, the sweeter she'd asked her questions. Yasmeen had joined in, the two of them making a veritable show of fawning over Bastian and all the "helpful information" he provided them. The captain's face had gone completely red with anger by the time they'd finished, and Sleth's suspicion had been replaced with amusement at the situation.

"Yes, that's why I acted so stupid," Larina responded. "Although I will admit I didn't mind making Bastian mad in the process."

Yasmeen smiled with exquisite innocence in return. "Why, Reagan, I have no clue what you're talking about."

"Me either. But I should get back to Dezrick now. I'll let you know if I learn anything else about the masked ball. Please do the same?"

"I will. Thank you for your help. I'm happy to know that I have someone trustworthy to lean on."

Larina returned the smile—and the compliment—with only a small pang of guilt. She still didn't like some of Yasmeen's choices, but perhaps she could understand why the sorceress had made them. Perhaps under Dezrick's rule, her friend could find some measure of peace without feeling like she had to give herself away in order to achieve it. Larina hoped so. She knew the prince didn't care for the woman who now warmed his father's bed, but a word from Larina on the matter might help to open his eyes. He'd proven himself to be remarkably levelheaded, even when faced with a reality he might not like.

When she reentered her room, she found the adjoining door open, and the prince himself waiting at her table. He dismissed the guards and asked her for an update.

"Bastian and Sleth tried to plan all of the security measures without us," she explained. "If your father hadn't mentioned it, we would have been completely in the dark."

"You know what they're planning?" he asked. "What a relief!"

Unfortunately, Larina could report no other positives. All her questions had led her to one simple conclusion— security would be tight. They might get to Elrin, but the one who struck the final blow had a slim chance of escape afterwards. She had no problem with the possibility of her death, but once again, she remembered her dream and the agony of seeing Dezrick and the others bleeding out on the floor. She couldn't let that happen. She wouldn't. After all, she was the Shadow, and her reputation had been built on planning perfect assassinations.

Elrin had proved to be the most impossible of them all, but still, she would accomplish it. There had to be a way.

Chapter Twenty-One

As the days passed and the ball drew closer, Larina and Dezrick fell into an unspoken schedule. They spent their nights at the smithy, helping Kyra and Alaris at the forge and finalizing their plans. During the day, Dezrick sequestered himself in his rooms. Although he claimed to be studying, in reality, the two of them caught some much-needed rest. As always, few people took note of the prince's behavior, although Larina kept a close eye out for Sleth. Even if he'd written Dezrick off as an unimportant player in the game, he would watch for any opportunity to discredit her.

She and Dezrick still hadn't discussed their kiss, and as the time passed without confrontation, Larina began to wonder if the whole thing would fade into memory. Dezrick must have calculated the risks of allowing their feelings to run unchecked just as she had, and as a result, they subsided into a comfortable and friendly partnership without any drama or tears. This should have soothed Larina's nerves—and it did—but it failed to suppress an inexplicable sense of loss. She'd never had his heart to begin with, so the emotion made no sense. She squashed it firmly and kept on with her work. She had too much to do in too little time to be mooning around.

Late one evening, as she cleaned out the forge, Dezrick approached her. She'd been running through the plans for the millionth time, trying to anticipate any new complications that she might have missed. In a solo job, she could improvise on the spot and often did, but in a complicated mission such as this one, with so many inexperienced operatives and independent pieces, she had to give full instructions. *If the guards stop you, go through the passageway instead. If your uniform attracts too much attention, stop at one of the caches and change into servant's garb.* And so on and so forth until each end goal seemed a certainty.

So absorbed was she in her obsessive planning that she didn't hear the prince's approach, and when she turned from the workbench with a sooty rag in hand, she nearly knocked him over. For an uncomfortable moment, they stood face-to-face, mere inches separating them. Then he backed away, forcing a laugh, and said, "Sorry I frightened you."

"It's my fault," she responded, flustered.

"I wanted to show you something. If you have the time, that is."

When she agreed, Dezrick gestured her over to the bench where he'd been working with Alaris. The two of them had inexplicably requested all the sooty residue from the bottom of the forge but had refused to explain the request when Kyra inquired what they were about. Perhaps now Larina would learn what they'd been up to.

"I've been working on that distraction you wanted," Dezrick said, gesturing to the table.

Larina perked up. Chaos would make it much easier to get close to Elrin. Unfortunately, Sleth and Bastian had done an excellent job of cutting off most of their opportunities to make it happen. The kitchens would be under heavy guard, so starting a fire there was out. The lookout towers were covered as well, removing the possibility of ringing the bells and signaling a fake attack. Every idea Larina had, the king's loyal servants had anticipated.

"Did you come up with something?" she demanded.

His answering smile said it all.

"Let me show you," he responded. "It took a while to get the mixture right, but I think we've got it. If you add the powder in this bag to the fluid here, it will emit flames and a heavy black smoke. It will ignite anything that's too close, so you need to back away as soon as the two are combined. The fire will spread on its own. I've mixed it to create quite a lot of smoke, so it will be difficult to see. That should help us get closer to the king, don't you think?"

Larina beamed at him. "I think that will be very helpful. How thick is the smoke? Will we be able to function if we're prepared for it? I think it's too late to fashion some contraption to protect our eyes."

"I'm honestly not sure. We tried only a pinch of it outside, and it seemed quite thick to us. But the only way to know for certain is to try it out. Shall I? We made plenty."

Larina nodded, and Dezrick picked up the small pouch containing the flammable powder.

"Stand back," he warned.

With painstaking care, he poured the powder into the flask of amber liquid. Thick black smoke began to pour out of the flask. No sooner did the prince back away than a great gout of flame came out of the top, spilling like lava to sizzle on the anvil. The smoke continued to leak out at an alarming rate, filling the room with a black haze. It stung Larina's eyes, but she could still see if she squinted. If she tied something over her nose and mouth to filter the air, she would be functional. Perhaps their seamstresses could modify the masks for the ball to incorporate a filter so she wouldn't have to worry about it at all.

They stepped out of the room and into the empty storage area beyond, coughing, and shut the door behind them. He turned hopeful, red-ringed eyes toward her, eager for her approval.

"It's brilliant, Dezrick," she said.

He shrugged, suddenly awkward. "Since he took your family from you on a night of blood and fire, it's only fitting that we use the same tools against him. I hope that doesn't bother you, or bring up memories you'd rather forget."

Later, she would reflect that it was the unexpected kindness that undid her. She'd carried the burden of revenge for so long, and the realization that she no longer carried it alone struck her hard. She threw herself into his arms and kissed him again, heedless of her promise to herself that she'd never repeat that mistake.

Without hesitation, he returned the gesture. They stood there, wrapped in each other for who knew how long, until the clearing of a throat across the room broke them apart.

Kyra stood at the opposite end of the storeroom and had been there for who knew how long. Larina had been so distracted by the smoke—and by Dezrick, a traitorous voice murmured in her head—that the smith could have been standing there the whole time. She would have seen every-thing. Larina's cheeks flushed, and Dezrick rushed to apologize.

"I'm so sorry, Kyra," he said. "We didn't realize you were there. We..."

He trailed off, looking at Larina out of the corner of his eye, unsure of what to say. She wanted to save him, but she had no idea either. She could kill a man with a knife at twenty paces, but she had little experience with relationships. If you could call their doomed kisses a relationship.

"No worries," replied the smith in light tones. "I'm not so old that I don't remember what it was like to be young and in love."

Dezrick burst into a wave of shocked coughing which might have been a delayed reaction to the smoke. Larina wasn't sure. She sputtered a bit herself, wanting to protest Kyra's statement but still finding herself at a loss for words.

"But if you don't mind the interruption, I have something for you, Highness," Kyra continued.

Larina stepped back to give her access to Dezrick, eager to move on from this uncomfortable subject. To her surprise, Kyra brought out a long, wrapped parcel and offered it to her instead of Dezrick. She'd gotten so used to hearing the prince referred to as "highness" that she hadn't stopped to think the smith might be addressing her.

Although she wanted to protest the honorific, she would have to do so later or risk hurting the smith's feelings. Kyra went down on one knee before her, holding up the long, unmistakable shape of a sword, wrapped in white linen. Her face wore a blend of pride and anticipation as she offered the weapon, and Larina couldn't make herself say anything other than a quiet thank you. Dezrick watched over her shoulder as she unwrapped it.

The cloth fell away to reveal a masterpiece of a weapon. The metal gleamed in the light, a short, fast weapon designed for precision work, its form beautiful and deadly. The figures of three dragons wrapped their sinuous bodies around the hilt, with the blade emerging from the open mouth of the middle dragon. Larina ran a finger over the creatures, marveling at the craftsmanship, then lifted it for the first time. The tapered blade felt like an extension of her arm, the perfect length and weight. She raised delighted eyes to Kyra, who answered her smile with one of her own.

"Thank you," Larina said, choked with an emotion she couldn't quite name. "It's beautiful."

"I designed a sword for your mother once," replied the smith. "Did you know that?"

"No! Why haven't you said something before?"

"It was a long time ago. But I was proud to do it. My father made swords for your grandparents, and he taught me the craft. For a long time, it was my dream that Alaris would follow in my footsteps and create a blade worthy of the next generation of Dracomeer royalty."

Kyra paused, seeming overcome by her feelings. Larina empathized, although she couldn't have explained her own swelling emotions. Somehow, the gift was bigger than just a blade. Holding it made her feel an inescapable loss and the bright joy in discovering something new and precious, both at the same time.

"I lost his bow," she admitted, somewhat nonsensically. "The one that Alaris made, I mean. I hid it the night I tried to kill the king, and I never did have a chance to go back for it."

Kyra patted her hand. "That's fine. There will be more bows. In fact, I think if you asked him to, he'd start on another one for you tonight. He probably wouldn't shut up about it either." She paused, chuckling. "We're honored to arm you, as we were honored to craft weapons for your family before you. May the Great Mother shelter you in your darkest moments and keep you safe. And if all else fails, my steel never will."

She held out a sheath, and Larina slid the blade home and settled it on her hip, where it belonged.

"I'll try to be worthy of it," she said, meaning every word.

"You still don't get it, do you, Larina Dracomeer?" asked Kyra, shaking her head so her blond braids skittered over her shoulders. "You already are."

The gifts didn't stop there. The day before the ball, Dezrick and Larina lunched in his rooms and had just finished their meal when a soft rap at the door interrupted them. He leaped up with excitement, and Larina hushed him before going to answer it. If he didn't settle down, someone would become suspicious. They would have to greet the envoy of Dunheim and endure the pomp and circumstance of introductions and bootlicking before they could put their plan in motion. He needed to calm down or Elrin would grow suspicious. She'd begun to think that maybe she would share her usual calming drought with him. He could use it.

Miriam stood at the door. The old nurse's face also wore an expression of delight, and Larina looked between the two of them with fond exasperation. They'd been cooking up some plot. It didn't take her Praetorian training to figure that out.

"What did you do?" she asked.

Miriam's eyes twinkled. "Carry that in for me, will you dear?" she asked, pointing to a fabric-shrouded figure next to her.

It stood nearly as tall as Larina, but she lifted it without much effort. The shape suggested a training mannequin, although the wooden body was much lighter than the mannequins she'd lugged around the keep as a trainee, and the bottom tapered down to a stand rather than fully carved legs. The rebels had probably had to make do with whatever they could find. It wouldn't matter; if seeing her practice with her new blade would set them both at ease, she would oblige them. It was the least she could do for people who had reminded her that she still had family left after all these years.

She set the mannequin down as instructed, and Miriam removed the fabric covering with a flourish. Larina blinked, startled by the sight of a dressmaker's dummy when she'd expected a training one. The wooden figure wore a beautiful blue dress that took on hints of purple in the light. It was a gorgeous gown, with light beading at the bodice and a simple sash at the waist to allow for easy movement. Larina had worn a few fancy gowns during her work, and she hated what they did to her breath, but this one appeared to be designed for comfort.

"Do you like it?" Dezrick asked, his face bright with excitement.

"It's very kind of you," she began before trailing off, not wanting to offend.

"I know you don't care for dresses, but even with the mask, you'll stand out in your tunic and trousers," he explained. "So Miriam and I had this made for you."

Larina tried not to frown. As much as she appreciated the gesture, she wouldn't be able to draw her sword without lifting her skirts to her waist. The scabbard wouldn't fit atop the full skirt.

"It is very kind of you," she said. "But I'm not sure I can use it. It's beautiful, and I thank you both very much, but I can't fight in that."

Their expressions, which had both fallen at the beginning of her speech, lightened up once more as she explained her concerns. Miriam gestured her forward to get a better look.

"Ah, but that shouldn't be a problem, child," she said. "Look at this."

She loosened a row of cleverly hidden buttons at the front of the skirt, releasing the front panel. It draped neatly off to one side, exposing a set of matching trousers underneath. A belt and sheathed sword sat tucked beneath the folds of the skirt. She could see now that the dress had been custom built, the skirt designed to avoid trailing on the ground and tripping her up as she moved, but long enough to shield a pair of practical boots from view. As she looked closer, she realized that the bodice featured a number of hidden pockets for knives. Their jeweled hilts stuck out of the fabric, blending in with the ornamentation. No one would realize how many weapons she carried unless they put their hands on her, and she didn't intend to allow that for a moment.

"You thought of everything, didn't you?" Larina said, looking between the two of them. Dezrick blushed and ducked his head, but Miriam smiled.

"We see you, Larina," she said. "And we love you. The Great Mother blessed us a hundredfold when she brought you back to us." She folded Larina into a warm embrace, stroking her head. "It's a pity that you changed your hair. It would have been lovely with the gown. But you're such a beauty that it won't matter."

Now it was Larina's turn to flush. She wasn't much for dresses, and most of the time she chose hairstyles for their ability to keep her vision clear. She'd never sought beauty for its sake alone. But when Miriam called her beautiful, it meant something.

"Thank you," she said, even though that felt insufficient. "It's..."

The old nurse patted her on the arm as she fumbled for words. "I know, child. I know," she said, and then she let herself out.

As the door closed, Dezrick let out a tense breath.

"You really do like it?" he asked. "I know you're not a fan of gowns in general."

"It's a very kind gesture."

"Then why do you look so uncomfortable?" he asked. "I feel like I must have done something wrong."

"That's not it at all!" She paused, trying to marshal her thoughts, but she didn't understand this unsettled feeling herself, so how could she explain it to him? "I'm...just not used to receiving gifts."

"Oh. That's fine, then."

But the prince didn't look reassured at all. His face remained pinched with concern, and his fingers drummed on the tabletop as he stared at the wall without seeing it. She sat down next to him, taking his fidgety hand in hers to still its incessant motion.

CONNOR ASHLEY & CARRIE HARRIS

"Honest, Dezrick," she said. "It's the nicest thing anyone has ever given me."

He blinked. "Oh, I wasn't thinking about that. If you said it's okay, then I'll do you the courtesy of believing you."

"What's bothering you?"

"I'm terrified." His hand clenched over hers, squeezing her fingers tight. "I'm responsible for all of this, you know. Kyra leads the group, but I brought them together. They all showed up because of my title. If things go wrong, their deaths will be on my conscience."

"They showed up of their own free will because they believe Oramis deserves better. No fight is won without casualties. They all knew that when they signed up," she said.

He gave her a bleak smile. "I understand what you're saying, but it doesn't make me feel any better. I wish it did."

"Me too," she replied. "I could name the circumstances of every innocent death I've witnessed. Everyone who died because I didn't do my job as well as I ought to. Every person I couldn't save haunts me, as does my family. But maybe stopping Elrin once and for all will put them to rest for good."

"I hope so," he said earnestly.

"So do I..." she replied.

Chapter Twenty-Two

In the gown, with her braided hair pinned to her head, Larina felt like a different person. As a girl, she'd taken any opportunity to dress up, sneaking into the throne room to climb up to her mother's seat and play queen. Anything frilly and beaded would have sent her into swoons of delight back then, but once she'd sought refuge at the keep, she'd abandoned finery. At first, the lace would have scratched at tender skin still healing from the burns. Later, she found that putting on a gown made it difficult to breathe. She'd chalked that up to the restraining bodice, but with the cushion of time and space, she realized that it had been nerves as much as anything else. Lacing herself into a dress brought back vague memories of her mother and sister in rustling silk, lacing her into tight bodices that made her complain. But she pushed those memories—and the weakness they brought with them—away. Since then, she'd avoided finery. It had been easy to stick to tunics and leggings, claiming this to be a practical choice to facilitate her Praetorian training.

Of course she'd worn dresses since then. During one long summer in Roshai, she and Nix had infiltrated a dancing troupe in order to get access to its patron, who had a large stake in the illegal slave trade. The dancers performed in tiny dresses and loincloths that barely qualified as clothing, and at first, Larina had quailed at the idea, but it had turned out to be one of her favorite jobs. Her friendship with Nix had been cemented while wearing those scraps of fabric, which was enough to make her look back fondly on them.

After that experience, she no longer worried about the expanse of cleavage exposed by a gown. Although she was modest by nature, she'd gotten used to frank admiration of her body and what it could do, and she'd taken pride in her acrobatic dance performances, blending strength and beauty in tantalizing ways. Still, she preferred not to wear gowns out of practicality. If given the chance between the standard ball gown and her skimpier dance costume, she would have taken the costume in a snap. It had been built to facilitate movement, while gowns encouraged their wearers to be immobile ornaments.

This dress didn't do that at all. She'd spent some time in it last night, running through her stretches to familiarize herself with the weight and movement of the fabric before taking a long soak and soothing herself with some hot tea. Dezrick had accepted her proffered cup and retired early. Hopefully it had helped him sleep.

Now she sat like a lady while Miriam fussed over her hair, pushing additional pins into place and murmuring to herself. Larina had protested when her old nurse had shown up at the door, but she had to admit that Miriam knew what she was doing much more than Larina did when it came to hairstyling. It wouldn't do to have her hair all come down at the moment of action, obscuring her vision and leading to yet another miss. She couldn't allow that to happen, not this time. This time, the plan would work.

After Miriam pushed the last pin into place, Larina picked up a delicately scaled dragon mask from the table. It would be tempting to remove the mask before she struck the killing blow, but if all went to plan, there wouldn't be time. She would have to make do with the knowledge that the last thing Elrin saw would be the symbol of her family's legacy.

Miriam clucked and cooed over her appearance, and Larina thanked her with a kiss on the cheek. Then the nurse bustled off to attend to her other duties for the evening. Each member of the resistance had an important job, such as distracting the guards at just the right moment, placing needed equipment at the right spot without detection, or watching Sleth or Bastian. They would all contribute to this evening's success. Larina had built redundancy into the plan to ensure that as situations developed and unanticipated complications presented themselves, others could help pick up the slack. It was as iron-tight as she could make it.

She was ready.

Her stomach turned lazy flips as she let herself into Dezrick's suite. Her placid calm had begun to give way to a vague and unsettling nervousness that made itself known at inconvenient times. Like now, for instance.

Dezrick sat at the table, waiting for her. He rose as she entered, a gesture of politeness that failed to surprise. Ever since those first few awful days, he'd been nothing but cordial to her. But for the first time since she'd arrived, he looked the part of a prince. The deep red of his clothing set off the warm tones of his skin, and the gold embroidery and detailing gave him just the right amount of pomp. His sword hung at his waist, and a black handkerchief in his pocket served as a gentle reminder of the mother he'd lost. The understated look spoke of restraint and leadership in turn, with the added advantage of making him look quite dashing in the process.

With a start, Larina tore her eyes away from him, flushing with embarrassment. She needn't have bothered. He'd frozen in place, staring at her with his mouth hanging open. She picked up the castle plans, which sat unrolled on the table after their last minute review, and whacked him on the shoulder.

His face broke out into a delighted grin. "What was that for?"

"You're acting like my wearing a gown is a miracle."

Instead of making excuses, he nodded. "I'm sorry. You're very beautiful," he said.

"Thank you. This really is a wonderful gown. I can move about quite easily in it."

Although she didn't often gush, she meant every word of it. Dezrick's face lit up at the praise.

"If this goes poorly, perhaps I'll become a dress designer," he said.

"It won't."

Larina spoke with a confidence she didn't quite feel. Her stomach flipped again, and she couldn't help but think about all the ways their plans could go wrong. She had anticipated so much, but after years of Praetorian work, she knew the impossibility of planning for everything. Something would go sideways this evening, and she could only hope that the people on the ground made the right choices, or innocents would die.

Despite her confident speech, Dezrick seemed to pick up on her nerves. He approached her in respectful silence, taking her mask and tying it on for her. He'd chosen an owl mask for himself, its ruddy feathers tipped in a deep red to match his tunic. She helped him to settle it in place. Then

CONNOR ASHLEY & CARRIE HARRIS

he took her hand, tucking it into the crease of his elbow and covering it with his own.

"I thank the gods that you're here, Larina Dracomeer," he said.

The quiet faith in his words bolstered her flagging confidence. She smiled at him from behind the mask.

"Shall we?" she asked.

With impeccable manners, he led her from the room. The security measures had been tripled at the very least, with guards posted at every intersection and stairway. Bastian had emptied his barracks for the evening on the advice of Sleth, leaving no one without a task. The sheer manpower on display boggled Larina's mind. At first, she'd worried that Sleth knew her intent, but how could he? Everyone in the rebellion had been careful to hide evidence of their plans. She'd picked up on no signs of pursuit en route to their meetings, nor any indication that their secret had been leaked. If it had, she did not think for a moment that Elrin would waste time in punishing the rebels. He wouldn't sit on the information when he could make a lesson out of them for the prince of Dunheim's benefit.

Dezrick had begged off the initial reception, claiming a headache, but Larina had watched the procession enter the castle gates. The Dunn prince appeared to be the bloated and egotistical type, accompanied by an honor guard and a full complement of servants to attend at his every whim. He appeared to have more in common with Elrin than

Dezrick did. The two greeted each other with a great deal of grandstanding, and it would have been a close contest to determine which royal's uniform bore the most golden braid.

As planned, Larina and Dezrick arrived in the throne room after most of the guests had arrived. The already grand space had been cleaned to a spit-shine. Ornate stained-glass windows ran along the walls leading up to the throne, depicting the dragons of Oramis and the Three Sisters who had tamed them. Candelabras dotted the space, hanging from the tall rafters on long chains, coating the assembled courtiers in all their finery with flickering light. In one corner, a small group of musicians played quiet music on priceless instruments. Along the opposite wall, a long row of tables sagged under the weight of a gourmet meal that would have made Larina's mouth water if nerves hadn't curdled her stomach.

In the already-crowded room, their entrance caused no stir at all, as Larina had intended. She wanted to remain inconspicuous for as long as possible. She dropped back to maintain the proper distance between bodyguard and client, keeping a lookout for anyone who drew too close to the prince.

Imposing in his guard disguise, Alaris took up position near the buffet. Another rebel, a woman who moved with a weary efficiency that leant an air of legitimacy to her servant's uniform, paused behind the shield of his body to drop a small package into the decorative plant that flanked the table. Alaris remained there for a few minutes after she'd left before moving on to his next objective.

Dezrick had confessed that he usually ate sparingly from the buffet before finding a spot in a corner at events such as this one, and deviating from this pattern would only attract unwanted attention. Larina stood by his chair as he nibbled on a plate of delicate pastries. They watched as Elrin made his entrance, flanked by Yasmeen and the prince of Dunheim, all of them easily recognizable despite their masks. Elrin's had been designed to resemble a golden bear with sharp incisors and the suggestion of a spiky crown atop its head. The Dunn prince wore a gem-studded atrocity that made a garish display of wealth and power, and peacock feathers arched delicately from Yasmeen's mask over her perfectly curled hair. The three of them didn't bother to speak to anyone but stood on display instead, allowing themselves to be admired.

Dezrick grunted with distaste, otherwise keeping his comments to himself. But as the first notes of music filled the room, he gestured Larina close.

"Dance with me," he said, taking her by surprise.

He must have had some reason to suggest deviating from the plan. Larina took a moment to scan the room, wondering if he'd noticed something she'd missed. But everything was proceeding like clockwork. As she watched, Kyra walked across the room in her guard's uniform, palming a small package passed to her by Miriam as they brushed past each other. She saw nothing out of place that needed tending, so she turned inquiring eyes onto Dezrick. He just smiled at her.

"Is something wrong?" she whispered in his ear.

He blinked as if he only now realized that the offer could be construed as alarming. This was why she preferred to work with Praetorians. Regardless of his intelligence, Dezrick lacked the background to understand that any last-minute changes increased the likelihood that something might go wrong. She understood the desire for a better vantage point; the dance floor would afford them a view of the antechamber where most of the preparatory action would be taking place even now. But the benefit wasn't worth the attention it would draw, and a prince dancing with his bodyguard—no matter how finely dressed—would be an instant scandal.

His words came out in a nervous staccato. "No. I just wanted to dance with you. This might be our last chance. If things go wrong."

Larina shut her mouth with a click. Suddenly, she found it difficult to meet his eyes. She felt exposed and awkward, and the emotion had nothing to do with the low neckline of her gown. They still hadn't spoken about their kisses; she'd hoped they were safely forgotten, but now they filled her mind. Even though she needed to keep her attention on the plan, and the attack that would begin any moment now, she couldn't tear herself away. If she did, he'd think she didn't care, and she couldn't stand to mislead him. As doomed as their relationship might be, he deserved her honesty at the very least.

"La—Reagan?" he asked, fumbling over the pseudonym. "Would you like to?"

"I would," she admitted, pitching her voice low to avoid being overheard by any number of passing couples, anonymous behind their masks. "But you know we can't. Your father would have a fit if he saw you fraternizing with a bodyguard. And...the timing isn't good. You know it isn't."

Dezrick's face fell, but he nodded in agreement anyway.

"I know you're right, but..." He took a deep breath, steeling himself. "I can't risk leaving this unsaid. You're smart, fierce, and kind. I've told you many times that I'm grateful you're here, but I'm not just referring to your much-needed skills. Being near you makes me happy."

He paused there, looking up at her with hopeful eyes, seeking some kind of encouragement that his words fell on welcoming ears. Larina wanted to give it, but what then? Even if she lived to see another day, she couldn't remain here once Elrin met his destiny. In her girlhood, this castle had been her rightful place, but not anymore. As much as it pained her to admit, she looked forward to exploring what her future could be without the burden of revenge hanging on her, and she simply couldn't do that here. It left her feeling torn, even though she knew leaving would be a kindness. Dezrick couldn't truly rule with the Dracomeer heir hovering over his shoulder.

He might not understand her logic now, but he would someday. Still, she couldn't leave him in doubt of her feelings. Honesty might be painful, but he'd earned it.

His face fell as the silence stretched between them. As he withdrew, she hastened to explain, searching for the words that would make him understand.

"Dezrick, I only wish we had the time to explore this," she began.

Before she could explain further, a scream of pure terror ripped through the room, silencing the music and stilling the occupants.

"Fire! The castle is on fire! Everyone out!" shouted Alaris from the door, his face alight with feigned concern.

As quickly as he'd appeared, he vanished from sight. The dancers stopped, scenting the air. Larina sniffed too, picking up the faintest tang of smoke. She reminded herself that she needn't panic, but painful memories still made her arms break into fearful goosebumps. A nervous murmur spread across the dancefloor, but no sooner did the first couple take a step toward the doors than Elrin clapped his hands for attention.

"Stay where you are!" he thundered. "I am in charge here, and the ball doesn't end until I say it does. My staff will get this under control."

In the sudden quiet, Larina could hear the distant shouts of alarm as the fire spread. Some of the guards would leave the ball to contain the blaze and preserve the food supply, and the guests at the ball would grow restive. When the smoke bombs went off by the buffet, she would take advantage of the chaos and strike.

She met Dezrick's eyes, wishing they had more time, trying to communicate everything she felt for him. She could have loved him. She lacked the opportunity to pursue her feelings, but that didn't make them less real. If only she could make him see that. His jaw tightened with resolve, his emotional declaration all but forgotten.

"Go on," he urged, determined to motivate her. "It's time."

"But..."

"If you don't go now, all is lost."

The flat reality of his words struck her like blades. She nodded. Perhaps later, after she'd settled down somewhere safe, she would write to him and explain everything. That would have to do. She'd always known that a relationship between them would be impossible; she couldn't get all melodramatic about it now. Larina would get him the crown or die trying. Somehow, her motivations had changed over the past few weeks. She'd gone from wanting to avenge the past to wanting to make a better present.

She nodded, offering her hand to help Dezrick to a standing position. He would approach his father and introduce himself to the visiting princeling, distracting them with his sudden interest in politics. Larina, as his bodyguard, would follow on his heels, taking up a position within striking distance of the king. At some point, the smoke bombs would go off, and Larina would take advantage of the chaos to end the king's life.

Dezrick stood without her assistance, straightening his clothes and marshalling his nerve. Then he led her toward his father, passing small clusters of masked dancers too afraid of the king's ire to leave outright. A small group of guards surrounded their liege, but otherwise the plan had worked. Most of the guards had left the throne room to fight the fire. Sleth still hovered nearby, but he couldn't cover all of the openings. If she played her cards right, she would have her shot.

The remaining guards parted to let them through, closing ranks behind them. The king eyed them with mild curiosity, like his son was a pet that sometimes amused him. Sleth smiled his oily grin, wiggling the tips of his fingers at her in a greeting that made her skin crawl.

Dezrick bowed with a flourish, placing all of his weight on his good leg to avoid overbalancing. He'd practiced this move over and over again until his lips went bloodless with pain but hadn't spoken a word of complaint.

"I haven't yet had the opportunity to be introduced," he said. "I am Dezrick, Crown Prince of Oramis."

The Dunn prince bowed perfunctorily, clapping

Dezrick on the shoulders like they were old drinking buddies.

"Cathar of Dunheim," he replied. "This place is falling down around you, eh? Pretty soon, you'll be needing more of our troops to set things to right again!"

He elbowed Elrin, who glowered at the impertinence. But the prince didn't seem to notice—or care—that he'd aggravated the king at all. If the twinkle in his eye was any indication, he might even have done it on purpose.

"As my father explained, it's under control," Dezrick said. "We've brought in many outside staff for this event. I'm sure that one of them simply overturned a lantern or had a mishap in the kitchen. I can barely smell the smoke."

Larina scented the air again. That had been a blatant lie; the scent of burning things grew stronger with every moment. A few of the dancers had begun to edge toward the doors, trusting in the protective anonymity of their masks to shield their identities from the king. But the ring of guards around them remained steady, ready to intervene should any danger present itself. Little did they know that the danger stood within their ranks. Larina folded her arms, trying to look as if she tried to warm herself against a sudden chill, while she rested her fingers on the handle of one of her daggers. One pull, and it would be free. If only Dezrick would shift just a half step to the side...

Prince Cathar arched a brow and stared at Dezrick for a

moment before breaking out into a wide grin, his cheeks ruddy with wine.

"I like you, Dezrick. Elrin was wrong about you. You aren't a spineless sop after all," he said.

Dezrick's ears went red, but he made no reply.

With a hiss and a thump of air, the smoke bomb hidden next to the buffet detonated, spewing a thick black cloud into the air. Terrified guests streamed toward the doors, heedless of their orders to stay in place. Larina tensed, evaluating her chances and finding them lacking. If she got into a prolonged struggle, she'd lose by virtue of sheer numbers. Sleth would see to that. She had to do something to even out the odds and guarantee that after so many failed attempts, Elrin would not escape this one.

A triumphant voice at the door interrupted her ruminations.

"We got them, Your Highness!"

Bastian sounded positively gleeful as he hurried in, clutching Alaris and Kyra by the backs of their necks like recalcitrant children. He pushed them onto the floor before him where they sprawled, beaten and bloody. Another guard followed him, holding Miriam and the woman in the servant's uniform. One by one, most of their co-conspirators came marching in under duress, bruises already rising on their faces. None of them struggled, but if the bloody, rumpled appearance of the guards gave any indication, they'd put up a fight.

Another set of guards popped the smoke bombs into jars under Yasmeen's watchful direction. The lids fastened on tight, cutting off the thick flow of smoke. A haze still hung in the air, and the few remaining dancers coughed as it tickled their throats.

Larina glanced at Elrin, who had his hand on the hilt of his sword, his eyes alight with invitation. He knew an attack would come from some direction, and he welcomed the challenge even if he hadn't yet found its source. In a fair fight, she'd best him, but he wouldn't play fair. Besides, Sleth wouldn't stop staring at her, his expression elated as he sucked in all the chaos and fear. He edged closer to the king, grinning in self-satisfaction. Then the emaciated Praetorian wagged a finger at her in mock rebuke.

"You ought to keep your hands off your daggers, little Shadow," he said. "Or someone will get hurt."

"That was the point, actually," she replied, but she lowered her hands to her sides anyway. A second set of daggers rested near her hips in reinforced sheaths. She might still find a use for them. If she couldn't get to the king, Sleth's neck would do.

"You shouldn't be so glib. Not now that your little ruse is uncovered. I've been following our friend Miriam for weeks now. You have the skill to watch your tail, but she trusts everyone. One night, she even gave me a copper to find a bed when she passed me begging on the street. Isn't that sweet?"

Sleth's voice dripped sarcasm. He leaned forward, whispering in Elrin's ear. The king jerked as the words hit him, his narrowed eyes pinning Larina in place. She didn't need to overhear the words to know what name Sleth murmured. She had finally been discovered. It was almost a relief, but she pushed the emotion aside, preparing herself for the inevitable moment where violence broke out. She would acquit herself well, and although the numbers were against her, they would underestimate her skill. The king could still fall beneath her blade if she played her cards right.

He straightened, lips drawing back from his teeth, and took a single step toward her, Sleth at his elbow, blocking her line of attack.

"We are now at an impasse, are we not, Larina Dracomeer?" Elrin purred.

Once again, his voice cut through the room like a knife, turning all eyes to them. The few remaining party guests murmured in disbelief, craning their heads to get a glimpse of her. The true heir! The implications of her survival sent ripples through the room, to Elrin's obvious fury. Prince Cathar clapped his hands in dark glee as he watched the drama unfold.

"A Dracomeer heir, alive after all these years?" he asked. "I'll get you the armaments you want if you'll give me her too. I like the feisty ones."

Without even looking at him, Elrin backhanded the

prince. He staggered backwards, putting a hand to his reddening cheek. The few members of the Dunn honor guard remaining in the throne room surged forward to protect their royal master only to be met by the raised swords of Bastian's guards. A tense silence filled the room. It might explode into violence, or it might slowly subside.

Larina edged around toward the king, but Sleth dogged her every move. His hands were empty, but they hovered near his throwing knives. There was no way to get to Elrin without going through him, and that delay would cost her.

She had been taught since her youth that sacrificing her life to complete a mission was an honorable trade, and Garret had seen to it that those Praetorians who made the ultimate sacrifice were revered for their bravery. But she had realized long ago how he benefited from such a policy. Garret pocketed the death cost for every slain Praetorian who had no immediate family to receive the benefits. She knew that, yet the lesson had been so ingrained in her that she followed it anyway.

For the first time, she had a reason to choose otherwise. Although she didn't fear the embrace of the Dark God, the others needed her. She had to survive until their safety was guaranteed, even if that meant letting Elrin slip through her fingers yet again. To her surprise, the thought didn't rankle as much as she'd expected. For the first time since her childhood, her hope was stronger than her need for vengeance.

She began to back away, drawing everyone's attention

with her. Sleth tracked her on one side, and Bastian began to circle around to the other, drawing his blade. The guards streamed toward her, Dunn and Orami alike, their weapons in hand. The Dunn guards carried shorter, blunt swords, while the Orami favored lighter weapons with a surprising reach. Standing against both at the same time would require her utmost concentration.

Dezrick, who had been dismissed as unimportant as usual, took advantage of this fact. At some point, he'd managed to draw his sword unnoticed, which impressed Larina under the circumstances. He raised the blade and swung it at his father with little skill. The larger man side-stepped without much effort, but Dezrick twisted, desperation lending him a burst of agility. Somehow, he managed to whack his father in the face with the hilt. The strike had little finesse, but it landed squarely nonetheless. Bone crunched, and the king let out a strangled cry of pain, his hands flying to his broken nose.

The Orami guards whirled on Dezrick, intent on protecting their king, while the Dunn guards hovered in momentary confusion, unsure of what to do.

Larina had little time for planning. She sprinted past the distracted guards, flung her skirts up to protect her arm and face, and hit the window at a full sprint. Leaving Dezrick behind pained her, but Elrin was too power hungry to kill his only heir, or he would have done it already. She would return for them both soon enough.

The shock of impact ran up to her shoulder, exploding in a haze of pain. She flew through the window, calculating with the confidence of experience how long it would take for her to reach the ground. The impact came only a fraction of a second later than anticipated, and she managed to roll into it enough to avoid serious injury. Still, her body throbbed with pain, pushed to its considerable limits. She flung her skirt down to free her head, bits of colored glass raining on the grass of the garden where she'd landed. The sounds of pursuit already reached her ears.

Larina sucked air into her aching lungs and ran for her life.

Chapter Twenty-Three

Blood trickled down Larina's forehead and into her eyes, blurring her vision. The thick fabric of the skirt had protected her face from major damage, and her training had helped her survive the fall, but she still bled from innumerable cuts and scrapes. Everything hurt. Her right arm, which had absorbed the bulk of the impact, twanged at the slightest movement. Although the reinforced bodice of the dress had protected her body, the fabric had shifted, and now one of her sheathed daggers poked her in the ribcage. At least the sheath had done its duty, or the dagger would be stabbing her instead.

Despite her injured state, she'd lost the guards without much trouble. That fact made her more paranoid than ever. She'd doubled back over and over again, but no one followed her. Perhaps Bastian and Sleth had lacked the manpower to protect the king, fight the fire, contain the rest of the insurrectionists, and chase her all over the city. She'd been deemed an acceptable loss.

By the knowing eye of the Black Robed Goddess, she didn't blame them. After she'd lost her immediate pursuers and checked to make certain she hadn't damaged herself too badly, she'd begun to circle back around to the secret passages, intending to return to the castle. But there, her invention failed her. The moment she showed her face inside those walls, the guards would lock her away until the gallows could be readied. With time and resources, she could have concocted a disguise that would allow her to roam the corridors without being recognized, but she had neither.

Despair overwhelmed her. The great and mighty Shadow had proven to be a disappointment after all. Not only had she tried and failed multiple times to kill the king, but she'd managed to get her companions sentenced to death in the process. Elrin would hang his own son and think himself justified in his barbarity.

Without supplies and a decent plan, intervening would only guarantee that she joined them in death. She had to get off the street.

Larina had bought her safe house outright, its cheap price a testament to its owners' desire to leave town as quickly as possible with no questions asked. She'd stashed all of her supplies there along with the drakon, paying a neighbor kid to care for her. Retrieving them still posed a risk, but so did wandering the streets.

Her mind made up, she snatched a tattered blanket from an unattended wash pile, covered her bloodied dress with it, and veered toward the safe house, which sat on the edge of the slums. Everyone she saw kept their heads down in an attempt to avoid trouble, recognition, or both. She did the same. She passed the boarded-up hovel next door to her safe house and circled around back, taking the opportunity to scout before she approached. But she noticed nothing out of the ordinary. On her rare visits, she'd left the curtains pulled tight and never cleaned the windowsills, using the dust that gathered there as a record of any interlopers. From the looks of things, no one had tried to break in.

Reassured, she let herself inside, locking the door tight behind her.

Zemora cocked her head to look at her from her spot next to the thin mattress. Larina's relief at seeing the impish creature took her by storm. Without a word, she crossed the room and put her arms around Zemora's scaly neck. For once, Zemora restrained herself. Instead of nipping at Larina's hair or throwing something at her, the drakon nestled in close. The comforting weight made things seem a little less bleak.

"I'm sorry it took me so long to get here," said Larina.

Zemora tossed her head and gave her the side-eye.

"I know. But I'm here now." Larina sniffed. "And I'm a mess."

It didn't take long to clean and dress her wounds. Then she washed the blood from her face and arms, dressing in clean clothing and plaiting her hair. The familiar motions soothed her jangled nerves, allowing her to clear her mind. Everything inside her begged to rush back and storm the castle, saving her friends from further pain at Elrin's hand, but that would only get them killed. So she distracted herself with these simple tasks until the urge faded and she could think things through.

She allowed herself to recline on the thin straw mattress with Zemora's head pillowed on her belly, resting her damaged body while she considered her options. Unfortunately, every idea she came up with had too many flaws. The map with all the secret passageways on it had remained in Dezrick's room. Although they'd hidden it well, Sleth would find it at some point, making the tunnels too risky to use. The smithy would be watched now, impeding her ability to acquire weaponry or more of Dezrick's smoke-producing concoction. All she had to work with were the basic supplies gathered here. Frustrated tears sprang to Larina's eyes as she realized the truth—she was helpless.

A light rap at the door interrupted her circling thoughts, and she started up from her mattress with a pang of fear. Had Sleth known about this part of her plan too? If so, the lack of pursuit had been a ruse, designed to make her feel all too secure in her escape. It had worked. She would have to fight her way out. Under most circumstances, this wouldn't be a problem, but she had taxed her body to its limits already.

She drew one of her daggers and crouched down, moving in painstaking silence. Her legs still screamed in protest, but she ignored them. Her assailant wouldn't expect her to be so short. She could hamstring them before they realized their mistake. If it went well, they wouldn't even have a chance to cry out.

She flung open the door, striking like a viper at the veins of her assailant's inner thigh. Moving with a surprising swiftness, he brought his sword to bear, blocking her attack. She glanced up at him, half expecting to see Sleth's leering visage. But it wasn't him. She blinked, unable to believe her eyes.

"Nix?! What are you doing here?" she gasped.

His surprise arrival combined with the stress of Dezrick's capture suddenly overwhelmed her. She threw herself into his arms for the first time in their long friendship. He stiffened in momentary shock before he hugged her back, pressing his lips to the top of her head. After a moment of indulgence, she pulled away.

He frowned, taking in her battered appearance and the way she curled in on herself, diminished by pain. Then he closed the door behind her. His familiar grip reassured her as he helped her sit down in the rickety chair.

"Hey, Reagan," he said, pretending surprise. "Funny seeing you here."

She snorted in amusement but couldn't relax just yet. Although she trusted Nix, Elrin had more influence—and more luck—than anyone had a right to possess. If he had turned Nix, she might as well give up and die now.

"Enough with the jokes," she said. "I don't mean to offend, but I'm in a huge mess and your appearance has gotten my hackles up. How did you find me?"

"Blind luck, mostly," he replied. "After you left the keep, I waited until Garret sent me out on a mission, and I took that necklace with me. When I had it appraised, my dealer told me it was a royal piece. Worth a fortune. The kind you can't sell without attracting questions." He fixed her with a pointed look. Larina only shrugged. "Anyway, I decided I should ask you those very same questions, so I abandoned my assignment and followed you here instead. I couldn't use my usual Praetorian contacts to locate you in the city once I'd arrived, because I'm sure Garret is eager to string me up for deserting. So the whole thing took longer than I wanted. To be honest, I was starting to worry that you'd already left."

Zemora sidled closer and shoved her nose into his hand.

"Hey there, you big jerk," he said, petting her.

"So...?" Larina urged.

"I got to Crestwynd last week. I made friends with a few of the guards, but none of them knew you. I figured you were lying low or you'd already left. I knew you hadn't gone back to the keep, because I've got people watching the docks and the southern gates. So I decided to get a job with one of the castle vendors to get inside and look for you myself. I was watching the gates, trying to find the right mark when I saw you fly out a window."

She snorted. "How'd you know it was me?"

"You didn't die," he said, shrugging.

"Fair," she said.

"I tried to follow you, but I didn't want to get taken in for questioning. I figured you'd go to ground in a shady part of town where no one asks uncomfortable questions, and you'd have to ditch the mask and dress before you got there. Once I found the mask, I handed out pennies to the street kids until I found one who had seen you. Apparently, you have a reputation for giving out sweet rolls."

"That's Dezrick."

"Either way, it made an impression. Few people are kind to street kids, but I know what a softie you are. So here I am."

"Here you are," Larina echoed in wonder. The sight of his friendly face eased her worries like nothing else had. "I'm glad."

"Good, because I'm about to yell at you. What in the Great Desert is going on? How did you get that necklace? Why did you jump out of the tower like fire-breathing dire lizards were on your tail?"

"You mean dragons."

"What?" he demanded.

"Fire-breathing dire lizards. Those would be dragons."

"Oh, fine then," he replied irritably. "Dragons. Answer the question, Reagan."

She took a deep breath. "Well, first off, my name isn't Reagan."

The story took a while to tell. As Larina spoke, Nix's eyes grew wider and wider, but he knew her well enough not to call her out for tall tales. He spoke only to clarify some bit of information, asking intelligent questions that reminded her how he'd always been underestimated as a bit of muscle and a pretty face.

When she finished, he let out a long, astonished breath.

"Wow," he said.

"That's all you've got? Wow?"

"Well, I can't believe I've been friendly with a princess all these years. Does that make me royal by association?"

Larina fixed him with a look of pure exasperation.

"Don't make fun, Nix. I can't stand it right now."

"No, I suppose not," he said, the teasing lilt fading from his voice. "But seriously, Reag—I mean, Larina. Why didn't you tell me? You know I would have kept your secret."

She paused, thinking. It was a reasonable question, and

after he'd gone to such lengths to find her, he deserved the truth.

"I didn't want to be a Dracomeer anymore," she said. As she spoke the words, she realized they rang true. "Larina Dracomeer lost everything. I wasn't hiding the truth from you as much as trying to keep from thinking about it myself."

He exhaled, the tension draining from his shoulders.

"Yeah, I guess I can see that," he said.

"I'm glad someone does. The rebels assumed I was going to pick back up where I left off, but that's impossible."

"I can't see you being all hoity-toity. I would have smacked you silly." He paused, pursing his lips. "Does Garret know?"

"Of course not. He would have sold me to Elrin without hesitation. I haven't spoken my real name aloud since before I arrived at the keep. If my old nurse hadn't recognized me, I wouldn't have brought it up at all. It's just an unnecessary complication."

Nix shook his head in admiration—or was it exasperation? She couldn't quite tell.

"Only you would refer to a royal title as an 'unnecessary complication,'" he said. "You're strange."

"Yeah, well, your ears stick out," she shot back.

The familiar ribbing evaporated the last of the tension in the room, and they grinned at each other. Larina's happiness lasted only a moment, until she remembered the rest of the rebels, waiting for their deaths—if they hadn't happened already—while she joked around.

"What now?" Nix asked, sitting down on the straw mattress. "What's the plan?"

"There is no plan. I messed up, and good people will die because of it. I'd like to make it right, but what can I do? It's just me against an entire castle full of soldiers, and they're on the alert."

He rolled his eyes. "Don't be stupid. You're not alone. You've got me."

"Great," she replied. "I can get you killed, too."

"That's enough of that," he snapped. "Your name might have changed, but you're still the Shadow. The girl I grew up with didn't give up, even when Garret told her she was hopeless and would never become a Praetorian. She found a way to make him eat his words, even when that meant sneaking into his bedchamber and drawing a flower on his face while he slept."

"It wasn't a flower," she countered. "It was a smiley face. It took a long time, too. I could only apply a little paint at a time, or he'd wake up."

"If you can do that, you can do this. *We* can do this," he said.

She nodded, swallowing against the lump in her throat. Nix would help her. After all, he had signed his death warrant as certainly as she had by abandoning his post.

They'd probably still die, but at least it wouldn't be alone. The thought brought tears to her eyes again. She brushed them away, trying to cover up her emotions by getting down to business.

"Let's get to work, then. You want something to eat while we plan? I've got mostly dried goods here, but it's better than nothing."

"Sure." A mischievous grin split his face. "You want to bring them to me? I've never been waited on by a princess before."

"Enough," she said. "Tease me later. This is serious."

He nodded, his smile fading. "Sorry. You know how I joke when things get messy. I'm taking this seriously, I promise."

"Thanks. I'm glad you're here."

"What else are brothers for?" he responded. Her eyes filled at the use of the word, and she had to duck her head until she had herself under control again.

"Okay, so here's what we've got to work with," she said, pulling out a piece of parchment and a quill. "It isn't much."

Nix sat up, all joking forgotten, and listened.

Chapter Twenty-Four

As they talked and planned, Larina's spirits climbed from the depths of utter despair to something approaching hope. The rescue attempt would probably still result in their deaths, but Nix's presence gave them a slight chance of success, and she found herself clinging to it. If they could only free Dezrick, the effort would be worthwhile. He could rally the people and try to topple Elrin with politics since he had proven to be impervious to knives. Larina likely wouldn't be around to see it, but at least she could go to the afterlife with some hope instead of nothing but regret.

Nix made a supply run and came back with fresh clothing, consumables for Zemora's saddlebags, and news. She could see it on his face as he closed the door behind him.

"What?" she demanded. "What did you hear?"

"The king has ordered the execution of the traitors tomorrow morning. Everyone in Crestwynd is required to attend or face his wrath. It's all anyone could talk about at the shop." Nix winced. "The people are afraid, Rea—I mean, Larina. Elrin may have gone too far this time."

"He'll do away with his detractors the way he always has if we can't get him off the throne." Larina frowned. "Any word about me?"

He hesitated. "Elrin wants you alive."

"He probably intends to make an example out of me."

"After he squeezes you for every ounce of information he can," Nix agreed in bleak tones. "He'll be after anyone you've ever known."

"Won't Garret love that," said Larina, with a flash of dark humor. "Okay, I think this news changes things. As much as I hate to say this, we should wait until morning. The crowds will give us the opportunity to get close to the castle without being spotted."

"I was thinking the same thing. Will you be able to sleep?"

"I'm not sure, but I'll try."

Zemora had let herself out into the backyard, bedding down against the high fence. Larina insisted on moving the thin mattress to the floor to cushion both of their heads. She'd been through the wringer, but they both needed to be operational. He'd grumbled about it but capitulated when she'd insisted.

They slept side-by-side on the floor with the mattress spread out like a long pillow. To her surprise, Larina drifted off right away, her body weary from all its exertions. A few times during the night, she awoke with her heart pounding from some unremembered nightmare, but otherwise she managed to rest.

Early the next morning, as the sun began to creep over the rooftops, Nix sauntered up to the castle with a seemingly unconscious Larina draped over one shoulder. She hung limply, her hands dangling, and tangled hair waving in the breeze. Overnight, her scrapes and bruises had intensified, so she'd needed no subterfuge to look beaten and defeated, especially in comparison to Nix's sizable brawn.

As they drew up to the gates, the guards standing behind the drawn portcullis shouted in warning. Through slitted eyes, Larina made a quick headcount. Fourteen that she could see, and possibly a few overhead with crossbows. She couldn't look without betraying her consciousness, and the back of her neck itched at being so exposed.

"Halt, by order of the king!" said one of the guards. "You're too early for the hangings. Come back later, or you'll regret it."

Nix stopped, as blasé as you please, and saluted them with insouciance.

"I mean, I *could*," he said, "but I think that king of yours will want my present."

"Drunk bastard," muttered the guard. "Haul off, or we'll put an arrow in your foot and you'll have to hop your way home."

"Okay, okay. So I should take the Dracomeer heir with me? I thought the king wanted her, but I guess I was wrong about that."

Larina's true name brought about instant change. The guards stiffened, craning their necks to get a better look at her. She focused on remaining as limp as possible, even though Nix's shoulder dug painfully into her battered abdomen.

"That git could be anyone. How do you know it's her?" asked the guard.

In lieu of an answer, Nix held up the Dracomeer gem. The faceted stone caught the light, and the gold shimmered as the pendant spun around. For a moment, no one spoke. The guards stared at the priceless bauble with mouths hanging open. Then the man in charge, a whippet thin guard with an imposing mustache, gestured for them to open the gates.

"Come in," he said. "Bounty hunter?"

"How'd you guess?" asked Nix. "I'm hoping this one will be worth my while."

"I'm sure it will. If you'll wait in here, I'll find out if the king will see you," responded the guard, gesturing to an anteroom.

The door clicked shut behind them, cutting them off from view. Nix set Larina down in a chair, where she remained slumped over until he finished a quick review of the room and gave the all clear.

"Okay," he whispered. "So far, so good. I was hoping they'd take us right up to him, though."

"As paranoid as Elrin is?" she responded quietly. "Never."

She glanced around the well-appointed chamber. It had been difficult to keep track of their location while she'd been swaying over his shoulder with her eyes shut, but she recognized this room, a receiving area reserved for unexpected guests that allowed them to remain under guard while reinforcements were called for. They would have to get out before they arrived.

The room sat at the northern end of the castle, with easy access to the stairs. Larina traced out a map with her finger, outlining the route to the dungeons. Nix nodded, committing it to memory, and then they got into position.

He opened the door, shielding her from view. The guard stationed outside turned his head to look questioningly at the Praetorian. More would be here at any moment; time was of the essence.

"I think she's stopped breathing," said Nix, his face

stricken. He'd always been an excellent actor. "Can you help me?"

The guard hesitated. "I can't leave my post. Bastian will have my job *and* my head."

Nix stepped to the side, revealing Larina's limp form, slumped once again in an overstuffed chair. He poked her, hard. Larina allowed her head to loll to one side, sliding further down toward the floor. Still, the guard hesitated.

"The king will be furious if she dies before he has a chance to question her. It's not my head if she croaks. Are you trained in healercraft?" Nix pushed.

"Only a little. What if I make it worse?"

"Then we don't mention it at all. We just say she fell over dead and hope for the best. But if we can save her, it would be better for the both of us." Nix clapped the man on the shoulder, looking into his eyes. "It's worth a try."

The guard nodded, entering the room and closing the door behind him. He hurried over to Larina, leaning down over her. The moment the tips of his fingers touched her face, she burst into action, driving the palm of her hand into his nose. He crumpled to the ground, dead. She paused a moment in silent regret, but it couldn't be helped. An unconscious guard could wake up and draw attention to their escape. This had been the only way, but she didn't have to like it.

Nix put on the guard's uniform as Larina pulled a dress and apron out of her pack, throwing them over her clothes.

She would have preferred to disguise herself as another guard, but the extra uniforms still sat in the smithy, too dangerous to retrieve. A servant's disguise would have to do. Moments before they left the waiting room, she lit the overstuffed chair on fire with a spark from her firestarter. The rich fabric went up rapidly. When the guards arrived, they'd find at least one charred body, and they'd hesitate to admit to the king that they'd possibly burned the Dracomeer heir to death. Elrin's fury would be deadly. Their hesitation would buy the Praetorians valuable time.

Nix preceded her down the stairs, making a point of loudly saluting anyone he saw and giving her advance warning to hide. Larina took a tray of sweetmeats from a salon she ducked into and held it before her to complete her disguise. The ruse worked, and they didn't need to kill anyone as they descended into the depths of the castle.

In the dungeons, a pair of guards stood at alert attention, as if Elrin himself might come round the corner at any moment, and they had to make a good impression or risk his wrath. But instead of an angry king, they found themselves face-to-face with two trained killers. Larina and Nix closed in quickly. She knew without needing to be told where his weak points were, and he hers, and they covered each other with the ease of long familiarity. The guards drew their swords, but the long blades in such a small space worked to their detriment as much as in their favor. Larina caught one blade with the hilt of her knife, dodged under

Nix's sweeping arm, circled in close, and downed her attacker with a swift strike to the throat. The blow crushed his windpipe, but she had no time to mourn his death, although she would pay her obeisance with her braid later.

Nix had already dispatched his guard with similar speed. When she turned to the cells, Larina saw quite a few familiar faces, including the woman from the first night she'd crashed the meeting and the older lady who had played the part of the servant at the banquet. But she didn't see Dezrick. Or Kyra. Nor Alaris or Miriam.

Nix began to work on opening the heavy gates as Larina pelted the prisoners with questions.

"Where are the others? When did they leave, and how many took them?" she demanded.

But of course, these people weren't Praetorians. They shook and cried, rattled by their ordeal and the wave of relief that had overwhelmed them at her appearance. Only the older woman—Clara—kept her composure.

"The prince never came to the cells, so we don't know about him," Clara replied. "But they came for Kyra, Alaris, and Miriam just a little while ago. Two guards and a little man who looked like a walking skeleton."

Larina's stomach clenched. Were they too late? The guards would likely take the prisoners out through the kitchen door, and from there out to the gallows. Her eyes lit on the table, where all of the confiscated supplies waited for someone official to dispose of them. The pile held swords and aprons, serving trays and fancy masks. In the middle sat a small heap of Dezrick's smoke bombs. Larina snatched them up, sifting through the pile for any other goodies.

"What are those?" asked Nix, looking on with curiosity.

"They produce smoke and fire. Dezrick also made something called a catalyst that you could rub on the outside before you hide it. The catalyst eats away at the outside, and as soon as it creates a big enough hole, the smoke comes out." She gestured vaguely. "He explained it much better than I did, but that's the basic idea."

"Where's the catalyst then?"

"I don't see any. Dezrick and Kyra carried extra around with them last night just in case, but it doesn't seem to have been saved. The guards probably didn't know what it was."

"So the bombs are unusable?"

"No, we'll have to crack them open manually and back away fast. You only have a few seconds before fire starts shooting out at you. But they make for good cover. Better than just a firestarter, anyway."

He considered them, stroking his chin. "Might work for a diversion. Stay on plan?"

"I think so." She turned to the newly freed insurrectionists, handing over a painstakingly drawn map. "Follow us. We'll drop you off at a tunnel that will get you out of here. Don't go home; they'll just pick you up again. Get to the safe house on the map if you can, and if not, hide out for the night and try again tomorrow."

Clara nodded. "I'll get them out of here."

That would have to be good enough. Larina led the group to one of the tunnels that had been marked on the map. She wasn't surprised to find another pair of guards standing near the entrance, but the two Praetorians took them out without fuss. After the prisoners had gone down the tunnel, they placed the bodies inside and closed the door. With luck, anyone who came searching wouldn't think to look there.

From there, they circled around to the kitchen door that led out to the gallows. Sliding open the viewing panel, Nix reported a small contingent of guards standing at the ready while Alaris, Kyra, and Miriam strung up the ropes themselves. It was cruel work indeed to make them manufacture their own deaths. Larina squeezed her hands, her nails cutting into her palms as she watched.

Nix arched a brow at her. "Okay, Shadow? Got a plan here? There are too many of them to take on our own."

"One of us lights fires while the other one helps the prisoners escape." She bit her lip. "But we're missing Dezrick. His father must be keeping him elsewhere. His suite, maybe?"

"Or the king's." Nix nodded. "I'm assuming you'll want to find him, too?"

"We need him. Besides, he would come for me if the situation was reversed."

"Good man."

"Yeah, he is," she replied.

He watched her for a long moment, as if he could see her muddled feelings for Dezrick written on her face. "Okay, then. You'll have to fetch him because I don't know this place like you do. Think you can handle that?"

She snorted. "Think you can handle the courtyard if I draw a few off?"

"Yeah. That old lady doesn't look too good though. I'm not sure how quickly she'll be able to escape."

Worried, Larina looked out toward the gallows. Bruises mottled Miriam's face, and the hard labor had taxed her beyond her endurance. She staggered under the weight of the heavy rope she carried, bumping into the executioner in his black robes. He slapped her in irritation, and she fell to the ground, too weary to stand again. Alaris tried to help her, but the guards restrained him as Kyra begged him to remain calm.

"Fetch Zemora," suggested Larina. "She'll help you fend the guards off."

Nix had ridden the drakon to the stables before turning Larina in, since they'd wanted to have a mount nearby in case they needed to make a quick escape. He agreed with the plan, and the two of them made their way through the hushed corridors toward the stables. They passed a few members of the castle staff, all moving with their heads down as they prepared for the execution of one of their own. No one questioned them.

When they opened the stall door, Zemora took one look at Larina and picked up a nugget of poop from the ground in her teeth, flinging it at her. She'd never liked waiting, and she'd had to do it a lot lately.

"I know," said Larina. "I'm sorry."

The drakon picked up another piece and tossed her head in warning. But she didn't throw it. Not yet.

"That's enough of that. Nix is going to ride you now," Larina continued in stern tones.

Zemora pranced over and dropped the turd on his shoe.

"This is going well," he said, kicking it off.

"I'll give you carrots. Lots of them." The bribe got no reaction, and Larina began to despair. She couldn't think of any other ideas, except... "You'll get to fight. There are guards out there just waiting for you to bite them."

Now Zemora looked at her, head cocked. Listening.

"You won't be in trouble. Think of all those tasty guards..." Larina said, feeling a bit foolish.

But it worked. The drakon put her head against Larina's for just a moment, a sure sign that peace had been restored between them again. She allowed Nix to stroke her long neck without trying to bite him, and she even allowed him to put on her saddle without shying away. Finally, he mounted up.

"I'll circle back around to the kitchen door and light the first fire there. That should draw most of them out of the way," she said.

"Okay. I'll get your friends to safety. If you don't return to the safe house by dark, I'm coming back for you."

She almost told him not to bother, but that would be useless. If the tables had been turned, she would have gone back for him no matter what he said.

"Okay. And Nix? Thanks."

He nodded in acknowledgement and then shooed her away. She made her way back to the kitchen without incident, opened the viewing panel to ensure that the smoke would attract attention in the courtyard, and cracked open one of the bombs. A small pile of kitchen refuse on a wooden table near the door served as the perfect kindling. The whole thing caught fire, smoke pouring out to coat the kitchen in a dusty haze.

Larina turned to leave and ran straight into Viola.

The servant girl was disheveled, and she kept glancing over her shoulders with obvious nervousness. Usually, she took some care with her glossy curls, pulling them back with a band, and she'd always kept her uniform neat, even if she'd chosen one that fit a little too small. Now her hair hung loosely in lank strands around her face, and her rumpled uniform had smudges at the wrists and across the bodice. She met Larina's eyes with a look of horrified recognition, opening her mouth to scream.

Before she could make a noise, Larina grabbed her and spun her around, clapping a hand over her mouth. Viola struggled, but she lacked the strength or training to accomplish much. After a moment, she gave up, her body sagging in surrender.

"I won't hurt you," Larina whispered in her ear. "But we have to move into the next room. This room is on fire, and if we stay here, we'll be hurt. I can march you around like this, or you can walk prettily for me without crying out. Can you do that?"

Wide-eyed, the girl nodded. Larina let her go with slow caution, but it appeared that Viola would keep her word. She shrank before the growing fire until Larina tugged on her arm.

"This way," she said.

Viola followed her into the storage pantry and Larina closed the door against the growing smoke. As soon as she did, the servant girl went to her knees, clinging to the hem of her tunic.

"Please don't hurt me," she begged. "I won't tell anyone you were here. Promise."

"What kind of nonsense tales has Elrin been telling the staff?" Larina shook her head before Viola could answer. "Never mind. I'm not sure I want to know. I won't hurt you. I'm here to save Dezrick."

"I don't believe you. You're a criminal."

"If I didn't care, I'd be long gone. You know how his father treats him. I won't leave him to that."

Viola stood there for a moment, frozen in indecision. Shouts from the courtyard signaled the discovery of the fire. They had to move, and soon. But Larina knew how much she asked of the servant girl, and she waited those excruciating seconds while Viola thought it through. Finally, her lips firmed with resolution, and she nodded.

"Okay. What do you need me to do?" she asked.

"I need to know where Dezrick is, and how many guards are with him."

Larina sent Viola off to search, hoping she hadn't misjudged. If so, she'd be at the end of a noose soon enough. She hid out in the bedroom she'd used right after arriving at the castle, pacing with agitation. No one had used it since she'd left, and it was safer than attempting to return to her old room next to Dezrick's. No one would think to look for her here.

A soft rap on the door announced the servant's reappearance, and Larina let her inside. The girl's pale cheeks were blotched with red and her eyes flashed with fury.

"You were right," she said. "I took my duster and went into the king's suite to clean, and they were all there.

Dezrick, the king, Bastian, and Yasmeen. Dezrick has bruises and blood all over him."

"But he's alive? Is he tied up?"

"He looked at me when I entered. Shook his head like he was trying to warn me away. But I'm not sure if he was tied down or not. Bastian told me to leave before I could really look around. He smacked me right across the face." Her eyes blazed with anger.

"Okay, and how many guards are between here and there? You counted like I asked, right?"

Viola nodded, sketching out the layout for her. Dezrick's condition and Bastian's poor treatment had dissolved any lingering misgivings on her part, and she was much more thorough than Larina had hoped for. She could deal with the guards, but Sleth's absence unnerved her. It would be a mistake to forget him.

"You'll save the prince, won't you?" begged Viola. "Dezrick is a good man. The best. When I first came here, one of the guardsmen took a liking to me, and he'd try and touch me when no one was watching, even though I told him to stop. I was too young to know what went on between men and women then, and definitely too young to be treated like that. Dezrick wasn't much older than I was, but when he caught that guard giving me a hard time, he put a stop to it. Most royals wouldn't even notice, and even if they did, they wouldn't bother taking care of a little serving girl."

For the first time, Larina saw the girl in a new light. She'd dismissed Viola as a boy-crazy chit with a crush on the most powerful young man in her acquaintance, but that had clearly been incorrect. She'd been attracted by Dezrick's kindness just as much as Larina had.

"I will save him," she promised. "But I need one more thing from you."

"Just tell me what to do."

"I need you to set these off for me," Larina said, holding up the smoke bombs.

Chapter Twenty-Five

"One hundred ninety-nine. Two hundred."

Larina finished counting off the seconds, allowing Viola to get a head start. Now she needed to move. With a regretful look at the beautiful tapestry on the wall, she opened a smoke bomb on top of the guest room bed, leaving only one unused bomb remaining in her possession. Flames spewed out, catching the bedspread. Within moments, the small room would be engulfed. She hurried toward the king's suite, taking one of the secret passageways that Dezrick had uncovered.

Distant shouts suggested that Viola had been successful in lighting at least one more fire and hopefully more. The passage was cloying and close with heat, but perhaps that was Larina's imagination at work, conjuring remembered flames from the past. Still, she took the precaution of covering her mouth with her tunic to protect her breathing as she neared the suite, drawing her knife.

She made quick work of the guards, hiding the knife from view with the borrowed tray until she got close enough to strike. Once she was in range, she brought out the weapon in a wide and sweeping arc, spinning in a dance of death as she made her way down the row. The bright blade flickered in the light before blood coated its length. The four of them made little noise other than chirps of surprise before they died. None of them even came close to touching her.

She slipped into the room like a shadow, noting with satisfaction that Viola had described it well. Dezrick slumped in a chair before his father, unconscious, one eye crusted shut with blood. At least he hadn't been bound; his hands hung limp at his sides. Elrin and Yasmeen conversed near the sideboard while Bastian watched the prisoner. Sleth was nowhere in sight, and that worried her. She would have to remain alert lest he stab her in the back.

The captain of the guard spotted her first, as she approached with her knife drawn. He grinned in anticipation as he drew his own blade. The movement attracted Elrin's attention, and he glared at Larina, his face like thunder.

"Stop!" he commanded, and Bastian froze in place. Like an obedient dog, he waited for instructions from his master, but his eyes flashed with impatience. "You have some gall, Dracomeer. Do you plan to hew down the entire castle on your own?"

"No. I came for the prince. If I can kill you, I will, but his safety is more important to me than you'll ever be. My family will understand that."

A weight had lifted off her shoulders, one that she hadn't even noticed until it was gone. She almost laughed as relief suffused her limbs, energizing her anew. She loved Dezrick. She had family in Miriam and Nix, and the beginnings of a strong friendship with Kyra and Alaris. For the first time since she'd been a girl, she had people. A community. A place to belong.

Elrin laughed at her, a hollow sound of pretend amusement.

"You waste your talents, little princess," said the king. "My son is useless unless you're in desperate need of a librarian. Your loyalty to him is quite adorable, but not worth your death."

"Loyalty? I'm surprised you know the meaning of the word," she said.

She sniffed in distain, buying time. The scent of burning things stung her nostrils. Out the open window behind the king, burning motes from the enflamed kitchen wound their way up into the sky. As she watched, bright sparks settled on the heavy velvet curtains, burning small black holes in the fabric. The prince moaned as consciousness flooded back in. She inched closer. Bastian twisted, tracking her every movement, his fingers caressing the hilt of his blade with eager anticipation.

"Hold your temper, Bastian," Elrin ordered. "Or you will suffer my wrath."

Bastian blanched, pulling his hand free of the weapon like it had caught fire too. But he did not back away, and Elrin didn't press the matter. He had returned his attention to Larina.

"I know more than you realize, Shadow," said the king. "I have watched you work for some time now. At first, I doubted your skill, but I was wrong. Your reputation doesn't do you justice."

The compliment took her aback when almost nothing else would have shaken her. She had imagined this moment for so long. Out of everything she had expected from him, flattery hadn't been on the list.

"You're stalling," she accused. "It won't work."

She could think of no other explanation for his compliments. A queasy sensation settled in her belly. Elrin's admiration troubled her.

"Ah, but turning a Dracomeer to my cause will quell those pesky attempts at rebellion, and you are just as brutal as I am when it comes down to it," he countered. "I've seen your work. I will make you a trade. You will take an oath of loyalty to me, and in return, I will spare Dezrick's head from the noose."

His fingers twined in the prince's long braids and lifted.

Dezrick had regained some semblance of woozy alertness. He blinked at her, his lips moving in a vain attempt to form words. The emptiness in his eyes tugged at her heart.

"Well?" demanded the king.

"You must be joking," she said.

"I am quite serious. The prince of Dunheim seems to think I owe them a debt for services rendered the night I ascended to the throne. I will not be ordered about in my own castle. With your skills, I'm certain we could put them back in their place. It's quite a good idea, don't you think? My dearest Yasmeen put it to me in the event that we managed to catch you, and I admit it has its advantages."

He ran a hand over Yasmeen's hair with a possessive sort of affection. She remained immobile as he did so, her expression unreadable. Bastian's expression grew darker with every passing minute, and that more than anything convinced Larina that the offer rang true. In a room full of liars, Bastian was the only forthright one among them. He made no secret of his desire to be rid of her. She could make use of that.

"Would I have Bastian's job?" she asked, feigning interest. "I don't take orders well."

"You can compete for it," the king offered magnanimously.

Bastian choked. He took a step forward, wanting to strike her down then and there, but a flick of the king's eyes in his direction froze him in place once more before he could take another step.

Once he was satisfied that his captain didn't intend to cut her down, the king continued, "Of course, if you displease me, the deal is off. If you accept, Dezrick lives on the strength of your performance."

Behind the king, the tiniest of flames began to lick at the heavy curtain. Larina glanced down at Dezrick, who sagged in his seat, still unable to support the weight of his own head. Confusion and guilt roiled around in her belly. As much as she wanted to deny it, Elrin had a point. Over the last few years, she'd left a trail of bodies behind her. The blood she'd spilled would fill a lake. Although she wanted to believe they were different, could she honestly say so? What would her mother say if she saw the killer Larina had become?

She didn't want to believe she belonged in the same category as Elrin, but maybe that was wishful thinking.

Dezrick groaned again, drawing her attention. He seemed to be trying to force words out of lips too swollen and numb to form them. She couldn't make anything out, but it didn't matter. Because the sight of him reminded her that she had come here willing to sacrifice her life to make things right. That alone separated her from Elrin.

She met his eyes, full of gleaming avarice, and recoiled.

"Come now," he said. "Submit to me, and I will be merciful."

Now his offer made sense. For Elrin, it wasn't enough just to kill her. He needed to dominate, to break her spirit. He needed to know that he had truly bested her before he was done. If she swore an oath to him, he would control her completely, or he would have her killed.

"That is a very generous offer," she said.

"I agree."

"But I'd rather die." She met his eyes, delivering the line with icy disdain. Before he could reply, she shook her gloved hand, bringing the final smoke bomb down from its hiding spot in her wrist. "I'm taking the prince, and we're leaving. Make one move toward me, and I'll break this open in my hands. I understand that the gout of fire it shoots out is quite hot."

An angry smile twisted Elrin's lips. "You wouldn't. You'd burn us all. Yourself and your precious prince included."

"Dezrick and I were both prepared to die if it meant freeing Oramis from the likes of you. That hasn't changed."

"Yeh..." murmured Dezrick, trying in vain to lift his hand.

"You are insane," the king began. A whuff of air interrupted his soliloquy as fire spread along the curtain. He turned, stiffening as he saw the blaze, and satisfaction ran shivers down Larina's spine as she watched him contemplate his end. But then, to her surprise and dismay, he smiled.

"You have done a good job of repaying me for the night of flames all those years ago, young Dracomeer," he said. "But in the process, you have made your escape rather difficult."

"It doesn't look like you'll be getting out either," she countered. "I can't say I'm sad."

"Ah, but there is one passageway that wasn't marked on your map. One that *I* built." Elrin took Yasmeen by the elbow and began leading her toward his bedchamber. "That leaves you in a sticky situation, doesn't it? You can't carry my son and fight off all three of us. You'll have to make your way through the burning castle, as you did all those years ago. I wonder if you'll make it out alive this time. Burns do hurt, don't they? I imagine you're an expert."

Larina shuddered in remembered pain. Her hands spasmed on the smoke bomb, but she couldn't make herself detonate it. The shiny skin of her hand and shoulder screamed in remembered pain. She lowered the bomb, ignoring the king's amused smile.

"We'll make it," she said. "And then we'll come for you. I promise you that."

"I can't wait," said the king, backing through the door.

Yasmeen shook herself free of Elrin's grasp, running toward Larina. "Wait!" she exclaimed. "Take me with you!"

Elrin tried to grab onto the sorceress, but she was too fast. She twisted from his grip, and he didn't dare come closer to Larina.

"Traitor!" he exclaimed. "Get back here!"

Yasmeen drew herself up with pride. "You will never touch me again," she said.

Instead of answering, he snarled in anger.

"Kill them all," he said to Bastian.

"Even your heir, sire?" asked the captain, shocked.

"I can always make another," said Elrin.

Bastian's face split into a slow, cruel grin as his king stalked into the bedchamber, the guards closing in to cover his retreat. Larina twitched as he disappeared. She knew she had made the right decision, but old habits died hard. Only Dezrick's presence and the desperate grip of the sorceress kept her from following him. If she didn't protect them, Bastian would gut them like fish.

Not on her watch.

She stepped forward, placing herself between the approaching captain and her vulnerable friends as Bastian stalked toward them. His eyes flickered from Dezrick's slumped body to Yasmeen's silks. Larina needed to catch his attention and keep it.

"Do you really think you can beat me?" she asked. "Perhaps your guards would like to take bets. The smart ones will put their money on me."

"They wouldn't dare," he grated.

"Oh, but I think they would. After all, they know I beat you before. Besides, I was holding back."

The taunts worked. Bastian charged, all thought and calculation vanishing in the face of his overwhelming fury. He lifted the heavy sword overhead, bringing it down in a devastating sweep.

But Larina wasn't there. She'd circled around him, cutting him with one of her knives. Blood welled along his forearm as she backed away, drawing him across the room. He followed mindlessly, taking their fight away from Dezrick and Yasmeen. Larina only hoped that the sorceress took advantage of the opportunity and led him to safety.

Bastian charged again, and once again, Larina sidestepped. But this time, he'd anticipated her, releasing the sword to punch her in the belly. His thick fist drove the air from her lungs in a pained gush. It felt like she was suffocating.

He pressed his advantage, slamming another fist into the side of her face. Her field of vision exploded in color and pain. She backed away, but the larger man just kept coming, pummeling her with brutal efficiency.

The agony was nearly overwhelming, but Larina had endured worse. Ever since the night her family died, her life had been pain. The pain of losing them. The pain of her burned skin and the sickly sweet scent it emitted when Captain Flynn changed the bandages. The pain of training at the keep. The pain of a thousand missions, with all the injuries that came with them.

So she endured. The longer he persisted, the more convinced Bastian became in his triumph. His strikes slowed so he could sneer into her face. He grabbed her by the hair, pulling her up onto her tiptoes, twisting her head to look at him. Her pained yelp made a satisfied smile creep over his face.

"See, little girl?" he said. "I was holding back too. But now they all know that I am the better—"

A cough cut him off midsentence. He rubbed his hand across his mouth and stared at it in confusion. Red streaked his fingers. Blood began to pour from his lips. He looked down, his eyes widening as he saw the dagger's hilt protruding from his stomach.

"That's...not fair," he protested.

She pushed the blade in further, turning his body to use it as a shield. Yasmeen hadn't moved. She stood with her mouth open in shock, pinned in place. So Larina walked Bastian over to them. He stumbled, trying weakly to resist, but a little tug on the weapon embedded in his guts convinced him to comply.

"Here," she said, pinning the guards with her stare. "Take your captain and get him medical care. I'm going to do the same for the prince. We do not need to cross blades today."

For a moment, no one moved. Then one of the guards stepped forward, setting his sword down on the ground.

"I'll take him," he said.

Larina handed over the injured man, alert for any sign of betrayal. But she'd whittled down their numbers enough over the past few days, leaving the guards reluctant to challenge her unless under direct orders. The man took Bastian and withdrew in the direction the king had disappeared, leaving behind a contingent of men to stand guard at the doorway, keeping her from pursuit. Larina didn't mind. She'd pierced Bastian's bowel. No amount of healing would save his life. It would only prolong his death.

She turned back to Yasmeen and Dezrick. The prince's head lolled as he tried to look at her. But his pupils responded to the light. He would recover, but it would take time. Time they didn't have. She began to heft him onto her shoulders, ignoring the protests of her overtaxed body.

"Take me with you. If you have ever been my friend, I beg you," Yasmeen continued. "You know the price I have paid to get here."

Her wounded gaze tugged at Larina's heartstrings, stirring up a wave of pity. She couldn't turn down her friend.

"Help me with the prince," she said. "We can't leave him here."

Yasmeen nodded. Larina tucked the smoke bomb into her belt and leaned over, sliding her hands under Dezrick's hips. All she needed was a boost to get him up onto her shoulders, and they could go. Perhaps they could make it to one of the other passageways. Perhaps it would be unguarded due to the fire. Perhaps they would make it free after all.

"Lift him up onto my shoulders," she ordered, looking up at the sorceress.

Yasmeen nodded, leaning down toward her. She lifted her hands. But instead of grabbing onto the prince, she held them up in front of her, blowing a sparkling powder right into Larina's eyes.

Larina shrieked in pain. Bright spots of color danced before her eyes. She'd been a fool. Tears streamed down her face and she staggered backwards in blind desperation, trying to evade the attack she knew had to be coming. She couldn't see, couldn't hear anything except the crackling of the flames, which sounded louder than they had just a moment before. Would she see the fire before it burned her? Or would she blunder into it sightlessly?

"Sleth!" shouted Yasmeen. "Your Shadow is in here, as promised. I will escort the king to safety."

Larina heard the click of the door to her father's old bedchamber. She rubbed at her eyes with her sleeve, but to no avail. Water might help. A pitcher usually sat on the stand in the corner. She fumbled in that direction.

"Left..." Dezrick said. The word still came out garbled, though much more understandable than before. But she didn't know what he meant. Yasmeen had left? She should go left? There was an enemy to the left? She needed more.

"What?" she demanded.

"Water. Left."

She turned in the direction he'd indicated and nearly knocked the pitcher over. Cold wetness slopped over her feet. She snatched at the handle and poured the entire thing into her face, forcing her eyes open. The pain stabbed into her skull, but she endured it. Her life—and Dezrick's—depended on it.

The water washed away the last of Yasmeen's stinging concoction. Her vision cleared, revealing a room swirling with smoke. Dezrick stood just a few feet away, clutching the back of the chair as he tried to keep his balance on legs still weak from whatever potion they'd dosed him with. His mouth twisted as he looked over her shoulder, calling out a garbled word of warning.

She whirled around to see Sleth with four guards at his shoulders.

"There you are," she said. "You almost missed the party. Did Elrin forget to invite you?"

"He left me to clean up your mess," Sleth replied. "I'll give him his castle on a platter, and you'll be the cherry on top." He flicked his hands toward her. "Take her alive."

The guards moved forward as one. Larina drew her knives, circling around to put their backs to the fire. She had to keep them on the defensive. They had greater numbers and longer reach, and as good as she was, she ached from a million different injuries. None of them would cause lasting damage, but they made her just a little slower. Just a little weaker. She would tire quickly, and then they would kill her.

She dispatched the first one quickly, drawing him in with a feint and then slashing his throat. The second came at her just a bit too fast, and she used his own momentum against him, driving him into his companions to her right. She pressed her attack then, forcing one guard back into the flaming curtains, lighting the leg of his uniform on fire. He backed off, rolling about on the floor in an attempt to try and put it out.

Her eyes still burned, and bright spots danced around her field of vision, but she could see. Her breath came heavy though, and a stitch in her side suggested she was near the end of her endurance already. Sleth had planned it this way. At her best she could beat him, and they both knew it. He would use the guards to bleed her and then finish the kill himself. Probably take all the credit for it, too.

The remaining guards went down all too quickly as she tried to figure out how to beat him. She knew his skills and fighting style. He would come at her with short blades, probably poisoned. She couldn't risk so much as a scratch.

The last guard fell. She stood panting over his prone body, waiting for Sleth to make his move. He stepped forward, drawing his weapon, his eyes alight with that familiar malicious glee. He carried *her* sword. The one Kyra had made for her, the dragons that gave her family their name twining up the hilt. *He had no right to her sword.*

Righteous fury filled her, lending energy to her tired limbs. She let out a howl of anger as she charged. His expression changed from self-satisfaction to complete shock as she did so, and he barely managed to bring the sword up in time to parry her first strike. She pressed the advantage as he tried to back away and gain the distance between them that would spell her doom. But she would not allow it. She nicked him on the arm. On the cheek. Her breath came in desperate gasps as she pushed on, the rush of adrenaline fading. She couldn't keep up this pace for long. She had to break through his defense.

As she swung her next blow, she knew the timing was off. Fatigue had set in hard and she had moved just a little too slowly to match his sword with her blade, drive it down, and swing the other knife at his exposed torso. The flat of the sword hit her, sending her knife tumbling down to clatter on the floor. She swung her second blade around to bear, her fingers clumsy with weariness, but Sleth smacked that one away too. Grinning, he kicked them away into the corners, far out of her reach.

She backed away, scanning for another weapon. Sleth stalked her around the room, feeding off of her desperation. She was so tired. Her arms and legs dragged, heavy like lead.

She tripped over the burning chair, almost losing her feet. Sleth giggled, delight lighting his gaunt features.

"I have waited so long for this," he hissed. "You should not have threatened me, Shadow. We could have coexisted without conflict, but you dared to pass judgment on me. I have waited years for the opportunity to put you in your place. I have been patient." A sadistic smile lit up his face. "And as we learned in the guild, patience is always rewarded."

Whack! A book slammed against the side of his head, taking them both by complete surprise. Dezrick toppled to the floor behind him, exhausted by the effort it took to deliver the blow. Sleth staggered, clapping a hand to his head. The point of his sword dropped toward the ground. This would be her only chance.

Larina lunged forward and drove her dagger into Sleth's belly, all the way to the hilt.

Chapter Twenty-Six

Sleth slumped to the floor, the blade of her dagger emerging from his guts. Larina followed him, her tired legs giving out beneath her. She would have to get up, of course, and try to find a way out through the fire, but she would do it in just a moment.

Dezrick crawled up next to her. Her eyes flew open in worry, but then he patted her shoulder.

"S'okay," he said. "We can rest now."

"Rest?" she asked. "The castle's on fire!"

The only response was a bleary mumble. He wouldn't have even suggested it if not for the herbs coursing through his veins. Appleroot and verwen, she wondered? A proper tincture could have caused this lingering weakness, but they would have had to dose him with a ton of it...

The crackle of the fire roused her. She had pushed her

body to its limits, and unconsciousness threatened to pull her under once again. Although most of the smoke still spilled out the open window, the fire had spread and would soon cut off their path to the door if they didn't leave soon. Larina pushed herself up to standing, every part of her body protesting as she did so.

"Come on," she said. "We need to go."

Dezrick grunted. She shook his shoulder and shouted in his ear.

"Your people need you, princeling! Get! Up!"

His eyes flew open. "Scales and tongues," he swore weakly. "You don't have to yell."

He made his shaky way up to hands and knees, but his limbs wouldn't support his weight. Together, they managed to maneuver him up against the wall, and from there, she slung him over her shoulders. He wasn't a heavy man, but still, she staggered under his weight. If she could just get down to the stables, they could steal a mount and make their escape.

The door handle turned just as she reached for it. Larina dropped into a ready crouch, ignoring the blood that spattered from her wounds to the floor and the weariness that weighted her limbs. Then Nix rushed in, sword drawn. Kyra followed just a few steps behind, a thick lump on her forehead and a stout, blood-caked cudgel in one hand.

"You okay?" Nix demanded.

Larina leaned back against the wall, wilting with relief. Alaris pushed his way into the room, taking Dezrick's weight off her shoulders. She thanked him with a weary smile as Dezrick protested in speech that was now only slightly slurred.

"I'm so glad to see you," she said. "But how in the blazes did you find me?"

He pointed out into the hallway where Miriam waited on Zemora's back. The drakon cleaned a smear of blood off one clawed foot with her long, pointed tongue. Once she realized she had an audience, she tossed her head, showing off.

"She knew exactly where to go," he said. "Keen nose, that one."

"Zemora," said Larina. "You're a jerk, and I love you."

The drakon whinnied as if it understood her. Larina staggered forward, put her arms around the animal's neck, and hugged her close. It was that or fall over.

Chapter Twenty-Seven

Z emora led them from the burning castle, pausing to run down three guards that had the gall to get in her way. Otherwise, no one tried to detain them. In all the smoke and confusion, the guards were more concerned with survival than fighting. That was probably for the best. The only thing Larina had the energy to do at this point was fall on them.

Once they'd gotten free of the castle, they took refuge in Larina's safe house, and a few of their co-conspirators trickled in through the night. The guards might organize a house-to-house search, but that would take time, and the city gates would be under heavy surveillance. The large group crowded the small space, even with Zemora settled out back. But at this point, they welcomed any safe refuge, no matter how uncomfortable. They all fell asleep without much conversation. It could wait until the morning.

Just after sunrise, Larina went out to the back pump to wash the film from her teeth and the blood and soot from her body. She found Dezrick already standing there, his braids glistening with moisture. He drew up short as she approached, his stance awkward and tentative.

"How's the water?" she whispered, trying not to wake the others.

"Cold," he responded. "But refreshing."

"Are you feeling better now? No lingering effects from whatever Yasmeen dosed you with?" Dezrick shook his head, but Larina pressed on just in case. "No double vision? Fatigue? Difficulties remembering things?"

"I'm fine," he insisted. "If anything, I remember too much."

"I'm sorry it took me so long to get to you."

"I knew you'd come."

But he refused to meet her eyes as he shifted from foot to foot, a restless gesture that appeared to be more than discomfort from his damaged leg and the tight quarters. Worry tightened Larina's throat. If he wasn't hurt, what was wrong?

"Dezrick..." she said, not knowing what to ask.

"I suppose you'll be leaving then?" he asked, staring at his shoes and blinking hard.

"Leaving? Why?"

"My father won't stop until he hunts you down. If you don't get out of the city soon, he'll kill you. I've got a connection at the shipyard; we might be able to smuggle you out that way."

Her blood ran cold.

"*We* need to get out of the city. All of us. Aren't you coming too?" she asked.

"I don't want to be in the way."

Larina sighed. Clearly, he hadn't forgotten the moment at the ball when he asked her to dance and she'd refused. She had to make him see that it hadn't been personal. She swept into a deep curtsey that made her injured legs groan with pain.

"What are you doing?" he asked.

"You asked me for a dance, didn't you? I wasn't at liberty to accept at that moment, but I'd like to accept now if the offer still stands."

She straightened, wincing slightly, and he chuckled, the awkwardness fading from his face.

"In the state we're in, I think we'd fall over," he said.

"You're probably right. But that settles it. You'll have to come with me so we can have our dance."

"I can't. I can't leave him here in charge, you know that. I've got to stop him."

"That's why we go. We need to regroup. Consider

getting reinforcements. Subterfuge didn't work, so it's time to try your way."

A smile flickered over his lips. "That sounds good, but what's my way?"

"Politics. Intelligence. Elrin must have made enemies. Those people are our friends." She held her hands out to him. "Come with me and help me find them."

The offer was self-serving in the end. Words couldn't describe how grief had washed over her when she'd seen him hurt. It had taken the possibility of losing him for her to admit that she didn't ever want to leave his side. She would when he became king, because staying in the city would only cause problems for him. But she would leave because she loved him. She needed to tell him that, but how could she do so when she didn't entirely understand the logic herself? She could only give in to her instincts and hope that they didn't steer her wrong.

"It would be my pleasure," he said, leaning his forehead against hers, the familiar gesture warming her insides.

Once everyone was awake and clean, they gathered inside to plan. She'd expected this meeting to go like many of the others, with Kyra taking the lead as the somewhat-official head of the uprising, and Dezrick doing the bulk of the talking as the heir to the kingdom and son of the despot they all loathed. Instead, all eyes turned to her. She remained silent, not quite understanding what they expected of her, until Kyra finally spoke.

"What do we do now, Larina?" she asked. "What is your advice?"

Larina wanted to protest, but she had to admit it made sense for them to defer to her expertise. Once their safety had been reestablished, the old organization would exert itself again and she would leave. After all, she had nothing to stay here for. She might even forget Dezrick, after a while. But the idea made her throat tighten, so she pushed it away and focused on the business at hand.

"The tower still smokes," she said. "You can see it over the rooftops. Once the fire is under control, the guards will be looking for us. We need to get out of the city by then. Dezrick might be able to smuggle us out on a ship, but we need to find the others first. We can't leave anyone behind."

"I'll compile a list," Nix offered. "I know a few of them fell in the castle. If we all contribute, we should be able to determine who we still need to look for."

It was a grim job, even for those in their profession. But Nix would undertake it with the respect it deserved. Larina tugged at her prayer braid and nodded.

"Thank you. So as I see it, we have two options. Anyone who wants to can hide out here as long as you like. There are some smaller gems off my old necklace that can be sold to a broker without arousing too much suspicion, and Dezrick has a ring and a broach that his father didn't take off of him. You can wait things out here, or hold off until things die down and head out to Roshai. I have some friends there who will take you into their caravan as laborers. Even if Elrin managed to track you to the desert, the caravans move around so much that it makes it nigh impossible to locate a specific one if you don't know exactly where to look."

"It sounds like you're not planning to do that yourself," said Kyra.

"I'm not. I'm going to take the second option. I'll be on the boat. I'm going to find a place to regroup, and then I'll come back to end Elrin once and for all. Dezrick and I are going to tackle this together. We can't leave Oramis in his clutches. I'm not as consumed by vengeance as I once was, but I can't just walk away."

She paused, looking around at the group, seeing nothing but sober expressions and nodding heads.

"Out of all of us, I'm the one who is most likely to be able to get to him," she continued. "You don't have to come with me. If you hide in Roshai, I swear on the memory of my family that I will come and fetch you when it's safe to return home."

"Don't be ridiculous," said Kyra.

"You won't be going into battle without me," said

Alaris. "I owe the king and his men some crushed skulls for putting their hands on my mother."

Nix patted the larger man on the arm, urging calm. To Larina's surprise, Alaris subsided, looking down at his feet.

"You know I'm with you, Shadow," Nix commented.

"Someone needs to look after you all, or you'll all march to your deaths," declared Miriam. "I'm coming, and I won't take no for an answer."

Larina broke into a wide smile. The smile faded as she thought of what that might entail, but she was ready.

She was the Shadow, after all.

Later that morning, they stood on the deck of the Venture. Captain Dormano had welcomed the prince with elaborate politeness before naming a price of two gems to carry their group out of the city.

"Two gems?" demanded Larina. "I could buy my own ship for that."

The captain gave Larina's injuries a pointed look, then turned to gaze up at the still-smoking castle.

"Maybe," he allowed. "But something tells me you're desperate. I won't put the Venture at risk for less."

Larina nodded with begrudging respect. "I can't argue with that," she said. "Two gems it is."

They shook on it.

As the boat pulled away, Larina reflected that this mission hadn't gone the way she'd expected. All of the rebels had chosen to accompany them on their mission, and although she kept trying to tell herself that they followed Dezrick, an uncomfortable voice at the back of her head insisted that they followed her. She worried they didn't know what that meant. What they risked following in her shadow.

Dezrick joined her at the railing, his limp even more pronounced than before. Of course, he changed the subject whenever she'd asked, but he'd hurt himself on the night of the fire. Or his father had done it, torturing his own son. Her blood ran cold as she contemplated that possibility.

He offered her a friendly smile, which she forced herself to return.

"You okay?" he asked, putting an arm around her shoulders.

"Yeah," she replied.

It took every ounce of strength she had not to pull away or to melt against him. Being friends was much better— much safer. She ought to be grateful.

"You sure?" he asked, frowning at her.

She shook her head. "Just thinking."

"About my father?"

Telling a lie was easier than admitting the truth, so she nodded.

"Don't worry," he said. "We'll set things right. My mother and your family will have peace. As will we."

Larina nodded, trying to focus on that. She would still have her vengeance on Elrin, but now it would be on her terms. She would find a safe place, discover what Dunheim intended, and return when the time was right. This time, her plans would not fail.

Elrin wouldn't know what hit him.

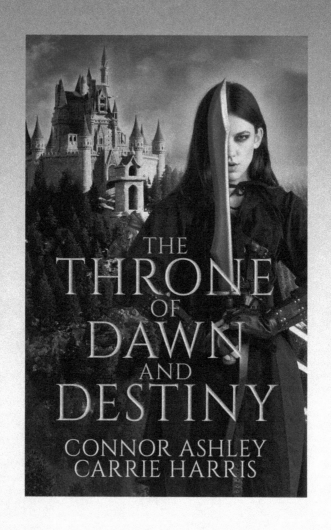

THE
THRONE
OF
DAWN
AND
DESTINY

CONNOR ASHLEY
CARRIE HARRIS

Book 2 coming Winter 2022!

THE THRONE OF DAWN AND DESTINY

NEVER MISS A RELEASE!

Thank you so much for reading THE CROWN OF BLOOD AND FIRE. We hope you enjoyed it!

We have so much more coming your way. Never miss a release by joining our free VIP club. You'll receive all the latest updates on our upcoming books, gain access to exclusive content and giveaways, and get a FREE book!

To sign up, simply visit www.connorashley.com/vip-club

Thank you for reading THE CROWN OF BLOOD AND FIRE! If you enjoyed the book, we would greatly appreciate it if you could consider adding a review on your bookstore of choice.

Reviews make a huge difference to the success or failure of a book, especially for writers like us. The more reviews a book has, the more people are likely to take a shot on picking it up. The review need only be a line or two, and it really would make the world of difference for us if you could spare the three minutes it takes to leave one.

With all our thanks,

Connor & Carrie